MURDER BY MAGIC

Sonoma Witches #5

GRETCHEN GALWAY

Eton Field

For my friends.

THE GARDNER FAMILY

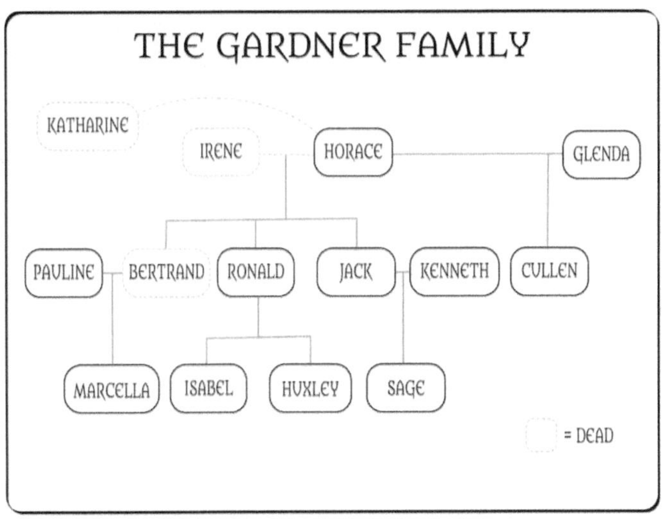

Chapter One

I met my former schoolmate near a cluster of fairies riding a baggage carousel at the San Francisco Airport.

"That one's mine," Marcella said, pointing at a purple suitcase as it rounded the curve. She didn't see the little green fairy sitting on it, but I did. I hesitated to pick up the bag until the creature had flown off. They were already annoyed at the rattle and bustle of the carousel where they lived. My ability to see them didn't mean I could understand why they'd chosen to live somewhere as overrun with humans and their ruckus as an airport baggage claim, but fae were not of our world. I didn't expect to understand them.

"I'll get it," I said, reaching for the suitcase. I gave a push of magic to gently nudge the fairy off the faux-leather handle, then grabbed it and hauled it to the tile floor.

"You didn't have to do that, Alma." Smiling, Marcella rushed forward to take it from me. "I asked for your company, not manual labor."

She'd asked for more than my company, but I didn't argue. She'd called me up a few days ago and asked if I'd be willing to provide extra security for her short trip from the airport to the city. I'd explained I wasn't a professional demon hunter anymore, but she'd insisted I was the witch she wanted.

It had been almost a decade since I'd seen her. We'd been students at a boarding school just south of the Oregon border, one popular among older witch families. After a series of other places, I'd ended up there for a couple of years before joining the Protectorate, the international witch governing body. Unlike me, Marcella hadn't been invited to apply for that great honor though her family name, Gardner, was even older and more prestigious than mine of Bellrose.

"I was closer," I said, swatting away the fairy who wanted to get back on Marcella's suitcase. He had a plastic cutlery knife in one hand and was aiming for the zipper. I looked up and saw Marcella staring intently at me, at my hand gesture at—to her—empty air. The fairy was able to hide himself and his knife from ordinary witches.

"Is something wrong?" she asked.

I kept my ability to see the fae a secret, even from people I considered friends. Witches didn't trust abilities they didn't understand, suspicious it might be Shadow magic. In my case, the distrust would be correct. I'd learned recently my biological mother had been possessed by a demon when she'd given birth to me. That was an even bigger secret I had to keep to myself.

"I've heard the fae can be pests here," I said. "I'm hoping to discourage them from following us."

"The fae? Oh right," she said, visibly relaxing. "I thought you'd seen demon sign. Or worse."

We began walking toward the BART train to downtown. "Worse than demon sign?" I asked. Most witches defined demons as the apex predator in our world.

"The real thing," she said. "Have you... have you ever actually... *seen* one?"

I had, even without the biological-mother connection. My job at the Protectorate had required me to hunt and kill them—and when I'd failed, they'd marked me with an Incurable Inability and fired me.

"I sense a lot of fae here," I said, pretending my awareness was dependent upon magical amulets and effort on my part. "Which is good for other threats. They wouldn't be here if there were any demons."

She stopped to adjust her grip on the suitcase. "Really? I didn't know that. I-I— So you mean, right now, right here, you don't think there are any Shadow beings because you sense there are lots of fae?" Her eyes darted around, squinting at the witches, nonmagical humans, service dogs, utility carts, light fixtures. In the five minutes we'd been together, she'd been as vigilant as a Protectorate agent on a stakeout.

"Yes. I don't think you have to worry about demons right now," I said. "Is that why you asked for my company today? You're afraid of possession?"

Marcella stared at me, nervously combing her fingers through her blond hair. She was pretty and had a tall, athletic build that others might envy, but she'd never seemed comfortable in her own skin. In school she'd been a loner, teased and excluded. I'd been a fellow weirdo, switching schools often, my dad an infamous thief. It was our family pedigrees, however, that brought us together. Both of us walked around with old witch family names that opened doors—but just as often prevented friendships. At the outskirts of school society or just lonely at lunch, we'd found each other and shared a few stories.

But we'd been kids then. In the years since, I'd grown up and had a few adventures (too many of them recently), but Marcella had moved to the opposite coast and lived alone in New York. She hadn't mentioned a career; I assumed she lived off her family's wealth.

"Yes," she whispered, visibly trembling. "I'm afraid of… of… possession. But who knows, maybe…" A full-body shudder ran through her.

I put my hand on my redwood-bead necklace, a magical object that amplified my power, and drew a bubble of defensive magic around us.

Feeling my enchantment, she let out a sigh. A flush of pink was returning to her cheeks. "Thank you. I do feel better."

I began walking again, focusing now on keeping extra defensive magic around her as well as myself. "Travel can be harder on witches than nonmags. It's easy to get worn out, isn't it? We pick up so many sensations they don't."

She gave me a fleeting smile. "I was afraid you wouldn't believe me. But this"—she gestured at my bubble enchantment—"really does feel better. Do you ever get that creepy feeling between your shoulder blades? Like a blow is about to land? I can't feel that anymore. Thanks."

"I could teach the spell to you," I said. We turned to follow the signs to the BART train. I'd insisted on public transit because it was safer than driving, not just because of nonmagical collisions but because of the need to concentrate fully on casting spells. Behind the wheel, a witch was limited and impaired. Distracted. In my Jeep, I wouldn't have been able to protect her properly.

"Thanks, but it's no use," Marcella said, hurrying just ahead of me. Her legs were longer, and she seemed to fear pursuit of some kind. She kept looking over her shoulder.

"Why not?"

"I'm hopeless," she said. "I've tried doing them myself. Had tutors, amulets, herbs. Doesn't seem to make a difference."

"But my defensive spells help you," I said. "Let me teach—"

"It's because you're doing them. It's the same with other witches I've… I've… asked to help me. It doesn't work if I do it myself." She glanced nervously at the woman passing in a wheelchair.

"Then I'm glad you called me for help." Curious and alarmed, I began scanning the people around us more carefully even though it pulled energy away from the magic I was using on the defensive spell.

"I didn't know who else to ask," she said. "I didn't feel safe making this trip by myself." We'd reached the BART station now, and after getting tickets and waiting at the platform, we got on a car headed north to San Francisco.

Standing near the doors, we found ourselves talking about old times—the teacher with the enchanted lead weights on his desk to impose discipline, the girl in our dorm who'd burned rosemary incense all night to keep away nightmares, the guy who suddenly got gorgeous after his fifteenth birthday because his grandmother had paid for beauty charms.

When our car was rolling into San Francisco, I brought our conversation back to the purpose of her trip. "You said something about visiting family?"

She flinched. "Yes. It's Granddad's birthday."

I thought back, remembering her telling me about her powerful grandfather. "You're good to come when it's so hard for you."

"It might be his last. My mother said I had to be there." Suddenly she straightened, looking around. "Did you feel that?"

I cast a quick scan over the train car, but I didn't detect anything particularly malicious. We were just coming into the Glen Park station. "No. What did you—"

"Let's get off," she said. "This one. Here. Now. Let's go."

Before I could stop her, she jerked her suitcase off the

train and onto the platform. I had to weave around the bodies blocking my way, barely making it through the doors before they slid shut behind me. Then the train continued without us, leaving us standing on the underground platform.

"What did you sense?" I asked.

Her skin was pale, and the sweat had returned to her upper lip. She lifted her shoulders in a shrug, then fumbled with a sachet of herbs—dill seed and borage flowers, I detected—tied to her belt. I felt a spell of calming magic wash through the air. It was her own fear she was trying to stop, not anything around us.

"Nothing," she said. "I think I just panicked. I'm like that. Jumpy. I can't help myself."

"No problem," I said. "Another train will come along. Your hotel is downtown, right?"

She ran a hand through her hair, digging her fingernails into her scalp. Her face was pinched, her breath shallow. "I need to get out of here."

I touched the wood beads around my neck and cast another scanning spell for danger, but I didn't find anything. Those who'd come off the train with us were already walking away, heading up to the street, none looking back at us.

"Now. Please." Marcella began jogging toward the escalator. Her suitcase twisted to one side, its wheels losing contact with the ground, but she didn't slow down, just dragged it harder behind her.

Chapter Two

I had to run to catch up, casting defensive spells ahead of me to include Marcella's departing form. If this was what bodyguards had to put up with, I was glad it wasn't my regular job. "Marcella! Please—wait!"

But she didn't pause, just kept going, pushing past a man on the escalator and disappearing above me into the station. I had to maneuver past the same man and hurry after her, my heart pounding with the exertion and shared fear. What had she sensed that I hadn't?

I got up to the street and realized she was already halfway down the block. Glen Park wasn't a neighborhood tourists would visit, and most of the people around me were commuters heading home. Over the steep hill to the north was Noe Valley, where the Protectorate office employed the local assortment of professional witches trained or hired to hunt and kill demons, research other supernatural threats, negotiate the biggest career ladder in witch society, and gossip.

My former workplace.

If we were in danger, we could go there, although the

hike over the hill would be tiring with countless shadowy corners for an assailant to hide. The sun was setting, the fog thickening, the light fading.

At the corner ahead, Marcella suddenly stopped and looked back at me, her chest heaving. When I caught up to her, she managed to say between breaths, "I'm so sorry. I had — I had to run. I— I'm sorry."

I cast another defensive spell around us. "Did you have a plan for how we'll get downtown?"

She shook her head, flinching. "Sorry. No."

"How do you feel about the J Church? The streetcar?"

"I don't know," she said. "I just need to see where we're going."

"Do you think whatever is threatening you is afraid of daylight?"

"No," she said. "It's not that. It's being underground."

"The J is aboveground here. We'll get off before it goes under."

"Great. Maybe that will work," she said.

I knew the area from my time at the Protectorate, so I led us down the street and across the footbridge to another station platform, this one located between lanes of busy traffic. I continued to cast spells, searching for danger, but the only thing I sensed was my own hunger, triggered by all the great restaurants sending their delicious aromas into the evening air. As I detected Chinese food, my stomach rumbled.

The train finally arrived, and we got on. Afraid Marcella might run off again, I didn't take an open seat but stayed on my feet. She did the same, although she didn't look nervous anymore. Her coloring returned to normal, and she began sneaking bites of a chocolate bar from her bag.

The ride was slow and bumpy, taking us into the edge of the Mission and along city streets north of the city center. My feet started to hurt from standing so long, but I didn't want to risk dropping my guard. As promised, I made sure we got off before the train went underground, then walked us to a bus stop. Marcella dropped the handle of her suitcase twice when the wheels hit a bumpy patch of concrete.

"Let me help," I said, turning to carry it for her.

She waved me away. "I'm fine," she said. "My fingers are just sweaty. Nerves."

The sun was disappearing behind the bank of fog to the west, streaking the sky with pink and purple. The city lights twinkled like fairies in the mist.

It had been a few years, but I still remembered how to get around on Muni. It would take us an hour longer—at least—than if we'd stayed on the original BART train, but I respected any witch's instincts about danger. Whatever she'd felt back there on the train had been serious.

"Thanks so much for all this," Marcella said, hauling her suitcase up onto the 22 Fillmore bus. It was crowded—the 22 was a popular line—but a few minor spells of mine opened up a little breathing room around us near the back doors. As the bus rumbled on, I cast jealous glances out the window at a Japanese restaurant I'd loved when I'd lived in San Francisco. My town in the boonies just couldn't provide the cuisine a big city could, even with magic.

"We'll connect to the 38 to get downtown," I said. "You still want to go to the Financial District, right?"

She glanced around before she spoke, as if afraid of being overheard. "Yes, my hotel is there."

"Is the party downtown?" I remembered her family had been from the Bay Area, but I couldn't remember which part. Maybe they were all meeting at the hotel.

She gripped the support bar with both hands and looked at her black boots. Some witch stereotypes were true—I liked to wear black boots too. "It's up at the family vacation house near Tahoe."

"Lake Tahoe?" I asked, surprised. It was about two hundred miles east over the Central Valley and up into the Sierra Nevada mountain range. "How are you going to get there?"

"There's a bus to train to bus thing," she said. "It doesn't take much longer. Really, it gets me most of the way. I'll meet one of my cousins for a ride from South Shore. Our house is in the wilderness. Nonmagicals wouldn't approve, but Granddad doesn't care. He's been hexing that corner of Lapis Lake for decades."

"Hexing?" I asked. That implied harm.

"Sorry," she said, rolling her eyes. "*Enchanting*. Whether the wilderness likes it or not."

"Given how hard it is for you to travel and how you seem to feel about your family and even the house where you're going…"

"Why didn't I just stay in New York?" she asked.

"Yes."

"I'm weak," she said, smiling in spite of her words. "Story of my life. I buckle under pressure. If I can't even get around San Francisco by myself, how could I stand up to my mother?" She reached into a bag she wore over her chest and took out another chocolate bar, handing me one and then tearing open the other.

"You will," I said. "Sometimes it just takes time."

She chewed, eyeing me. "I envy you, you know. Even when we were in school, you seemed like you didn't need anybody."

"Don't be jealous of a lie. That's what I wanted you to think. I would've hexed the eyeballs out of a baby kitten to have a family like yours."

Snorting, she shook her head and took another bite. "Liar."

I glanced at the nonmagical people around me to confirm none were paying attention. "Cast a truth spell. It's true. I would've killed for respectability like yours."

She elbowed me. "You couldn't even kill a demon, from what I've heard," she said, scoffing.

My smile fell. The word had gotten around, but it still hurt to hear my professional failure had reached a non-Protectorate witch in New York. "Ah. Right." I handed back the chocolate bar, still in its wrapper.

Face turning red, she held her hands up, refusing to take the chocolate back. "I'm so sorry, Alma. I was trying to be funny. Which is always a mistake. I didn't mean any criticism. Totally the opposite. I hate witches who are always casting spells, hurting things, trying to make themselves feel big."

I slipped the chocolate into her jacket pocket. A tingle of defensive magic, one of her boundary spells, lightly singed my fingers—since it was her candy, it didn't hurt very much. "It's OK. I'm just surprised you'd called for my help today if you knew why I'd left the Protectorate."

"Because it's your defensive magic I want," she said. "I need it. I can't seem to do it myself."

"Marcella," I said. "If you're in that much danger, maybe you really shouldn't go. Maybe you could explain to your mother—"

"No, can't do that," she said. "Mom's fed up with my excuses."

"You know your family better than me," I said, still annoyed about the joke about me being fired. After a few more stops, I said, "OK, we're getting off here."

Once again we left our ride, pushing through a crowd to

Fillmore Street where we'd have to walk to catch another bus. Hopefully it would be our last transfer.

We began walking, Marcella striding ahead of me with her suitcase, but now it was me who froze in fear.

She couldn't see them, but there were goblins all around us.

The same size and coloring as river trolls, goblins were night creatures who sought out crowded spaces and fed on Shadow. I'd never seen so many. They covered every inch of the sidewalk where we were trying to walk. On the other side of the overpass was Geary Street, where we could catch the bus to downtown—if I could make myself walk through the hostile fae without giving away what I saw.

They must enjoy the frigid wind off the ocean that rushed down Geary Street. We were above it on the overpass, so I could only imagine how many were gathered just below us in the cold underbelly of the bridge. Like bats, except not at all helpful and furry.

I stopped walking, reminding myself they weren't technically dangerous to the people walking by, although they did encourage drunkenness and irritability.

Marcella, realizing I wasn't with her, turned around. "What's the matter?"

I wasn't sure I was going to be able to walk through them. They weren't solid, so other humans were passing directly through their spiritual presence, but I was able to see and hear them. The thought of letting my body be mingled with one of their green, sticky, prickly, shiny, naked bodies…

A shudder began in my shoulders and rolled down my back.

Marcella stared at me, alarmed by my behavior. As she stood there, I watched more goblins creep over the concrete wall from below and approach her, gather around her, smile hideously at her. Two flew up to her head and hovered near her mouth as if wanting to climb inside.

"Alma," she called out, her voice rising, "what's the matter?"

I had to stay calm for the sake of my reputation and her nerves.

"Low blood sugar," I said, forcing a laugh. "I should've eaten your chocolate after all."

She relaxed slightly. "Japantown is nearby, isn't it? I came here with my parents once."

"Do you mind if we take the long way around?" I gestured in the opposite direction for her to follow me. More goblins were swarming around her head now, and I had trouble seeing her facial expression. "We can get some soup or something and then catch the bus?" My voice was too loud. I wasn't controlling my panic.

She responded to my tone immediately by running over. "Something *is* wrong. Tell me."

I was relieved to see her fast movement had outrun the fae, at least for a few seconds. With a smile, I took her arm, touched my redwood necklace, and thought of light, summer breezes and sleeping puppies. The Shadow energy around that bridge was stronger than my happy thoughts, but it did slow down the goblins for three seconds, long enough to get to the other side of the overpass.

Then another bus went by, discharging people with their array of energy, plenty of it negative, and the goblins turned their attention to them.

"Are you going to explain?" Marcella asked. "Is it me? Is there something after me?"

I picked up my pace, pulling her along with me. The purple suitcase caught on a cracked corner of the sidewalk, and she had to pause to stabilize it.

"Not you," I said. "I felt a lot of Shadow back there and didn't want to walk through it."

That was true enough. Not the complete truth, but enough.

"Do your wood amulets give you that kind of vision?" she asked. "Do you think I could use them? I'd pay you. You sell them, right? Of course. That's what you do now. I'd love to buy a dozen of whatever you've got. If I thought I could just see if something's out there, maybe I could relax."

"The beads would help you amplify your power," I said, "but they won't show you anything new, I'm afraid. That was… kind of a freak situation."

I regretted not being able to explain. She was anxious enough, and I'd just made her feel worse. Seeing the fae was a trigger for *me*, but most humans couldn't feel their presence, even that of malicious goblins.

"Let's find another way to get downtown," I said.

"I thought you were hungry."

"You know, I'd rather just keep going," I said. The faster I could get far away from the Geary overpass, the better. "How about a walk to California Street? We could take the cable car downtown. That's always fun." Shadow creatures would hate the cable car with its happy tourists and fun-loving locals, its history of whimsy.

"That would be great because it's open air," she said. "Good idea."

So we walked several more blocks through the rolling city streets, past the people seeking food, drink, entertainment, hookups, and handouts, to the top of a hill for the California cable car. There we heard a couple talking about an accident in the BART tunnel that had stopped all the trains— suggesting our detour hadn't added much of a delay after all.

As expected, there weren't any malicious fae on the car when it came, and we reached downtown without either of us casting a panicked defensive spell. We jumped off in the Financial District and made our way to her hotel.

"I really owe you," Marcella said, stopping to face me.

Since the start of our journey at the airport, with the evening offshore winds and fog, the temperature had dropped twenty degrees. I zipped my jacket up to my chin, looking forward to getting into my Jeep, currently parked under an invisibility spell just outside the entrance to the Union Square parking garage.

"Don't worry about it," I said. "It was nice to connect. I'm bad at keeping in touch with people. Trying to work on that."

Her mouth curved in a tentative smile. "Do you mean that?"

"Absolutely." And I did. Marcella and I hadn't been close in school, but I'd always felt like we could be, even—or especially—after the weirdness of our tour of San Francisco. I could relate to weird.

"Then will you come with me to my Granddad's birthday party?" she asked.

Chapter Three

My smile froze. I'd walked right into that one.

"It's this weekend," she said. "I wouldn't ask but…"

If I'd thought I'd be reuniting with Marcella's family, I wouldn't have come to see her today. I didn't remember much about her mother, but her dad had made a strong, negative impression. Stingy and verbally abusive, he'd taken one look at me on a school visit and told her to do better.

"Bad blood," he'd said while I was still standing there. "Stay away from her."

Sensitive about my father's criminal history and my lack of a reputable nuclear family, his remark had made me feel small and ashamed. I would've avoided Marcella from then on, but she'd been brave and ignored her father's command. She'd even told him so at the time, refusing outright, not sneaking around. That loyalty was probably why I'd answered her request for today.

"I don't know, Marcella. I've got a boyfriend who's kind of clingy—"

"Bring him along!"

No, my changeling boyfriend couldn't sleep under the same roof as a family of witches he didn't know. "And there's my dog Random—he's also pretty needy—"

"Him too! It's Tahoe. Dogs love Lake Tahoe."

I wrapped my arms across my chest, feeling cold. "Do you remember when I met your father? He hated me. I don't think he'd want me to cross the threshold of a family home."

"He's dead," she said.

I stared blankly at her. Part of me was thinking, *good riddance.* The rest was trying to hide that thought from my face.

"Boating accident," Marcella said. "Up at Tahoe. My mom survived, but barely."

"When was this?"

"Not long after we got out of school. Nine years now. Can't believe it's been that long already."

"I'm sorry for your loss," I said.

She gave me a pained look but didn't challenge the sincerity of my statement. "Thanks," she said. "My mother took it really hard. They were everything to each other."

Her tone wasn't that of a happy child but that of one who'd been excluded. Although my father had many flaws, I knew he loved me. Marcella didn't seem as if she'd ever had that comfort.

"I just don't know," I said, stalling for time. "I'm not good in groups. You need somebody who—"

"I'll pay you."

I drew back, a little offended. "I'm not that hard up that I take money to be with my friends."

"Well, I was trying to acknowledge the hard labor you'd be doing, but you're right. I'm sorry."

Her self-deprecation made me uncomfortable. "It's not hard labor to join a friend at a family party."

"Oh yes, it would be. Let's not pretend it wouldn't. Look,

Alma—I've felt better today in your company than I've felt in years. The anxiety that's always with me, the pressure coming at me from all sides, even under my own skin—with you, it was easier." She gave me a dazzling smile that I'd never seen before. "I bet I could drive a car with you at my side. Demon's balls, I bet I could fly a plane!"

In spite of myself, I felt a warm pride bubbling up inside me at the thought I'd helped her that much. "I've learned a lot of defensive magic the past year," I said, silently reflecting on the murders, assaults, mysteries, hexes, enchantments, shape-shifting, and demon possession I'd dealt with. "A lot. The Protectorate teaches hunting and killing, but I've learned other ways, other techniques, other tools. I could teach them to you. Then you wouldn't need me."

Her smile fell. She looked away. "It's not your magic that helped me," she said.

"You said you didn't feel the threats when you were with me." Back on that bridge, she hadn't seemed to notice the goblins crawling over her face.

"There is no threat," Marcella said. She was quiet for a long moment. "It's all in my head."

"What?"

"I'm so sorry. I didn't think you'd help me if you didn't think there was real danger. You're former Protectorate. You've seen demons, and I can't imagine what else." She turned and gave me a pained look. "I have an anxiety disorder."

"You're a witch. Did your doctor know about us? Probably not. Your senses aren't like a nonmag person."

"In this way they are. Believe me, I wish this was a magical thing."

I took a breath, thinking back to the hours we'd been together, the pervasive sense of fear. "You mean... All that running around the city, taking trains and buses, wasn't to avoid anything in particular?"

She shook her head.

"But your senses were overloaded with it," I said. "I could feel you feeling it. It was all around you. In your bones."

"It's like that sometimes. Doesn't mean it's real." Tears pooled in her eyes. "It's why my own magic doesn't help me. Deep down I know I'm just crazy."

I thought about how she'd hurried off the train at Glen Park. "If we hadn't gotten off BART, we might've been in that accident we heard about," I said. "Maybe your fear is protective."

"That was a coincidence. It always is. Brightness, I'd love to be wrong. But not once, in all these years, my whole adult life, has anything ever turned out to be actually dangerous. I feel like it must be real—it must be—and I'll break out my magic, start running, ask for help, and then… nothing." Her voice was getting louder, more angry than embarrassed. "I hate it. My family has no patience with me anymore. I've lost friends, and it gets expensive to pay for bodyguards. Though you'd be totally worth it. Please, please let me pay you."

"I'm not going to accept your money for doing a friendly favor."

She shook her head. "That's really nice, but I'd feel so much better if you'd let me. Look what you did for me today. If you'd let me compensate you somehow, I wouldn't feel so bad about it. I scared you. I should've told you there wasn't anything out there. You were wasting your energy setting up those defensive spells for nothing."

"It's never a waste of energy. You don't know what's out there."

She slapped her hands over her ears. "Don't say that. That's exactly the voice in my head that makes me so paranoid all the time."

"There were dangers today, Marcella," I said. I couldn't tell her about the fae, but she knew there were all kinds of supernatural beings in the world. "We made our way through a crowded, diverse, energetic, unpredictable city with lots of bodies and spirits in it. Maybe your vigilance is a gift. You pick up subtle dangers as well as big ones."

"No, please don't say that. It's enabling. I need to face my fears as the pathology they are. One reason I came to California this time, after lots of other invitations and pressures to come back, was my therapist told me I needed to expose myself to my greatest fear if I was going to ever get past it."

"California is your greatest fear? Or traveling?"

She ran her hand through her hair, then pulled her hood over her head and tightened the drawstring until only the tip of her nose was visible. Her entire body began to tremble.

"My Granddad," she said. "I'm terrified of him."

Although she'd said my magic was useless over her psychology, I grabbed my necklace and cast the strongest defensive blocking spell I could muster—including our feet, which were often forgotten and therefore allowed a tendril of danger to break in—and wrapped it around us. Then I reached up to put an arm around her shoulders—she was taller than me—trying to support her body, which was shaking so badly I thought she was going to fall on the sidewalk.

"It's all right," I said. "I'm here."

After a few slow seconds, she released her grip on the hood drawstring, slumped against me, and inhaled a long breath. The shaking had stopped. I reached up and pushed the hood away from her face. Her eyes opened and met mine.

"Please," she said, bare and vulnerable. "Come with me to Tahoe. If not for money, then for karma. I'd be so grateful."

Chapter Four

Well, there were many different kinds of enchantments, and guilt was certainly one of them. Or maybe it was a hex. Yes, guilt was definitely a hex. Those blue eyes of Marcella's had gone right through my thickest, sturdiest defenses and lodged into the soft underbelly of my soul.

I didn't make any promises before I left her at her hotel, but by the time I got home a few hours later, the remote little town of Silverpool dark and quiet in the wee hours of the morning, I knew it was hopeless. I'd have to go with Marcella to her family party.

It was raining and had been for months. I drove slowly through the narrow street to my house on a bluff overlooking the Vago River, wishing her family's vacation home were in a desert or tropical beach instead of the cold, snowy mountains where people had once infamously been trapped and eaten each other. Or more than once, who knew?

But snow was better than rain, especially after months of the unusually wet winter we'd endured on the north coast. No drought this year, which was good, but there could be too much of a good thing. The river had flooded downtown twice, threatening my friend Birdie's bookstore on Main Street. She'd had to learn how to cast water-repulsion spells and was still busy cleaning up the damage that had been done. Even the magical Wellspring of Silverpool had been submerged in the river's high waters a few times.

The sun seldom shone; either it was rainy or foggy. Willy, the gnome who lived under the redwood tree in my backyard, seldom came out to visit anymore, not just because he was depressed from his latest reunion (and latest breakup) with his centuries-long wife, but because he said the rain was bad for his velvet coat and extinguished his pipe.

I parked my Jeep in my driveway and looked at my soggy, neglected garden. The soil had been too saturated to cultivate, and with Willy hiding underground, the few plants I'd tried to grow had suffered without his help, succumbing quickly to rot and mildew.

Even snow had to be better than this cold, damp misery.

Not everyone was suffering. My boyfriend Seth Dumont, whose spirit was a lake fairy, loved water in all its forms—pooling, flowing, dripping, soaking, freezing—he was happy company. I found him asleep on the couch in my living room with Random curled up on his feet. Because he had his own house next door, I was surprised to find him there. Willy wasn't fond of Seth, and until now, I wasn't sure he'd allow Seth to be in the house without me. Maybe Willy was allowing him there to perform his dog-sitting duties.

It was the middle of the night, but Seth sat up quickly, his voice alert, no hint of sleep fog clinging to him. "You're about to tell me something you're worried about," he said, but seemed cheerful about it. He was usually cheerful, sometimes annoyingly so. Most of the time, however, I found it irresistible. As appealing as his dark good looks.

I turned on a lamp and was fascinated by his blue eyes'

lack of a reaction to the sudden light. "A friend wants me to join her at a family party this weekend," I said.

"Same witch who needed a chaperone from the airport?"

I sat beside him, and Random jumped between us, wriggling and licking and wagging, his claws digging into my thighs. He was a quiet, medium-sized, mixed-breed dog with black hair, a mutt who never drew attention to himself—just the reason my father the career thief had used him on night burglaries before I'd rescued him.

"Yeah, Marcella," I said. "Turns out she's got an anxiety disorder."

I got up and began preparing for bed. For most witches, that involved taking off not only layers of clothing but a dozen or more pieces of metal and botanical jewelry, stone amulets, fabric accessories, herbal sachets. Some also had to wash off runes they painted on their skin with clay, charcoal, or flaked minerals that held various magical properties.

The hassle for me tonight was I had to unwrap the tight fabric sleeves I'd worn to hide the circular black rings around my lower arm that had appeared on my skin over the past year. The first mark appeared after I'd killed a witch in self-defense with his own hex, and his tattoos had been transferred to me. Since then, I seemed to keep acquiring them, always after a magical conflict with another witch—which also seemed to keep happening. Some witches believed the rings meant I was a killer—quite the opposite of the truth— so in consideration of Marcella's feelings, I'd made sure they were well covered today.

"Where's the shindig?" Seth asked when I climbed in next to him.

"Some secret spot near Lake Tahoe," I said. "Her family —the Gardners are as old as the Bellroses—has had it for generations. In the wilderness on a little lake."

He nodded as if he knew already, which maybe he had.

He kept secrets from me about his fae nature, the extent of his powers, and I struggled to accept the boundaries he'd left up between us.

"We'll make a vacation out of it," he said. "We haven't traveled together yet. It'll be exciting."

"You can't come," I said. "It's a witch party. They'd make you miserable. Or worse—dead."

"We'll make the drive together, but Random and I will find another place to stay." His face lit up with enthusiasm, which confused me if we weren't going to be spending it together. I'd also wanted to make a trip together, some romantic getaway, but I'd imagined us actually being in each other's company.

"Why are you so happy about spending time apart?" I asked.

He got a sly, playful look on his face. "Miss me already?"

"Maybe," I said. "Or maybe I'm suspicious. Why are you so eager to go?"

"Alma. Please. You want to know why I'm excited to go to Lake Tahoe?" He pushed Random out of the way and took my hand. "Have you forgotten what I am so soon?"

My first insecure, irrational thought was that he was reminding me he was a sneaky, amoral flirt of an almost-human man who was also rich, supernaturally powerful, good-looking, and sexy—and why would he be happy with just me?

As was often the case, he seemed to read my mind—and was only too happy to tease me about it. "Jealous, darling?" He nuzzled my neck, inhaling and kissing.

I allowed the display of affection. We'd only been together for a few months, and I was only human. Well, mostly.

"Is it"—I tried to concentrate as he touched me— "because it's a"—I ran my hand through his hair—"a lake?"

Water of all kinds filled him with delight. Our neck of the woods had a river, tributary creeks, a seasonal pool, and the Pacific Ocean down the highway, but no lakes.

"Not just any lake," he said. "It's two million years old and over a thousand feet deep. I haven't been up there for months."

The thought of sharing the drive with him made me feel better about the trip. "I don't know exactly where Marcella's place is, but it's near South Shore. I'll need to take the Jeep."

"Still lots of snow up there. There's a storm forecast for the weekend. Heard some guys talking about it at Cypress Hardware. They're going up to ski. Spring's around the corner, and they want to enjoy it while they can."

I yawned and turned off the light. Three in the morning, and the caffeine and enchanted peppermint I'd consumed to stay awake was wearing off. "Great. A blizzard." I sank against him, enjoying his warmth, wishing we could forget Marcella and snuggle in some warm snowed-in cabin, just the two of us. "If I get stuck in the snow, promise to rescue me?"

He was quiet for a while, and as I began to fall asleep on his shoulder, I heard him mumble, "It's not the snow I'm worried about."

Chapter Five

Marcella was so grateful I was going to accept her invitation she sent me flowers with a glittery balloon saying Thank You. They were cottage garden flowers—white camellias, yellow daffodils, black hellebores—sent from a florist in Occidental, a small town not far from Silverpool. The flowers carried a witch's magical fingerprint, and I made a note to visit the florist someday, preferably in the summer when it was warm and sunny, not the endless rain we were currently experiencing.

And so two days later, Seth, Random, and I set out for South Lake Tahoe. As per her original plan, Marcella had gone the day before by herself on Amtrak. Much of the journey was actually on a bus, not a train, but as long as she wasn't driving, she said she'd be able to protect herself.

Because Seth was coming, I hadn't offered to drive out of my way to pick her up in San Francisco and go together. She hadn't expected me to—if I was driving through heavy traffic in the snowy mountains, I'd be too absorbed with that to be any use protecting her with magic—but I still felt a little guilty.

But I had no choice. Seth wasn't comfortable around witches, and I wanted to keep the existence of my changeling boyfriend a secret, even from Marcella. Part of that was my somewhat pathological tendency to protect my privacy. But I was also afraid Marcella, from no intention of her own, might give away his existence to her powerful family. And if the Gardners learned a changeling was living near Silverpool, the story would soon get out into witch society—and he'd have to flee for safety. Or worse—be killed by the Protectorate.

I didn't want to lose him.

"I hope it's cold enough for the snow to be dry and fluffy," I said to him as we drove through Sacramento. "Not that wet, mushy stuff that makes you cold and miserable."

"Doesn't make me miserable," Seth said brightly, patting my arm, then Random in the back seat. "I like wet."

I did the driving while he chose the tunes and handed out snacks. He'd baked fresh cinnamon rolls for breakfast, which magically didn't make me feel nauseated like most heavy pastries did, and kept my insulated cup of hot tea filled. His domestic talents were very fae, and I appreciated them more than I was comfortable with. Having a boyfriend provide a steady supply of sensory pleasures—taste, smell, touch, sound—was ruining me for human company.

What if it didn't last?

How *could* it last?

I took a bite of cinnamon roll, frowning at the snow-capped mountains in the distance. "Just another two hours if the snow doesn't slow us down too much," I said. "Can you tell if there's a blizzard at the moment?"

He pulled out his phone.

"I thought you'd use your fae powers," I said.

"This is easier." He tapped the screen and read. "Yes, there's snow. On the ground and more coming down."

"So maybe three hours," I said. "The traffic on a Friday will be terrible. We should've left earlier. Maybe I'll need chains, even with the four-wheel drive. I can't believe I'm doing this. As if the weather isn't bad enough in Silverpool. Marcella must've hexed me to get me to come. Why—"

Seth brushed his fingers along my cheek, and my anxious discomfort vanished. "You're beautiful when you're ranting," he said.

I wanted to be annoyed, but I smiled and leaned into his hand. It was warm, strong, and smelled like cinnamon rolls and charm, which was basically the same thing. "I'm stressed."

"Maybe you should listen to your feelings. They're telling you not to go."

"My feelings are always telling me not to go anywhere," I said. "If I listened to them, I'd never leave the house."

He found a strand of my hair and twirled it around his finger. Random, jealous, pushed his head into the front seat between us and tried to get Seth's fingers to pet him too.

"Do you think these witches will have reliable internet?" Seth asked. "I want to be able to talk to you. Frequently. Make sure you're OK."

"I think so. Marcella emailed me from there." I glanced at him—only a glance, because the weekend traffic between the Bay Area and Lake Tahoe was a nightmare. Sacramento, like all of urban California, held an overloaded network of intertwining highways, and the Jeep was moving through over a dozen lanes filled with cars, trucks, and motorcycles weaving and creeping and stopping and racing. I didn't understand how nonmag people could drive and stay alive without defensive spells.

"Is it going to snow over the next few days?" I asked.

"Let's see," he said, scrolling through his phone again.

"You really can't use your fairy magic to tell me that?"

"Meteorologists have way better equipment than I do." He gave me a rakish grin. "In that area."

He might have been part fae, but he'd also been raised—and socialized—as an American human male. "Don't make assumptions," I said.

"Have you ever dated a weather man?"

I had to admit I had not. "No."

"There you go," he said. "They've got nothing on me. If they did, you'd be with one of them instead of a changeling you tried to kill once."

My last job at the Protectorate had been to kill a creature they'd identified as a demon. But when I'd found Seth Dumont, he'd been something else, although I didn't know what until months later. But even though I'd thought he was a demon, I'd been unable to kill him. He'd been my first and last test of all the training I'd received. When I'd let Seth throw my partner off the Golden Gate Bridge (and then rescued him, no harm done), that had been the end of my career. If I couldn't kill a demon, I wasn't much use to them. Even the genealogists and archivists in the library could kill demons. One little silver knife—poke—job done.

Except I hadn't.

I braked to avoid a car who had braked to avoid another car and so on, all along the road to the East Coast as far as I could tell. "Demon's balls!"

"Maybe I should let you focus on the road." He snapped his fingers, and the electronic K-pop song turned into something with a harpsichord and a children's chorus. "Ah, the music of angels. Remember them? They're like demons, but nicer. But you knew that, didn't you? Met one. Probably are part one yourself—"

"Don't say that." The argument about demons being on a spectrum with angels on one end and many more in the middle, not worth killing or loving, was one we'd had many times. The creature who had possessed my biological mother had been—and was, because I'd met her, although she was bodiless at the moment—a demon. Not an angel, which I wasn't ready to admit existed. To a modern witch, angels were like Santa Claus. Children believed in them; adults learned not to.

I was losing patience, and the road was wearing me out. "I thought you were going to let me focus on driving," I said.

"You're right," he said. "Sorry." With a kiss on my cheek, he handed me another cinnamon roll.

Chapter Six

After enduring the bumper-to-bumper slog up the mountains into the snow, I dropped Seth and Random off at a cute cabin a short drive up from South Shore, right across the highway from the huge, deep blue lake spanning California and Nevada. I had actual physical pains when I saw the two-story, five-hundred-square-foot dwelling with snow piled on the roof like a white hat; I wanted to stay with him. But I'd promised Marcella, so I kissed him, scratched Random behind the ears, and took off without looking back.

I was less than a mile away when I heard his voice speaking out of my phone—without my pushing any buttons.

"I'm always here if you need me," he said. "By the way, if any of those witches happen to be meteorologists, I'm coming to get you."

Laughing, I set up my phone to guide me to the address Marcella had given me. It wasn't on any maps, but somehow the family had gotten Google to navigate to a secret address they'd arranged. *Five Thousand and Nine Lapis Lake Way.*

The harpsichord angel music was still playing, and I let it. The sky was a dark, cloudy gray, snow was falling heavily, and I was sad about leaving my two favorite guys behind. My life was ice, chunks of salt, slush, dirt, cracked pavement, potholes, and more traffic.

I turned right into a residential neighborhood, took that for a mile or two, then turned again onto a narrower, icier road into the wilderness. The Jeep was good in the snow, but if it weren't for the enchantments I'd cast on the wheels before leaving—and my 4WD—I would've slid into a snowbank several times.

For the first twenty minutes, locals in trucks and SUVs had passed me, knowing where they were going. But then I followed the phone's navigation to turn again, and Seth's magical harpsichord faded away into silence. From that moment onward, I didn't see another soul.

Fairies, yes. They were out in large numbers. Forest folk similar to the coastal redwoods back home, but in heavier clothing, fluff and fur, flying around the Jeep like moths around a porch light. I knew I couldn't hurt them with my car, but it was hard not to brake or swerve when they stood on the road in front of my bumper.

It took longer than I'd like to admit before I realized they were guiding my way. Along the coast, the fairies tried to lure you off the road into the forest, and it was a bad idea to drive at night, when the human mind was more vulnerable to tricks and distractions.

But these fairies were happier than the ones near Silverpool. They were singing. Laughing. Waving at me and at each other. It reminded me of the way the fae partied at the magical Silverpool Wellspring during the winter solstice.

Maybe that was why they were so happy. The blizzard was their magic, their season, their joy.

The road beneath me seemed to disappear—at least, I lost

all sense of it. I hit the brakes, felt myself slide as I gripped the wheel, cast out a spell of safety and stability. Heart pounding, I paused, unmoving on the road, my front bumper wedged in a snowbank, waiting for my breath to return to normal.

The snow was not *my* joy. Had I really been griping about rain? Rain was nothing compared to this. This was deadly.

I waited for Seth's voice to tease me through the phone, but I hadn't heard his voice for miles. Could he see me right now? He had strange powers, but I didn't think they were as extensive as he'd like me to believe. I hoped not. Because I'd just done some pretty bad driving.

Through the white flurries beyond the windshield, a figure suddenly appeared. At first I only saw a vague outline, the faint shape of a woman, but then I saw a black hoodie and…

Shorts. The woman—it was Marcella, who should've been freezing in the storm—was waving at me to keep driving. I pointed at the bumper caught in the snowdrift, tapping the gas to show my wheels were stuck—

But then I slid right through the snow, which disappeared, and drove into a warm, bright summer day.

Marcella pushed her cotton hood off her blond head, shook off the snow, and waved again, smiling. She came over to the driver's side, and I rolled down the window. Chunks of snow fell through and landed on my lap.

So it was real snow, but…

I twisted around in my seat to look behind me. It was like looking at a large-screen movie of a snowstorm in the mountains. Everything was there, the poor visibility, the cloudy sky, the snow-blanketed trees and shrubs blasted by white, freezing wind. But now I was watching it from a safe distance in warm sun.

"I'm sorry I couldn't tell you about the enchantment

before you got here," Marcella said, reaching through the window to lift a chunk of snow off my arm. "That's part of the magic. None of us can talk about it with outsiders when we're not here. It keeps it secret. Listen, why don't you get out and stretch your legs for a few minutes? Sometimes visitors get headaches from the enchantment if they push through too quickly."

Doing as she suggested, I got out and studied the boundary of the warm-weather spell. The snow and ice simply ended, leaving the earth and granite bare to the sun. Sweating, I tore off my fleece pullover and long-sleeved shirt, leaving me in an old T-shirt. A garment I hadn't intended to wear by itself, but I was too hot to cover up with my more presentable sweater. At least it was black. Practically formal wear.

Looking at the summer scene stretching out before me, I wished I'd known to bring different clothes. I wouldn't be wearing my flannel shirts, wool socks, or fleece joggers.

"How do you manage it?" I asked. "Does your family combine their powers while they're here?" It would take an enormous amount of energy to fuel the enchantment for more than a minute or two.

Her voice got low and serious. "Granddad has a wand. Ancient and powerful, handed down the generations through a blood oath."

I exhaled, impressed. "What's it made out of?"

"Pewter. With a Jeffrey pine handle—cut from a tree up here," she said. "I think it looks like a giant pushpin. I said that once when I was little, and everyone made fun of me. Back then, even my father thought I was cute. That was before I started getting afraid of everything. That made him angry. But the angrier he got, the more fearful I became."

"Of course you did," I said. If she wanted me to complain about her father, I was ready to join in. *Bad blood.*

"Don't judge him too harshly," she said. "You see… they need me to be stronger than that. The whole family is relying on me. Especially since my father died."

"Why you? Don't you have uncles and cousins?"

She looked at her feet, slow to answer. "I didn't tell you before because it's a bit of a family secret, but since you're here, you need to know. I'm the heir to the wand. The blood oath follows the line of firstborn children. When my father died, I became the one. Much to everyone's horror. They knew it was going to be me eventually, but they'd hoped my father would live past a hundred like Granddad. Maybe I'd get better as I got older. Stronger. Or… something else. But here we are." She showed me her hands, which were trembling. Runes of confidence and safety were inked around her wrists and fingers.

"Wow," I said. "You poor thing."

"No, don't feel sorry for me. Feel sorry for them. They rely on that wand to keep this place going and all the other family investments, properties, enchantments—and I think we all know, when he dies, so does that." She stretched out her hand, taking in the poppies and lupine, the butterflies, the singing flower fairies she couldn't even know were there.

"You don't know that," I said. "The wand might give you the power you lack. Including confidence. You've had your family expecting the worst from you for so long it's become a self-fulfilling prophecy. With the wand—"

"I can't blame them for my reaction. I should be stronger than that." She threw her head back and closed her eyes. "Every atom in my body is telling me to run away and never come back to this place. Yet if I do that, my family will hate me."

"Maybe you should listen to your atoms and to Shadow with your family."

She gave me an agonized look. "I can't do that. They're all I've got. And they're relying on me."

I had no idea what it would be like to be part of a large family with emotional obligations and complicated inheritance rules. It had always just been me and my father. Until now, I'd envied people like Marcella with so many living relatives, a family home, shared traditions. But now I could see the advantages of being free.

Well, there was my spiritual demon mother who liked to stalk me, but she'd always been affectionate. Marcella's family seemed like mean, spiteful bullies.

"I'm sorry for your troubles," I said. Lame, but I was tired.

"Just you wait," she said, offering me a nervous smile. "I'll get in your car with you. It's just a short drive, and there aren't any freeways to worry about."

Even without her anxiety disorder, I had understood her reluctance to drive around San Francisco. In city traffic, it was much harder to use defensive spells. We climbed in, and I continued along the narrow road.

The ice and snow were gone, but the asphalt was badly pitted with holes, and although it was less than a mile, it was slow going. Apparently the magic that controlled the weather didn't extend to road repair.

Suddenly there was a view of a snowy field—no, it was a frozen lake—between the pine and cedar. Clinging to its edge was a large house in the classic Tahoe style—big, brown, and rustic, with a sharply pitched roof to dislodge the snow.

But tonight there wasn't any snow. The enchantment had kept it warm.

As I drove closer, I kept glancing at the lake to see how far the summer enchantment went, but my eyes were unable to focus. It was like when you had a dust mote in your eye; whenever you tried to look at it, it moved farther away. My guess, however, was that given the amount of magic required to hold such a powerful, unnatural spell, the summer weather didn't extend very far. Marcella had walked out to meet me; the house was probably the center point.

"I'll show you where to park," she said. "It's all family—well, and staff—but it's a big enough group. It can be tricky to find a spot that doesn't block the drive."

Breathing in the scent of flowers, noticing the sound of birdsong, I followed her instructions and drove past the rear of the house, where I parked in a patch of gravel. Near us along the lakeshore to our right were four small, identical cabins under the pine trees.

I was used to magic, but the enchantment was a shock both to my thoughts and my body. I got out and stood beside the Jeep, enjoying the sun's warmth, but Marcella didn't join me.

I bent over to look inside. She was staring ahead with the anxious look I remembered only too well from our journey in San Francisco.

"What's wrong?" I asked, afraid to hear the answer.

Chapter Seven

"Do you mind if we take a few minutes to hang out before we go see my family? I have to introduce you, of course, but I think you should know more about who's here." She got out and gestured toward the cabins. "Maybe a little walk?"

"Sure. Of course." I was in no hurry to hang out with her family.

We headed away from the house, past a kitchen garden that flanked the cabins. It was the kind of garden a hearth witch would love—and I did—planted in the remains of an old volleyball court. The net was now holding vining cucumbers, pole beans, tiny golden tomatoes. The mountain slope just above us was heavy with snow and ice, but down here it was late summer.

It was a complex enchantment that seemed unnecessary to me in a place like California. If a witch family wanted warm weather, they only had to travel a few hundred miles south.

"Do you do this every winter?" I asked, trying to keep the judgment out of my tone.

"Oh no. A week or two at most, usually at the end of fall or beginning of spring, just to extend the season. And late December, of course. It gives my grandfather an ego boost to override the actual winter solstice with his magic wand." She looked over her shoulder as if afraid of being overheard and continued more quietly. "He's done it all winter this year though. My mother said they don't expect him to see summer again, so this is one last hurrah. Even if it annoys the fae."

"But if he's dying, doesn't doing all this magic drain him, shortening his life?"

"Apparently not," Marcella said. "That's the power of the wand. It doesn't take energy from him—it gives it. Wait until you see him. You'll never believe he's well over a hundred. He's as terrifying as a witch half his age."

A visible shudder ran through Marcella's body. She looked over her shoulder again, tapped the runes on her wrists, muttered a few words under her breath, and hugged her arms over her chest.

The patriarch of a large, ancient witch family often inspired fear in his descendants because of how many things of value he controlled. There was real estate, intellectual magic property (such as secret spells), access to social events, jobs and careers, family heirlooms both magical and nonmagical, and even love, which could be given and withheld like a silver dagger through the heart.

"Do you believe this is his last winter?" I asked, thinking she had to be secretly looking forward to him passing on.

"I should, because my mother does, and she's always right about these things." Marcella led me over to the garden, where she picked a green bean off a tall vine and handed it to me. "She has a touch of the sight. More than a touch. When I was a kid, it drove me crazy how she always knew I was about to do something like have a cookie right before dinner."

"That had to contribute to your anxiety," I said, "feeling like you were always being watched."

"Exactly! I'd never say that to her though." She found a purple pod hanging near the green ones, tugged it free, and took a bite. "Funny how people who are so good at giving out constructive criticism are the worst at hearing any."

"Well, she's your mom. I hear they're like that."

Marcella flinched. "Brightness, you're right. You must think I'm so annoying." She threw the stem from the purple pod to the ground. "I have *no* right to complain. I've always had food, a roof over my head, pearl earrings on my ninth birthday, a platinum ring on my fifteenth, the boarding schools of my choosing, and now that I'm an adult, a stipend to cover rent and living expenses—in Manhattan."

Silently I agreed it all sounded pretty good. I could see the pearls and feel the steady power of her platinum ring, but I hadn't known about the free New York apartment. The rent on my two-bedroom cottage in a rural backwater was almost due, and I was going to have to ignore the water bill to cover it.

But I didn't want to worry about money while I was enjoying a few days of magical sunshine after months of gloom. Marcella had mentioned the fae being annoyed, but the ones I could see were happy, even celebratory. There were about a dozen palm-sized, green-clad fairies living inside the shelter formed by the bean tripod. When Marcella had been picking them, the fae had held the stem for her, though she hadn't noticed. Over near a trellis heavy with tomatoes, a thin fairy in a brown dress and green boots was guiding the honeybees to each yellow star-shaped blossom.

"You've gotten quiet," Marcella said. "Did I offend you with all my poor-little-rich-girl talk?"

I tore my gaze away from the fairies. "No, of course not. I've had lots of privileges myself. We can't control what we're born with or what we're given as children. Just what we do with it as we grow older."

She pressed her lips together, nodding. "I agree. Which is why I get so mad at myself. I should be doing more to help the world, but I'm so afraid all the time. It can be an ordeal just to leave my apartment."

"You're here and you didn't want to be," I said. "You pushed through really bad anxiety to get here, just to make your family happy. That counts."

Laughing, she gave me a quick hug. "You're better than my therapist. And that's saying something."

A tiny brown fairy with black wings was fluttering around her head, making it easy to laugh along. Sometimes I just couldn't believe other witches couldn't see them. They were so obvious, as diverse and numerous as insects.

"Have you had any incidents to suggest the fae are unhappy with the summer enchantment?" I asked.

"Brightness yes," she said. "Follow me."

She led me through the garden to a path between the middle cabins. I sensed there were people inside but none I could see. In case they were listening, I didn't ask her any pointed questions until we were all the way past them to the rocky slope that led down to the water. All of the small lake was covered in ice and snow.

"See?" Marcella pointed below at the shoreline. "The lake fae despise us. See how the snow comes all the way to the edge? Warm sand, then ice, all within millimeters. This lake is deep enough not to freeze over, but they want to spite us."

"How do you know that? Has anyone…" I didn't want to let on that some witches could see and hear the fae if she didn't already know that. "Has anyone had evidence of that?"

"Before my time, but the family says the wand used to

warm up enough of the lake to paddle around on a kayak or even swim. Now it's frozen through, but you'd never want to skate on it. I wouldn't put a pinkie toe on that ice."

Seth often said his lake fairy family members were amoral, hard, vindictive creatures. Cruel even to their own kind, their own children. They made their children changelings, sought vengeance, nursed grievances. He missed the water and all its life and beauty, but not so much his own kind.

I'd lived along the coast or in cities all my life and hadn't known lake fae except through stories and Seth, and the occasional conflict in Silverpool, where they were off their own turf and outnumbered.

But Lake Tahoe and its satellite lakes… deep and wild… old… the fae here had to be quite unlike any I'd ever known.

"You mentioned spite," I began.

"They killed my father's dog."

I sucked in a breath. There were rumors about the fairies in Silverpool hurting pets near the wellspring, but I'd never seen proof of it. "How do you know it was them?"

Marcella turned to me, her voice lowering. "They found him under the ice."

Involuntarily, I took a step away from the lake. Then, consciously, I took another one. "That's horrible."

"My father was only a teenager, and Granddad had warned him not to bring the dog up here, but of course he didn't want to leave Hoppy at home. One night, he went missing. In the morning, everyone set out to go looking for him, and then they realized the lake, which the day before had been warm enough for a kayak, was now solid ice. And there, just off shore, was Hoppy. Frozen, unmoving, trapped under the ice." She turned away from the lake, arms crossed over her chest. "Granddad never tried enchanting the lake water again."

"Did you… recover the body?"

She gave me a pained look. Nodded. "My father buried him at their house in Carmel. I planted an aloe on his grave. It made me so sad to think about him."

Stricken with a chill, I touched my necklace and drew a warming spell over myself. Fae were supposed to be amoral, neither Bright nor Shadow, but that felt evil to me.

"I'd stop coming here altogether if I'd seen that," I said.

"Yes, well, it was my father's dog, and he was just a kid at the time," she said. "Granddad wasn't the one crying about it. Obviously I wasn't there, but I could feel my father's pain when he told the story. Whenever we came up here when I was a kid, my father would stay inside the house and pretend the lake wasn't there. He hated coming here."

"Maybe that's why you have a hard time too," I said.

She glanced over her shoulder at the lake. "Maybe. I don't know. I kind of like coming down to the shore, looking for the fae, wondering what they're thinking, if they still hate us. It's the humans that I worry about."

We walked back through the cabins to the kitchen garden. I was eager to get the meet-and-greet over with and settle into one of the cabins to rest.

But as we walked past the gravel lot where the Jeep was parked, she stopped.

"Wait," she said. "I need to tell you something."

I stifled a groan. I really needed to use a bathroom. "Yes?"

She put her face in her hands and spoke from behind them. "You might want to turn around and leave. I wouldn't blame you."

The story about the poor dog had already creeped me out, and now I felt the hair on my arms stand up. "What's wrong?"

She dropped her hands and met my gaze. "I didn't tell them you were coming."

Chapter Eight

emon's balls. If I hadn't been invited, they and their defensive boundary spells might treat me as an invader. Marcella's magic, especially given her anxiety and family avoidance, might not be enough to protect me.

I looked up at the house. There were several cars, but nobody was walking around outside, and I didn't see anyone in the windows. If I was truly unwanted here, which was very common among witch communities, they could hex me from out of sight, but it would be weaker than within visual range. Otherwise the trouble would happen when I crossed the building's threshold.

I turned back to Marcella. "Should I put up defensive spells?" My hand was already on my necklace, drawing on my power to weave a boundary from my feet to my head.

"No, no, at least I don't think so." She forced a smile. "There's no reason they wouldn't want you here. That's why I invited you. We have friends—well, my mother and aunts and uncles and cousins have friends—come up here all the time."

"But you're not sure," I said.

"I don't know." She massaged her temples. "All I know is when I called my mom to tell her I'd invited you, I had a panic attack before I could speak. So then I waited a few hours and tried texting. She hates texting, but whatever. But —same thing. I started hyperventilating, thought my heart was going to burst, believed I was really dying this time. Every time I thought about trying again, the panic came back. So I stopped trying."

I clenched my teeth, afraid of what I might say. My bladder was full, my stomach was empty, and I'd been looking forward to a shower and a free meal. Maybe even a cocktail. I'd been on the road for over five hours, half of that through heavy snow, and my boyfriend was cuddling with my dog in a cozy cabin miles away.

Her face was red, embarrassed and angry with herself. As much as I wanted to snap at her, I didn't have the heart. And it wouldn't help anything.

"Will they let me into the house?" I asked. The bathroom in particular.

"I don't know. Let me go ask. I'm so sorry."

I cast my gaze over the cabins with a sigh. "Which one is ours, hopefully?"

"The one farthest from the house. It's got two bedrooms, so you'll have some privacy."

"If they don't hex me," I said.

"You've gotten this far," she said. "Granddad's enchantment let you through. I think it'll be fine."

But she didn't sound confident. Then again, Marcella never did.

"I'll go talk to them," she said. "Wait here, OK?" She strode away without looking back. Afraid to meet me in the eye, I guessed.

I told myself it wasn't too bad. If the family didn't want

me, I had Seth and Random waiting for me relatively nearby. I could already taste the cinnamon rolls.

But after several minutes, Marcella came out of the house with a bright, relieved face and waved wildly at me. I made sure I had my favorite redwood-bead necklace around my throat, felt both wrists for other charms and beads, and began walking up the hill.

"They're cool with it," Marcella said breathlessly, jogging over to me. "Well, I only saw my mother, but that's enough. She's got seniority as the widow of Granddad's firstborn by his second wife."

It sounded like an old-fashioned cult. She'd never talked about this at school. "Excuse me?"

"I know," she said. "It's complicated. And weird. I've never told anyone outside the family about it. There's a blood oath. The firstborn is a really big deal with a blood oath."

"I've heard about blood oaths," I said. "First child born of woman, not man, isn't that right?"

"Because with men, you never know if it's their first. So it hinges on the mother." Marcella began chewing on a fingernail. "That's why I'm the heir. I'm the first child of my mother, who was married to my Granddad's first child by Irene. She was Granddad's wife number two."

My head was spinning. "How many wives has your grandfather had?"

I wondered if we were far enough from anyone in the house to eavesdrop with ears or magic, though Marcella didn't seem to be sharing any shameful secrets with me. It was just family tree stuff. But maybe that's why she hadn't talked about it in school, knowing how intrusive our classmates could be, gossiping with each other and their parents. Even young witches were obsessed with family trees because power and property were often controlled through bloodlines.

"Granddad has had three wives. The first two, including my grandmother, died—don't worry, it was natural causes—decades ago. The third is still living. She's here right now. She's always with Granddad. That's Glenda—my step-grandmother. She's younger than him, of course. She's not like a supermodel or anything, but she is younger than my mom, which can be a little awkward."

"Glenda," I repeated, trying to remember. "Step-grandmother."

"She's all right," Marcella said. "Her son is Cullen. About our age. Granddad's favorite. Mine too, I suppose, though I've been away for a few years. He gave me a ride from South Shore."

I tried to visualize the family tree she was describing so I'd remember—Horace and his second wife were Marcella's grandparents. Horace and his third wife were Cullen's parents. There had to be lots of other relatives here for such an old man with so many wives. Would they mind if I took notes? Remembering names was not my strong point, and I was already stressed.

"We better go in while my mother's still there to break the ice with the others," she said as we approached the entrance, a pair of beautifully carved double-entry doors. I admired the abstract design for a few seconds, imagining the enchantments that could be hiding within the wood. "I'll fill you in on the rest later. There are a few cousins. My dad had two brothers, and they each had kids. Mostly in their twenties. Well, Huxley's still a teenager. They're all fine. I mean, I'm not close to any of them, but they shouldn't give you a hard time." She glanced down at how I was gripping my redwood-bead necklace.

Whenever I crossed a witch's threshold, I wanted to be prepared. Marcella reached out and gripped the iron door handle, pushed forward, and I felt a scanning spell hit me in the belly and extend simultaneously downward, upward, and out. My spine tingled, and I saw stars for a moment as if I'd been slapped.

I could only imagine what it would've felt like without Marcella's company or my redwood beads.

"Here we go," she said, smiling nervously at me.

We stepped inside an entranceway that was both rustic cabin and luxurious lodge, with warm wood paneling on the walls and exposed ceiling beams. I heard instrumental folk music playing faintly in the distance.

There was a woman standing just inside the door who I guessed was Marcella's mother, but only their tallness and golden hair marked them as related. Pauline Gardner was round all over, especially in the face, which was pink-cheeked and dimpled. Like all witches who could afford the spells and nonmagical treatments, she looked twenty years younger than her actual age, giving her the appearance of a woman in her late forties. She wore a black sundress and gold-toned sandals.

I did a double take. Gold-*plated* sandals. An enchantment made them flexible.

"Welcome to our family home, Alma Bellrose," Pauline said.

I felt the peaceful charm wash over me, and I relaxed. "Thank you," I said. Was it too soon to ask for a bathroom?

"I don't know why Marcie didn't tell us you were coming, but of course we're glad to extend hospitality to a former schoolmate," she said.

"Thank you," I said again.

"Were you born a Bellrose?" Pauline asked.

Marcella made a noise of protest. "Mom, please."

Offering me a frosty smile, Pauline didn't look at her daughter. "I only mean she might have married into it. It's a witch's way to wonder these things."

"I was born with it," I said.

Pauline nodded, softening a little. "I was a Hawthorne before marriage," she said. "In Connecticut, where I was raised, our school's library had a Bellrose Room. The collection was why my parents chose the school for me. I was their only child, and they didn't hesitate to invest in my future. Very old, powerful books were kept there. There was a Celtic tome—France, not Ireland—with gold lettering kept in a glass box. You must have seen it."

"No, I'm afraid not," I said.

"Mom, she's a Californian." Marcella suddenly sounded much younger. "They don't care about that snobby East Coast stuff."

"She was at the same school you were," Pauline said, "so somebody cared enough about that—as you call it—snobby stuff. Tuition there was a fortune."

Although the school had seemed unstructured and Bohemian, which was ironically the preferred vibe of prestigious witch schools, only the richest children could go there. Or, in my case, the children of a well-connected man with a respected family name who could find forbidden, often stolen goods on the Shadow market to use in the place of cash tuition. Blackmailing of former clients might also have played a role.

"I'd be curious to learn more about the Bellrose Room at your old school if you have time later, Witch Pauline," I said politely. "Thank you."

She nodded, frowned at Marcella, and turned to escort me deeper into the house. We'd been standing in a weather-friendly, slate-floored foyer, but now we passed through a doorway into a great room with a high ceiling and panoramic views of the lake. It had the classic Tahoe log-cabin look, with boards and beams and planks composing all the surfaces and furnishings, and a massive stone fireplace to one side.

In a witch's house, the stones in the fireplace would make any potions or ashes made there have extra power. I wondered if there was a second stone fireplace below it on the lake level. Exponentially more powerful enchantments could be made in tandem with two hearths working together, and I thought of the defensive spells or healing ointments that might be possible.

But looking around, I didn't see hearth magic being displayed; although the architecture was an ode to wood and therefore the botanical powers of old-fashioned hearth magic, the furnishings showed the harder tastes of modern metal witches. Steel frames in the chairs and sofas, glass tables, crystal vases and candlesticks, iron metalwork in the wall sconces.

For me, however, the old plank floors and the old-growth redwood timbers spoke to my soul. My magical powers thrived with trees. As I soaked in the beautiful wood all around me, the urgency of my bladder ceased, and I walked into the room to meet Marcella's family with an involuntary smile, the joy of life bubbling inside me.

I knew instantly that the old man by the window was her grandfather. Horace Gardner sat with his back to the room— a show of strength, confidence, and superiority. Out the window in front of him stretched the frozen lake where the defiant fae ruled over their chilly domain. I wondered if he watched and plotted his revenge, just as the lake fae, long-lived and vengeful, certainly did.

Magic brought creatures together—human and fae—who never would've been able to communicate otherwise. Even conflict was a kind of communication.

"Horace, my daughter is here," Pauline announced. "She's brought a friend."

I followed Pauline and Marcella across the room to the back of his chair, where we stood and waited.

He still didn't turn around. He had the narrow, hunched shoulders of a man who had never been large but was now at the farthest end of an enchanted human lifespan. He didn't seem to be using any spellwork on his appearance; only a few strands of white hair clung to his skull, faint as cobwebs. His pale skin was spotted, with visible scars and dry patches. And his breathing was audibly raspy.

But he was still powerful. I could feel his magic touch me, probing for danger, talents, surprises. Usually eye contact or touch was necessary to probe a subject, suggesting he was as strong as Marcella said he was.

Then I saw his faint reflection in the window glass shadowed by my stronger one and realized he was using magic to alter it like a mirror, giving him a clear view of me. To be polite, I looked off to the side as if admiring the view. Meeting his gaze in the reflection would seem aggressive, and if just for Marcella's sake, I didn't want to insult him.

He cast another probing spell over me. This time I blocked it. Appearing weak could be just as dangerous as looking too strong.

He made a waving gesture with one hand, and a woman suddenly appeared and turned his chair around for him. She was about thirty, redheaded, and petite—around five feet tall, maybe a little less. In spite of the summer weather, her dark, tailored clothes suggested the office.

"Thank you, Sarah," he said. "Now check my mail again. I should be hearing from that lawyer. Very important."

"Of course, sir," Sarah said. She nodded at me, gave Marcella a quick smile, completely ignored Pauline, then hurried away.

"My PA," he said, then looked at me. "Who are you?"

Chapter Nine

"Alma Bellrose, Horace," Pauline said. "One of the old families."

He patted his lap, and suddenly I could see the wand Marcella had described. It really did look like a big pushpin. The Jeffrey pine handle was more interesting to me than the pewter wand, although I knew they'd dismiss the wood as only a practical substance that contained the more powerful metal.

He gave me a cold half smile. "Bet your father would love to get his hands on this, wouldn't he, girl?"

The crack about my father made me wonder how much else he knew—had he watched my journey through San Francisco with his granddaughter and then my arrival here at his enchanted property?

It was safest, and wisest, to assume he did. "I'm sure he would, Witch Horace," I said.

"It was just the two of you, wasn't it, when you were a child?" he continued. "Did you learn any of his tricks at his side, the way any apprentice will learn from a master?"

I froze, holding my breath. The joy I'd felt from the old-growth timbers vanished. In just minutes, Horace had unearthed a secret I'd managed to keep hidden from casual acquaintances. My superiors at the Protectorate had known, since all trainee agents go through intensive background checks and interrogations. But my peers and, certainly, random grandfathers I met on getaway weekends, didn't know I'd been trained by one of the best witch thieves in the world.

My father had used me as he'd used metal, stone, herbs, and animals to steal. As a small child, I'd been his lookout. I'd climbed through windows and set off traps. I'd been a decoy, a distraction, a warm body with small fingers.

Until I'd gotten old enough to say no and finally gone to school like normal children. Well, normal for witches. One of those schools was where I'd met Marcella.

"Yes," I said. "But only when I was very little. Since then I've devoted my life to Brightness."

Unexpectedly, he smiled. "I know that, child. I hear from my sources in the Protectorate that you've been quite helpful with a few unpleasant incidents this past year or two." He pulled a throw blanket tighter over his shoulders, and I saw the heavy gold chains around his wrists, the many gemstone rings, and vivid abstract tattoos on his skin. They weren't enchantments like mine but designs he must've had inked by an artist. "It's rather diverting to have you cross our threshold."

I wasn't sure if he was playing with me, if the compliment was genuine. "It's my pleasure."

He pursed his lips and nodded. "You don't really know my granddaughter very well though, do you?"

"Well, we have lost touch—" I began.

"Of course you have." He scowled at Marcella. "While

you've been taking risks—with some setbacks, of course, but also triumphs—she has been hiding."

"She was able to come for your birthday this week, Horace," Pauline said, managing to say something supportive of her daughter while also sounding disappointed.

"What an accomplishment," he said. "Oh, come on now. Let's not pretend it was. Exorcising demons, dominating fae, fighting Shadow—these are accomplishments a family can be proud of. Taking a first-class flight from New York to California is hardly that."

I felt my face get hot for Marcella's sake. Her own grandfather was humiliating her, or trying to. I paused to let Marcella speak for herself—because if I jumped in now, it would only confirm the insulting comparison that I was somehow stronger and better than she was.

But Marcella said nothing. Her face was blank, her eyes downcast. I looked at Pauline, who was staring intently at her daughter as if, like me, she wanted Marcella to speak. Fight back.

"Well, that's just what I mean," Horace said. He patted the wand in his lap, shaking his head. "Tell Sarah to call that lawyer woman if we haven't heard back yet. Marcella, make yourself useful and go find her. She should be in the room across from my office."

Marcella bowed her head and hurried away without a word.

"I wish you wouldn't browbeat her like that, Horace," Pauline said. "It only makes her worse."

"That girl is incapable of learning," he said. "A hopeless case. She's been coddled too much."

"We may be witches," Pauline said, "but we're still human. She's got a disorder. The doctor said so."

"A disorder." He dropped his hands into his lap. The

chains on his wrist clinked against the wand. "There you go. She's dysfunctional. Impaired. My own granddaughter. Supposedly my heir. Such a shame."

"People improve with treatment." I let my irritation show in my voice. "And *support*," I added.

Horace pointed at me. "See? That's courage. You're here under my roof, only inches away from the most powerful wand in the country, yet you speak up. You defend your friend, as you should. And what has she done for herself? Run away. She should've been a tree fairy. Tiny, fearful little things. Not like the lake fae. Those demand respect. You see that ice out there? That's what strength does. It fights back."

"The tree fairies are a lot better company," I said.

He scowled at me, then burst out laughing. "Indeed! You are a Bellrose, aren't you? I knew a cousin of yours—well, this was over a half century ago, era of your great-grandfather, perhaps—he was a prime debater. The head mage at the school locked him in the latrine at least once a week for disrespect."

My father had told me very little about my family, so I couldn't help but be curious. "Where was this?" I asked.

"Oh, this was Canada. They liked to send young witches to the Yukon back then, thinking it would toughen us up— and it did. You don't see any graduates of those schools quivering in fear when somebody says a harsh word to them." His gaze moved to a point behind me, and I turned and saw Marcella returning.

"Sarah says the lawyer hasn't replied yet," Marcella said.

"Then go tell her to make sure she does," Horace snapped at her.

She turned and hurried away again.

"She disgusts me," Horace said.

Flinching, Pauline met my gaze. Her discomfort seemed

more about the fact I'd heard what Horace had said, not that he'd said it at all.

"I think she's a wonderful human being, and I'm determined not to lose touch with her again," I said.

But Horace just laughed and pointed at me again, as if it were a game and I'd made the move he'd expected.

Chapter Ten

"Excuse me, but it's been a long drive," I said, turning away. If he was going to laugh at my rudeness, I'd go ahead and do it some more. "I need to use the bathroom."

I left them—Horace still chuckling—and went in the same direction as Marcella, past the foyer into a long hallway.

I found a bathroom easily, thank Brightness. When I was done and washing up, feeling much more relaxed, I noticed a repeating visual motif of a teardrop shape in the decorating. The wallpaper, the light fixture, the handles over the sink—all contained the teardrop shape.

When I left the bathroom, I noticed it again in the crown molding and then again in the wood inlay of the hardwood floors. I realized that the double doors at the entrance had been carved with the same shape.

Witch families often had a symbol to go with their name, much like an old-fashioned European crest. Were they honoring the lake fae and their love of water? But they were locked in an antagonistic relationship with them, and I couldn't see Horace honoring them with so much work even if he did respect their toughness.

A thought came to me, and I turned back to look at the bathroom wallpaper again.

A repeating teardrop—in burgundy.

It wasn't water, it was blood. What had Marcella said? The wand was held and inherited via a blood oath, one that predated the house itself. Wherever you looked was a drop of blood. Horace hadn't wanted anyone to forget it.

I heard the sound of Marcella's voice and followed it down the hall to a small room on the left. Inside, Marcella was talking to Sarah, who sat on an office chair behind a narrow computer desk. The room—there was no window, so it must've been a converted closet—was filled with file cabinets, bookshelves, and storage boxes. Sarah's workstation was cramped in the middle, surrounded by the clutter.

Marcella sat on the edge of the small desk, eating out of a bag of tortilla chips Sarah held out to her. "He sent me to nag you again about the lawyer. I'm really sorry."

Sarah's pale blue eyes were locked on her computer. "I know, I know. I think this is it. It's not easy to follow up on his business correspondence when the legal stuff is in code. He never gave me the key, so I can't read it." She clicked a button and sighed. "But this looks like the one. Sometimes I don't realize I'm giving him pornographic spam."

"Brightness," Marcella said, horrified. "What does he do then? I'd be terrified."

Sarah gave a little laugh. "It's no big deal. It makes him happy to see I haven't cracked his little code." She reached over to the printer and lifted out a sheet of paper. "Don't let him push you around, Marcella. It's worse when you do. He likes a fighter. He respects it."

"How can you stand it?" Marcella asked. "I've been here ten minutes, and I'm already stress eating."

Sarah shrugged. "Not sure I'm doing much better," she said. "Those are my chips."

"You're amazing." Marcella saw me and jumped off the desk. "Oh good. You escaped. Let's go to the cabin—"

"Is this where all the cool kids hang out?" a man said behind me.

I turned to see a tall, sandy-haired guy with warm brown eyes and a smile. He wore the typical metal items of a modern, privileged witch—gold necklace and watch, copper and platinum rings, stainless-steel studs in his jeans, silver belt buckle.

"Hi, Cullen," Marcella said.

"Who's this?" he asked, smiling at me.

"A friend." She looked proud. "Alma Bellrose."

"What bad luck got you here with us?" he asked me. "Step on a toad? Break a mirror at midnight under a full moon?"

"I asked her, and she was nice enough to say yes," Marcella said.

He put his hand over his heart and bowed to me. "Whatever she told you about me, it's all a lie."

"She said you're not too bad," I said.

Marcella groaned. "Oh Brightness. He'll never let me live that down."

"Not too bad? Faint praise," Cullen said. He gestured at the door across the hall. "I'm going to get a mineral water out of my dad's minifridge. He keeps one next to his desk. Anybody else want one?"

We declined—bad luck to take a drink from a hostile host—and watched as he used a brass key from his pocket to open the heavy wooden door. It closed with a thunk behind him.

I looked at Marcella, who was staring at the closed door. Her happy mood had vanished.

"Something wrong?" I asked.

She continued to stare at the door, so I turned to study it. Each wood panel on the door held a teardrop shape the size of a human head. Even the doorknob was in a teardrop shape.

Marcella shook her head. She wrapped her arms around herself and began to rock slightly.

Cullen returned with two bottles of European water, setting one next to Sarah's keyboard and opening the other.

"I'm sorry you and Dad don't get along," he said to Marcella. "He's just old-school, you know? He really doesn't mean any harm."

"I know, I know. You're right," Marcella said. "Ignore me. How's he doing, by the way? Is he…?"

"He's not taking the medicine he's supposed to," Cullen said. "My mom tries to get him to take it, but he won't. Thinks he's the boss."

Marcella hugged herself. "He *is* the boss."

"Not like he used to be." Cullen's tone turned serious. His lips pressed together, and I realized he was choked up.

"How long…?" Marcella prompted.

Cullen ran a hand through his floppy hair. "Not long enough. Months at most."

Horace was over a hundred years old, and his decline couldn't be a surprise, but he was still Cullen's father. Cullen was about my age, and as much as I complained about my thieving dad, I wasn't in a hurry to have him leave this earthly plane.

The whir of the printer sounded in the closet office. Sarah got up, pulling the pages off the tray, and moved toward the crowded doorway. "Excuse me. He's been waiting for this email all day."

We all made way for her, and she walked out into the hallway, headed for the living room.

Marcella watched her go. "I hope Granddad doesn't blame me for keeping her away from him for too long. I don't know how she stands it."

"You really can't let him bully you, Marcie," Cullen said. "One of these days you should really let him have it. Your life will improve dramatically. Promise." He nodded to me, then strode away in the same direction as Sarah, calling out to her to wait for him.

With a sigh, Marcella turned to me. "How about we go rest awhile in the cabin?"

"Yes please. That would be great."

Instead of leaving through the front door, Marcella walked to a staircase that led down to the ground floor. Like upstairs, it was a living area with couches and chairs, but it was on a smaller scale with more pillows and blankets, over-stuffed cushions, and wool and animal-skin rugs on the floor. It had the same lake view, however, and the duplicate fireplace I'd hoped to see. We passed through another heavy wood door to a deck and then down a stone path to the lakeside cabins.

Marcella didn't speak while I got my bags out of the Jeep or as we walked by the kitchen garden where I silently greeted the fae still enjoying the pole beans. It wasn't until we were inside the simple two-room cabin at the edge of the summer enchantment when she let out a long, audible breath and said, "Brightness help me, I wish I'd stayed in New York."

"I'm sorry," I said. "Is it that bad?"

She took my suitcase and brought it to the bedroom that had a view of the lake. "I was going to give you this one. Or would you rather have the garden view?"

I looked past her at the smooth, white ice. The mountains around the lake were also heavy with snow, and the contrast with the blooming red geraniums on the deck was still unnerving, even to me, who'd seen a lot of enchantments before. "This is great, thanks."

She looked relieved. "Good. Most people like the view."

"Don't you?"

"Well…" She walked over to the sliding glass doors that opened onto the deck and pulled them open. "I admit the lake fairies do make me a little edgy sometimes."

I joined her out on the deck, scanning the shoreline for sign of fairy activity. I saw summer-loving flower fairies and tree sprites, but no fae on the icy side of the enchantment. There was an aura of menace, however, wafting faintly in from all sides, but that was typical of any witch dwelling. Wherever we settled, magical creatures—and historically nonmagical human creatures—tried to get rid of us, or consume us, co-opt us. To get a sense of how hostile and powerful the lake fae were, I'd have to get out of the bubble of Horace's influence over the environment and scan it from the natural, winter side.

"Do the lake fairies make other people uneasy?" I asked.

"Are you asking if my anxiety is reasonable or just a symptom of my generalized anxiety disorder?" Her tone was mild and inquisitive, not annoyed.

"I think it's reasonable to be afraid of the lake fae," I said. "I wondered if the others had the same sense we do."

She smiled. "Thanks for saying that, but you don't have to. I know there isn't any danger as long as I stay on the summer side. Granddad's wand has incredible power, enough to extend his life and keep this enchantment. Did you see how he held it in his lap?"

"Yes. Does he always have it nearby?"

"Always," she said. "He's like a gadget that only works when it's plugged in. His natural battery has worn out, so he needs a constant supply of energy."

"I could feel it the second I walked into the room. Have you ever held it yourself?"

She snorted. "Not that I remember. Maybe when I was a baby they thought it would be cute to bring it near me, but never since then." She went back into the cabin. "I think he'd stab me with it now if I even tried to touch it."

I followed her in. "Really?"

She turned, saw my serious expression, and laughed. "Can you imagine? I wonder what my mom would say. I'd be bleeding out on the floor, and she'd be like, 'Oh, Horace. You're only going to make her more afraid of you.'"

We both laughed.

"The only time I've ever seen him yell at Sarah was when she touched the wand," she said. "It had rolled off his lap when he fell asleep in the chair. She bent over to pick it up, he woke up, bam. Shouting his head off."

"Powerful objects like that can hurt people," I said. "Maybe he was afraid she might get hurt."

"Yes, because that would be so like him to care about other people," Marcella said, and we laughed again. "Besides, it only hurts you if you try to use it. I've seen Glenda pick it up lots of times."

Given the way he liked to have it on hand all the time, even in the family room with guests, I was relieved to hear there were safeguards. "That's good."

"Well, I'll give you some space," she said. "We've got about an hour until dinner. Granddad likes us to be on time."

When she reached the doorway, I said, "It's beautiful here. Thanks for inviting me."

She paused, turned. "No, thank you for coming. With you here, I'm actually having a nice time." Suddenly she flinched and rapped her knuckles against the doorframe. "Knock on wood."

When she was gone, I did the same.

Chapter Eleven

A little before seven, we set out for dinner at the big house. I'd changed into the lightest-weight shirt I had (without holes) and a pair of clean black leggings (with pockets), but something felt wrong as we walked up the road in the darkness. The air was unusually warm for an evening in the mountains, which made the flower fairies dance and glimmer. And the smell in the air was odd—the incense cedar had the rich aroma I expected, but the surrounding snow gave the wind a sterile, indoor quality.

As we walked up the steps, I realized the darkness itself was unnerving, too. If it truly had been summer, the sun would still be in the sky, and we might be eating outside on the deck, watching boats and birds on the lake. But of course the enchantment was only a local one, and no witch on earth had any influence over the sun.

Before we went inside the house, I paused at the double front doors to study the teardrop pattern carved into the wood. Each drop was about the size of a human hand, all pointing upward. Framing them was a series of pointy arrows — No. It was a silhouette of the wand, its shape repeated dozens of times, aiming out. Blood and protection, blood and attack.

Staring at all those blood droplets compelled me to fill out the family tree in my head before I risked a dinner with them. If Marcella had no standing with her own relatives, I'd probably have even less—and they were witches. I'd have to be on my guard.

"Tell me about your other relatives before we go in," I said. "Just a quick summary." I should've asked her in the cabin, but she'd closed the door on me to meditate. Given her condition when she'd come out, I guessed she'd taken several calming herbs as well.

She stepped away from the door, obviously happy to delay the social event. "Sure. I mentioned Huxley," she said. "My dad had two brothers, Ronald and Jack. Ronald's wife left him to raise the kids by himself. Those are my cousins Isabel and Huxley. They're younger than me."

"Your dad was… Bernard?" I asked.

"Bertrand, or Bertie." She stroked her arm where a protective rune was tattooed around the wrist bone. "Bertrand, Ronald, and Jack. Three brothers. Two living. I'm the eldest cousin, the heir."

"Other cousins?" If her inheritance was a point of resentment, she probably had several cousins who disliked her.

"Jack's married to Kenneth. It was hard for Granddad to accept at first, but he seems to have gotten over it. Their daughter is Sage." Marcella gave me a pained look. "She hates me. I mean, really hates me."

"Is she adopted?" I asked. Maybe all the fetish for blood relations made her dislike the one who was fated to benefit most from it.

"Yes. Pardon me if I don't introduce you," she said. "I avoid her at all costs. She'll be the one giving me the evil eye. Literally. I'm wearing a necklace just to repel her hexes."

"And Cullen," I said. "Does he have any brothers or sisters? A child of his own?"

Marcella was smiling.

"What?" I asked.

"I'm imagining Cullen having a secret baby out there somewhere," she said, laughing. "That would never happen. He's too careful. And Glenda would make sure the lucky girl got screened by the family first."

I thought about that. Even witch mothers couldn't control what their children did. Or especially not them since their kids were witches too.

"That's everyone?" I asked.

"You won't need to remember any of this. Other than this dinner and tomorrow night's birthday party, feel free to hide in the cabin or go hiking as much as you want." She looked down at her body and brushed a piece of lint off her chest. Unlike me, she'd known to bring a sundress. Her fair hair looked light and cheerful with the floral fabric—in contrast to her actual mood.

I pulled up the waistband of my leggings, feeling underdressed. "The birthday celebration is tomorrow?"

"It's going to be low key, thank Brightness. Just a cake."

"Knowing a few names is good," I said. "It helps me relax."

She sighed and opened the front doors. A wave of boundary magic tingled through me again, scanning my body for danger.

"I wish it did the same for me," she said. "I'm great with names, but it has no effect on how I feel. Ready?"

"Ready."

We went into the house where Marcella's mother stood in a sleeveless linen dress and a long necklace made of antique gold coins that sent out a buzz of magic I could feel in my teeth. From her position near the door, I guessed she'd been waiting for us.

"Is something wrong?" Marcella asked, clutching her hands together.

"Let your friend talk to Granddad," she said to Marcella. "He seems to like her. That can't be bad for you, no matter what unflattering comparisons he draws between you."

"Hi," I said.

She gave me a tight smile. "Try not to shine too brightly, will you? Marcella needs her grandfather to think less badly of her. It's terrible it's gotten to this point, but there's no going back in time, at least not with the magic I have."

"Does it matter what he thinks of her?" I asked.

Both Marcella and Pauline turned horrified faces toward me.

"Does it *matter?*" Pauline asked. "Of course it matters. It matters more than anything." She whispered something into Marcella's ear before walking away without another word to me.

Marcella showed me her hands, which were shaking. "I hope there's wellspring punch tonight. She told me not to ruin her life."

"I just don't understand why you put up with all this," I said.

"Money," she answered. "That's basically it."

"But we're witches. Money isn't half as useful as magic."

"In this family, they're a package deal," she said. "When Granddad dies, whoever inherits the wand gets everything else too. Houses, amulets, investments, everything."

"But if you're the heir under that old oath, you don't have to worry about what they think of you," I said. "It's set in blood."

She looked down, clasping and twisting her hands together. "I worry anyway. It's supposed to be fate, but I don't feel like I'm ever getting that wand." Her voice grew faint. "I've always felt like something terrible is going to happen to stop it. It means so much to my mother."

I reached out and took one of her hands in mine. Just brief skin-to-skin contact from a friendly witch could feel soothing. "She's not going to starve," I said, thinking of the gold sandals.

"Granddad pays out a good allowance to everyone in the family," she said. "Mom relies completely on that allowance, but there's no guarantee of more to come when he dies."

"I think she'll be fine," I said. "Maybe what you're afraid of is that you won't be able to support yourself."

"Oh no, I'm not actually worried about me, not that way. I can work. Staying in New York would be too expensive, but I don't mind moving somewhere cheaper." She raked her fingers through her blond hair, exposing a row of gold earrings and steel cartilage piercings. "But my mom is too old to lose all this. I'd never be able to earn enough to make up what she has now."

"Wouldn't the rest of the family help her out?" I asked.

Marcella glanced over her shoulder, where the voices of a large gathering were building. "You're about to meet them. You tell me."

Chapter Twelve

We must've been late. A large buffet was set up on a long table in the great room, and everyone was already picking up plates and filling them with food. There were about a dozen people, not counting the cooking staff in white shirts. I recognized Horace and Cullen and of course Pauline. I didn't see Sarah. While the age and ethnicity of those in the room varied, a quick scan told me everyone was a witch, including the employees.

Some witch families entrusted nonmag people with their secrets in exchange for extra pay, job security, and magical gifts. But if a family was rich enough, they hired only their own kind, which gave them both security from exposure (and potential blackmail) as well as the status within witch high society.

Marcella and I walked to the end of the buffet and were the last to get our food. As I discreetly probed each dish for harmful magic—very discreetly, because it was insulting not to trust your hosts—the others took their seats in two age-defined groups. The older generation took the pine table near the window with the best view. The four younger ones got the couch, chairs, and floor.

"The bald one is my uncle Ronald," Marcella whispered to me. I looked over and studied the man with a shaved head, looking for a resemblance to Marcella but not finding any. He was talking to Horace. "The green polo shirt is Jack. Kenneth is the thin guy next to him with all the earrings."

I studied the two men, noting the obvious differences in their appearance—Jack was round and pale with shaggy red hair, and Kenneth thin and brown—but then they met my gaze, and I had to look away.

"And Glenda, of course," she continued, lifting a roll from a silver platter. It was enchanted to keep them warm. "Not exactly a trophy wife, but close."

Glenda must've been the fashionable woman at Horace's side. She had pixie-cut champagne-blond hair, a long neck, and impressive amounts of gold jewelry that would be heavy to wear.

I followed Marcella over to a couch just as Horace shouted, "Cullen, son. Join me."

Perched on an ottoman near the same couch, Cullen paused with his fork in midair. "I've already settled over here, Dad," he said. "The crab salad is amazing, by the way. Have you tried it?"

Horace raised his voice. "What's that? Come over here so I can hear you."

Cullen, flushing, gave his cousins an awkward smile and got to his feet. "Excuse me," he mumbled.

"Have fun," a teenage boy on the sofa said, snickering. His black hair was cut in a trendy, masculine style, but his clothes were a mix of gender identities: a floral skirt over hairy legs, a black tank top showing off his muscles.

"Oh Chosen One, we shall miss you," said a young

woman on a chair. She had an eyebrow piercing, a nose ring, and a sarcastic tone.

Marcella whispered to me, "That's Isabel. And Huxley, her brother."

I studied Isabel. She had long dark hair and golden skin and wore so much makeup that I wasn't sure I'd recognize her without it. The rest of her style was plain white, a blank canvas: T-shirt, jeans, sneakers. When she noticed me staring, she stared back and cast a probing spell at my eyes.

Blinking, I turned my attention to my plate. Extremely carnivorous, the menu had included beef, crab, and chicken. I took a bite of the crab, as Cullen had recommended, and cast a stronger self-defense spell around my head.

If Isabel did that again, I'd end up with a migraine. Her attack had surprised me with its socially unacceptable timing —the dinner table with family—and its strength. She was about my age, but she hadn't worked at the Protectorate like I had, and I didn't usually expect that kind of power from normal witches under thirty.

While I chewed, I prepared a mirroring defensive spell, one of my specialties, then looked at her again. She immediately probed me again. This time, however, my magic turned it back on her, amplified.

Eyes widening, she made an audible yelp.

"No magic at dinner!" Horace shouted. "Isabel, I can feel you hexing again. Cut it out or I'll have you wash all the dishes by hand."

She flushed and looked at her plate. "Sorry, Granddad."

Huxley, my attacker's little brother, grinned. "Who's your friend, Marcie?" he asked, making a sandwich out of a roll and some of the meat. He had a mountain of food on his plate.

"This is Alma Bellrose," Marcella said quietly. "We went

to school together. Alma, this is Isabel and Huxley, Ronald's kids, and Sage, Jack and Kenneth's daughter."

"Nice defensive spell," Huxley said to me. "I should learn more of that stuff, but my thing is music. Did you notice it when you came in?"

I paused to listen. It had been loudest near the front door, but I could still hear something Irish and folksy playing in the distance. "Yes," I said. "Fiddle?"

He nodded and swallowed. "I studied in Dublin."

Isabel snorted. "You were in a hotel there for four days."

Ignoring his sister, he touched a silver pendant hanging from his neck. The music in the other room became louder. "I'm going to really study as soon as Dad says it's OK." He lowered his voice. "He needs to get the funds from Granddad."

Isabel looked over her shoulder, then poured something from a vial in her pocket into her wine. "If it were *Cullen* wanting to go somewhere, there wouldn't be any problem," she said. "But one of us? We don't count. Look at the golden boy over there, buttering up the old witch like he always does."

"He's his father," Marcella said, surprising me with the force of her words. "Of course Cullen has a different relationship with him than we do."

"We? That's Bright, coming from you," Isabel said. "You get the wand. What do you care about the rest of us?"

Marcella flushed red but said nothing.

One of her cousins—a twentyish woman with strawberry blond hair I guessed was Sage, Kenneth and Ronald's daughter—hadn't spoken yet, but I noticed her suddenly become interested in the conversation. She set her plate aside, smashed her napkin into a ball, and dropped it on the unfinished food. "Cullen would at least have the skill to wield the wand."

A cold silence fell over the group of cousins. The older family members were listening to Horace talk about the weather outside the enchantment, the feet of snow he'd prevented from falling on his property.

"It's not my fault I'm firstborn of the firstborn," Marcella said, her voice still quiet, defensive.

"But you should at least let it go to somebody else," Sage said. She wore a black T-shirt and shorts that made her fair skin look as pale as the snow on the mountains. "It's a miracle of magical engineering. Totally unique. Priceless. It should go to somebody with the talent to wield it."

Nobody spoke. I wanted Marcella to tell them to all hex themselves, that an inheritance from a blood oath wasn't something she could choose to reject, but she had shrunk deeper into her seat and was staring at her food.

Isabel reached over and put a supportive hand on Sage's shoulder. If her Granddad hadn't already scolded her for using magic at dinner, I thought she would've given her cousin a comfort spell.

"As you know, life is *not* fair," Isabel said. "Especially with magical bloodlines."

Sage shook off Isabel's hand and lifted her chin. "Just because I'm adopted doesn't mean I'm nonmag," she said. "I have as much power as any other Gardner."

"*You* do," Isabel said.

I stabbed a hunk of chicken with my knife, silently begging Marcella to fight back. They respected power and would respect any self-defensive move she made. But I saw her hand trembling on her glass, and the tight line of her lips, and knew she was going to stay silent, just waiting until it was acceptable to run away and hide again.

An argument at the other table broke out, interrupting the cousins' attack on Marcella. While Horace was waving the wand in the air like a conductor with a baton, Jack banged his hands on the table and stood up.

"You've gone senile," Jack said.

"It doesn't matter what you think," Horace said, continuing to wave the wand. "It has never mattered."

Cullen, at Horace's side, looked just as upset as Jack did, but he sat red-faced and silent.

"I'm going to have to leave before I do something I regret," Jack said to the thin man with a dozen earrings—Kenneth, his husband.

Kenneth stood and put an arm around him, trying to get him to sit. But Jack pulled free and strode away. A few moments later, the front door slammed.

I looked at Sage, who looked unhappy but not surprised. She picked up her glass and took another drink.

"They've never gotten along," Marcella said to me.

Sage turned on her. "Oh, and you have?" Her anger allowed tiny magical sparks to fly out of her mouth with tiny droplets of spit. "Granddad hates you. He hates how weak you are. Don't talk about my father."

Marcella recoiled and closed her eyes. She became so withdrawn I thought she might drop the plate on her lap, so I picked it up and moved it to the coffee table. Then I lifted my wineglass and drained it. These witches were unpleasant. I realized how lucky I was to never know any cousins. Or uncles, aunts, siblings, or grandparents.

"Marcella and I are going to say good night," I said, standing up. I bent over, took Marcella's hands, and pulled her to her feet. Like a toddler, she let me guide her away from her family out of the great room and then the house itself.

The night was still warm and smelled of jasmine. I inhaled a deep breath and told her to do the same. Then we walked down the hill past the vegetable garden, where the fairies slept, to the sanctuary of the cabin.

I locked the door behind us and hung a sachet of bay leaves I had in my pocket on the doorknob to support my protective boundary spell.

"It's always worse than I remember," Marcella said, leaning against the wall. "I know they're going to be horrible, and they are. That's fine. They're family, they're witches, they're jealous and insecure, and our parents have set us against one another. But what I never remember…"

I was eager for her to finish, but the silence stretched out for several long seconds. "Yes?" I asked.

"I forget what happens to *me*," she said. "How I feel. How I fall apart. How I just can't… can't… I don't know. It's like a dream. A nightmare. And I can't get out of it, and I can't wake up."

She held up her hands, and then before I could stop her, she slapped herself.

"Don't do that!" I cried, grabbing her hands. They were as cold as the frozen lake.

"They're right," she said, her voice rising. "I'm not strong enough. It's too strong, whatever this is. It's always there, always hanging over me, and it's bigger. It's stronger. Alma, I'll never be strong enough. I know that. I've always known that. They're right. How can I defend myself from them when I know what they're saying is true? I know it better than they do!"

I didn't think what she needed was for somebody else to tell her she was wrong, so I just stood with her, holding her hands, trying to give her my strength.

I didn't realize then how much of that she was going to need.

Chapter Thirteen

"You don't have to come," Marcella said. "It's a family tradition. A ritual. Please feel free to sit it out."

We were enjoying our breakfast on the deck, sitting in shorts and T-shirts as we watched a hard, northerly wind tumble across the ice and kick snowflakes into the air. The family had a selection of loaner summer clothes for surprised guests, and I'd found a pair of men's cargo shorts with wood buttons that had a fun botanical vibe. The Gardner family wore more metal than any family I'd ever seen. On a walk early that morning, I'd found a massive pine cone and had broken seeds off to store in the shorts' many pockets. The power in flora could be wild and unreliable, but I had a knack for pulling energy out of it, much more than with silver, gold, pewter, copper, platinum, or steel.

"I'd like to come," I said. "What's the ritual?" I popped a fresh cherry tomato from the garden into my mouth. The magic of the wand had created artificial warmth to let it grow, but the short days hadn't provided enough sun to make it very sweet. It was a little better than a grocery-store tomato in January, but not much.

Marcella pointed at the edge of the lakeshore where snow met bare, warm rocks. "We meet at the edge of summer. Sometimes it's farther away, sometimes closer, but always the western edge at the lake. Then we hike around the boundary. See how far it goes this year, note what the landmarks are. When we reach the lake again"—she moved her arm in an arc, then pointed at the shore to the east—"we stop and, you know, celebrate."

"Summon a demon?" I joked.

She smiled, then got serious. "I wonder if a demon could get through Granddad's enchantment?"

I glanced around at all the fairies. There were so many in the trees and plants, climbing over the rocks and just bobbing around in the air, that I decided they'd come from miles around to enjoy the summertime. The density was much too high for long-term peace.

But with so many around, there couldn't be any demon threat at the moment. The fairies would disappear if they sensed a malicious spirit out to consume them, as demons did with fae. Unlike other witches, even those trained to hunt demons, my sight of the fae gave me a secret warning system for demon presence.

"I wouldn't worry about demons," I told her.

"Really? That means a lot, coming from you. Former demon hunter. Protectorate agent." She took a sip of the chamomile tea I'd made, which I'd mixed with a few dried borage blossoms for courage. "Though I'm worried anyway, because of course I am."

"I'd like to join the family hike if I'm welcome," I said. "I'm fascinated with the wand's enchantment. The boundary might be interesting."

"If you're sure," she said. "I'd love to have you there."

"Are there any rules about what I can bring?"

"Nope. Load up," she said. "I'm wearing all my jewelry. Do you have beads you're not wearing now?"

I patted my pockets. "I do, but I was thinking about the pine seeds. They're giving off a really cool buzz. Can you feel it?"

She tapped me with a gentle magical probe. "Barely. Honestly, I'm so loaded up on boundary spells it kind of dulls what I can sense on other people."

I started to tell her that it was dangerous to dull your senses, then wised up. The last thing she needed from me was a list of new ways to worry. "You said you measure the summer enchantment zone. Does that mean you write it down somewhere?"

She gave me a surprised smile. "Yes, Granddad does. There's a book. It's fun to look at, see how the area gets bigger and smaller some years."

"I'd think it would be smallest this year since you think your grandfather is at the end of his life."

She shrugged. "I guess. It doesn't seem smaller. Except for the lake being frozen, the area seems as big as ever."

A man from the kitchen staff came by walking around the outside of the cabin to collect our empty breakfast dishes. Marcella told me the staff only came in during the day and lived over the snowy side of the boundary on the road back to South Shore. He walked away with our tray toward the neighboring cabin, hidden behind a thick hedge.

"Who's got the cabin next to ours?" I asked.

"Probably Sage. Jack and Kenneth prefer the house." She got to her feet. "Usually it's me, Huxley and Isabel, and Sage out here. Like at dinner. The older generation likes more comforts."

"How about Cullen?" I asked. "Where does he sleep?"

She smiled. "The main house. Granddad insists."

"Or maybe he likes the comforts too," I said. And for all his geniality, he might feel uncomfortable with the jealous teasing from those his own age.

We went into the cabin and put on hiking boots, checked our beads and necklaces and sachets, sun hats, glasses, then walked along the shore toward a pile of granite boulders along the lakeshore. Just beyond was a slope of snow rising up the mountainside.

Ronald and Jack were already there, as well as Huxley, Isabel, and Sage. They were facing away from us, pointing at the snow, arguing about a pole sticking out of the rocks that Jack insisted was where they'd marked the boundary last year, but Ronald said it had been years earlier.

"Morning," Marcella said, but she spoke too quietly for anyone to hear. Or they didn't care enough to respond.

"It's already rusty," Ronald said. "That thing's been there more than a year, Jack. Three or four at least. Last year's must be out there in the snow somewhere."

Jack shook his head and started to argue, but then he was distracted by Horace's arrival with Cullen. Sarah walked behind them, carrying a red leather journal on a silver tray, as if it were breakfast.

I leaned over to Marcella. "No Glenda?"

"Not the outdoorsy type," she muttered. "Neither is Kenneth."

Keeping to the back of the group, Marcella and I followed the others as they walked up the slope along the snowdrift. Cullen and Huxley, the two youngest males, each took one of Horace's arms, guiding him over the rocks, lifting him when necessary. We came upon a cliff that was too steep for anyone to climb, so we turned and walked along the bottom until we could meet up with the boundary again in a meadow.

The presence of so many other witches made it hard for

me to study the enchantment. At the head of the group, Horace kept shouting out landmarks to Sarah, who marked dots on a map folded out from the book, and then making Cullen double-check her work.

I was glad I was walking in the back because the flower fairies were swarming in large numbers and I was having to concentrate on pretending not to see them. About the size of butterflies and sparrows, the various fairies were flitting around my head, sitting on my shoulder, my feet. I tripped over a few that surprised me by jumping out of a gap in the rocks.

"Are you OK?" Marcella asked me. "What's wrong?"

In my preoccupation with the fairies, I'd stopped paying attention to Marcella's shifting moods. But now, hearing the high-pitched tone of her voice, I realized she was back in an anxious state.

"Nothing," I said. "Just out of shape. I haven't hiked in a while."

She was staring at my face. "Are you sure? You looked as if you'd seen something."

I wasn't going to lie to her, but I also wasn't going to tell her my secret. "It was fairy sign," I said.

"Oh, here? Do you think they came out of the lake?"

"With all the flowers, there are bound to be fae who are thrilled to get a break from winter," I said.

She frowned at the pinkish-blue blooms of penstemon growing on the slope next to the snow boundary. "Do you think they hate us as much as the lake fae?" she asked, drawing a new protective spell around herself.

"No," I said. "I would guess they like the summer weather."

She continued to frown, sending probing spells at the harmless flowers. Horace and the others had stopped and were just a few feet away, stretching a tape measure between a huge pine tree and the snow. As he orchestrated the measuring, Horace's elbow bumped Marcella in the back. She jumped and scrambled away, but he didn't seem to notice.

When the others continued on, Marcella didn't move. Her face was pale, her lips bloodless.

"Marcella?" I asked.

"I feel like I'm dying," she whispered.

"You're not—"

She sucked in a breath. Her eyes were unblinking, staring at her hands. "I know. I know I'm not." She started panting. "Panic. It. Feels like. Brightness. Like I'm dying."

I put my hand on my beads and touched her throat, trying to calm her, open up the airways. When that didn't seem to do anything, I cast a comprehensive defensive spell around her that would muffle all sensations, not just magical ones—like putting on noise-canceling earphones but for sound, scent, and touch. Her vision would soften, but not completely go black, which would only alarm her more.

It seemed to work. Her shoulders lowered, her breathing steadied, and she blinked her eyes. The rest of the group had gone on ahead without us, and we stood on the slope with the snow on one side and flowers on the other. I watched as a bee flew away from the flowers and bounced off the seasonal boundary as if it were mosquito netting.

"All right, you can take it down now," she said, her voice muffled behind my spell. It was a two-way enchantment, putting her behind a sensory wall from me as well.

I removed it. My head was swimming.

"That's amazing," she said. "But aren't you tired? Didn't that wear you out?"

Seeing she was better, I let myself bend over and sit on the ground. Magic always had a price, and my beaded necklace and bracelets had paid only some of it. My body had paid the rest.

"Why don't you go ahead without me?" I asked. "I'll be able to catch up in a minute." Her family would be much more judgmental of her than they would be of me for falling behind.

"No way. What kind of person do you think I am?" She put a hand on my shoulder, and I felt strength pour into my magical well of power. "I'm a mess, but I still have a few tricks."

It was surprisingly effective. The fatigue left my limbs. With her support, I got to my feet and we hiked up the rocky slope after the others. She seemed to have recovered from her panic attack, but now I had a headache.

When we caught up to them, they were gathered at the edge of a dry creek bed. The main road was just to the left, crossing the creek on a concrete bridge. Cullen was walking along the snow, calling out the landmarks to Sarah.

"Same as last year," she said about a boulder as tall as she was, only half-covered in snow.

Horace nodded, wiped the sweat off his brow, and then, seeing Marcella and I had rejoined them, scowled and turned away.

"The falls must be dry this year," Marcella said to me. "Frozen, I mean. Sometimes some of the water melts and we get a nice trickle here. But not this year."

We jumped over dry rocks and hiked under an overhanging snowbank that would be impossible without magic. Huxley had his phone out, taking pictures, and Cullen and Horace talked about the potential of bits of granite collected now, when under the wand's enchantment, to have more spell power. Isabel walked with Jack and Sage, laughing about something I couldn't hear. Jack wasn't angry like at dinner, and he and his daughter seemed to get along well; overall the mood was much more relaxed than the night before.

For everyone except Marcella. Since we'd rejoined the

others, her anxiety had returned. I noticed her digging her fingernails into her arm, enacting the tattooed runes until she'd hexed her own skin. A pink glow surrounded the scratch marks.

I gestured for her to slow down with me a moment. "Maybe you should go back to the cabin."

She shook her head. "No. I refuse to give up." She pulled down her sleeves to cover the glowing welts on her arms. "I came all this way. I can't let him see me give up."

I nodded, and we kept walking.

"You've got tattoos too." She gestured at the thin black rings on the skin around my wrist.

In the heat, I'd pushed up my sleeves. I wore heavy bracelets around both wrists, but the marks on my skin were still visible if you were looking for them.

"Yes," I said.

"I know what those mean." She met my gaze. "Or I think I do. You battled another witch, right?"

It would take too long to tell my whole life story, so I just nodded. "Something like that."

"And you won." She smiled, her anxiety vanishing for a moment. "That's why you're here. I know I can count on you. You can protect me. I know it."

I lost my patience. "But from what, Marcella? Something that's really dangerous or just your feeling that there is?"

Smile falling, she shrugged. "Is there a difference?"

"Yes," I said. "There is. There really is."

She looked unconvinced.

Chapter Fourteen

We hiked up toward the waterfall; far outside the summer zone, however, it was still covered in ice. After Sarah noted the location in the book, everyone turned to walk back down the trail. Horace was supported at each side by Cullen and Huxley, the two youngest men, while Ronald, Isabel, Sage, Marcella, and I walked behind them. Bored, I studied the elaborate braiding of Isabel's dark hair. And she was wearing just as much makeup as she had at dinner. How did she find the time? I'd done a quick probe to confirm it wasn't an illusion. Witches who spent so much time on their appearance always confused me. Why not use magic? A little spell, quick and easy, could make you *look* as if you'd spent an hour on your eyeliner. Why do it for real?

I was looking forward to the end of the hike, for Marcella's sake as much as my own. There was something exhausting about the Gardner family—the alliances, resentments, friendships, grudges—but maybe it was that way in all large families, especially affluent witch ones. They had a lot to gain, a lot to lose, and too much of the deciding power in the hands of a very old, very irritable witch.

"Watch your grip, child," Horace snapped at Huxley, who was using both hands to hold his grandfather up by the elbow. "You'll leave a bruise. Don't you know any antigravity spells?"

Huxley looked over his shoulder at his father, Ronald, silently begging to be relieved. Ronald turned away and took a picture of a distant hawk circling overhead. I wondered how far into the air the enchantment went, if they'd ever tried to measure that as well.

While I was looking up, Horace suddenly let out a cry. Sparks exploded in every direction, and both Huxley and Cullen collapsed, dropping their elderly burden onto the trail. Horace rolled down the slope, struck a granite outcropping, and lay still.

Heart pounding, I grabbed my necklace and cast a quick defensive spell around me and Marcella. Had there been an attack from the forest? And who was the enemy—fairy, demon, or witch?

Amid the cries and shouting, Ronald ran down the hill and was the first to reach Horace's side. "Father? Talk to me. Are you conscious?" Ronald looked over his shoulder at Sarah. "Run and get Glenda. She'll want to be here."

Huxley and Cullen scrambled to their feet and hurried down the trail where Ronald knelt next to his father.

The old man lifted his head. "Demon's balls, nobody go anywhere." He slapped Ronald's hand on his arm. "You think I'm dying, that it? Can't wait to see me pass on, can you?"

Ronald leaned back on his heels. "That's not true, Father. Of course it's not—"

Horace lifted himself on an elbow and pointed at Cullen. "Help me get my wand out." He fumbled with his chest.

Cullen, rubbing his forehead—the explosion had been

magical, and he looked dazed, as if it had captured him too —staggered forward and helped Horace unbutton his shirt. Underneath was the wand, its handle wrapped with a leather strap, which was connected to a long leather cord hung from his neck.

I felt its magic from twenty feet away, like music in my mouth. It was just the sort of unique, powerful object my father would covet. I'd never been a willing thief, but now I felt an urgent desire to possess the wand for myself, take it away from these petty, mean-spirited witches and do good with it. What would the pine handle feel like against my skin? Would it sizzle or soothe? Was it hot or cold?

We all watched and waited as Horace, white hair visible on his pale chest, held the wand against his cheek with both hands. He was bleeding along his cheek, and his jacket was streaked with dirt.

It was Cullen who finally braved the question. "What happened, Dad?"

Horace clung to the wand with his eyes closed for several long seconds. Then he lowered the wand and gestured for Cullen, who was kneeling at his side, to help him up. Huxley tried to assist, but Horace waved him away, relying only on his youngest son.

"I was attacked, that's what," Horace said, casting a narrow-eyed glare over the group. "One of you witches is in a hurry for me to go to the other plane of existence."

"What are you talking about?" Cullen asked. "That's ridiculous."

"Don't you tell me what's ridiculous," Horace snapped. "Somebody hexed me. Clear as day. Shot me right in the chest. If I hadn't been wearing the wand, I'd be dead. Right now you'd be pretending to be sorry I'm gone."

"I'll get Kenneth," Jack said. He looked at Sage. "Dad can help, don't worry."

Cullen put his arm around Horace and said, "You've had a scare. Let's get you back to the house."

"You, I trust. And Sarah. But the others, stay back." Horace glared at Huxley, Ronald, Isabel, and Sage and even me, and then, finally, Marcella. "If you weren't completely incompetent, I'd think it was you who hexed me."

I felt Marcella stiffen at my side.

"But maybe you had help," he continued. "Maybe that's why your friend is here."

I opened my mouth to defend myself, then thought better of it. He was very old and had had a shock. He might be seriously injured. He could've broken a rib or fractured his hip—the wand was protecting him from the pain now, but it wouldn't last if he needed true healing.

"Let's get you home," Cullen said.

"Only you can touch me," Horace said.

Ronald was offended. "I'd never hurt you. And neither would my children."

Horace put an arm around Cullen. "Save your breath," he said. His other hand continued to clutch the wand, pointing it at the ground like a cane. His posture straightened as the wand provided invisible support.

They hobbled away down the path together, Sarah behind them with the book. The youngest generation—Sage, Isabel, Huxley, and Marcella—hung back to let others deal with the crisis and, I guessed, to avoid their grandfather's temper.

"He needs a doctor," I said to Marcella.

"Jack went to get Kenneth," she said. "He can help. If Granddad lets him."

"He's a doctor?"

"Cardiologist." Marcella looked at Sage, who was scowling at us. "Right? He's works at UCSF?"

"Stanford," Sage said. "Don't pretend you care."

Marcella sighed. "I had nothing to do with Granddad—"

A blast of magic came at Marcella like a tidal wave. Already on guard and standing close to Marcella, I was able to push it away with a blank wall of defensive magic.

Sage, struck with her own hex, tripped on the rocks and fell.

"Wow," Marcella said.

Sprawled on the ground, Sage pointed at me and said to Isabel, "Do you see what she did? Maybe that's what she did to Granddad."

Isabel reached out a hand to help Sage get off the ground. "He'll take care of her. Don't worry."

"She put up a defensive block," Huxley said. "Sage was the one who struck first."

"We can't trust her," Sage said. "We can't trust either one of them."

Isabel bent over and picked up a rock. When she clutched it in her fist and drew an arc over her head, I sensed the signature of granite magic. I put out a hand to stop Marcella from walking into the weakness spell Isabel had drawn in front of us.

I stood there with Marcella and watched everyone else jog ahead.

"They'd love it if I left now," Marcella said.

"They might see that as an admission of guilt," I said.

She turned and sat on a log. A tree sprite she couldn't see ran away from her and climbed into a rotted crevice. "It won't make any difference. They already hate me."

"But why?" I asked.

It was too much. Other than her anxiety disorder, Marcella was inoffensive. She didn't seem the type to inspire passion of any kind, positive or negative. She had average talents, above-average looks, a kind disposition, and never hurt a soul. She was their cousin, niece, granddaughter. Why did they hate her so much? If they'd believed she'd attacked Horace, they would've taken her into custody, interrogated her, punished her. But they didn't actually think she'd done anything. She was just a scapegoat.

"They really do think the wand deserves somebody better," she said. "They just hate the idea I'm going to have it and wield it over them, doing whatever I want, probably as long as they're alive, because it will also give me extended life."

"You think they'd hate a different cousin if they were the one inheriting?" I asked. "You think Sage would be rude to Isabel if she was going to get it?"

"Absolutely," Marcella said. "You know how families are."

"I guess I don't."

She withdrew a pouch from her pocket and poured out a handful of dried herbs. When she crushed the leaves between her fingers and drew protective circles on each cheek, I smelled sage. Although it was a common hearth witch's spell to calm one's system, I thought it was ironic her remedy had the same name as her hating cousin.

"It's one of the oldest stories there is," she said. "Brother killing brother."

"It seems so irrational to me."

"Of course it is." She handed a few sage leaves to me. We'd reached the road again, and the house was a short walk to the right, the cabins to the left. The frozen lake, surrounded by snow-capped mountains, shimmered in the morning sun ahead of us. "Human nature is witch nature."

"Terrifying," I said.

"You're telling me." Marcella looked at the house, then over at the cabins, then back to the house again.

I studied her profile, saw so much suffering in her eyes, her lips, the hold of her jaw. "If it makes you feel better," I said, "I'm glad I came." I meant it literally—if my being there made her feel better, I was glad I'd come. I liked to be useful.

"I can't do it, Alma," she said softly.

Thinking she meant being the wand-wielding family matriarch someday, I said, "Then don't. Choose your own path. Fate isn't written. Even witches can't see the future."

She smiled at me. "I meant lunch."

I laughed. We'd planned on eating in the house with the others. "I'm not afraid of them," I said. "But you should take a break. Recharge for the next challenge. Cast a calming Circle and sit in it a few hours. I'll find out how your Granddad is doing."

"Thank you. I'll need to rest to face the family tonight, especially if Granddad has any broken bones and they're going to blame me for it."

"Agreed."

"You don't have to have lunch with them, you know," she said. "The kitchen can send a tray to the cabin. That's what I'm going to do."

"No, I don't want them to think we're afraid of them."

"Too late," she said. "They already know I am."

"Then even better they know I'm not." I put my hand on the braided jute-and-redwood-bead bracelet I wore, intending to use it to cast a quick feel-good spell on her, but then took it off and held it out to her. "A gift."

She looked down, her eyes widening as she sensed the magical friendship charm I was attaching between us. Hand trembling, she reached out and put her hand over mine, trapping the bracelet between our palms. I closed my eyes, pictured her face—smiling, relaxed, glowing in sunlight without the suffering—and released my grip on the bracelet.

"Thank you," she said, bringing it to her chest, holding it against her heart.

"Maybe that will help a little," I said. "I can't promise it—"

"Of course it will help." As she strung it around her wrist, I noticed her eyes were shining. "It already is. I wish I could do something for you in return. I'm such a drain on people."

"You said you have friends in New York."

"That's different," she said.

"Why?"

She shrugged. "It's easy there. Nobody knows me. I take the subway, eat at the deli, hang out at the library. I volunteer at the hospital. Work part-time at a spa."

From the way she'd been acting, I'd thought she'd lived as a recluse, not too unlike my life in the forest. "You know other witches? Or is it all nonmag?"

"Lots of witches, are you kidding? It's New York," she said. "The spa was a witch operation. They said I did a great calming spell."

"I bet."

She put her hand over the bracelet. "Thank you again. Can I combine it with herbs?"

"It can amplify whatever magic you're already using," I said.

"I owe you, Alma. I don't know what to say." With a wave, she walked off toward the cabin, her head lowered, her shoulders hunched.

The way her family crushed her spirit made me angry. Fired up like an avenging angel, I walked quickly to the house and marched over the threshold without acknowledging the magical scan. It felt like an electric shock in my brain, but I was angry enough not to feel it.

Chapter Fifteen

Just inside the door, Ronald was looking at his phone and frowned when he saw me. "Maybe this isn't a good time."

Ronald was Marcella's oldest uncle, and I had the impression he didn't think as badly of her as the others did. He hadn't joined in any of the pile-ons, and his expression with her was serious but kind. Well, maybe not kind, but at least neutral.

"How is Witch Horace?" I asked, ignoring the hint I should leave.

Ronald put his phone in his pocket and shrugged. "He's one hundred and thirteen, and he just fell down a mountain."

It would be rude to cast a probing spell, but his casual attitude confused me. Was he glad Horace was going to be dead soon, or were his injuries not serious?

"So… he's going to be all right?" I asked.

"Ken's taking a look, but he seems as strong as ever. Nothing broken. A few scrapes and bruises." He took a small glass vial out of his chest pocket and tipped a few drops of a green liquid onto his tongue. Once again, my manners and self-preservation stopped me from casting a spell to study him. "Glenda's making him rest."

"That's good," I said.

He ran his hand over his bare scalp, looked around, and nodded at me to follow him to the stairs. He led me to the cozy room on the ground floor and sat on the brick hearth in front of the fireplace.

"You're Protectorate?" he asked, picking up an iron fireplace poker. "You aren't now, but you were trained there?"

It took me a moment to be sure he wasn't threatening me with the poker. "Yes." I sat down across from him and picked up the little broom, wood and straw. My magic told me it was as old as Ronald was—and nicely powerful.

He looked at the broom in my hands and smiled faintly as he put the poker down. "Sorry. Habit. Marcella's dad used to pick on me as a kid, and this was my preferred self-defensive weapon."

I put the broom down. "I couldn't feel anyone attack your father," I said, "if that's what you're asking me. I know it wasn't Marcella though."

"Of course it wasn't Marcella," he said, rolling his eyes. "Pitiful thing. How Bertie's only child could turn out like that is… It's wrong."

"She's not—"

"I'm sorry, of course she's your friend. I mean no disrespect. She was a nice kid. My brother didn't bond with her, but I always thought she was sweet."

I smiled tightly, although I thought it was weak of him to let the rest of the family bully her. "Who do you think hexed your father?"

"That's just it. You're Protectorate and you couldn't feel anything. You know what that means."

I met his gaze. His eyes were as dark as the iron poker. "What does it mean?" I asked.

He leaned toward me, lowering his voice. "It means he did it to himself. He's very old. He overestimates his strength. That wand was on his chest, right near his heart. He'd been using it to subdue winter—did you feel how hot he made it today? Eighty degrees at nine in the morning? That's warm for July up here."

"And what—he drained his energy?" I thought back to the moment he fell. "There was definitely a blast of power."

He looked around the room. His voice was still low and conspiratorial. "I think he just lost his grip on the enchantment. It rebounded. He's tired, distracted, maybe a little confused. One hundred thirteen. Even with magic, the brain ages."

"Does anyone else think what you're thinking?"

"All of them, I imagine," he said. "Except Sage. She really does think Marcella's an agent of Shadow here to ruin the family. Which is insane. But maybe she's being self-protective."

"Of what?"

"Oh, you know, a good offense is the best defense," he said. "Adopted children can have a rough time in witch families. Goes back to the old days. Paranoia about changelings. And of course the fetish for bloodlines. So many of our traditions are garbage from the past. Why should a firstling inherit more than the second? Obviously I'm biased—Bertrand was my older brother, and even though he's dead, I and my descendants are completely disinherited—but I think Marcella would be very happy to step aside and let somebody else take the family burdens as long as her mom was taken care of."

"She would," I said.

He nodded and got to his feet. "Well, please relay my

good wishes to Marcella when you see her. I wanted to make sure she knew one of us didn't suspect her of hurting her grandfather. I don't blame her for staying away. Never will."

I watched him walk off and disappear up the stairs.

Uncle Ronald didn't impress me with his courage. He wanted me to relay his good wishes but wasn't going to actually tell her himself or display them in front of the others. He believed his father had hexed himself but wouldn't risk saying so to his face.

Or was it possible he was lying to me? Maybe he did know who had attacked his father. He just wanted to make sure I didn't.

❧

I WENT UPSTAIRS and found Cullen with Isabel and Sage, talking close together near a side table laid out with coffee and sandwiches. They gave me mixed looks—Cullen was friendly enough, but the women frowned—and I decided getting a quick lunch was enough of a show of bravery.

"Help yourself," Cullen said, stepping aside to give me access to the plates. "Sorry it's not much. We're all a little freaked out at the moment."

"Of course." I took only one plate so a hand would be free to defend myself if necessary. "How is your father doing?"

Cullen rubbed his eyes. "Better than I am. His fall scared the Shadow out of me."

"I bet." Hoping Marcella would eat, I took two baguettes stuffed with meat and cheese. I also took a serving of marinated green bean salad which I guessed had come from the enchanted vegetable garden. I wasn't entirely sure eating it would be safe—the spell might have left some residue on the beans I'd rather not imbibe, similar to a toxic pesticide—but I'd run a deep scan on it when I got back to the cabin.

"The cheese is from Sonoma County," Isabel said suddenly. "Isn't that where you live?"

"Yes, in Silverpool. Up north, not far from the coast." I waited for her to say something nasty.

"I went to Bodega Bay once," she continued. "It was really beautiful. Peaceful." She reached over and took a strawberry from a fruit platter.

"I've been there," Sage said. "But I was little. All I remember is my dads got me saltwater taffy."

Afraid they were testing me somehow, I stood frozen and tense, prepared for an insult or criticism. But they just looked at me, mostly bored, picking at the buffet.

I made myself open my senses more, drop my guard. So far as I could tell, they were making honest small talk.

"I hope Witch Horace makes a full recovery," I said, lowering my guard completely so they could, if they wanted, cast truth spells over my speech.

They smiled politely.

"Thanks," Sage said.

Isabel nodded to me, then gave Cullen a reassuring pat on the arm. "He's tough."

Cullen sighed. "He really is. I keep telling myself that."

After another few awkward seconds, I wished them well and made a run for it to the cabin.

What was going on? The women had seemed to hate me before. Maybe Ronald had talked to them. Believing Horace had been the one to hurt himself and not me would make it a lot easier to be pleasant at the buffet table.

As I walked back to the cabin, I enjoyed the warm sun on my cheeks and looked forward to my lunch. The green beans seemed fine. If they hexed me, the worst that could happen was probably indigestion. A butterfly flew by me and landed on a branch of a quaking aspen already occupied by a flower fairy. I smiled, feeling joy with such a beautiful day.

It was when I got to the cabin that I realized what had made it so pleasant. Marcella hadn't been with me.

It made me feel guilty as well as sorry for her.

Chapter Sixteen

Dinner began the same as it had the night before, with a buffet, casual seating, and an anxious Marcella attracting hostile attention. But as we were finishing eating, Glenda stood and cast a chiming spell with a pink puff of light to get our attention.

"Birthday cake and champagne as soon as the plates are cleared," she said, clapping her hands. The pink light flashed again, and she laughed.

Next to me on the couch, Sage said, "She's in a good mood."

Isabel looked up from her pork chop. She was sitting on the floor with her plate on the coffee table. "Hush. She can hear you with that spell."

Sage lowered her voice only a little. "What's she so happy about? That spell was ridiculous. The room is pink now."

"Maybe she's happy Granddad didn't die today," Huxley said.

"Either that or she got into the wellspring water stash," Sage said.

Isabel stood up. "I'm not going to hang out with you

guys if you keep talking like that. One of them is going to send a hex over here, and I refuse to get hit again."

I'd be surprised if Glenda could overhear us from across the living room, but I didn't know the extent of her powers. Did she have any access to the wand's powers as Horace's wife? She was with him now at the dining table with Cullen, Ronald, Jack, and Kenneth. Sarah was also in the room tonight; she'd been absent from dinner the night before. She wore business clothes, however, and stood near the entrance to the kitchen, obviously reluctant to be there at all. She held a stack of paperwork and her phone like a shield, as if to reassure the group she had no illusions about her support role. She was at the birthday party as an employee, not one of the family.

"Glenda, excuse me," Pauline said. She had to shout to get Glenda's attention through the sizzling pink party spell. "I thought we were moving the cake to tomorrow. It's been a difficult day. Wouldn't it be better after a good night's sleep—"

"What in demon's balls is that pink smoke?" Horace demanded.

Glenda clapped her hands, and the pink cloud vanished. "Just a celebratory atmosphere, darling."

"I want the cake tonight," Horace said. "Like I said."

"Of course," Glenda said. "After the plates are cleared and the coffee's ready."

Pauline looked at Ronald, who was dropping that weird liquid on his tongue again. I glanced at Huxley, who saw me looking at his dad and flushed red.

Whatever Ronald was taking, it was something his kids were ashamed of. I guessed it was a wellspring water extraction of some kind. It was illegal, potent, expensive, and highly addictive. A terrible combination for many witches.

Feeling bad for Huxley, I pretended I'd been looking out

the window at the lake and not at his dad. "Do you ever go ice skating out on the lake?" I asked.

"No, since we don't have a death wish," Huxley said. "Want to try? We could probably find some skates." Trying to regain his cool, he'd gotten obnoxious.

"Don't trust the ice?" I asked.

"It's the fairies that'll kill you," he said.

"The lake fae have never adapted to our presence here in the winter," Isabel said.

Although Marcella had already told me about the lake fae, I was curious to hear how they described the fairy people and the wand's effects on local magical politics. "How do you know it's them? Maybe some other witches live around the lake. Or other fairies." I glanced at Marcella to make sure she didn't undermine my approach by revealing she'd already told me the dog story. I didn't need to worry; Marcella was curled into a ball in the corner of the couch, counting the beads on the bracelet I'd given her. She was actually getting worse with the family exposure, not better.

"Maybe we know because we're not nonmag idiots," Huxley said. "Of course it's the lake fae. Fairy magic out of the lake. You think just because we weren't trained at the Protectorate, we can't recognize fairy fingerprints?"

I managed not to get mad at Huxley and his rudeness. He was still a kid, fighting shame he felt about his father; I could relate to that. "I didn't say that," I said. "I believe you. What did you see?"

Huxley moved to the edge of his seat and spoke to me. "Last winter, one of the fairies swam up the creek and broke all the cars' mirrors. Inside and outside. Without touching any of the windows."

"Maybe it was some crazy witch who wanted you to think that," Isabel said, shooting a look at Marcella.

It really would be better for Marcella if she'd sit up straight and stop counting the beads under her breath.

Huxley turned his rudeness on his sister. "Oh sure. And Granddad couldn't tell the difference," he said with a sneer.

"He said it was lake fae?" I asked.

"Totally," Huxley said. "And there was that story about Uncle Bertie's dog—"

He was interrupted by another pink cloud and jingle of bells. Glenda stood holding a decorative iron star with bells at each point, shaking it to get our attention. "Cake time," she said.

We all got to our feet and turned toward the dining table where Horace sat with the upright wand in his hand as if it were a wineglass.

A moment later everyone, even Marcella, began to sing. "*Happy birth—*"

Suddenly there was a flash of white light, freezing everyone's mouth on the second word. On instinct, I struggled to throw off the spell by touching my necklace, but my entire body was immobile. Only my eyes could move to watch the one man able to get up and walk across the room, the wand glowing faintly in his hand.

Horace.

"I have an announcement to make," he said.

Chapter Seventeen

"I'm sure you'll understand in a moment why I'm having to hold your tongues. As well as your limbs," he began. His voice was strong, but he had to brace his weight on a nonmagical cane. "The crisis of this family's future has been building for some time." He looked at Marcella, then Pauline.

I deeply resented the hex on my body, but none of my efforts to move had any effect. He had me.

"The situation came to a head when my first son died, but it had already been evident his child at that time was not adequate for this family's needs," he said. "It had been evident since her infancy to those with the skill to see it." He held up the wand to emphasize his claim of unique magical insight. "Until his departure from this plane of existence, there was still a chance for another heir, a suitable one. Pauline is a Bright witch and a good woman, but tragedy often strikes those who least deserve it, as we are all aware. Were she and her daughter to have perished, tragic though it would've been, another child by my first son could've been heir." Horace let out a long sigh, shaking his head at the misfortune.

If I'd had the use of my body, I would've knocked the cane out of his hand and smacked him with it—which almost made me glad I wasn't able to do so. Almost.

He continued talking. "With Bertie's premature demise, however, this preferable future became impossible. It would have to be another firstborn. Obviously Ronald was the second child from his mother's womb, a nonnegotiable reality we all have to live with." He gave Ronald a sad yet dismissive smile. "It would have to be another firstling to carry the wand's burden. Luckily, and I do not say that lightly, for I believe Fate knew what She was doing, Glenda had already given birth to a child who is more than qualified to carry the burden of this family's responsibilities."

I couldn't move most of my body, but my disgust was strong enough to make bile rise in my throat. It lingered there, sour and burning, as Horace droned on about his favorite child's qualities: his magical powers, his good looks, his strength of character.

But then, seeming to realize that even with his spell holding our bodies in place, he was unable to hold our attentions, he returned to his most passionate subject: his disapproval of Marcella.

"This needs to be done. It's obvious to all of us!" He waved the wand, and a spotlight formed on Marcella.

She flinched and closed her eyes. It killed me I couldn't help her.

Horace's voice boomed. "Everyone of importance who knows us pities—*pities!*—our misfortune. And for her as well! The poor unworthy witch seemed destined to be forced to bend to a blood oath she never chose to make, originating multiple generations before her birth."

Marcella's eyes opened slowly and regarded him curiously. Even hopefully. But then…

"Let us discuss her birth," he said.

He had everyone's full attention again.

"It was a painful one," he said. "There was trauma for all parties involved. Bertrand was quite miserable as the hours dragged on, waiting to meet his firstborn, and of course it was quite difficult for the mother. Her suffering, however, and her father's as well as all of ours, was only just beginning."

I managed to close my jaw enough to swallow the acid in my mouth.

"Perhaps it would be easiest to blame her birth, the time of transition—a liminal time period, most powerful with magical kind—before and after she drew her first breath. As it was twisted with pain and dysfunction, it was natural for the spirit afterward to be permanently weakened." He shrugged his thin, bony shoulders. "We can't blame anyone, least of all the child. I admit I too have occasionally taken out my disappointment and fear on the… the victim. We can only blame fate. And when fate is the culprit, we know what to call it. We know what needs to be done."

From a dozen frozen mouths, sharp breaths were suddenly inhaled.

I was afraid, very afraid. Would he really say Marcella was—

"She is cursed," Horace declared. "Yes, I've said it. No witch so burdened can add her Shadowed luck to an entire ancient, illustrious witch family."

"*No*," Pauline said. A growl.

He turned a pitying look on her. "You always were a strong witch. It just makes it more tragic that your daughter would inherit none of your strength," he said. "She was a weak child from the beginning. Too quiet. A wallflower.

Flinching if you spoke to her. I was amazed she wasn't kicked out of those schools you sent her to, but I imagine my name and fortune was too tempting to reject."

I didn't know what Marcella had been like as a small child, and I wasn't even sure of her magical abilities, given how her anxiety seemed to drain them, but I did know she'd been a decent student. There would've been no reason to expel her. None.

"Perhaps you think it's cruel to state these truths aloud," Horace said. "But I must do so. I must. Tomorrow I will do it with a witch advocate who will preserve this evidence in a magically binding document. As I am nearing the end of my life, I must care for the next generations." He looked at Cullen, and his expression softened and glowed. "Marcella will be eliminated from the line of succession. The wand requires more. The wand requires an alternative. An exceptional one. My firstborn son by my beloved wife Glenda will thus be the heir."

Chapter Eighteen

ould he do that? I wondered. Was his low opinion of Marcella enough to override the wild magic of a blood oath?

"I've said my piece," he declared. Swiping the wand through the air like a sword, he pivoted uneasily and hobbled away.

When a door slammed down the hall, the spell on our bodies broke.

"He can't," Pauline said, her voice shaking. "He can't. It can't be done. The wand won't permit it. The oath. It's a blood oath."

"I'm sorry, Pauline," Glenda said. "But you heard what he said. In extreme cases—"

"Silence!" Pauline held her fingers rigid in front of Glenda's face.

Glenda stared, frozen by another hex.

"Let her go," Marcella said. She sounded dazed but calm. Relieved? "Mother, it's fine. You heard him. If he's got a witch expert who can change the inheritance—"

Pauline swung around and pointed at Marcella, casting

the same silence spell on her she'd used on Pauline. "It is not fine!"

But Marcella was far enough away, and maybe had enough warning, to deflect the hex. Holding her wrist with my bracelet aloft, she stood. "Please release Glenda, Mom. Granddad will be angry."

"Granddad! Angry!" Pauline marched over to shout at her daughter from close range. "How do you think *I* feel? You don't even have the… the… guts to be angry on your own behalf!"

"Which is his point, don't you think?" Marcella asked softly.

"Aunt Pauline," Cullen said, "release my mother or I'll have to enact a counterspell against you."

Making a sour face over her shoulder, Pauline waved her fingers in the air.

Glenda coughed and gasped. "My spirit is Bright enough to forgive you for that. You've been through a lot. I'm sorry it had to come to this."

Cullen turned on her. "You knew," he said. "You knew he was going to do this."

Glenda rubbed her throat. "Of course. We share everything with each other."

"It's wrong," Cullen said. "She's the firstborn of the firstborn. It's not right. It's not going to work."

"Even a blood oath has conditions that permit flexibility," Glenda said. "That's what the expert told him."

Cullen lifted his hand to his head, twisting the large gold-and-diamond stud in his left ear. "You should've told me. We need to stop this."

Glenda picked up a wineglass and drank deeply. Head high, she put it down on the table and looked out the window at the lake. "It's too late. He's been planning this for a very long time." She turned to her son. "Nobody can stop him now."

❧

"I will not let this happen," Pauline declared. She walked over to Glenda, holding her hands in a neutral prayer position between them. "If you love him, and I believe you do, you'll set him straight on this. He's a very old, very confused man."

Glenda frowned at Pauline's hands. They could quickly turn into an assault pose, fingers wrapping over the many rings and gems she wore. "He's not confused. I'm sorry, Pauline. He shouldn't have told everyone this way. It was embarrassing, I'm sure."

"Embarrassing?" Pauline moved her hands apart but didn't attack—yet. "Don't you dare patronize me. I've been part of this family for a lot longer than you. My husband was the original firstborn, an honor you can't imagine. It's too bad—"

"Bertrand was *not* the first," Glenda said. "He was the second. Katharine had a baby before Irene did."

Pauline shook her head. "That was—what—ninety years ago? Almost a century. And the child died."

Curious, I looked around the room. Horace's first wife had given birth? The information didn't seem to be news to anyone. I'd have to remember to ask Marcella about it.

"It doesn't matter how long ago it was," Glenda said. "You claim an honor you don't deserve."

The family watched in silence, frozen by curiosity, not magic.

Pauline lowered all fingers but one, a threatening index finger. "Your self-interest has blinded you to the senile derailment he's going to drag this family through," she said. "This is one thing he can't buy or bully his way into getting. It's magical law *and* human law. Marcella inherits. No question."

Calm and smiling faintly, Glenda rose to her feet. "If you believed that, you wouldn't be so upset." She looked over at Marcella with a pitying look. "I really am sorry about all this. I'm sure you'll be relieved when this is settled in a new way. The family burden can fall on Cullen. He's a natural for it."

Pauline put one hand on her necklace. Everyone in the room held their breath.

Glenda didn't seem worried, however. She kept her gaze on Marcella. "Maybe you could tell your mom the truth about how you feel. Save us all a lot of awkwardness."

Marcella stared back at her with an expression I couldn't read. Anger, guilt, temptation.

"It's not up to any one of us to change the path of a blood oath," Pauline said. "Ronald? You're going to just sit there while your father's new wife tries to divert the family's destiny to her own son?"

"Makes no difference to me," Ronald said. "I've been cut out from the beginning."

"But your brother's child!" Pauline turned on Jack, who was also silent, leaving her to protest alone.

Pushed too far, she put her hand on the thick chain of gold around her neck and blasted a hole in a dining chair. Everyone jumped back, the chair banged on the floor, and Pauline marched out of the room with her temper blazing as hot as the charred pine.

Glenda stood with her hands over her heart. "She's gone insane," she said, drawing a defensive spell around herself. "Marcella, we're begging you. Speak up. Tell her you welcome the change. Think of somebody other than yourself for once."

We could hear Pauline banging on Horace's office door down the hallway. "Open up, you old witch!" she shouted.

"Demon take you, talk to me or you'll regret it. I swear to Brightness you won't get away with this!"

Cullen came over and leaned down to Marcella. "I'm sorry, but I have to stop her."

Marcella didn't look at him. "Go ahead," she said calmly, picking up a wineglass and bringing it to her lips. Her hand's shaking, however, gave away her distress; red wine sloshed on her chest, staining her white shirt.

Cullen glanced at me and his cousins, looking pained, then turned and went after Pauline.

Marcella set the glass down, nearly missing the table, and began to fruitlessly dab at the red stain. Her face was colorless, expressionless.

Pauline's shouting continued. "The only curse will be on your head, Horace Gardner!" The banging got louder, then stopped abruptly. Cullen must've reached her.

I was afraid Marcella might faint. Without any allies in her family, it fell to me to help her.

"Let's go to the cabin." I reached over and touched the beaded bracelet I'd given her. She hadn't removed my magical fingerprint, allowing more of a bond, an opening, between us. If I'd been her, I wouldn't have trusted me with that kind of access. Flattered, I pushed a spell of calm goodwill at her.

"No, I should help my mother," she said, getting up.

Isabel snorted. Sage shook her head.

"Later," I said. "Let her cool off." I scowled at her cousins, then her uncles. They thought Marcella was weak, but none of them ever put their necks out. They were the true cowards.

With my hand still wrapped over my beads on her wrist, I pulled her out of the room. Nobody asked her to stay, but Isabel and Sage followed us.

When we got near the front door, Pauline came down the

hallway and charged at Marcella. "Don't you dare leave this house right now."

I cast a strength spell through the bracelet into Marcella. "She needs to be alone for a little while," I told Pauline.

She ignored me completely, her unblinking, furious gaze locked on her daughter. "You're going to talk to him right now. You're going to show him you're a Gardner. You're Bright. You're a competent witch. And you are the heir to that wand and the future head of this family. No matter what he does."

I felt the shock of a compulsion spell strike the air in front of us. Still holding Marcella's wrist, I began to prepare a defense, but it wasn't necessary. Marcella, perhaps because she'd grown up under Pauline's maternal thumb, cast a neutralizing spell before I did.

"Sorry, Mom," she said, walking ahead to the door with me dragging a little behind her.

To keep my eye on the others, I crossed the threshold backward, my heart beating fast, and was very glad to pull the door shut.

I sucked in fresh, pine-scented air, worn out from the combination of defensive spellwork and social anxiety. Marcella slipped her hand out from mine and broke into a run, headed for the cabins.

Brightness help me, I was too exhausted to run after her. I began walking as fast as I could manage, regretting the wine and heavy meal.

As relaxing weekend getaways went, I'd had better.

Chapter Nineteen

The stars were bright overhead, shining through the pine and cedar. The continuing presence of happy, relaxed fairies assured me at least there was still no demon threat. I enjoyed the fresh forest air, accented with the cool taste of nearby snow. Without the wand, it would quickly blanket the trees and buildings, smother the out-of-season tomatoes and sage. If Cullen took the wand, would he end the enchantment? Would Marcella?

The moment I got inside our cabin, Marcella locked the door and cast a spell that created nine new dead bolts in a rainbow of metals—copper, rose gold, yellow gold, platinum, steel, iron. The metal was an illusion, but the magical boundary was not.

"Will I be able to get out?" I asked, holding my open hand over the sizzling energy.

"Oh yes. Of course," she said. "It's just for intruders. Besides, I doubt I'd be able to lock you in even if I wanted to."

"You all right?"

"This is going to kill my mother," she said.

I was impressed she was more worried about her mom, not herself. "Did you have any idea your grandfather was going to do this?"

"Everyone has always said it's impossible. As much of a failure as I am, the blood magic is too strong." She kicked off her shoes and went to her room. "Old magic wasn't supposed to care about achievement. Just breathing was supposed to be enough for it. Didn't need an education, athletic prowess, charm, beauty, a prestigious career—just the right blood. Not very American, is it? Drove Granddad crazy."

Next to the bed on the nightstand was an old pine box with an uneven lid. Some witch schools taught students to make their own storage cases for their magical treasures, and that's what this one looked like. She opened it, took out a small glass vial, and uncorked it.

I sensed wellspring magic, but it was oddly strong for such a small quantity. "Is that springwater?" I asked. It was common for witches to collect small amounts of wellspring water for special occasions, although it was forbidden because it attracted supernatural trouble—demons and fairies, mostly.

"Good thing you're *ex*-Protectorate," she said, lifting the bottle. "Got this from Uncle Ronald."

"What kind of wellspring water is that?"

"An extract. Crystallized and reconstituted with yarrow root in a seawater solution." She rolled the little bottle between her fingers. "I'm afraid Uncle is an addict. You probably noticed. Huxley and Isabel get really embarrassed about it."

"What does it do?"

"General feel-good poison," she said. "Analgesic, narcotic, psychedelic, intoxicant, sedative, hypnotic, stimulant—whatever you need it to be. Makes it very addictive."

"Your uncle is unkind to share it with you then."

"Yeah, you may have noticed kindness isn't a family trait." She continued staring at the bottle, then corked it and handed it to me. "Take it. My mother doesn't need more problems. An addicted daughter would be the last straw."

I had a natural immunity to the negative side effects of springwater and was relieved to take it away from her and put it in my pocket. "Want to leave?" I asked. "I've got the Jeep. We could make a run for it. Your mother will get used to the new arrangement eventually."

"Thanks, but I can't do that to her. Besides, it's too good to be true. Granddad can't break a blood oath. I wish I *could* give it to Cullen." She collapsed on the bed and pulled a pillow over her head. "Unfortunately, I'd have to die before that could happen."

"And you know there aren't any other eligible descendants?" I asked. "Your grandfather lived over a century."

She set aside the pillow. "Positive," she said. "My grandmother, Irene, only married Granddad because the blood oath would guarantee her firstborn descendant was heir. *Her* line would get the wand. That is, me. Or my first child if I had one."

I thought again of Horace's first wife. "But what if Katharine had a child who grew up and had another child," I said. "Glenda mentioned there had been a baby."

"She didn't grow up," Marcella said quickly. "She died."

"Are you sure?"

She wriggled upright, got out her tablet, plugged it into the power on the nightstand, and propped it on her lap. "Yes. Really sad, actually. I saw the gravestone once. Somebody brought me to it when I was little. I remember thinking it was sad people could die before they became grown-ups. Before then, I'd thought only old people could die. It made quite an impression."

"You were exposed to a lot of creepy stuff when you were a kid," I said. "Gravestones, blood oaths…"

"Yet another price of being a witch heiress." She ran a finger over her screen. "I'm going to numb out for a while. See what the rest of the world is up to."

Happy to do the same, I went to my room. It was early, but I got ready for bed and relaxed online myself for a couple of hours—or tried to. Nothing kept my attention for long. The fairies outside on the other side of the cabin walls were singing about green beans, putting me into a fae-flavored drowsiness. Before I fell asleep completely, I called Seth, even though I knew hearing his voice was only going to make me miss him more.

"Hey," I said. Given his fairy nature, he'd probably guessed I was about to call, and I didn't pretend he hadn't.

"Promise me you won't go anywhere tonight," he said. "I've got a bad feeling."

I smiled. He could be a little protective—not unreasonably, because I did tend to get into trouble. "You know I can't promise you anything like that."

"Promise you would if you could," he said. "Promise you'd try to make an effort to maybe consider being careful because it stresses out your besotted beloved."

I snuggled deeper into the covers, cuddling the phone against my cheek as if it were him. "I promise."

A faint knock sounded at the door. It was almost a scratch. Marcella probably felt awkward about bothering me so late.

"What's that?" Seth asked.

I could hear her breathing heavily at the door. "I should go," I said, putting my feet on the floor. "I think that's Marcella."

"You probably know I love you," he said.

My drowsiness fell away, and suddenly I felt hot all over. "You picked this moment—?"

From the other side of the door, Marcella's voice was strained, anxious. "Alma?"

"Seth," I said, my heart fluttering. "I can't— I have to go."

He made a kissy sound and ended the call. Flooded with longing, fear, happiness, and irritation at Marcella, I went to the door.

"I'm… sorry." She stood in the dark hallway with both hands gripping her head. "I'm… I'm— I wouldn't ask— I feel— Can't breathe. Sorry. I'm… sorry."

I still had on my favorite redwood-bead necklace, and I put my hand on it and scanned her for magical attack or injury. I found nothing. "It's OK. Can I touch you?" Skin-to-skin contact would give me more accurate information.

Slumping against the wall, she nodded. I put my palm on her cheek and cast another probe over her, searching for hexes.

"It's nothing," she gasped. "Right?"

A significant part of my mind and all of my heart was still preoccupied with Seth, but I scanned her again. "I can't feel anything."

She grabbed my wrist. "Give me the drops. My uncle's. No, no. Don't. Sorry." She slid to the floor and curled into a ball. "Can't. Breathe."

I'd been half-asleep a few minutes ago, but now my heart was pounding. "Do you think you're being attacked? Can you tell?"

She shook her head. "P-panic," she gasped. "Panic. Attack."

Even if there wasn't an antagonist other than her own anxious brain, I had to do something for her. I had herbs that were good for relaxation, but this seemed too intense for lavender and chamomile. "Hold on," I said, then ran into my bedroom, grabbed my travel case, and returned to her on the floor. I pushed aside a black velvet bag with mouse bones—from owl pellets, good for allergies—and found the mud patty I'd made under the full moon in my garden just a week earlier. Seth had been with me; maybe his fae magic could help her.

Face shiny with sweat, Marcella was staring at me in terror.

"I'm going to put this under your shirt, OK? Promise I'm not hitting on you." I forced a laugh and pushed the dried mud, sewn into my old linen pillowcase, into her bra so it was over her heart. "Hold it there." I helped her put her hands over the mud and keep it in place.

After a few long seconds, her breathing seemed to deepen.

My own quirks made me cast three quick boundary spells around us, including our feet, even if there wasn't an external attack. It drained my magic, making my knees buckle, so I sat on the floor and panted for breath next to her.

"We're a pair," she said, smiling weakly at me. "What is this? Under my shirt?"

"Dirt."

"I think it's helping."

"I'm glad," I said. My vision was sparkling. My boundary spells were strong enough to muffle the sound of anything but our own voices and breathing. I couldn't even see the lamp next to my bed, just the unfocused light.

"Maybe you could teach me that," she said. "Sensory deprivation spell, right? Mine isn't nearly so good."

I was nodding off, exhausted from the long day and the unexpected spellcasting. "I can teach you, but it's only for emergencies." I yawned, heard my ears pop. "It'll suck the juice out of you. Wipes me out every time. But it should last a few hours."

"Thank you."

"I hope you didn't want to go visit anyone," I said. "We're stuck in here until then."

"You mean even if I wanted to go talk to my grandfather, I wouldn't be able to?" she asked.

I got to my knees, straightened, helped her up. "But you don't want to, do you?"

"Of course I don't, but I should," she said. "I was about to go when the panic hit."

I noticed then she was wearing shoes. "Do you think it would do any good?"

"I'd be able to tell my mother I'd done my best," she said. "I'd know I had."

I picked up my travel case, took out a few spare bracelets and another necklace, and slipped them on for recharging. My toes curled against the wood floors, pulling some of their old energy into my muscles. "If you really want me to, I'll break a hole for you to get out." In my hurry, I'd set up a rigid boundary that wouldn't be able to move with our bodies. The only way to release it would be to destroy it completely.

We stood in the dim hallway, lit only by the spell-diffused lamps in each of our bedrooms. Marcella wiped the sweat off her forehead with the back of her hand. "No, of course I don't want you to. I'd fall apart again." Her voice cracked. "What's the matter with me? Why can't I do such stupid, simple things? He's my grandfather. I should be able to visit him without having a heart attack."

"It's been a stressful trip—"

"But nobody else is falling apart, just me!"

"Nobody else living was raised as the heiress of that wand," I said. "Maybe it *is* a curse."

She stared at me, eyes wide. "I've thought that many times. Especially when my dad died. That's when things really got bad."

"Then this might be your chance to escape it," I said. "Find another way to help your mother. Go back to school. Join the Protectorate. Find a new path."

She clutched the mud patty sachet over her heart. "I wish I could believe it was possible. But I don't. I can feel fate itself holding me back. It's always been there. Whenever I think of breaking free, it punishes me. A blood oath can span countless generations. What does one little human life matter to wild magic like that?"

I was tired and losing patience. "Maybe you should go to bed," I said. "I know *I* need to sleep. The boundary spell wore me out."

"Oh Brightness, of course. I'm sorry. I'm so sorry." She bowed her head and turned toward her room. "Thank you. Thanks for everything."

"So, you *are* going to bed?" I asked. "You're staying in the cabin?"

She paused and gazed at the door, her face twisted. "Sometimes I feel like one arm is tied to a bus and the other one is tied to a train and they're going in opposite directions." She closed her eyes. "Except it never ends. I'm still here. I get torn apart, but I'm still here."

Chapter Twenty

I slept fitfully under my own boundary spell, unnerved by the lack of sound or sight. When the sun finally rose, shining the snowy mountains in cheerful bright light, I got dressed—in one of my own T-shirts and borrowed shorts—and decided to have breakfast at the big house by myself. I disbanded my spell while Marcella snored in her bedroom. Glad for a break from her anxiety—and feeling guilty I was relieved to be spared her company—I hiked up to the house with a small smile on my face, knowing I'd be going home with Seth soon.

Love. He'd said the *L* word. The fae were supposed to be above—or below—such things. The human upbringing in Minnesota had made a greater impression than his lake fae mother had ever anticipated, and I was glad. Goofy with it. Being with Marcella and all her fears was showing me that I myself had been too afraid of taking risks. I'd put my body and soul at risk many times, but my heart? I'd kept that behind muffled, sensory-blocking boundary spells as rigid as the one in the cabin last night. Time to tear them down.

The long table in the living room was laid out like a hotel

breakfast room—coffee, juice, self-serve breads, bacon and sausage in heated casseroles, bowls of fruit, cereal. The spell last night had taken a lot of calories, and I filled a full-size dinner plate with a bit of everything.

Only Jack and Kenneth were there, talking quietly together on the couch. I nodded at them and took a seat at the empty dining table. Sarah walked by in her business clothes again—wasn't it Sunday morning?—carrying a tray of toast, coffee, and a file folder.

I'd given up coffee last year after a hex ruined it for me, so I tore open a tea bag and eyed a bowl of fruit on the table next to a vase of delphiniums. The bananas were green. All this magic and they couldn't get ripe bananas?

A woman screamed from the other side of the house. I swung around to see Jack and Kenneth get to their feet, start to run toward the sound. Throwing aside the tea bag, I cast a protective spell around my body and moved toward the door to the deck in case I needed a quick escape.

I stood there, breathing hard as I waited. The noises coming from the kitchen sounded like typical, everyday cooking tasks. The deck outside the sliding doors from the living room was empty except for a pair of tree sprites sitting on the decorative wooden ball on the top of a closed patio umbrella, which assured me no demons were nearby. Other than me and a young woman setting out smoked salmon next to the bagels, the great room was empty. All activity seemed to be coming from down the hall. From Horace's wing of the house.

Since none of the Gardners were there to see me, I picked up a silver candlestick and used the metal power like an antenna to hear better. Yesterday the hallway with Horace's office had looked like a dead end, and it seemed like a bad idea to go farther until I knew what I was walking into.

But why go farther? Why not run out of the house, get my Jeep, enjoy a real vacation with my boyfriend and dog?

There were many logical reasons, but the real one was that I was too curious. As I'd been told by an older friend of mine, witches coveted knowledge more than any amulet, herb, or spell. It might kill us, but it was the price of our power.

So I kept the candlestick in my hand and walked down the hallway. It was empty, but voices and flashes of magic came from Horace's office. I cast a probing spell of my own, and amid the mess of spells coming out of the office, I sensed an absence. Jack and Kenneth were active, but the third man's magical fingerprint was stale.

Horace. His mark was fading.

My mouth went dry.

Sarah stepped out of the room, walking backward, a blank look on her face. I came up beside her, lowering the silver weapon in my hand and tucking it under my arm.

I looked inside. Horace was on the floor, the men bending over him. I knew instantly he was dead.

"Sarah?" I asked. She was rigid, unblinking. "Sarah, it's me, Alma. Can I touch you?"

Her eyes moved slowly toward mine. She nodded once. I took her hand and held it between my palms, rubbing warmth and a gentle, soothing magic into her skin. When she finally took a deep breath, I looked into the room to get a better look at Horace. Jack was kneeling near his head, stroking his forehead; Kenneth was trying to pull him away, telling him he was gone and the room needed to be scanned properly.

It was not a natural death, that was obvious. Not only were Horace's rigid limbs outstretched in four directions like an X, but his strands of white hair were standing on end, avoiding the floor as well as his scalp.

I looked at Sarah again. Blood had returned to her face, and she was blinking. "What did you see?" I asked.

"He was like that when I went in," she said. Then her professional demeanor kicked in. "I didn't touch anything."

"Good." I saw she'd put the breakfast tray on the floor at our feet. Inside the office, Kenneth had managed to pull Jack away from his father's dead body, and they joined us in the hall.

"He's dead," Kenneth said.

Rubbing his mouth, Jack stared at the body. "Killed. On his birthday!"

"The Protectorate should be called," I said.

Jack turned on me. "No."

His refusal didn't surprise me. Old families—or young ones—never wanted Protectorate agents poking around their homes, uncovering illicit magic, dragging relatives and friends to a field office for questioning. One murder might lead to the prosecution of a dozen other crimes—most of them involving forbidden objects from the Shadow market— and even a sweet elderly Auntie might be sent to jail in the Mojave Desert for the rest of her life.

"He's been murdered," I said.

"Obviously," Jack said, "but two wrongs don't make a right. No Protectorate."

"Glenda needs to be told," Kenneth said.

"Now we know they don't share a bedroom," Jack said. "Or they do and she's the one who did this."

"Jack," Kenneth warned.

Jack sighed. "All right. I suppose she's going to be upset." He looked at Sarah, who was leaning against the far wall, arms wrapped around herself. "*You* can tell her," he said.

Sarah's eyes widened.

"It would be better if it came from family," I said.

Jack turned on me. "Why in Brightness would you think that? I think it'll be much better if it doesn't."

"Jack," Kenneth said again.

Sarah pushed away from the wall. "I don't mind. You need to stay with the—with Witch Horace," she said. "Glenda has a bedroom upstairs. I'll… wake her. She usually sleeps in."

I didn't envy waking a witch to break the news her husband had been killed. An extra boundary spell would be a sensible precaution. Or a weapon.

"Would you like this?" I asked, holding out the silver candlestick.

Jack snorted—a muffled laugh—but Sarah shook her head and walked away.

Kenneth said, "That's right. You were Protectorate. *You* could probe the scene."

"Hardly. She's a prime suspect." Jack turned to me. "Are you sure you want to stick around? They're going to blame you and Marcella for this."

"Of course nobody is going to blame Marcella," Kenneth said. "Look at him. He was killed with his wand in his hand. The witch who did that…" He trailed off.

We knew what he meant. Such a witch would be very powerful, certainly stronger than Marcella had ever been.

"Your parents were Protectorate," Jack said to Kenneth. "You know the protocol. You've complained to me about them always bringing you to work. I think we'd all be more comfortable if you scanned everything."

"I'm family," Kenneth said.

"You should be, but they've never seen you that way," Jack said. "Besides, you're even a real doctor as well. Bonus."

While they went back and forth, hashing out old grievances about their mutual in-laws, I did a probe of the office from the doorway.

Face locked in an enraged grimace, Horace lay faceup on the floor in front of his desk. His dead hand was still clutching the wand, which gave off the same thrumming power as it had when he was alive.

That explained why the climate outside the house was still warm and sunny. Until another witch took command, an object under a blood oath might still be bonded to a dead master until his spirit departed completely.

"Let me see him!" Glenda shouted.

She was running toward us down the hall. I quickly moved away from the office door. I could hear how upset—and furious—she was, and I didn't want to get caught in any magical, vengeful crossfire. She began to run into the office, but Kenneth stopped her.

"It's a crime scene," he said. "I'm sorry."

She spun around, looking for somebody to blame. Unfortunately, her gaze locked on me. "You did this. You helped Marcella."

Cullen came around a corner with Sarah. "Mom, what's happened? Is it true?" He strode over to Glenda and put an arm around her as they looked into the office.

"They won't let me in," Glenda said.

"He's been hexed," Cullen said, his voice cracking. "Look at him."

"I told him not to make any announcements until the paper was signed," Glenda said. "I warned him! And now look. Look!" She burst into tears.

The cousins were arriving—Isabel, Sage, Huxley.

"Maybe he died of natural causes," Huxley said.

"Sure he did, genius," his sister snapped at him. "That's why his hair is like that."

"Could've been an accident," he said, annoyed. He rolled his eyes and looked around. "Where's Dad?"

"Sleeping off his bender last night, what did you think?"

Isabel pushed him out of the way. "We need to comfort his spirit. It might still be nearby. Granddad? Can you hear me?"

"What's going on?" Pauline appeared behind Isabel. "Where's my daughter?"

I realized Marcella, still asleep in the cabin, didn't know what had happened, but I was too curious and suspicious to go to tell her. One of these witches must have killed him.

Glenda was crying. "I need to be with him," she said, moving into the doorway. "Isabel is right. His spirit is nearby. I need to say goodbye."

"What should we do with the wand?" Jack asked.

"Cullen can take it," Glenda said. "He's the true heir now."

"Sorry, Glenda," Kenneth said, "but the body and room needs to be scanned properly. By me or somebody else with training. Unless you want to call the Protectorate."

"Of course not," she said.

From the hallway, I sensed power coming from the room that felt increasingly wild, even dangerous. The wand was missing its master.

Chapter Twenty-One

"I think it would be safer to put the wand away," I said. "Did he have a velvet bag? Special box?"

"On the desk," Sarah said. I hadn't realized she was there until she spoke. What would she do now that her boss was dead?

Kenneth stepped forward. "I'll do it. Is that acceptable to everyone?"

Nobody argued.

Kenneth went into the office, walking as far from the body as possible, and touched an old wooden box on the desk. It was black with age, battered and coarsely crafted—typical for the treasure box of a wealthy witch. The value would be on the inside.

Perhaps because Horace had been using it himself before he died, it was open. With one hand on one of his gold earrings, Kenneth muttered a protective spell and reached in and took out a long and narrow velvet bag, black with a white drawstring. Then he squatted down and slipped it over the wand. When the fabric touched Horace's dead fingers, the wand slipped free of his grip and disappeared into the velvet. The distracting magical pressure in the room eased slightly.

"Cullen will take it now," Glenda said.

"Marcella is the heir," Pauline said.

"Everyone heard his intention last night," Glenda said.

"His intention changed nothing," Pauline said. "The oath and the will remain as they were."

A thick, suspicious silence fell over the group.

Glenda turned on Pauline. "You went crazy when he wouldn't see you. Maybe you got desperate."

"I never entered the office," Pauline said. "A simple scan will prove that."

Glenda gave Cullen a skeptical look. I didn't know how powerful Cullen might be, but she didn't seem reassured he'd be able to uncover any of Pauline's tricks, if any existed. "We'll see."

Pauline adjusted the silver combs in her hair. "The heir needs to be alerted," she said, walking away. "I'll do it."

Kenneth put the wand in the box, and it snapped shut by itself with a flash of light. "The wand will stay with his other amulets until the matter is settled officially."

"If Aunt Pauline didn't go into the office, maybe Marcella did," Isabel said.

"I was with her all night," I said. "Neither of us left the cabin."

"You can't be sure of that," Sage said.

I looked at her, raised an eyebrow. "Yes, I can." Years of dealing with both sides of Protectorate interrogation had given me the ability to fill my words with conviction. She recoiled as if I'd poked her with a pin.

Glenda began to cry softly. "It's a conspiracy."

"Mom, I doubt that," Cullen said. "Come on, let's sit down. I'll make that potion you like."

"I don't want any potions. I want my husband," she said,

but let him take her by the arm. I felt a cloud of subdued, quiet magic envelop them as they walked away. Cullen's magical fingerprint had the gentle flavor of a kind witch.

"We should all go to the other room," Kenneth said. "Too many witches are messing up the residue. There might be clues."

"We can't just leave him there," Jack said.

"With a sentry until the room can be formally probed. A sentry who won't inherit." Kenneth turned to their daughter. "Sage? Would you honor the family by standing guard?"

Sage began to complain—she'd be missing out on the drama—but then seemed to recognize the situation was too serious to argue. "Of course." She pointed at Sarah, who had retreated to her office across the hall. "She can help me."

Sarah looked up from her desk. She'd been typing something on the computer, and I had the darkly humorous thought it was an application for a new job. She cast an uneasy look at everyone. "I'm not qualified to do any magic that would stop a witch from getting in."

"That's fine. We just need witnesses," Kenneth said. "Everyone else meet in the living room. I need to go upstairs for a minute."

"Demon's balls, Ronald still doesn't know," Jack said suddenly. "I'll go with you."

Leaving Sage and Sarah at Horace's door, I walked to the living room but stayed on my feet near the sliding doors to the deck to allow a quick exit if necessary. Glenda and Cullen sat together on the couch, and Isabel and Huxley sat on separate chairs.

"I'm not sure we can trust Kenneth," Glenda said. "Your father would've wanted you to be in charge."

"He's a Bright witch," Cullen said. "And a Stanford doctor. We're lucky to have him."

Jack returned with Ronald at his side. Ronald must've

cast a quick clean-up spell on himself because he looked spiffy enough for TV—crisp white shirt, perfectly creased trousers, clear-eyed and clean-shaven.

He didn't sit down. "I'm going to look at him before I join the rest of you. I need to see for myself."

While he was down the hall, Pauline strode in with Marcella. From the way Pauline's fingernails were digging into Marcella's forearm, I guessed Marcella hadn't been eager to leave the safety of her cabin.

Pauline pushed her slightly as she let go, then sat on the couch and crossed her legs.

In spite of everyone staring at her, Marcella looked calm. She cast a sleepy gaze over the group, then came over to stand with me. "I'm so sorry to drag you into this," she said. "If I'd had any idea…"

"Good thing I *am* here," I said. "I'm your alibi."

She took a stick of lip balm out of a pocket. "That's what Mom said. I don't know how I'm ever going to make this up to you."

I stared at her as she casually dragged the stick across her lips. Her high anxiety of last night seemed gone. *Maybe I should become a witch therapist,* I thought. Blocking spells, wood beads, herbal sachets—who needs to talk about feelings or past trauma when you've got magic?

Ronald returned, shaken but silent, and stood near Isabel's chair. The spell he'd cast over his appearance was wearing off, perhaps from the shock; now his shirt was wrinkled and had a wine stain over the left breast pocket.

He looked at me. "What is she doing here?"

"She stays," Pauline said. "We can use her experience. Protectorate trained without the baggage."

"She's hardly without baggage," Jack said. "She's a suspect. Kenneth isn't."

I wanted to assure everyone I wasn't going to investigate

anything, but I said nothing. My tongue was still under the influence of my own conviction spell I'd used when talking to Sage a few minutes earlier—which required honesty—and I'd be lying if I said I wasn't going to poke around. My friend was in danger of being framed or losing her inheritance—and I was too curious. How could I not?

"If you suspect her, do you really want her wandering off by herself?" Marcella asked, surprising me and everyone else.

At that moment Kenneth returned with a black-and-white wooden box about two feet long, marked with geometric carvings. He set it on the dining table, tipped it open, and took out a multicolored glass ball slightly larger than his palm. Waves of attention-grabbing magic struck the room, like a beacon from a lighthouse.

He held it aloft. "This was my mother's," he said. "It's a truth ball."

People leaned closer to get a better look. I felt a cascade of probing spells mix in the air, feeling the ball's magic.

Jack got up and stood at his side. "Everyone should tell it where they were last night. In front of everyone else. Agreed?"

"What, now?" Glenda asked. "We've only just found him. Am I the only one who—whose heart is breaking?"

Cullen hugged her close. "We don't have time to wait. The evidence might not last."

"How do we know the ball is potent enough?" Ronald asked. "Or that Kenneth has the skill to work it?"

"Would you rather call the Protectorate?" Jack asked. "The San Francisco office is always happy to send agents out to meddle in witches' lives, especially if there might be valuable amulets to 'borrow' during their investigation."

That terrified everyone enough to sit up and stop talking. My former employers had earned a reputation for making excuses to steal magical objects from anyone they investigated. I'd had some of my own things taken and then, after a painful delay, restored—but only because I had insider contacts. This family had nobody currently working at the Diamond Street office who could advocate for them.

"Let's start with the first person we know tried to see him," Kenneth said. "Pauline, will you come speak to the ball?"

She sprang to her feet and walked over, obviously eager to speak. Kenneth held the glass orb between them, level with her chin, and cast a truth spell I could feel from ten feet away.

"Speak," he said.

"Everyone knows I tried to speak to him after dinner," Pauline said. "I was upset, obviously. But he wouldn't open the door. He wouldn't see me. So I left and went to my room, where I was all night."

The ball glowed hot pink, then returned to its dim, rainbow sheen.

Kenneth nodded. "It believes her."

Smiling, Pauline met Glenda's gaze and returned to her seat.

Kenneth looked around at the others. "Did anyone see him after that?"

There was a pause as everyone looked around the room.

"You might as well speak up now," Kenneth continued. "Before I take the ball to each of you. It'll save us time."

Jack smoothed his shirt down and cleared his throat. "Well, I talked to him around ten," he said. "When Pauline was finished with him. So to speak."

"How dare you," Pauline said.

Kenneth frowned at his husband. "You didn't tell me you talked to him. I asked you not to."

"It's a good thing I did." Jack leaned over and kissed him on the cheek, then stepped back, arms at his side. "Hold that sucker up. I've got news for everyone."

Chapter Twenty-Two

After a pause, frowning more deeply, Kenneth lifted up the ball. "Go on."

Jack cast a triumphant smile over his shoulder, then turned back, breathing deeply. "My father was reluctant to open the door at first—probably thought I was Pauline—but then he let me in."

The ball shone pink.

"What time was that?" Kenneth asked.

"Ten, like I said."

"You came back to the room around ten thirty." Kenneth spoke into the ball, and it continued to shine pink.

"Exactly."

"How was he when you left him?" Kenneth asked.

"Same. Old, irritable, pain in the—"

"How was his health?" Kenneth prompted.

"Fine. So far as I could tell. But listen—he told me the new will would include a generous provision for Sage. As well as for you and me." He faced the group. "We had nothing to gain by his death. In fact, now we're screwed. The winner takes all. Winner being Marcella."

Everyone fell silent, absorbing that news, watching the glass ball continue to glow pink. Next to me, Marcella stiffened.

I had to speak. "You may believe what you say," I said, "but that doesn't mean what you say is true. He may have been lying to you."

Every head turned to look at me. Unnerved by the glares of a group of witches unified against me, I felt myself flush.

"The new lawyer can back me up when she gets here," Jack said. "She was going to write up the new will with the provisions to divide the property more equally among all of us. Buck, the old lawyer, wouldn't do it."

"I already had Sarah tell her not to come," Pauline said.

Glenda's mouth fell open. "What?" She leaned against Cullen, shaking her head. "You had no right."

"It would be wasting her time," Pauline said. "Her client is dead."

"Convenient," Isabel said.

"I didn't hurt him," Pauline said. "The ball knows I'm telling the truth."

Isabel shook a gold bracelet in the air, sending white sparks around her fist. "Then Marcella did."

"But we need to listen to Jack. He had specific plans about the new will. It just hadn't been seen by the lawyer yet," Glenda said. "We should make the case this was the wish of his heart before he died. We can create it from what he told Jack, confirm it with the ball, and have it signed posthumously."

"Just how is he going to sign it now?" Ronald asked. "Are you going to hold a paper up to his dead hand?"

"We have to at least establish what was in the new one," Jack said. "It explains motive. Isn't that what we're trying to do here?"

"Yes," Glenda said. "Pauline and Marcella wanted him

dead. The rest of us did not. That should simplify things enormously."

Jack shook his head. "Not so simple as that," he said, turning to the group. "He told me the new will also included an extra stipend for Pauline. A very generous one. So it's more complicated than it seems."

"But she didn't know that," Glenda said. "Horace didn't let her into the office."

"Actually, I did know it," Pauline said. "He told me weeks ago he was trying to leave me a fortune in the new will. I told him not to do it. This is *not* about me. It's about what's right. Marcella is the heir. Trying to buy me off was never going to work."

"I don't believe you," Glenda said.

"Scan me," Pauline replied, stretching out her arms.

Cullen grabbed his mother's hands before they reached her diamond earrings. "No, please. Kenneth is going to do the scanning. We can't have duels breaking out. For Brightness' sake."

Marcella walked to the middle of the room. "I'd like to go next," she said, her voice wavering. "I've been accused. I have the right to defend myself."

She'd called upon a powerful tradition, and nobody could argue.

Kenneth held up the ball. "Tell your story, Marcella."

She walked closer, gripping her wrists. I hoped my jute bracelet was giving her strength. "I was in my cabin with Alma," she said. "We were there from after dinner until this morning. I couldn't have left even if I'd wanted to."

"Why not?" Kenneth asked.

Marcella lowered her head. "I was having a panic attack." She sighed, then cast a look around. "I know, hard to believe. Anyway, to help me calm down, Alma had to cast a spell that cut us off from the outside world.

Completely. Sound, smell, touch. We were both stuck inside it."

"That worked?" Ronald asked, sounding surprised. "It didn't make you sick? I knew a witch who could do that once. It always made everyone vomit."

"Not at all. I felt better than I have in a long time," Marcella said. "Still do."

Kenneth held up the ball, still shining pink without a flicker. It absorbed the words and felt the truth of them.

"Maybe she believes what she's saying," Ronald said. "That doesn't mean it's true. As you've already pointed out, Alma Bellrose. It's your testimony that we need."

Having expected that, I walked over, feeling the hairs on the back of my neck stand up as the other witches watched me, and stood before him at Marcella's side.

Kenneth lowered the globe and put his hand over it. "One problem."

"What now?" Glenda asked.

"It's bad luck to interrogate a guest," Kenneth said. "We should compensate her in some way."

"That rule's ancient," Jack said.

"No, he's right." Glenda sighed, running her hand over her eyes. "Cullen, give her a stone, will you? There's a vase by the door."

Cullen strode out of the room and returned a moment later with an unpolished hunk of rose quartz. To a nonmag, it would look no more special than a landscaping rock. But given to a witch guest, it would provide me with extra protection within the home.

"Please accept this apology from us," Cullen said, dropping the stone in my hand, avoiding physical contact. "Thank you for your friendship and your speech."

I closed my hand around the hard rock, smiling as its cool magic wiped away the stress response in my body. It would fade after a few minutes, but fresh from gifting, it was a nice, potent pleasure to hold. "You're welcome," I said.

Kenneth cupped his glass ball in both hands to reset the spell, then held it out to me. "Is Marcella telling the whole truth? You were with her all night in the cabin?"

I looked into the glass and opened my mouth. The truth enchantment was in my lungs immediately, swirling around my mucus membranes, my throat, my brain.

"Yes and yes," I said, feeling another rush of pleasure as the enchantment rewarded me for my honesty and sent pink light flowing out of the ball.

But right away I sensed a flaw in the ball's magic. Maybe because I'd been Protectorate trained, or because I'd been unpopular with the Emerald mages there and had therefore been interrogated more than usual, I could see a way to wiggle around the enchantment and lie without being detected. It was just a gap in the magic, a trapdoor. If you could identify the pleasure the spell was giving you, it could be turned aside like any other temptation—not forever, but for a few seconds of questioning. Similar to holding your breath underwater.

Was I the only one to see the ball's weakness? I concentrated on keeping a blank face. I wanted them to believe me.

"Marcella and I were in the cabin all night, from just after dinner until this morning," I said.

The ball rewarded me again with a hit of dopamine, but if I'd wanted to, I could've said I'd flown to Mars in a helicopter for pizza. Like now, the ball would still glow a bright pink.

"Thank you, Alma Bellrose," Kenneth said with a slight bow of his head. Did *he* know the ball wasn't trustworthy?

I nodded and hurried back to my station near the door, hoping the thudding of my heart wasn't audible to the others.

None of the questioning was trustworthy. Any of them could be lying. I only knew I could trust myself.

"I saw him right after that," Cullen said. His voice was rough, weakened, very young. He got up from the couch and went over to Kenneth. "It was almost eleven. I didn't stay."

Kenneth held up the ball. "And he was in good health?"

A pause. When he spoke, Cullen's voice cracked. "As far as I could tell, but I didn't run any scanning spells. He forbade it."

"That was usually true, wasn't it?" Kenneth asked. "I know he wouldn't let me check on him unless he asked first."

"Sometimes he let me, but he was still in a bad mood, I think, from dinner. I wanted to come in, just to hang out. We all knew his… his… days were limited, but he wouldn't even let me through the door." Cullen paused, shaking with the effort to hold back his emotion. "He hadn't changed for bed yet, and I told him it was late, that, he should, you know, brush his teeth, get some rest. He slept in his office. He had the bed under a disguising spell. But he said he had more to do and to stop fussing over him."

"So you left?" Kenneth asked.

Another pause, as if he hated to admit it. "Yes."

The glass ball glowed pink, and after finally giving in to his sobs, Cullen returned to the couch where Glenda drew him into an embrace.

If I'd been the one wielding the ball, I might've been able to sense a lie, but I wasn't. So far as I knew, however, Cullen would've wanted his father to live to make a new will.

"Did anyone else see him after Cullen's visit at eleven o'clock?" Kenneth asked.

After everyone shook their heads, Kenneth went to each of them to state their denial formally for the glass ball. Having lost faith in its power, I let my attention wander.

Marcella was doing well, considering, even though her cousins continued to send her evil looks.

When everyone was officially cleared, Kenneth returned the glass ball to the box. "I will scan the office in depth now. Any objections?"

"I want to see him," Glenda said. "He's all alone in there. It's not Bright. His spirit needs company. Mine and Cullen's."

Kenneth didn't seem to think he could refuse, and Pauline insisted she be included as well.

When only Ronald and the younger members of the family remained in the living room, Huxley asked, "What happens to the body?"

"You stupid goblin," Isabel said. "Have some sensitivity."

"I'm just asking," he said. "We can't just leave him there, and we can't have the nonmag funeral people or whatever come in here and take him away. They'll kind of notice it's summer here, don't you think?"

Ronald—his face covered with stubble, his eyes blood-shot—went over to him and put a hand on his shoulder. "We'll figure something out."

"Are we sure it wasn't just a heart attack or something?" Huxley asked.

"We're sure." Ronald pulled him into a hug, then he gestured for Isabel to join them. To my surprise, she moved into his arms, and the three clung to each other, crying softly.

They were close-knit, a loving family of three, even with Ronald's problems. I wondered who their mother was, if she'd ever been to the vacation house, if there was bad blood.

Sage walked past me, bumping my shoulder, and yanked open the sliding doors to the deck. "Don't think we don't know that ball has limitations," she told me. A ruby hanging from a silver loop in her left ear emitted a high-pitched magical whine that made my teeth hurt. I followed her outside, my temper flaring, preparing to strike back, but she was already jogging down the steps to the shore. I decided that throwing one of the Gardners into the frozen lake that morning might not be diplomatic.

Marcella followed me onto the deck. "I've been trying to think how I can make this up to you," she said. "If I do end up with a lot of money when this is over, maybe I could buy you a new car or something. Of course that would only make them convinced you'd conspired with me. By then it won't matter. Might makes right."

"I just can't understand why they hate you so much," I said. "It seems so intense for just an inheritance."

"You know, I never really thought about that until this trip," she said. "I just took it as a given. But it's kind of crazy, isn't it? We were friends when we were little."

"Maybe as they got older, they started to realize what they'd lose," I said. Their cars, houses, prestige, security.

Marcella took out her lip balm again and popped off the cap. "Whatever it says on paper, I'm not going to take everything for myself. I wish they'd believe that."

"Fear brings out the worst in witches," I said.

"Don't I know it." With a sad smile, she ran the balm across her lips.

Chapter Twenty-Three

"You seem remarkably calm," I said.

"I know," Marcella said. "It's terrible, but I feel better this morning than I have in years. Ever since you put that spell around us last night."

We walked down the path to a stony outcropping overlooking the cold beach. Just inches away, the wind was filled with ice particles. And below that, under the frozen surface of the lake, dwelled wild, ageless, amoral creatures who resented the witch invaders.

Without the wand, witches wouldn't be able to become their neighbors of perpetual summer. Was it possible they'd had something to do with Horace's death? A battle over the inheritance, historically speaking, could lead to an entire witch family wiping itself out. Fairies might have seen this for themselves. Were they trying to spark a reenactment of ancient history? A blood oath without blood might free the wand from any master—or return it to a magical cousin. Some said the fae had imbued the oldest amulets with their power, which we'd stolen.

"Do you feel anything?" I asked Marcella, studying the

butterflies. They seemed as energetic as they had before Horace's death. The bees were buzzing around a large purple salvia bush. "Summer seems as strong as ever."

"Not a thing," she said. "I wonder if Cullen does."

"It can take a while for an object like that to change masters," I said. "His body is still here. His spirit might be clinging to that wand like static electricity."

Marcella shuddered and wrapped her arms around herself. "Ugh. I hope he finds peace somewhere far, far away from here. I love this place. I'd like to come back."

"Really? I thought you hated it."

"I only hated—" She stopped herself.

"Dear old Granddad?"

"I won't say that." Putting one hand over her heart and another over a gold chain around her neck, she looked at the house, the trees, the mountainside. "I'm sad we couldn't be close, Granddad. Safe travels into the beyond."

If I weren't friends with Marcella, I would've been suspicious of the sincerity of her kind words. "You're too forgiving," I said.

"It's bad luck to hold a grudge." She smiled at me again. "Let's eat. I'm starving, aren't you? They'll bring us something at the cabin. Sound good?"

I agreed, and we walked back. A half hour later, I learned my enclosure spell still lingered around the cabin enough to block out the sound of the kitchen guy knocking on the door when he brought our lunch basket. He had to send Marcella a text, asking if we wanted it brought somewhere else— nonmag communication filling in the limitations of magical.

When we were done with our sandwiches, Marcella asked my advice on which outfit she should wear—black sundress or blue? The inheritance of the wand would determine more than Marcella's financial status; if she suddenly began controlling its magic, her family would stop questioning her talent, charm, and guilt. Power would bring her the respect they'd denied her until now. Maybe she realized this—explaining her good mood and a greater interest in her appearance.

While she showered, I went for a walk to see if there was any change in the winter boundary. I hiked the entire perimeter, seeing no changes in the snow or ice, the fairies' behavior, not knowing if that was significant.

As I was walking by the house along the lake road, Ronald, Jack, and Cullen came out carrying Horace's body. A white SUV was parked out front, and Glenda walked over and opened the hatch at the back. She was holding a ski jacket.

Horace was still rigid in an X shape, but somebody had smoothed down his hair. I watched with horrified curiosity as they loaded him inside as if he were lumber. Sage and Isabel came out of the house with their arms overloaded with winter coats, hats, scarves, a pair of snow shoes which they put into the back with the corpse.

Marcella came up behind me. "They're taking him to the house on the snow side."

"There's another house?" I asked.

"Just a small one. The cook lives there. We use it for deliveries mostly. It's near where I met you, at the edge of the enchantment." She brushed the hair out of her eyes, and I noticed she'd chosen the navy dress. It made her look older in a good way—closer to thirty than thirteen.

"So what's the plan?" I asked. "Dial 911 from there, pretend he died in his sleep?"

"I think so."

It was a good idea. Nowadays it was necessary to have a death officially recorded by nonmagical society because of all the legal and financial matters. The Gardners didn't want to waste any time, risking questions about time or manner of death.

"They'll have to explain his odd position," I said. "And the shocked look on his face."

"He's so old. Do you really think they'll pay much attention? As soon as he gets away from the wand, he's going to look every minute of his one hundred thirteen years."

"I suppose not," I said. "They'll see what they want to see. As usual."

The SUV drove away with Ronald at the wheel, Cullen in the passenger seat, and Glenda in the back. Both men would be needed to carry the body. The others watched them drive away, then went inside.

"Brightness to you, Granddad," Marcella said quietly.

The somber moment was interrupted by her mother striding out of the house. "Marcella! Where have you been? You need to go find Kenneth and get scanned again. Right now."

I wondered if people had raised questions about the glass ball's effectiveness.

"Why?" Marcella asked. "What happened?"

Pauline came over, not speaking until she was very close. "Something screwy is going on. They've found traces of you all over the office."

"What kind of traces?" I asked.

Pauline frowned. "All kinds. Physical and magical."

"But that's not possible," Marcella said. "I didn't go in there."

"Kenneth claims he's found your magical fingerprint on the chair, the floor, the desk—*and* on the body." Pauline was staring at Marcella. "I don't want to know. Don't tell me. But whatever you did with Kenneth earlier, do it again. Tell him you weren't in there."

Marcella glanced at me for help. "But it's true! I never went into the office."

"Kenneth found your hair and some of that herbal tranquilizer you use. The stuff I think smells like bedtime tea."

"It *is* bedtime tea," Marcella said. "It's chamomile and lavender."

"Well, it's yours and it's in his office." Pauline looked at me, lips pressed together, then at her daughter. "I don't want to know. For Brightness' sake, don't tell me anything. So far I've managed to only tell the truth."

"But there's nothing to tell, Mom. I—"

"They found the spell residue of the chain your grandmother left you. That one." Pauline tapped Marcella's necklace. "Tell them you took it off and it was stolen, then turned up this morning."

"I can't say that. You know I never take it off. I couldn't even if I wanted to—it's spell-clasped. Her nurse put it on me at the funeral, saying it was her dying wish."

Pauline closed her eyes. "This is a problem. I'm proud of you for taking action, but this complicates things."

"Mom. I didn't—"

"Shush. Find Kenneth. Tell him what you told him before. Be even more convincing this time." Pauline gave me a sly smile. "Alma will help you."

She went back to the house while Marcella and I stood in shock, watching her go.

"What's going on?" she asked.

"I don't know," I said, my mind racing. Marcella had been with me all night. Hadn't she? Was there any chance I was wrong about that?

"I better see Kenneth. You don't have to come, no matter what my mother says." She began walking to the house.

Too curious not to, I followed. "I'd like to come," I said. "Do you mind?"

"Of course not. I'm grateful. But—"

"Don't worry about it. It's what I want to do," I said. Curiosity had me again.

We found Kenneth in the office, holding the glass ball in his hand. Instead of people, he was interrogating the furniture. It looked silly, but if he had talent, he'd be able to hear its response. The antiques in Horace's office were made of wood, wool, silk, metal, and steel—all carrying their own memories of a previous existence on earth. The plastic pen wouldn't have any information, but the natural items might.

Marcella and I waited in the doorway, watching. He didn't see us.

"Show me again," Kenneth said, waving the ball over the seat cushion. Only he would be able to see what the chair showed to him. He didn't seem to like whatever it was.

"Uncle Ken?" Marcella asked.

His head jerked up. Blinking, he looked back at the chair, then at Marcella again. "Oh. Hello. I suppose your mother spoke to you."

She nodded. "I want to make my statement again."

Kenneth lowered the ball and came to the doorway. "Yes, but you'll want to stay in the hallway. For your own sake." He looked at me. "I'm glad to see you. I was hoping to get a second opinion. An unbiased one is impossible, of course, but I'd appreciate a Protectorate eye on this nonetheless."

I was relieved he was going to let me. "Happy to help."

He held up the ball. "Marcella, would you mind telling the glass again about your movements last night?"

"Of course," she said. "I don't know why there would be any mark of me in this room unless somebody put it there."

Kenneth and I exchanged a look. Magical fingerprints were difficult to fake. The perpetrator wouldn't be able to prevent leaving a personal trace as well. If he let me do a thorough magical screening of the room, maybe I could find some evidence of another witch.

He held up the ball at eye level, sending more spell energy into the air this time than he had that morning, and Marcella repeated exactly what she'd said earlier. The glass ball, as it had earlier, glowed a steady, bright pink.

"Well, that's that," Kenneth said, lowering his arm. "Thank you, Marcella. You can go now."

"But—"

"Trust me, honey," he said. "You don't want to set foot in this room. There's enough evidence of you in here already. Any more will make it impossible to clear you."

Marcella looked at me. "You know I didn't leave the cabin. Somebody is trying to frame me."

"If that's true, then you should convince your mom to call in the Protectorate," I said. "Their agents have the power to do seriously unpleasant"—I glanced at the glass ball—"but foolproof interrogations. If somebody did want you to take the blame, they're counting on the Protectorate not being involved."

"We can't," Marcella said. "They might take the wand, and then people would really hate me."

"They probably wouldn't take it," I said. Then I thought about how they'd confiscated my magical wooden staff, and only a personal favor got it back to me. "Well, they *might* not."

"Can't risk it," Marcella said. "You'll have to clear me. You can, right? I'm sure you can. I know you were going to go home tomorrow, but— Please. Please stay and help me. You're the only one I can trust."

"The stakes are too high. It's your life, Marcella. I can't promise—"

"Of course you can't promise to succeed," she said. "But you can promise to try."

As much as I'd been looking forward to going home with Seth, I felt my resistance break. "I will try to find the truth," I said. "No matter what that is. Are you sure you want to risk that?"

"I'm innocent, Alma."

I looked at Kenneth, who was watching intently. "That gives you cover with the family," I said. "If they ask why I've gotten access to the office, tell them I'm working to clear Marcella's name. She's hired me."

He nodded. "That's a formal claim. What payment does she offer?"

I thought about the pink quartz stone still sitting in my pocket. Its pleasing charm had worn off, but I liked its potential for spells of my own. "Another stone from the guest bowl," I said.

"A new car," Marcella said.

I smiled. "I don't need a new car."

"You will someday. Whenever that is, I'll get you one."

"What if I fail to prove your innocence? You won't be able to—"

"You will." She grinned. "Every cell in my body is telling me to hand over my life to you. I haven't felt this good since I was a kid. I trust my instincts. They're usually telling me to run for my life. For once they're telling me something good. I'm going with it."

Chapter Twenty-Four

M arcella gave me a thumbs-up—a completely nonmagical gesture—and walked away. Her lack of nerves made me wonder what herbs she'd imbibed that morning. Or maybe it really was just having an ally to face the hostile forces of her family. The mind was a funny thing.

I turned my attention back to the office. I'd been a lowly Flint-level agent when I worked for the Protectorate and had never been trusted to scan a crime scene by myself. After magical crimes, however, I'd been part of teams of agents tasked with searching for evidence—and with witches and inhuman entities, that involved studying every item from the physical world as well as from the metaphysical. Residue could be spit or spell.

Other agents complained about it being boring, but I'd loved it. It had been my favorite part of the job. Breaking in, snooping, stealing—for the good guys—had taken advantage of all my childhood training as a burglar's daughter. And more than training, to be honest. I'd inherited some of my father's personality as well: the curiosity, independence, hostility to authority… It was a wonder I lasted at the Protectorate for more than a week.

"I need to do this by myself," I told Kenneth.

"I don't think I should leave you here without a witness," he said.

"Please." I searched my many pockets for the rose quartz and something else I could use, deciding on a few sharp seeds from the sugar pine cone. "I won't tell. You can say you were here."

He moved past me to stand in the hall. The air in the room shifted, the molecules of magic realigning themselves. "I could watch from out here," he said.

Already annoyed by his intrusion into my concentration, I squeezed the pine seeds into a fist and walked into the room, leaving a curtain of impenetrability behind me. It would take some of my energy, but I didn't want to risk being interrupted again. Some evidence could only be seen once; magical fingerprints didn't always survive the measuring and prodding from another witch. If I found and inadvertently destroyed something that might help Marcella, she could have my memory scanned for her trial.

Of course only the Protectorate would give her a formal trial. Her family might kill her first. So it was a tricky business, and a good reason to have Uncle Ken stay outside. I bent down and dropped the seeds in a star pattern on the floor to lock it in place, then began my scan of the room.

Horace's presence was huge and overwhelming, as dominant as a habanero in a bowl of baby food. But it was equally distinct, and once I recognized it, I would be able to ignore it and look for other people's.

The first thing I noticed was the path of movement from the doorway to the desk. People had come in, walked over, sat or stood, walked back to the door, departed. The energy pattern had the texture of tire ruts in a dirt road. Nobody seemed to stay, meander to the bookshelves, have a drink from the bar, hang out. The space Horace shared with others, even his own family, was very proscribed and very narrow.

That made it easier to analyze it. I stepped off the well-worn path and studied it from the side. There was the recent upheaval, but he'd been dead by then, so I focused on any of the magical fingerprints that had been interacting with him. That would eliminate today's visitors.

I couldn't find any recent sign of Pauline. Jack's mark was strong, consistent with him staying a few minutes in the evening. There was a lot of Cullen and Glenda in the room, but I couldn't establish how recent it was.

Everything matched the statements given to the glass ball —with one horrifying exception.

Marcella.

She was everywhere. Her hair, her magical fingerprint, the indentation of her foot in the carpet. There was even a strand of jute fiber from the charm bracelet I'd given her on the chair facing the desk.

I swallowed hard, trying not to lose my grip on my scanning spells, but I was upset. After wiping my sweaty hands on my cargo shorts, I touched my redwood-bead necklace again. Maybe I was only picking up so much of her essence because I'd been with her, touching her recently.

No. It wasn't a false reading. The debris was hers, nobody else's. And her distinctive aura was mixed with Horace's.

I squatted down and studied the eyelash-sized piece of jute that was clinging to the edge of the seat. Without touching it, I ran a probe over the leather upholstery. More Marcella. It felt as if she'd been there for quite a while.

The high concentration meant it had been as recent as Cullen's visit. Last night. Or could her state of high emotion have left more of a print than somebody else, and she'd actually visited a day or two ago?

That's what I'd advise her to tell her interrogators. For her defense. Because the evidence in her grandfather's office was overwhelmingly bad for her.

I didn't think she'd left the cabin, but my earlier certainty was wavering. I had to find something else to explain why my scan showed so much *Marcella-ness* in that office.

Clasping the guest rock for protection, I touched Horace's antique oak desk with my bare hand and invited it to tell me what had happened. Wood was my thing; I had a few more local cedar seeds in my pocket, and I was wearing redwood beads from my home. The tree essences might talk to each another.

Ugh. A sharp, acrid taste hit my tongue, making me jerk my hand away. Shadow energy was all over the desk. The old oak tree's purity had been vandalized with cruelty, violence, hate. The residue was recent, too fresh to attribute to Horace's difficult personality; it had shown up yesterday. If it were the winter solstice and fewer fairies were around, I'd think it had come from a demon summoning.

I let out my breath and walked to the door, eager to get out of there, have a cup of herbal tea. I'd brought some spearmint and lemon verbena from my garden, which should help wipe away the stain of Shadow magic I felt on my skin.

I began to pick up the pine seeds, which would open the door to Kenneth again, then paused.

What was I going to tell him?

Chapter Twenty-Five

I broke the spell in the doorway and put the seeds back in my pocket. Kenneth stood there, arms crossed over his chest, his face unreadable. He was a well-respected doctor nearing retirement age in the nonmagical world, held his own as a gay son-in-law in a cutthroat witch family, and seemed like a deeply self-possessed man; it would probably take more than my rude blocking spell to get him to lose his cool.

"Well?" he asked.

I wanted to trust him, but that could be part of his own personal magic. Perhaps the entire scene with so much evidence pointing to Marcella was a trick, and lying about what I'd seen might be what they wanted me to do to frame her—and therefore me. I'd have to tell the truth.

"There's a lot of Marcella's essence in that room," I said.

"From last night," he said. "Correct?"

"Looks like it." I stepped out into the hall and closed the door behind me. "I don't understand how. She was with me in that cabin all night. Scan me again. You'll see I believe that."

"I believe you believe that," he said, pinching the bridge of his nose, sighing. "But that's not enough to counterbalance the evidence. I have to tell the others. She should be locked up."

"*Locked?*" I hadn't expected that at all, not from him. Surely he could see how badly that would go, how easily they would scapegoat her. "No. Where?"

"There are bedrooms upstairs that could be used. Jack and I could move into one of the cabins." He looked pained. "I'm sorry, Jack and I have been together for thirty years, but I'm still an outsider to these witches. I can't afford to look disloyal."

"There isn't anyone here I'd trust to—what—what's the plan—interrogate her?"

"What choice do we have?" he asked.

"Call the Protectorate. I'll tell Raynor to keep his grubby agents from stealing anything."

He raised an eyebrow. "Raynor? You're on a first-name basis with a Director at the Protectorate?"

It was embarrassing, but I was. Sometimes you had to drop names to help a friend. "Yes. I'll call him right now—"

"Absolutely not." Suddenly a gold ring embedded with a hunk of sapphire was in front of my face. "You will not call the Protectorate." A complex coercion spell snaked into my nostrils and began to climb up into my brain.

I jerked my head to one side and blew my nose without even pausing to get a tissue. Just as he'd hidden his annoyance with my spell, I pretended not to be bothered by his. But unlike him, I'd overcome his effort to control me; if I wanted to call Raynor, I still could.

"Give me time to investigate for myself for a few days," I said, wiping my nose with my hand. Then I carefully rubbed it on my T-shirt from home—not the borrowed cargo shorts —in case somebody in the family had talents with bodily fluids and would use the garment against me. "Please? I won't call Diamond Street—yet."

"If she kills again—"

"She didn't kill this time! You must know that."

"The only evidence in that room points to Marcella."

"It was planted somehow," I said. "How long have you known her? You said you've been with Jack thirty years. That's her entire life."

"Yes, I was at her birth welcoming ceremony."

"Has she ever displayed the power necessary to kill a witch like Horace, even without an amulet like that wand he controlled?" I turned and pointed at the closed room where the wand rested inside the old treasure box. "He was holding it in his hand. Whatever killed him had been strong enough to overcome it."

He took a step back, lifting the hand with the sapphire between us. "I've restarted hearts with this ring," he said. "And you disarmed it like it was nothing."

I cleared my throat. A faint taste of his attempt to control me lingered in my sinus passages. "I've had a lot of practice with defensive magic. There were a few Shadow attacks where I live recently…"

He kept the ring raised between us. "Two days," he said. "Horace's body will be cremated by then. He's forbidden any ceremony, any funeral. The wand will have to choose a new master. If it's Marcella, so be it. End of story. But if it isn't, and she's somehow responsible for his death, perhaps with help, she needs to be punished."

"I didn't help her kill Horace." I smiled, trying to look harmless. "Ask around about me. I'm kind of famous for not being able to kill anything. Not even demons. That's why I lost my job at the Protectorate. They think I'm pathetic."

"I doubt that." He took another step back but lowered his hand. "Director Raynor wouldn't take your calls if he thought you were pathetic. Some of us have talents that are more subtle, and the Protectorate would be aggressive in co-opting them for their own purposes. I've worked with plenty of those witches. They use lies like spells. Deceit is its own magic. Whatever your story, being harmless isn't the truth of it."

I wanted to laugh in his face. I truly had been fired by Emerald mages who'd thought I was an incompetent loser, but in the years since, strange things had happened, magical mysteries had unraveled, and I'd discovered powers inside me that Raynor had wanted to exploit for the Protectorate. And had. So while it was funny to think I was some stealth assassin, it was true I wasn't a shrinking violet fairy.

"I always work for Brightness," I said. "And I'd never help anyone to kill even if they were as Shadowed as I suspect your father-in-law was."

He stared at me, still with that flat expression, then looked at his watch. "Four-oh-nine and ten seconds. You've got two days. Starting now."

Chapter Twenty-Six

I didn't get a chance to talk to Marcella alone before the evening meal. She wasn't in the cabin before or after I took a necessary nap—all the magic I was doing was wearing me out—and so I went to go look for her.

And to find dinner. I didn't want to be a demanding guest, but I needed a hot meal. The sleep had restored only some of my strength. If necessary, I'd break into the kitchen and make it myself.

As soon as I left the cabin, however, I saw the family gathered outside near the lake under a canopy of floating lanterns. When I got closer, I saw the two picnic tables had been draped with white tablecloths, formal china, flowers, wine—and I could feel a steady magical hum of the antique silverware.

Out of habit, I checked on the population of fairies in the area to make sure a demon hadn't appeared in our midst. Somebody had put Marcella's prints all over her grandfather's office, and it had taken unusual magic to do it without leaving a trace mixed with hers. Jack had been in the room, but I'd seen no proof of him interacting with Marcella or her residue—not with the jute or footprint.

To my relief, there were many dozens of tiny gnat-sized fae near the glow of lantern light, and several larger tree sprites sitting on the pines' lower branches. Whatever Shadow was at work at the Gardner lake house, it wasn't a demon.

The white ice covering the lake was within a stone's throw of the tables, but everyone was wearing clothing for a summer afternoon at the beach—sundresses and shorts. The wand was obviously still fueling the enchantment, even after the removal of Horace's corpse.

In spite of the heat, I shuddered. Some amulets went rogue. How many generations had the wand traveled down the line of firstlings? More years would make it a stronger bond. Fewer would make it vulnerable to other beings taking it for themselves. A wand powerful enough to change the seasons seemed to have a fae signature—certainly not exclusively human. It would require too much earth magic. Ancient energy that predated humanity.

I glanced warily at the lake. I bet the lake fairies were ancient—unless, like some animals, they lived on land once long ago and then returned. This evening they were making loud, painful noises that only I could hear. Was it celebration? Or continuing frustration that the land was still under an unnatural heat wave?

When I smelled garlic and melted cheese, my stomach rumbled. I was so hungry I almost didn't mind the awkwardness of no empty seat near Marcella, who was with her mother. Unlike the previous dinner, the tables weren't arranged by age. Pauline, Marcella, Ronald, Jack, Kenneth, and Sage were squished together at one table. The other only had Glenda, Cullen, and Huxley. The Gardners were taking sides. I hoped that boded well for Marcella.

I started to take the empty seat across from Cullen, but Glenda stopped me.

"Excuse me, no," she said. "Sarah will be sitting there."

Having a flashback to miserable birthday parties as a kid, I moved over. So long as I got some of the—I looked at the dish on the table—whatever that red pasta casserole thing was, I would be content. There wouldn't be much investigation possible at a crowded meal anyway.

Huxley looked up from his phone, offered a half smile. "Fun times." He lifted the salad bowl and offered it to me. "It has beets in it. Sorry."

Surprised by his hospitality, I took it, smiled back. "I don't mind them. Thanks."

When Sarah came out carrying a silver platter of desserts cut into small servings, Glenda stopped her. "You shouldn't be working for the cook. You weren't hired for that. Join us."

Sarah's eyes darted around the table. She looked as if she'd rather jump in the frozen lake. "I like keeping busy."

Glenda stood, took the platter, and set it on the table. "But you don't have to. We'll give you a good reference."

When she seemed to realize Glenda wouldn't take no for an answer, Sarah nodded and sat down between me and Cullen. A witch, she gave off a magical aura, but it was subtle and faint, common with the untrained.

Huxley continued to critique the food. Scooping a second serving of the pasta dish onto his plate, he said, "Not the greatest lasagna I've ever had."

"It's vegetarian," Glenda said. "To honor the dead."

"Since when do witches honor the dead without body parts?" Huxley asked, shoveling in a bite. "This isn't the middle ages."

"Dude," Cullen said warningly.

Huxley flinched as he'd only just realized he was sitting with the wife and son of the recently departed. "Sorry."

I liked the lasagna, which used the garden tomatoes and squash, and ate a big plate of it. Huxley, chagrined, had stopped talking, and Sarah stared at her plate. Glenda and Cullen held hands across the table, comforting each other as they ate in silence.

Because our table had fallen quiet, we could hear the conversation at the other one.

"Vegetarian?" Ronald asked, clearly annoyed.

"Out of respect for the recent death," Jack said.

I glanced over. Ronald was shaking his head, picking at his plate. He was part of the generation of witches that ate raw beef at a funeral. Sushi. Blood sausage. "He wouldn't respect this at all," he said.

Somebody shushed him. Glenda and Cullen had stiffened but weren't responding.

"Did anyone collect some of his hair?" Jack asked. "Clip his fingernails?"

"Don't be disgusting," Ronald said.

"Don't be wasteful," Jack said. "The night before his one hundred and fourteenth birthday—imagine what was in his cells."

Glenda stood up, her face red. "Quiet!" She lifted both arms and cast a silence spell over the other table, enclosing them like a garden cloche over a cold-sensitive seedling. "You ghouls. He was the love of my life. He *was* my life." Her voice shook, rising with each word, and when Cullen pulled her back down into her seat, she was crying.

The silence spell faded away, and the voices of the others became audible.

"I apologize, Glenda," Jack said, coming over and leaning down. "Really. It's just gallows humor. I'm gutted he's dead. He was my father, for Brightness' sake."

Cullen gave him a smile, then hugged Glenda. "We've all had a horrible shock."

"Not all of us," she said, shooting a dark look at me, then at the other table.

Sarah and I bumped hands as we both reached for the desserts at the same time. Sisters in misery, I thought.

"You first," she said, withdrawing.

I picked up the plate and held it out to her—she hesitated, then picked up a white petit four with a tiny pink flower on top. My own choice was a fudge brownie, which tasted as rich as it looked. We shared a commiserative glance as the Gardner family argued with each other.

Just a few steps away, snow was falling on the ice. The sky was white with another storm, and it was hard to see the other side of the lake. I wondered if the ambulance carrying Horace's body to South Shore had made it to the morgue or if fairies or other creatures, sensing the powerful body within, had swept it into a snowbank to take its spiritual energies.

"Do you know where they took him?" I asked Sarah quietly while the others were distracted. Jack and Ronald were now arguing about how much of Horace's hair should be removed before cremation. Tradition allowed ten hairs per descendant.

"No, but they've already picked out a funeral home," Sarah said. "For when they release the body. Most witches around Tahoe use it. They know the rites."

"Nobody is taking a hair from his head," Glenda said. She was standing now, pointing her hands at the other table as if she'd like to do worse than a silencing spell.

"You have to allow us some traditions, Glenda," Ronald said. "You aren't the only one grieving."

"You're greedy for his power, just like always. You *all* are." Glenda shook off Cullen, who was trying again to calm her, and strode off. White sparks kicked off her heels as she stormed up the wood staircase to the house.

I looked back at the faces of the Gardners at the other

table. Jack and Kenneth had resumed eating; Ronald seemed genuinely offended, and the cousins rolled their eyes.

Pauline, however, was smiling like a gnome with a four-leaf clover.

❧

BACK IN THE CABIN, I called Seth.

"Who died?" he asked.

"You heard?"

He let out a breath. "You're kidding. Seriously?"

"Marcella's grandfather was found dead this morning." I heard the defensiveness in my voice, as if I should apologize to him, as if I'd killed the old witch. "He was almost a hundred and twenty years old." I rounded up a little.

"It was natural causes?"

"Well, no."

Seth laughed. "I love it. You should warn people who invite you places. How many bodies is that so far? Ten? Eleven?"

I moved the phone away from my ear for a moment, annoyed with him and also concerned Marcella might somehow overhear—some witches could tap into phones even after a call and eavesdrop on the residue of the spoken word. "Just a moment," I said as I peeked out of my room. Beyond the sliding glass doors, Marcella was on the deck with a candle, saying her goodbyes to Horace. She wouldn't be able to see the tree sprites watching her from the railing, but plenty of moths and gnats were flying around her, attracted by the flame. I didn't expect her to stay outside much longer.

"I've offended you," Seth said.

I closed the door. "It's nowhere near eleven."

"Enough that I bet you've lost count," he said.

"Aren't you worried about me at all?" I snapped. Part of me had been hoping he'd be worried and insist I leave and rejoin him. A protective, manly response.

"You're probably safer now that he's dead. But yes, my beautiful one, I ache for your company, to climb into your lap and purr like the familiar I am to you." Seth's mocking tone was just like the charmer he'd been before we'd started… dating. Whatever it was. There hadn't actually been any dates, unless I counted the time he'd brought burritos for three and we'd sat under the redwood tree, hoping Willy would join us. (He'd waited until Seth left to claim his.) "When can I see you?"

"I don't know. Not yet. Everyone's uneasy here." I'd intended to protect him from the details so as not to worry him, but his flippant response had changed that. "They think I helped Marcella do it. I'm not sure if I'll survive."

"I'm sure the only match for you in that group was Horace Gardner," he said. "From what I've heard, the rest of the family has been riding his wand-tails for decades."

"From what you've heard?" I asked, my temper rising another notch. He was a terrible boyfriend. He made wonderful cinnamon rolls, but the teasing made me want to break things. "What have you heard? Why didn't you tell me earlier?"

He was quiet. I wondered what else he was hiding. We'd both accepted the need for a witch with demon ancestry and a human with the soul of a fairy to keep up a few boundaries, but he had more secrets than I did. The fae simply couldn't share everything.

"I'm sorry to upset you," he said finally. "I've been snooping around today. The Gardner family has been coming up to the Tahoe area for generations. There was a witch at the hamburger stand who'd dated one of Marcella's cousins a few summers ago."

My irritation faded away. "Just today?"

"Yes. I tried to call you around three to tell you about it, but you didn't pick up."

"I was scanning the office with the doctor uncle," I said. "Which cousin?"

"Arabella, Isadora, Annabel, something."

"Isabel," I said. "And?"

"Nothing really. She liked skinny-dipping when lots of people were around, using magic to hide, thinking it was funny."

"That sounds like her," I said.

"Anyway, she wasn't as good at it as she thought. More than one person saw through her little spell. The ex-boyfriend who gave me an excellent hamburger told me she just wasn't a very good witch."

"Maybe she was just an exhibitionist," I said.

"Not according to Jaden of the Burgers," he said. "The cheese fries were good too. Almost as good as at my high school in Minnesota."

His good cheer was lifting my mood as it always did. At first I was annoyed he didn't share my fears or temper, but then his unrelenting fairy calm seeped into me and I began to relax with him. "There are lake fae here," I said.

"Of course. There's a lake."

"I mean, they've made themselves known to the Gardners over the years. They hate the wand making it summertime in the middle of winter so close to their home."

Seth's tone changed instantly. "What happened?"

Now I regretted starting the conversation, but it was too late to stop. "They took a pet. A dog."

"Maybe I don't want to know this," he said.

"I don't think you do. Sorry I brought it up."

"I'm rooting for the fairies—I can't help it—but on the other hand, your life is precious to me," he said. "Do you think they're dangerous?"

I breathed in, listening to the moody, sour singing coming through the cabin walls from under the ice. A shiver ran through me. "Yes," I said.

"Be careful, sweetheart."

I shivered again, this time from pleasure. Getting the concern I'd wanted had come at a price, but maybe I was willing to pay it. I missed him and was embarrassed I missed him so much. "Maybe we should've come up here just the two of us."

"Three," he said. "Random knows how to behave."

"How's he doing?" My dog was wonderful, and I missed him almost as much as Seth. After a long day, having him flop on the couch or bed next to me, warm and furry, brought comfort and joy.

"He keeps melting the snow with his fire breath," he said. When my father had owned Random, he'd kept the dog enchanted as a miniature dragon—when he wasn't using him to assist in burglaries. "I have to keep making sure no humans are around to see the impossible."

"I thought my father's magic would've worn off by now," I said. "How is he regressing?"

"I may have given the old spell a little refresh," Seth said.

"Please don't let anybody get hurt."

"Same to you," he said. "No, I take that back. Let others get hurt if it means you're safe. Throw them into the lake. Let my water kin embrace them in an icy grave."

"Hey."

"Sorry. Sometimes I can't help but quote dear old Mom."

"She really sounds horrible," I said.

He paused. "Circumstances weren't kind to her. Living

too long, forgetting nothing, losing everything." He sighed. "It didn't help that she'd never had a moral core anyway."

"Yet you do."

"I had a human mother to pick up the slack. And my dad was great." He lowered his voice. "And your influence can't be overstated, darling."

Chapter Twenty-Seven

T he next morning I skipped breakfast with the family and went walking along the lake, searching for signs of the lake fairies. I heard a low moan that might have been their voices muffled by the ceiling of ice, but I couldn't see any figures. From what Seth had told me, they favored the deep water, the rocks and weeds, the hulls of sunken rowboats on the lake bottom. Could Seth rejoin his kin, even for a few minutes, now that he was locked into his human form forever? I knew he could apparate for short distances—maybe long ones—and his control of air and water was more than any witch's. I didn't know if he'd ever trust me enough to share everything. Maybe it would be too frustrating to explain. If I'd never been fae, how could I understand the joy of climbing the slimy weeds from the sandy bottom of a Minnesota lake to the loons paddling on the surface?

I inhaled sharply, my heart pounding. The image in my mind had been vivid, and I could taste algae on my tongue. Sweat dripped down my forehead, and I wiped it off, still caught up in the vision. Was it something here at Lapis Lake?

Were the fae trying to tell me something? Threaten me and any witch with a connection to the Gardner wand?

I closed my eyes and tried to bring it back. Deep water, northern pike, weeds, clay, shallow waves, water bugs, loons again. Minnesota. Seth's childhood. I smiled, no longer afraid. The memory was a gift from my boyfriend. I wondered how long it had been waiting there in my mind for me to discover it.

I wiped the sweat off my face again. It was hot today, hotter than it had been the day before. I looked down and studied the shoreline where a ribbon of water had appeared between ice and beach.

The enchantment was getting stronger, not weaker. I pulled my T-shirt away from my stomach to let air get underneath. It was only eleven, but already it had to be ninety degrees.

Was the wand malfunctioning, or had somebody taken command of it in secret?

Could both be true?

"Alma!"

I turned and saw Isabel walking toward me with something in her hand. She wore a pink tank top and jean shorts and, with her gladiator sandals and straw sun hat, looked like an ad for a beach vacation. Knowing she was not, in fact, a harmless fashion model, I put my hand on the mixed wooden beads on my left wrist and strengthened my defensive spells.

"Yes?" I asked. The sun was behind her, and I had to cup a hand over my eyes to see her face.

She held out the bundle in her hand, something wrapped in wax paper. "Banana bread. We missed you at breakfast."

I eyed it warily. This woman was not my biggest fan, had pretty much accused me of a conspiracy to murder her grandfather, and now she wanted me to hold and consume an object she gave to me.

Still, I couldn't be outright rude. I'd have to play the game.

"Thanks." I took the bread in its wax paper and didn't open it up. "Do you mind if I have it later? I'm not hungry yet."

She was already turning away. "Sure, whatever. If you're looking for Marcella, she's on the deck with my brother and Cullen. Sage too, I think. They've got a guitar out. Huxley's pretending to play."

"Cool," I said. "Thanks." The bread was warm in my hand, but that could've been from the air itself. It felt as if the temperature had risen another five degrees just as I'd been standing there. Were we in any danger? Should we all be staying close to the boundary in case we needed to jump into the snow? I didn't want to end up as cooked as the bread.

I unfolded the paper, legs braced, my elbow cocked, ready to throw it away in case it exploded.

Nothing.

Still, I wasn't going to eat it. I folded it again and walked to the house, following the sound of acoustic guitar. As Isabel had said, the younger Gardners were on the deck only half listening to Huxley struggle through a Irish folk song. Cullen was talking to Marcella, looking sad but making an effort, always the charmer, trying to please. He had a book in his hand and was pointing at the trees. I followed his gaze, alarmed because there were three dancing tree sprites where he pointed, but then saw the little gray bird and realized he was birdwatching.

"That's a mountain chickadee, I think," he said, showing Marcella the book. "See the white stripe above the eye?"

She looked at it and nodded. Her blond hair was pulled up in a loose ponytail, and with her smile and sunglasses looked as commercially photogenic as Isabel. "I think you're right."

Sage made a disgusted snort, audible during a pause in the music. "Who gives a Shadow about birds? One of you must feel the wand by now. Can't you turn down the heat?"

Cullen looked up from his book, meeting Marcella's gaze. They sat for a moment in silence, saying nothing.

"Well?" Sage demanded. At least *she* hadn't suddenly changed personality overnight.

"I don't feel anything," Cullen said slowly. "I wouldn't expect to. Dad only died yesterday."

Marcella let out a long breath. "I don't feel anything either."

"And you think that's normal?" Sage asked. "Something is happening. Look around. The beach is visible now. The creek is flowing a little. Somebody should hike up to the falls and see if it's melting."

"Go ahead," Isabel said.

"Am I the only one who's wondering about this?" Sage flung her arms out in frustration. "My dads think the wand might be going haywire without a master, and we're just sitting around listening to— Demon's balls, Hux, will you shut up?"

Huxley stilled his hands over the guitar and looked around. "Is it that bad?"

"No, it's pretty good," Isabel said.

"You're a natural," Cullen said.

Sage exhaled loudly—a growl of annoyance. "Maybe the wand needs us to do something."

"Maybe you need to relax," Isabel said. "If it gets too hot, you can jump in the lake."

"And have the fairies eat me? Thanks a lot." Sage grabbed a mug from the table and drank.

"They don't eat people, do they?" Huxley asked as he

resumed playing. "They just hold on to you underwater for a while. They don't care if you die, but they don't eat you."

"I care if I'm dead, thanks," Sage said. "I'm going to pack. Bag in the car. Ready to go, just in case."

Marcella caught my eye. "Should we do the same?"

"Why are you asking her?" Sage asked. "You're the one who should know. Or maybe you don't. That says a lot too."

Isabel raised her voice to be heard over Huxley's playing, which had also gotten louder. Sage was making everyone edgy. "Didn't you hear Cullen? It's too early—"

Just then Sarah stepped out onto the deck. The heat was bothering her too; instead of her business clothes, she wore a white tank top over black running shorts, and her face was red and shiny with sweat. "Cullen, your mom wanted me to tell you—but really, you'll all want to know this—the lawyer is coming at one."

"Little late for changing the will now," Isabel said.

"It's not to change it," Sarah said. "This is the family attorney. Ambrose Buck. He's on his way to read the old one."

"The one that matters," Sage said. "Since Granddad met his untimely end at the hands of totally mysterious unknown forces nobody could ever guess."

I tried to catch Sage's eye to see if she really believed Marcella and I had killed Horace or if it was all an act. She could be protecting somebody. Herself? But Sage had her head down and was playing with the gold bangles around her wrist.

"Thanks, Sarah," Cullen said. "Have some banana bread. Isabel made it herself."

Huxley strummed a menacing chord. "It's got a secret ingredient," he said with a smirk. "Granddad's fingernails."

Isabel kicked him. "I'll give your guitar to the fairies if you don't shut up."

I sent a quick probe into the bread in my hand, curious to see if it was true. If she'd ground them up, making them palatable, I wouldn't mind; the powder could provide a nice hit of magical energy. Sadly, my scan suggested Huxley was only joking.

"What about the other lawyer?" I asked. "The one who said she could break the oath?"

Everyone looked at me, annoyance or amusement about the fingernails forgotten. I felt myself flush—hotter—to be the sudden object of attention.

"What about her?" Sarah asked.

I waited for Cullen to speak. If Glenda had asked her to come as well, would he share that with the group?

No. His face gave nothing away.

"Is she coming too?" I asked. "Pauline had told her not to come, but Glenda said she might ask her. I was just wondering. Sorry, not my place."

The cousins seemed to forgive me, because they were looking curiously at Sarah.

"Well?" Isabel asked her.

"I haven't heard anything," Sarah said. "I'm— I'll be leaving soon. The lawyer will get his account passwords from me before I go and anything else you need. Email, phone, all that."

"Leaving, like, today?" Sage asked.

Sarah looked off toward the snowy pines. We'd all moved under the shade cast by the house or patio umbrellas, but it was still uncomfortably warm. In spite of my wise hesitancy to consume anything, I was tempted to pour a big glass from a pitcher on the table that held something pink and icy.

"As soon as I can," Sarah said.

Lucky her.

I EXCUSED myself from the group on the deck and followed Sarah into the house. If she was leaving, there wouldn't be a chance to ask her any more questions. The Protectorate would've kept her there for a few more days, but they hadn't been called.

Kenneth was in the living room by himself, standing by the window, looking in the direction of his daughter and the lake. I wondered how much, if anything, their branch of the family would inherit under either of the wills.

I approached him and asked quietly, "Kenneth, did you know Sarah was leaving?"

He turned, frowned. "Yes. Do you think that's a problem?"

"I don't know. Did— Was there any evidence in the office that might implicate her?"

"But what motive would she have?" he asked.

"Who knows? He couldn't have been easy to work for. And I heard he probably left her a little something."

He scratched his chin. "I didn't find anything in that room that pointed at her. So far as I could tell, she made a point of never using any magic in there. Horace might have insisted on it. That wand gives off a distortion field that could confuse other spells. My father-in-law wasn't the type to trust in the competence of others."

Since it was obvious Horace had been killed by magic, it was critical to find magical fingerprints to implicate anyone. The cook couldn't have crept in with a candlestick and smashed his head in; Horace had been hexed.

I lowered my voice. "Do you think anyone would mind if I put a tracking enchantment on her car? Just in case?"

"I suppose *she* would mind, but I'm not going to stop you," he said.

Frustrated with the family's refusal to call in real investigators, I left him to talk to Sarah while I still could.

She was in her closet office, working on the computer. On the other side of the hall, Horace's room was locked and warded to keep everyone out. The wand was still in there. I felt its power, muffled inside the velvet and wood of the box.

I tapped on Sarah's open door. "Hey, do you mind if I ask you a few questions?"

From the way she jerked her head up, I saw she hadn't noticed I was standing there. Witches who hadn't been raised as I had been—in crime creation and then in crime detection—always seemed so vulnerable, like children toddling after a bouncing ball into the street. Didn't she remember a man had been killed? Wasn't she a little nervous? One tiny warning spell at the doorframe could've alerted her I was nearby.

"What?" she asked, more confused than hostile.

"I'm trying to help the family figure out what happened," I said. "For Marcella's sake, you know? She and I went to school together."

She pushed away from the computer and regarded me. "I hear you used to be Protectorate."

"Briefly," I said. "A few years ago."

That made her curious, as it did with so many others. She invited me to come in and sit next to her in the tiny space. "What happened? I hear some people get the training and then go private," she said quietly. "Cash in."

"Some do that."

She raised her eyebrows, watching me. "Is that what you did?"

To get her to answer my questions, I'd have better luck if I answered some of hers. "No. I got kicked out because I have an Incurable Inability."

She grimaced. "That doesn't sound good. Mind if I ask what you can't do?"

"Kill," I said.

"You're kidding," she said with a laugh.

"Nope."

"Funny that isn't the default," she said. "For humanity, I mean. They think it's weird you *can't* murder people."

"Weird for the Protectorate," I said. "Killing demons is a nonnegotiable thing with them."

"Oh," she said. "You couldn't even kill *demons*?"

"Not when they're inside humans. And—" I cut myself off. When I started talking about the complex types of spirit beings who might take possession of human bodies on a wide spectrum of Shadow to Bright, other witches started to look at me funny. The Protectorate and modern witches saw all spirits who took possession as demonic and evil. That ruled out the merely curious, like the demon who had possessed my biological mother, and the outright angelic, like one not-quite human I'd met last year. It also made them want to kill Seth, which was obviously unacceptable.

"Has anyone else tried to go into the office?" I asked, changing the subject.

"Not that I know of, but when I'm in the zone working, I don't notice anything. Bombs could go off," she said. "I'd be a terrible Protectorate agent."

I smiled, having just thought that myself. "What are you working on? I hope you'll get paid."

"You're telling me," she said. "But I doubt it. Horace paid me in cash. Well, gold. It suited both of us. As soon as the lawyer says I can go, I'll go."

"Why wait for him?"

"I don't know," she said. "Seems like the closest thing to an authority figure there is. Other than Kenneth. If you were still Protectorate, would you let me go?"

"No."

She looked stricken. "That's what I'm afraid of. I hope Mr. Buck does. I knew it would be risky working for an old witch like Horace, but he paid well and was nice enough. Most of what I did was basic computer stuff, translating modern tech for him. When he was a kid, they didn't even have electricity in his house. I printed out all his emails and texts and gave them to him in a folder. He had to work on paper."

"So you must know a lot of family secrets," I said casually, playing with a bead on my bracelet.

"You've already heard the only big one I can think of. He wanted Cullen to get the wand."

Because she'd already claimed to be too weak to defend herself well, I tried a probing spell. "How about *little* secrets?" I asked, pushing the question into her head with a tap of magic.

Her eyes went out of focus. "I'd bring him springwater cocktails at bedtime to help him sleep," she said. But then I felt a sharp snap as she drew a boundary around herself. "Hey, don't tell anyone that. Or at least don't tell anybody I was the one to tell you."

"I'm not going to tattle about a witch having their own stash of springwater," I said. "Most do."

She sighed. "Not on my salary. After rent, I'm lucky if I can afford a protein boost in my smoothie."

I thought about how my perspective was distorted from living so close to a powerful wellspring, one that I had unusual year-round access to. "Where do you live? Are you from the Bay Area?"

Did she hesitate slightly? "My current apartment is in Redwood City, but I'm going back to LA as soon as the lease is up." She began arranging piles of folders on her desk.

I peeked at them, seeing they were each dated and stacked in chronological order. His email printouts, maybe. The paper inside was white, seemed all the same size.

"You grew up down there?" I asked. "I moved around a lot as a kid but usually lived in Northern California."

"I'm from the valley. San Fernando, not Silicon. Mom and Dad wanted me to go to medical school—they're both nonmag doctors—but I didn't have the brains or the guts for it. Looks like I'll be moving back into my childhood bedroom until the next gig comes along." She smiled, rolling her eyes. "Again."

The phone rang, and she excused herself. I lingered long enough to overhear her tell someone that yes, Horace Gardner had passed away the day before…

While she was busy, I hurried out of the house, one of her pens in my hand, and used her sweat on it to guide me to her car. She'd just been holding it, and her aura was easy to pick up. There was a row of cars parked in the gravel shoulder along the driveway, and I tapped the pen on the hoods of likely vehicles—the Subaru Forester, an old Camry—skipping the luxury electric SUVs that reeked like Gardners from ten feet away.

When I saw the twenty-year-old tan Honda CRV with a mismatched black bumper, I knew it was hers even before I tapped the pen on its hood and felt a kinship tingle in my fingers. I looked over my shoulder to make sure nobody was looking, then squatted down and put a tiny earth magnet behind the rear trailer hitch.

It was more secure than any botanical spell I might try to attach to the car—if I'd rubbed sage and blueberry leaves on the door, for instance, the snow outside would wash it off before she reached Sacramento. Unmagnetized metal was also too easily dislodged.

As I walked back to the house, I wondered why I was being so careful with Sarah when I was pretty sure she hadn't killed Horace. It was more than my humility, being aware of my limitations; another part of me expected the Protectorate to be involved later, if not sooner, and I wanted to be able to jump in and say where she was. Part of me still wanted to show them I could save the day. That I was amazing.

Distracted by my disgust with my own ego, I forgot to protect myself as I passed over the threshold into the house and had to endure a painful scanning that made my knees buckle.

Just inside, Pauline and Marcella were arguing.

"It's not up to any lawyer who gets the wand," Pauline was saying. "You are the first child of my womb, and believe me, I'd remember otherwise."

"I'm just saying I look forward to it being over," Marcella said. She saw me and waved. "However it goes."

"You can't talk like that. You have rights. Horace married Irene, Irene begat Bertrand, I begat you. That's all that matters."

"Begat?" Marcella asked. "What is this, the Old Testament?"

I had a sudden memory of her back in high school when she told jokes in the herb garden behind the teacher's back. It was nice to see that side of her again.

Pauline put her arms around Marcella, taking her into a motherly embrace. "Just remember, honey. None of that old man's bitter power plays can change your destiny," she said, kissing her hair.

Marcella gently pulled herself free, an awkward smile on her face, and turned to me. "Were you out on a walk? Enjoying the heat?"

"It seems to have leveled off," I said. "If it kept getting warmer, we'd have to think about evacuating."

"Don't be ridiculous," Pauline said. "All they have to do is give Marcie the wand. It simply needs its master."

Chapter Twenty-Eight

From my seat on a large hunk of granite beside the driveway, I watched Ambrose Buck get out of his black SUV and wipe the sweat off his brow as he marveled at the summer conditions around him. From his behavior, I decided he'd never been invited to the lake house under its enchantment before, although he was almost as old a witch as Horace had been.

Ronald came around from the passenger seat and helped Buck take off his suit jacket. The lawyer cut an interesting figure, somewhere between Santa and Marine. He was short and round, with the hair on his head cut high and tight, the bare parts of his scalp now shining with sweat. Much of his face, however, was hidden behind a glorious alpine-white beard, long and curly, conditioned and brushed in gleaming ringlets. Even for a witch it was a remarkable achievement.

He wore a shocking amount of platinum: cuff links, necklace, belt buckle, buttons on suit jacket, zipper in wool trousers, eyelets in his shoes. Nothing that would stand out in nonmagical society, but the magical aura was deafening.

He also wore a white-gold wedding ring and a watch inlaid with diamonds.

Pauline came out of the house, carrying a tray of cold drinks. "Witch Buck, welcome to Lapis Lake." She stood before him at a polite distance out of spell range, and he reached forward with a smile and took a glass.

I could tell by his delighted reaction to the first sip that Pauline had offered him wellspring water. "How marvelous," he said, bending over to sniff a nearby rose between sips. "How marvelous."

Glenda was nowhere to be seen. Cullen, however, had been with Ronald to greet the SUV. He touched the back hatch. "Did you have luggage, Witch Buck?"

"Oh, I won't be staying the night, but thank you." He set the empty glass down, then opened the back seat and took out a briefcase and a folding stool.

Cullen looked at his watch. "Are you sure? It's a long drive back to Sacramento in the snow, and it's already one o'clock."

"Yes, I know," he said. "That's why I'd like to get started right away, if everyone could be gathered. At the place of death is best, but of course if that's not possible…"

Pauline opened the door for him. "Of course it's possible. He passed in the office. We've set up chairs." She led him inside, and the others, including me, followed.

I hoped that in their obsession on hearing the will, nobody would think to demand I be excluded. A forget-me spell I'd drawn about my body while I was sitting on the huge hunk of granite outside, enhancing its power, should help.

Holding my breath, I slipped into the office behind Huxley and sat in the darkest corner. The others were already there. A few seconds passed, the remaining Gardners took their seats, and my heart began to steady. They'd forgotten me.

"Let's get started," Buck said. He unfolded the stool he'd brought, placed it beside the desk, and eased himself down. Clearly a witch who didn't take chances. "My condolences, of course. Brightness be upon him and you, all that." He cleared his throat and took a heavy binder out of a thin briefcase that looked too small for it. A handy enchantment for an old lawyer—making documents small and lightweight.

"Did he tell you he had written a new will?" Glenda asked. She'd taken the chair nearest to where Horace had died and was stroking the leather-upholstered arms with both hands.

"But he hadn't," Cullen said quickly. "He did speak of it, but it never happened."

Buck shrugged that off and put on a pair of reading glasses. "He never could accept the commands of the blood oath. I gave up trying to convince him years ago." He had to turn sideways to set the binder on the desk, then glanced around the room over his glasses.

I held my breath again but didn't risk doing any more magic in the room. Seemingly uninterested in just another young witch in the family, he looked down and began to read.

Without preamble, he began to list the addresses of residential and commercial real estate, then various pieces of jewelry, artifacts, amulets, works of art, vehicles, intellectual property, and investment accounts. There were also horses, exotic birds and reptiles, and a collection of rare orchids, as well as—

"Excuse me, Witch Buck," Ronald said.

The lawyer looked up from the binder. "Did you need me to repeat that last one? Forgive me, I can't be sure I'm pronouncing it correctly. Pha… Phalaenopsis—"

"Actually," Ronald said, "I think we'd like to get the, ah, big picture before you dive into the details of each orchid species and whatnot."

Buck frowned, glancing around the room. "I see. Well, the values of these items will need to be formally established, of course, although the cash investments are straight-forward—"

"I think he means we'd like to know who gets what," Jack said.

"It all depends," Buck said. "I thought that was understood."

"I told you," Glenda said.

"Depends on what?" Ronald asked. "My father was known to say things for dramatic effect. I'd like to know what's written down in black and white."

Buck sighed. "I can certainly relate to that. Unfortunately, what's written down in black and white is precisely what is subject to change. Due to the blood oath."

"So we're back to that," Ronald said. "The wand."

"I'm afraid so," Buck said. "Given the power it wields, there was no point in pretending a nonmagical document could split up the property. Whoever has the wand will have the power to determine who has the money."

"But without the wand?" Ronald asked. "If there was no blood oath and we had to go by the old will, who gets the… the phalaenopsis and whatnot?"

"But there is a wand," Glenda said.

Ronald raised his voice. "Humor me."

I saw his firm profile and tried to imagine what it would be like to be a middle-aged, second-born son, raised in privilege, single father of two children, facing sudden poverty. He was an addict who might have been spending every penny from his allowance. Maybe he hoped there was a trust fund, a cash account, an orchid noted in the will to save his future.

"In this will, all the nonmagical property, every item, goes to his firstborn son's firstborn child," Buck said, looking over his glasses. "Marcella Gardner. All distributions of all types will be up to her. As noted, she'll have the wand to enforce matters."

"And if she doesn't?" Glenda demanded.

Buck frowned. "It's quite nonnegotiable."

The room was quiet. It wasn't a surprise, but hearing it from the lawyer's mouth probably made it seem more real.

"All right," Ronald said finally. "You might as well read the other one then."

Pauline turned on him. "There is no other will. The woman who—"

"I don't mean that," Ronald said. "The original. The blood oath was recorded on something. Do you have it, Buck?"

He put his palms flat down on the three-ring binder, caressing the unread pages—it was five inches thick—and nodded. "Of course. Shall we skip ahead?"

Chapter Twenty-Nine

Buck snapped the binder shut, reached into his bag again, and took out a thick brass canister about a foot long. A wave of energy struck me between the eyes and drifted down to my breastbone, where it began vibrating like a cello.

Now *that* was old magic.

He unscrewed the silver lid embedded with gems and took out another canister, this one wood. Simple pine. He snapped that one open—it was hinged with brass—and took out a black velvet bag. Inside that was a stained scrap of linen, which he unfurled to reveal a roll of parchment.

He jammed the linen back inside its velvet pouch, tugged the drawstring tight, and took a deep breath. The dark, splotchy stain on the linen had been blood, and every witch in the room would've been able to feel it as I had, like a fist around the heart.

Buck held up the rolled parchment in a pincer grip. "This document predates and overrides any human intervention," he said. "No matter what that intervention might be. Not me, not any other lawyer, not any other witch. If there was an individual claiming otherwise, Horace was a victim of fraud."

Glenda spoke up. "This other lawyer said the issue of a beneficiary's… *unfitness*… was relevant. That even a blood oath had exceptions."

Buck looked uncomfortable and glanced at Marcella, his face reddening over the white beard. "He and I disagreed on that point."

"So you don't really know," Glenda said. "That old paper might already be moot."

"Please," Pauline said. "You've been scheming for over twenty years to take what wasn't yours. Give it up. You've lost."

I looked at Marcella, who sat hunched over, playing with the rings on her fingers.

"Your daughter herself knows she isn't up to the challenge of this inheritance," Glenda said. "The weight of the family's destiny."

Marcella lifted her head and spoke with a firm, steady voice. "Don't tell me what I think. It's true I don't want the wand but not because I'm not capable of handling it."

Silence. Her family didn't believe her. Her mom was happy though. Pauline smiled triumphantly and rested her hand on Marcella's shoulder.

"Just read the Shadowed thing," Ronald said.

Buck, nodding, put on black velvet gloves and unfurled the parchment. A smell wafted through the room. Burning hair, blood, sweat, roasted meat. My stomach turned. Sitting in the armchair between her two dads, Sage groaned and touched one of her gold earrings.

Buck held the parchment at arm's length and began to read. "I love you. Darling. I love you. Let this silver, let this pine, let this blood carry our bond through the ages, down our line, linking us in the chain of united love forevermore.

Signed— It's just a scribble. A letter K, I believe. I understand it to be his first wife's hand. And the blood should be hers. A mage could certify that if you need—"

"We know it was Katharine," Ronald said.

"Horace did say she was a very emotional woman," Buck said. "He blamed her red hair."

"But didn't Dad sign the blood oath as well?" Jack asked.

Buck shook his head, rolls the parchment. "Just her."

"But it was a wedding vow," Jack continued. "Wouldn't they both sign?"

"Not if it was hers before the wedding," I said, forgetting I wasn't supposed to be there. "Sounds like she gave it to him during the vows."

Everyone turned around and looked at me. So much for my hiding spot.

Buck agreed. "Perhaps it was her dowry."

"Perhaps? Don't you know?" Glenda asked.

"This is the first time I've been permitted to see it for myself," Buck said. "He was quite insistent it could only be read upon his death. Given the magical nature of the document, it seemed safest. These old papers can be quite dangerous. Self-defense enchantments to kill the unqualified. Protecting itself from destruction, burning, whatnot."

"So he got the wand from Katharine," Ronald said. "I wonder where she got it."

Ronald was shaking his head. "He said it was a family heirloom that went back centuries."

"He just neglected to mention it was *her* family," Pauline said. "Typical man."

Buck pushed his glasses up on his forehead. "That's why the master's control over it will be so strong. Their marriage vows, enhanced with this blood bond, ensured the wand would continue to follow the bloodline no matter what— theft or loss, for instance."

"It sounds like trying to take it away from its rightful owner would be out of the question," Pauline said. "It would take more than a sexist grandfather to change the rules of succession."

"Sexist? Who said—" Glenda clapped her hands together. "Cullen's gender has no bearing. Unfortunately it was obvious from a very, very long time ago that Marcella—in spite of her coping quite well today, which is remarkable and we have to consider it is due to some outside influence—is mentally and magically unstable."

"There's no mention of first child of woman born," Jack said.

"It's the usual rule with blood bonds," Kenneth said. "The unique power in a woman's first child. I've… I've seen it in my practice with some of my witch patients from big old families who are expected to inherit. The pressure gets to them sometimes. They end up with heart trouble." He was too diplomatic to look at Marcella.

Buck put his glasses back on and looked at the parchment again. "Yes, there's no question. It will go to the first of his firstling's firstlings."

An awkward silence fell over the room.

"My work with past clients has shown that the object will show you its owner eventually," Buck said. "With time for the old spirit to depart, a new bond can form." He rolled up the parchment, paused, untied the velvet bag, grimacing, and put it all back together. When he was done, he put the parchment back into his bag.

"So we'll wait and see," Glenda said.

Buck patted the thick binder. "As I said at the beginning. Everything rests on the wand."

EAGER TO GET AWAY from the buzzing, nagging irritation of the wand's energy, I slipped out of the office before the others were out of their chairs.

Something was bothering me, teasing at my mind, trying to get my attention. Something about the blood oath. Too many witches with their metal and their gemstones, their arguing and desires, were making it impossible to concentrate. I made my way through the house to the downstairs fireplace and sat on the brick hearth.

There. Even in summer, I could feel the house breathing through the old chimney. Its heart pumped from deep below, out of range of the wand's enchantment and even the lake fairies. I splayed my fingers over the brick and closed my eyes.

What are you thinking? I asked the part of myself that was trying to get my attention.

The parchment came to mind. I pictured a woman's hand, heard a woman's voice, tasted a woman's blood on a pricked fingertip.

I love you. Darling. I love you. Let this silver, let this pine, let this blood carry our bond through the ages, down our line, linking us in the chain of united love forevermore.

The sentiment was genuine. Passionate. Horace's first wife had felt true love when she'd bonded herself to him in marriage, and she'd used the blood oath and the wand to lock them in an eternal—well, she'd hoped—union. When had that been—? Eighty years ago? Maybe more. Horace had died just before his one hundred and fourteenth birthday. Like all humans, witches could get carried away with romance at a very young age, and witches back then were even encouraged to marry as teenagers if others could benefit from the contract. Obviously the wand would be an attractive dowry.

Down our line...

I needed to know more about Katharine. How had she died? Marcella had mentioned a baby who died too. There had to be a record. In the early twentieth century, witches weren't as integrated in the nonmag world, so I couldn't just go online and flip through hospital or census records, but an old family like the Gardners would certainly have an archive of family lore. The bloodlines were too important to them to leave it as oral history.

Would Marcella know? I'd have to ask her away from the others.

I opened my eyes, pressing my fingertips into the hearth, suddenly aware of the energy in the bricks from a woman's touch. Horace's aura, loud and masculine, dominated the rest of the house: its walls, windows, ceilings, and floors. But here in the overlooked, overworked heart of the house, there was a woman's warmth, her smokiness, earthiness, messiness…

I love you. Darling. I love you.

Katharine. It was her voice. But the house was too new for her to have actually lived here. She'd died before Marcella's father had been born, at least seventy years ago.

I reached my hands deeper into the fireplace—the oak logs weren't lit, of course, since it was so warm outside—and touched the iron grate.

Ow! I jerked my hand away, my brain screaming about a severe burn. Electric pain shot through me from finger to shoulder.

Demon's balls, why hadn't I used my defensive spells first? Did I want to get cooked in a strange witch's fireplace far from home, away from Seth, my friends, my dad, my dog?

After I'd silently berated myself, I put my sore fingers in my mouth and worked to counteract the hex. My vision began to sparkle as if I'd stood up too quickly. It was exhausting, but I refused to have another witch's mark on my dominant hand. The magic had been strong enough to blister, but I finally healed the damage.

"Forgive me, sister," I said aloud. "I meant no disrespect."

If it was Katharine's spirit that haunted the fireplace grate, she might recognize me as a potential ally. Woman to woman. Outsider to outsider.

I waited, but her spirit gave nothing away. Still sucking my fingers, I frowned at the iron grate. It didn't look remarkable at all, but I wouldn't be touching it again, not even if I engaged every redwood bead I had.

Somebody had brought that grate here. It could've been when the house was built, carried from another, older Gardner property—that wouldn't have been unusual, given the power of the hearth. A loyal servant to the family might have brought it here when they had the Lapis Lake house built. Her relationship with Katharine would've protected her as my lack of one hadn't saved me.

Or it could've been put here recently.

I needed to know more about Katharine, and I wasn't going to learn it at the fireplace. Hoping the Gardners were still preoccupied with the will and the lawyer, I went upstairs and ducked into the kitchen, where I'd never been before. As in the old days, the cooking area was walled off completely from the rest of the house. The counters and appliances were stainless steel, which at casual nonmag glance would appear modern and commercial, but was actually an affluent witch's way to infuse more power into the food cooked there.

"Looking for coffee?" a woman asked. She was about my age and had her hair pulled to either side in braided pigtails, then clipped up on top of her head. Pink-cheeked and pale blond, she looked like a European peasant girl from another century.

I introduced myself as a guest of Marcella Gardner. "Just wanted to give my thanks to the cook," I said. "That lasagna last night was really good. Any chance I could get the recipe?"

The woman's pink cheeks turned tomato red. "Of course! It's my mom's recipe. I've never cooked it here before. The family usually goes carnivore."

"So you're the chef?" I let her see my surprise. Usually witch families hired older women to cook for them.

She nodded, beaming, and took out her phone. "Can I text it to you?"

I shared my contact information, and a second later my phone chimed with the recipe. Her name was Tori. "Thanks so much," I said. "I'll make it when it's actually summer and I'm overflowing with tomatoes."

"It's so weird, isn't it? Every night I'm shocked to be in the cold again. They told me I'd get used to it, but I don't think I will."

If she was new to the house, she probably didn't have much to tell me. "This is my first time here. How long have you been working for the Gardners? Did you drive up with them from the Bay Area?"

"Brightness no. I'd hate it, all the traffic, the crowds. I'm fourth-generation Tahoe, third-generation chef. I went to culinary school in Napa and came back here as soon as I could." The timer went off on the stove, and she ran over to it, lifted a lid, and poked at something inside.

"So," I said, trying to sound casual, "is this your first winter here in this house?"

She lifted a bottle of olive oil, sniffed it. "No. Second. Why?"

Unlike Sarah, she had a self-preservation instinct, and it had just kicked in. I could feel her defensive spell waft through the room like steam from the massive pot on the stove.

I lowered my voice and glanced over my shoulder as if

sharing a secret. "I'm dying in this heat. Do you ever get used to it? I'm actually jealous of people on the other side of the boundary."

She relaxed her defensive spells and leaned in to me. "I know, right? It's never been this hot before. I asked my staff what they thought—I've got two guys who've been working for the family every winter since they were kids—and they said they think it's because Witch Horace died." She clasped both earrings, patted a silver chain around her neck, then knocked on a wood cutting board. "They think it's dangerous here. I hope Glenda agrees to hazard pay to keep them here because I can't do everything by myself."

"Dangerous—how? Too hot to work in the kitchen?"

"Too hot to breathe. Hot enough to set the forest on fire. It's not like the Gardners would call in the fire department," she said. Another timer beeped, and she ran back to the stove again. "Listen, I need to get back to work. Don't tell them what I said, OK? They're already upset, given the old guy's passing. I like this job and would rather not lose it."

"No, of course not." I tapped my lips and cast a demonstrative silence spell she'd be able to feel from across the room.

She smiled. "Thanks. Demon's balls, it's hot. I hope somebody takes control of that wand soon and turns the thermostat down."

Somebody would. But who?

Chapter Thirty

It took an hour before I could get Marcella alone and out of the house. While the sun was setting behind the white mountains, we sat inside the cabin next to the sliding glass doors, sipping glasses of iced peppermint tea.

I made sure a fresh anti-eavesdropping spell was around us before I spoke. "I keep thinking about Katharine," I said. "Your grandfather's first wife. Do you have any more information? When she died? How the baby died? Its name?"

"Sorry, no. My mom might, but I don't think you want to deal with her drama right now," she said.

Or her possible lies and omissions. I didn't expect Pauline to tell me anything that didn't benefit her and her daughter. "Everyone is certain the line with Katharine died out?" I asked.

"Yes, of course. I told you I saw the child's gravestone."

I thought it was interesting somebody had brought her there. "Your mom wanted you to see it?"

"No, she wouldn't. She didn't like to be reminded my father wasn't the first firstling."

"So who did?" I asked. "Your father?"

"Brightness no. He wouldn't have."

"Then who?"

Marcella stared at me. "Wow. Come to think of it, I have no idea. Do you think it's important?"

"Maybe not, but you never know."

"If you say so. Let me try to remember." Marcella squeezed her eyes together and began muttering a memory charm under her breath. I reached over and put a fingertip on her bracelet, trying to help.

But after several long seconds, she opened her eyes and shook her head. "Sorry. I was too little. That should keep it in California though. My dad didn't like to travel."

"Did you feel safe with whoever brought you there?" I asked, trying to get a sense if it was a relative, which would narrow the field.

"Wouldn't I— Wait. No." She closed her eyes again, her jaw going slack, and suddenly she shivered. The eyes that met mine were wide with remembered fear. "I *was* scared of her. She— It was a she."

I waited, feeling a buzz of excitement. There *was* something to uncover.

She licked her lips, getting excited now. "Somebody I saw all the time but didn't know very well."

"A servant, maybe," I said.

"We weren't rich enough for that. Dad was the heir, but we were never rolling in dough. My mom complained about having to do all the cooking and cleaning. Of course my dad wouldn't do it. It took her breaking her leg in a car accident for him to agree to—" She stopped and stared at me. My pulse kicked up, seeing she was remembering something important. "To pay somebody to help. But that was only for a month or two. I barely remember it. Mom still complains about it, how he almost killed her with reckless driving and then complained about having to pay for a cook. A cook! She was a cook. Brightness, I'd forgotten all this."

Yes. Finally we were getting somewhere. "How old were you? Do the memories fit?"

She took a long drink. "Yes." Her forehead was sweating. "Yes, I think it may have been the cook, whoever she was. Demon's balls, I had no idea that memory was in there."

"Can you remember anything about the child? Whether it was a boy or a girl, a name?"

She stared off into space. "A… girl. I think. That's another reason it scared me. I identified with her. I realized death could happen to me, a little girl."

"No name?"

Shaking her head, Marcella reached for her iced tea, took a sip, set it down. "I need a real drink."

"Where were you living then?" I asked. "If a woman was living with you only briefly, she wouldn't have been able to take you away for very long, or there would've been fallout. It had to be close enough to get there and back within a day."

"We were in Sunnyvale," she said. "Where I grew up. Well, before they sent me off to school."

I took a drink, trying to think of how I could track down a witch's grave in Silicon Valley without leaving Lapis Lake.

There would be documents at the Protectorate. A witch genealogist could unearth a lot of secrets with a few clues and enough time. But time isn't something Marcella had. She was suspected of murdering her grandfather, and his wand was on the verge of setting a wildfire and barbecuing the entire family, the staff, and myself.

"Don't mention this to the others," I said.

"You've noticed I don't really have that kind of relation-ship with the rest of my family."

"Not even Cullen," I said. "I don't know why you would,

but just in case you're talking about the past, please don't bring this up, OK? At least not now."

She frowned. "I wish I could trust people."

"Someday, maybe," I said. "But for now, keep everything to yourself."

She hesitated. "You're right. Of course. I'll be sure not to mention it to anyone."

I took another drink from my glass, draining it to the ice cubes. Even inside the cabin with a fan blowing, the air felt thick.

Witch families were aggressive about keeping secrets. So much was at stake—property, reputation, power—and bloodlines were still overly valued. To dig deeper into the official story, I'd need help.

The year before, I'd met a famously wealthy witch and his wife. He was no longer living—long story—but his widow, a well-regarded witch society genealogist, had kept in touch.

"Do I have your permission to ask a genealogist acquaintance of mine to look into this?" I asked.

Marcella played with her glass on the table for a moment. "I don't know. My mom would hex me if she found out."

"This witch is totally, utterly discreet," I said. "I trust her completely."

Marcella sank in her chair, avoiding my gaze. "I believe you, but if word got out… I mean, the family already hates me. The Gardners are snobs, if you hadn't noticed. If they learned I'd hired a random stranger to unearth secrets, I'd never see most of them again. Even my mother—"

"It's Zoe Thornton," I said. "Would that make a difference?"

Marcella stared at me. "You don't mean— Not *that* Zoe Thornton, as in *Phil* Thornton?"

I nodded, both proud and embarrassed I knew somebody so famous. "We met last year. She might have time to look into things a little bit. Find that gravestone, make sure you're the heir."

"Or Cullen," she said, "if Granddad's wishes come true."

"Or Cullen," I agreed. "But somebody killed your grandfather. Maybe they thought they'd get the wand. Maybe they will. So far neither you or Cullen is feeling any connection to it, right?"

Marcella still looked stunned by the news I could call up Phil Thornton's widow to help us out. He'd been one of the richest witches of our times, with a public profile in nonmag society as a philanthropist and space explorer. Well, until a Protectorate agent had driven a silver stake through his chest. They didn't believe a demon could be a Bright force in the universe, but Phil had been just that. And now, after the demise of his body, his spirit lingered around Zoe, protecting and loving her.

"I don't feel anything," Marcella said, "but I can't speak for Cullen. He might not tell me if he were slowly feeling the wand connect to him. Trying to protect my feelings or whatever."

It was still early for the wand to demand a new master—Horace had barely been dead two days—but the hot weather was alarming. And the clock on my two-day reprieve from Kenneth was running out. "So, do I have your permission to talk to Zoe?"

"I can't believe you're on a first-name basis with her," she said. "Do you believe her story about her dead husband being an angel?"

Zoe had just published a memoir, and the Protectorate was refusing to discuss its claims about Phil, although the mages there certainly did *not* believe in angels. It was as crazy as nonmag people believing in spellcraft.

I myself believed something more complex than pure-Shadow demons, but I wasn't sure what to call them. The demon who had possessed my biological mother wasn't evil —in fact, she'd sought to do good whenever possible, although cutting too many corners to be Bright in a pure sense. The last human she'd possessed had been a child abuser, but taking her body had been the equivalent of a death sentence without trial.

"I don't know," I said. An honest answer. Humans had too few words for the mysteries of existence.

"Wow. That's amazing. I hope it is true. I hope angels are real." She smiled, her face lighting up. "I'd like to live in a world with that kind of Brightness."

"Live as if there is," I said. "If it makes it easier to get through the day."

She patted my arm, still smiling. "Make me a T-shirt that says that, and I'll wear it." Taking her mug, she left me to make my call.

Hi Zoe, it's Alma, I texted. *I need your help.*

Chapter Thirty-One

Zoe phoned me two minutes later. "Phil told me to be ready for your call," she said.

I let that sink in. Phil was dead, but I believed it. "Tell him thank you."

"Of course," she said. "I've been thinking about you. I hear stories and worry the Protectorate is taking advantage of you. They aren't always considerate."

I snorted. "No. Don't worry. I'm well aware of that."

"What can we do for you?" she asked.

Silently noting the *we*, I gave her a quick summary of the Gardner family, Marcella's situation, and Horace's recent unnatural death.

"Ooh," Zoe said. "I'd love to dig around into that family. I've never had an excuse before. They go way, way back. But if his first wife brought the wand into the marriage with a blood oath, her lineage might be even more prestigious."

"I don't know her birth surname," I said.

"Oh, that's my job," Zoe said.

Zoe's fees as a genealogist would've been out of my league even before she became famous after Phil's death. Now they would be utterly impossible. "I won't be able to compensate you," I said, "but if Marcella inherits, she might be able to repay you in some way, but I can't guar—"

"Please. Don't insult me. Of course I won't take your money—or your friend's money." Her tone hardened. "I'd be in a Death Valley jail if it weren't for you. Phil can help me in some ways, but the magic around a Protectorate prison would be too strong."

I didn't believe Zoe would actually be in witch jail if it weren't for me, but I had done my best to make sure justice was done. "Thank you. I'm sorry to say I need you to hurry, too. Things are getting a bit tense up here."

"Like I said, Phil gave me a heads-up, so I've already reserved my time," she said. "I'll get back to you as soon as I can. Is this number safe, or would you rather I find another way to contact you?"

"This number should be safe," I said. "Thank you."

After we ended the call, I took out my bay leaf sachet, rubbed it over my screen, and set a fresh alert spell on my phone. A normal phone was the safest way to communicate, but a witch could use magic to interfere. The Protectorate had taught me excellent phone protection spells that had turned out to be far more useful than all the methods of killing things.

While Zoe looked to see if there was anything in the Gardner family tree that might explain Horace's death, I'd have another lovely, relaxing evening meal with the living members.

❧

I survived dinner but didn't feel any closer to understanding who had killed Horace. Pauline had motive, but she hadn't left any incriminating magical fingerprints behind. Cullen had motive if the will had been changed, but according to Ambrose Buck, that hadn't been possible. The others thought Marcella had the motive, though she truly didn't want the wand and its responsibilities, but not the skill.

It was almost eleven when we got back to the cabin. Exhausted, Marcella went to bed as soon as she'd brushed her teeth. After a mushy phone call with Seth, I too turned out the light and fell into an uneasy sleep.

Zoe woke me at four in the morning. I hadn't expected to hear from her so quickly, and I'd been having a bad dream about demons eating fairy sandwiches in my bed (they weren't—I checked), so I had a hard time concentrating on her words at first.

"There was a girl," she said.

"Yes, that's what Marcella remembered," I said. "She died as a child. What was—?"

"No, another girl," Zoe said. "I'm not sure if she's Violet's, but the dates match up. There's a record of a baby witch born in San Francisco during the year Violet ran away."

"Hold on, hold on," I said, jumping out of bed. With shaking hands, I set down the phone and put on the jewelry I'd taken off to sleep. It wasn't safe to write anything down, so I'd have to use a spell to make sure I memorized the details. I clasped a silver chain around my ankle and looked out the window at the lake, but there was no moon and everything was black. I picked up the phone again. "Who is Violet?"

"Sorry, sorry," she said. "It's late, and I'm getting a little punchy. Katharine had a daughter named Violet. That's the grave your friend Marcella visited. Violet's."

"But she was a child," I said. "You think she could've had a baby herself?"

"Violet was fifteen when she died, poor thing," Zoe said. "A child, yes, but old enough to have had one of her own."

The implications of this made me lean back against my pillows and close my eyes. Who else had known there was another possible heir to the blood oath?

"What was Violet's child's name?" I asked.

"Lena. But again, I'm not positive it's hers," Zoe said. "Here's what I know. In 1943, Horace and Katharine's child ran away from home or was abducted. There was a confidential plea sent to the Protectorate to assist the family in searching for her—I found the letter in the archives. Only the one letter, and I couldn't find any record of a response or resolution. But nine months later, there's a birth record in San Francisco. A fifteen-year-old girl calling herself 'Poppy'— I believe it was really Violet—gave birth to Lena, a female witch, five pounds six ounces, nineteen inches, brown eyes, curly red hair, good health, no evidence of Shadow."

"The father?" I asked.

"None noted. Genealogists hate that, of course, but it's typical of the era. Women witches didn't like giving that information away if they didn't have to. A lot of power in the knowledge. And possibly a payout, if blackmailing the father was possible down the road. She was probably too young to think of that, but she was a witch from a witch family and would've been taught to be tough."

"Is there any way you could find out who the father was?" I asked. "If he was young like her, and she went with him willingly, or…" I tried not to imagine the worst.

"With enough time, maybe," she said. "I've got some calls out. What I don't understand is why the Gardners didn't raise the baby themselves. As a firstborn, they would've wanted to keep her close. But you say your friend insists the line died with Violet?"

"Yes," I said. "That's what she believes."

"Well, what the older witches in the family know and what they say are probably different, with such a fortune at stake," Zoe said.

"Do you know if Lena is still alive?"

"Not yet," she said. "I just found her birth. Now I'll trace the years after. If she's still alive, she'd be in her early sixties."

"Thank you, Zoe," I said. "If anyone could do this, you can."

"You're very welcome. Phil says hello—in his own way. It's more of a feeling than a word, if you know what I mean."

I hesitated. I actually didn't know what she meant. Was it like when I talked to my demon mother, an apparition in a Summoning Circle? Or more like the casual, everyday chitchat you'd have with any departed relative, never expecting a reply but imagining their presence?

"If Lena is still alive," I said, "she'd be the heir to the wand and everything else. And if she had a child, or that child had a child…"

"Yes, I completely understand," Zoe said. "Those old blood oaths were terribly strict about firstlings. I'm glad they fell out of fashion. Very dangerous. I appreciate their gender-neutral approach to inheritance, with the realistic emphasis on the mother as deciding parent, given the tendency of male witches to spread their seed indiscriminately, forgetfully, dishonestly, accidentally, enthusiastically, anonymously…"

"Yes, but the firstborn requirement is just asking for trouble," I said. Or murder.

"Phil and I have set up a modern legal will with magical triggers," Zoe said. "All the beneficiaries have to endure a period of requalification after I die. Our trustees have the authority to use magical scanning to confirm they're worthy. That's what Horace would've liked to do, I'm sure. When you acquire a lot of property, you become attached to it and want to control it as much as possible, even beyond the grave. I can sympathize with his dilemma."

I looked in the direction of the room where Marcella slept. "I don't. He's been horrible and cruel to my friend for her entire life. She's traumatized."

"But the system was almost designed for him to do so. Let me tell you, the eighteenth century was the worst for that sort of abuse," Zoe said. "Your friend is lucky she wasn't killed. You know, *accidentally*. The archives are filled with heirs—especially heiresses, the poor girls—meeting untimely deaths."

We both fell silent, honoring their memory.

Then a thought occurred to me. "Do you think that's what happened to Violet? She was abducted by somebody wanting to wipe out that inheritance line? She ended up pregnant, maybe in an effort to kill her in childbirth?"

"Or she ran away because she was afraid of staying at home," Zoe said. "Who knows? I only just learned of her existence. I'll need more time to poke around."

"Please make sure to keep this confidential," I said. "I promised Marcella it wouldn't get back to her family. They give her a hard time about breathing."

"Of course. You don't have to worry about that." Her tone warmed. "Phil makes sure tongues don't wag."

That both encouraged and terrified me. "Great," I said.

Chapter Thirty-Two

round nine in the morning at the big house, only
cold food was laid out on the buffet table for breakfast: cereal, yogurt, fruit.

Kenneth had given me two days, which would be only
that afternoon. I was running out of time. My stomach was
uneasy, but I had to fuel up for my energy stores.

I appreciated the light meal on another hot day, but
Pauline stood there, unhappy with the offering, and told
Marcella to go into the kitchen to see if there was any coffee.
A moment later Marcella came out to say it was the cook's
day off, and the two guys who worked for her seemed to have
put out a few easy things on the table and gone home. The
kitchen was deserted.

"I could make us some eggs," Marcella said. "Would you
like that?"

"How about you make us coffee and bring it up to my
room, will you, honey?" Pauline asked her. "We can have girl
talk. Catch up in private."

Marcella shot me a concerned look, but I gestured she
should go ahead. Pauline headed for the stairs, Marcella went

into the kitchen, and I prepared myself a bowl of raisin bran. Kenneth was alone near the window, reading on his phone. Of the cousins, only Isabel was on the couch, also reading on her phone, drinking a Diet Coke and eating trail mix out of a plastic bag.

I sat next to Kenneth with my back to the lake, something the family avoided doing, feeling threatened by the lake fairies. My own fears centered on the human beings, and I wanted to watch people come in and out, so I kept my gaze on the doors.

I wanted advance notice of being overheard or interrupted.

"Morning, Kenneth," I said, offering a smile. "How are you?"

He frowned at me over his glasses, then looked around the room at all the empty seats farther away I hadn't chosen. "All right, I suppose." He put his phone down and rested his hand over it with a boundary spell. Magical phone lock. Perhaps habit or perhaps something he didn't want me in particular to see.

I turned my attention to my cereal, hoping he would lower his guard. While I ate, Marcella walked by with coffee on a tray for her mother, and we nodded at each other.

The dining room might get busy again, so I couldn't wait any longer. "I need to ask you a few questions," I said to Kenneth, who had gone back to his phone. "I hope you don't find them too intrusive."

He made a face and lifted a mug to his lips. I noticed he was drinking chamomile tea for breakfast. Was he secretly a tense, neurotic man under his calm exterior, or did he actually enjoy the taste?

He dropped the mug back down on the table with a thud. "What do you want to know?"

My question was going to upset him, but I had to ask. "Do you know anything about Sage's birth parents?"

The look he gave me made me want to apologize and run away. I imagined being an internist or nurse at the hospital and getting that look. I felt guilty, ashamed, afraid, desperate to please, to confess all. It would come in handy as a Protectorate agent—and then I remembered his parents had both worn silver jackets in their service there. The long, merciless arm of magical law.

"Why do you ask?" His voice was soft but scary.

I had no choice but to explain—as little as I could. "If Katharine has a living firstborn descendant, that person might have a claim on the wand," I said. Then, to make it less about murder and accusation, I gestured at the sun outside. "What if it keeps getting hotter? The issue of who gets the wand might not be able to wait until Horace's cremation and spiritual departure."

"You think Sage might be Katharine's granddaughter?"

I watched him carefully. "Or great-granddaughter," I said.

Leaning back in his chair, he regarded me for a long moment before he shook his head. "Fascinating theory. But it's impossible. It was an open adoption. We knew her biological parents. Witches, of course. No interest in parenting."

He seemed relaxed, but his parents and experiences must've trained him well; I couldn't read him at all. "You researched their family's histories?"

"Of course," he said. "We hired a genealogist."

I gave him a polite smile. "Great, thanks. Sorry to intrude."

"I hope you won't be redirecting this question to Sage herself," he said. "She can get a bit sensitive, especially when we're visiting the Gardners. They never let her feel like she belongs."

If she hadn't been so hostile to Marcella, I thought she

might've found kindness there, but it was probably too late now.

"I don't think I need to talk to Sage," I said. Given how she'd direct her anger against Marcella, I'd avoid talking to her if I could find the information in other ways. She'd probably lie anyway.

"I'd also suggest you not mention this to Jack. He's almost as touchy as Sage about feeling excluded here." He dropped his voice so low I could barely hear him. "That's what upset him the night Horace died. There was usually some blowup about it."

"Jack was upset about Sage being left out of the will?" I asked.

Kenneth gave a tiny nod. "I hope you understand it's not the money. It's the principle. A symbol of belonging. That's why he was so touched by his plan to add something specifically for Sage. Unfortunately there wasn't time to see it done." He got to his feet. "Now if you'll excuse me, I need to call the hospital."

"The hospital?" I asked, alarmed. Now what?

He took out his phone, ran his thumb over it, and turned away. "I'm a doctor, remember? The real world needs me."

Feeling stupid, I watched him go. Witches loved to hurt each other, so why wouldn't somebody have suddenly ended up in the hospital? Maybe they'd tried to resurrect Horace's corpse instead of cremating him.

A minute later, I plucked the tea bag out of his mug, put it in mine, and walked after him, pretending to drink. But instead of going upstairs as he had, I went down the hall toward Horace's office.

Nobody was standing guard anymore, but the door was locked and had a security spell around the doorframe. I could feel the thrumming pulse of the wand inside its velvet-lined pine box. Had it gotten worse, or was I just stressed?

I looked up and down the hall, then slipped into Sarah's office.

As I'd hoped, she'd left no protective spell behind. Her security measures had been extremely lax—there wasn't even a nonmagical lock on the door. Maybe she and Horace had assumed nobody would be interested in the assistant's workspace even though there were rows of binders crammed on the shelves that must've belonged to Horace.

I cast an invisibility spell at the door to hide my presence, then set the mug on the desk and began my search.

Chapter Thirty-Three

Sarah had departed, and the laptop she'd used was gone. I'd heard the lawyer, Buck, had taken it. Hearing footsteps in the hall, I froze. Jack, talking on his phone, walked by, stopped at Horace's office door. He tested the doorknob, shook his shoulders as the zap of power struck him, then continued on. He never looked behind him at Sarah's office. Just an assistant, and she'd left anyway.

I closed my eyes and touched my redwood beads to refresh my hiding spell. Jack's proximity had eaten away at it, and anyone could see through it if they concentrated.

On the walls to either side of Sarah's alcove desk were shelves filled with binders. I pulled a random one off the shelf and saw a month's worth of his printed emails and text messages. It was from July of last year and dealt mostly with an auction in London, the pieces of art and furniture he was interested in, their estimated value with an appraiser, details about the doubtful authenticity of a walnut table. It went on for weeks. I got drowsy just flipping through it in a hurry; it was the sort of thing my father would mock. "Just take it if you like it, sell it if you don't," he'd say. "If a fake gives you pleasure, who cares?"

Of course, he'd never be happy with a fake. But he believed others should be. To his credit, he'd never knowingly sell a counterfeit—though that was only because it might reflect badly on him personally someday.

Finding something relevant in so many pages of correspondence would take weeks. There might not even be anything of interest in this unsecured closet. But if there was…

On the corner of one of the pages of emails about the walnut table, there was a smudge of something brown and greasy. I hoped it was Horace's fingerprint while eating. I tore the stained paper, placed the coin-sized piece on my palm, then lifted Kenneth's soggy tea bag out of the mug and set it on top of the paper. After a glance at the door, I spit on it and closed my fingers.

Aggressive male energy thrashed in my fist. Horace was dead, but only recently—plenty of his magic was left in his things. Kenneth's spit had just mingled with the chamomile —I was always amazed when an experienced witch started drinking tea without taking the bag out first, because it left them vulnerable to magical intrusion. With Protectorate parents, he would know that. Perhaps being a prestigious doctor had made him feel invincible.

I waved my fist over the row of binders, gritting my teeth as Horace's voice echoed in my mind. There was too much of him to sort through the words, so I focused on my sense of Kenneth imbued in the lump of chamomile mixed with a drop of his spit.

Nothing… nothing… I moved my hand to another bookshelf and waved it sideways, up and down…

Nothing again. Maybe I was wasting my time, using Kenneth as a focusing agent. He was a son-in-law, not—

Wait. There. My fist was drawn to a binder in the middle of the third shelf. I hesitated, then took it down and opened it with my free hand.

Bingo. Family emails.

Using Kenneth's energy signature, I unfocused my eyes and felt myself be guided to a page in the middle. They weren't all printouts—the one that was speaking to me was a handwritten letter on old-fashioned stationery. I could feel the linen threads woven into the paper, organic material that gave the correspondence between witches extra weight. Centuries ago, a witch would've used parchment or animal skins. These tiny scraps of linen in recycled wood pulp were weak, but anything was more powerful than digital.

It was a letter from Jack to Horace, one paragraph long, asking for money due to an unexpected crash in their investments. Kenneth's doctor salary wasn't enough to get them out of the hole. Dated a month ago, it suggested meeting in person to discuss it.

I turned the pages and found another request, same paper, from six months earlier. In between the stationery from Jack were requests from Pauline, Ronald, and even Isabel asking for payments of various kinds for nonmag dental work, roof repair, school tuition. They had *all* asked him for money. No responses from Horace were recorded, making their relationships seem desperately one-sided, though the letters did mention their thanks for previous sums he'd given them.

Would Jack and Kenneth have wanted Horace dead in the hope of getting some of his money? Or had he been worth more to them alive? The question applied to all of them. If money was the motive, every one of them was a suspect.

I heard voices in the hall. Getting caught reading through files in the office would be awkward. With the powerful wand just across the hall, my stealth spell was weakened, exhausting to maintain. I put the binder back on the shelf and dropped the mass of chamomile and paper into an empty velvet bag I kept in one of my pockets. It had probably given me everything it could, but I couldn't just leave it in Sarah's wastebasket.

If there were printouts in the office about the new will or lawyer, it could take weeks to find, and I suspected truly sensitive materials would've been burned anyway.

A single file folder sat on the edge of the desk where the laptop had been. It was just like the ones Sarah had carried around with her for Horace. I picked it up and flipped it open. Although it looked well-worn—its unmarked tab was crumpled and the corners bent—there was nothing currently inside.

Fire. An image of the downstairs fireplace flashed in my mind. I ran my bare hand across the folder and cast a tracking spell for lost items. There was a chance the paper might feel attached to documents that had been taken and destroyed, especially if they'd been touched by the wrong person. The person who had killed its master.

There was a faint trail that led away from the desk into the hallway. I stepped out and quickly bent to tie my shoe, aware it wouldn't fool anybody if they truly cared what I was doing near Horace and Sarah's offices but enough to blend in if they were distracted. I saw the cook—Tori, with the lasagna recipe—walk across the living room in an obvious rush, setting a steaming casserole dish on the buffet table and then jogging back to the kitchen.

Part of my mind registered that Tori had come in on her day off, but I set that information aside to follow the faint tracking spell to the stairs. Papers had been taken to the living room many times, but they'd been returned. It was the path that led down the steps that gave the simple paper consciousness a shiver of terror. *Fire*.

I followed the shiver to the hearth and sat down to look inside. No hint of the papers remained, but I was sure this was where some had been destroyed. For some reason I was disappointed, but I don't know why. Had I thought I'd find drafts of Horace's will sitting here in pristine condition? A signed confession on calfskin, marked with a penitent drop of blood from whoever had killed him?

Leaning closer, I set my hand on the ash and brick, opening my senses to money, blood, human conflict, but I couldn't piece together anything coherent. The sensations were as muddled as the voices in a crowded theater. Yes, papers had been destroyed, but what they'd said was lost.

I removed my hand and brushed off the ash on the rug, not wanting to bring any of it, which would be contaminated with the essence of the Gardners and their troubles, with me. Remembering the limited cleaning staff, I felt guilty for giving them more work, then thought of Tori. She'd come in on her day off because her helpers were afraid of the heat. A thought nagged at me. Something I'd missed.

Heat in the kitchen… Too many cooks in the kitchen…

My work spying in the house had worn me out. I went outside through the door facing the lake and walked along the shore, trying to clear my head, to think, to figure out what was bugging me.

Sarah had said her family had been at Lake Tahoe for generations. Was that it? Or… Aha. Cooking. Her mother had been a chef as well. Had she also worked for the Gardners?

Marcella had been taken to Violet's grave by a cook who worked for the family. Could it be a coincidence?

The universe didn't give me any answers. I paused at the vegetable garden and squatted down to look for the fairies hiding behind the leaves and vines of the twining green beans. Inside, a family of three were enjoying the shade, using bright yellow squash blossoms as chairs. When they looked at me, I smiled and withdrew, not wanting to upset them.

The enchantment was wonderful in some ways—the fairies clearly loved it—but it was fragile. If the wand suddenly cast the area into subzero temperatures, the nonmag animals would suffer, maybe die, even if the fae tried to help them.

As I walked back to my cabin, my thoughts kept returning to the fireplace. It was a cozy spot and would be nice to sit there on a true winter day with a fire lit. I imagined the logs on the grate.

The iron grate.

That's what had been bugging me. It had hexed me yesterday, but today—

Today it was gone. Somebody had removed it.

But who? And what did it mean?

Chapter Thirty-Four

I went upstairs to the kitchen, where Tori was preparing something involving celery. She was alone.

"I hear it's your day off," I said, putting sympathy into my tone.

"My dudes wouldn't work today," she said. "You'd think they were nonmag. Seriously. A little magic heat spell and they noped out."

I looked at the stalks of celery next to her on the cutting board. "Can I help?"

She frowned at me, then laughed. "You must want something."

My face flushed, giving me away. I hadn't prepared a spell in time to hide my emotions. "You're right," I said, laughing with her. "Sorry."

"I know witches."

"Good instincts." I looked around the kitchen, seeing lettuce, garden tomatoes, and a hunk of feta cheese, and smelled chicken roasting. "You could work for the Protectorate."

"No way. I'd miss the kitchen." She pushed aside the celery and set down the knife. "What can I do for you?"

I studied her for any sign of anxiety, deceit, animosity, but found none. Although she'd caught me out, she hadn't used magic to do it, just common sense.

My hand was in my pocket, holding a detached strand of redwood beads. If she could see me grab them on my wrist or neck, she might block my spell before I got an honest answer, so I'd hidden them in my pocket. "Did you take the metal grate out of the downstairs fireplace?" I asked. My question carried the force of a Protectorate interrogation spell.

Her eyes widened as she felt it hit her tongue. "*No*," she said with a long, drawn-out vowel, as if forced to speak—which she had.

Satisfied, I broke the spell. "Thank you," I said. "Sorry about that."

She was furious. "Who in Shadow do you think you are?"

"I'm acting for Marcella, a member of the family you serve, to clear her name."

Scoffing, Tori picked up the knife and banged it down on a stalk of celery. "I don't even know what you're talking about. There's no grate in that fireplace. They never use it." She banged the knife down again. I was glad I wasn't a stalk of celery. "Glenda had it painted black last summer and put a vase of fake flowers in it. I mean, seriously? She calls herself a witch? The ground floor hearth is the best one."

Realizing she'd spoken too loudly about the lady of the house, she pressed her lips together and looked at the door.

"Don't worry," I said. "I've got a silence spell around us. Nobody can hear what you say."

She scowled at me, holding the knife in midair. "You're making me nervous. Do you mind leaving now so I can finish making lunch? They're still upset about the cold breakfast."

"Of course," I said. "And thanks."

"You didn't need to hex me. I would've answered you honestly without it." She resumed chopping.

"Sorry," I said. "I needed to be sure." Releasing all the magic I'd been weaving—which was wearing me out, even with all my focusing beads—I left the kitchen and immediately walked out of the house for fresh air and some distance from the Gardner family boundary spells.

So it wasn't Tori who had put it there. That suggested Sarah, and she'd taken it with her. Or was it just a coincidence, and one of the Gardners had brought the Shadowed object for their own purposes?

I climbed up the slope above the house below a snowbank and sat down on a large, flat hunk of granite under a tree that was still in internet range. Using my phone, I typed in the address I'd memorized from the letter for Jack and Kenneth's house in Los Altos Hills. I wanted to know what was it worth, what had they paid for it, that sort of thing. If money was at the root of the murder, I'd have to find out who was most desperate for it.

Even knowing real estate near Stanford would be expensive, I whistled to see the eight-figure price tag of their hillside estate. Kiwifruit vineyard, swimming pool, miniature riding train, botanical garden, guesthouse, aviary…

Wow. I wished I was using a bigger screen to appreciate the photographs. It was excessive but… somehow not entirely selfish. The aviary was shared with a nonprofit bird rescue organization. The kiwis were given to food banks. The little train was open at no charge for preschool field trips. The natural pool that had a view of the San Francisco Bay from its infinity-edge waterfall used aquatic vegetation as a biological filter and used no harsh chemicals.

Lost in real estate fantasies, I scrolled through all the photographs before realizing the listing was current. It had already been on the market for two weeks. That suggested they hadn't gotten the money from Horace and had made plans to work through their troubles on their own. Would that rule them out for his murder? Or put them at the top of the suspect list?

I put my phone away and closed my eyes to think. The natural swimming pool came to mind. What an amazing place to live. I loved my forest, but I wasn't a monk—and who wouldn't want a kiwi farm? Though it hadn't made Sage happy, had it? Loving parents, luxurious home, private schools, magical talent—but she wasted her energy hating Marcella. Money wasn't everything. Maybe downsizing would be good for all of them.

Easy for me to say. I myself had downsized so much I could practically fit in a moss fairy's pocket. Losing your home was painful no matter how rich you were. I reminded myself to be more compassionate about Sage's bad mood. We never knew what other people were going through.

I wanted to take a nap on the cool, solid rock in the shade, avoiding the family for my mental and physical health, but there wasn't time. Within several hours, Kenneth would go to the others and tell them he'd found Marcella's magical fingerprint all over the office.

For the first time, I wondered why he'd agreed to wait, given how much he had to lose. The rest of the family, especially Glenda, would have his head—and in the true, ancient witch way, with a sharp blade, not in the figurative you're-in-trouble sense.

I thought of their pool and kiwi farm. Only a generous infusion of serious cash would help them pay for that kind of estate. Cullen seemed like a nice guy, but if I were Kenneth, wouldn't anxious, meek Marcella seem like an easier target for money requests?

Kenneth had made his bet: support Marcella now, and count on her being grateful later.

But was that a plan they'd made after Horace's death, or before?

My head hurt. Too much magic, too many temperature shifts. Too many suspects.

Cullen was the obvious one, and his mother, of course. Ronald kept a low profile but was miserable. Could he also be homicidal? I knew nothing about his financial picture. Two older children depending on him, an addiction to an expensive substance. And who was their mother? Was she entirely out of the picture? I realized I should've asked Zoe to track her down. Another possible link to Katharine?

Too many questions. The first thing to do was to see who benefited most from Horace dying before a new will could be made. Even if such a will would be invalidated by the blood oath, the murderer might have wanted to be quite sure the status quo prevailed.

Nobody wanted that more than Pauline. I hadn't found any evidence of her in Horace's office, but what if her magical fingerprint was so similar to Marcella's, being her mother, that I hadn't recognized it?

I'd have to ask Kenneth if I could scan the office again. With my new theory about his motives, maybe he would. As I got off my rock and hiked back down to the big house, I wiped the sweat off my upper lip and wondered how much more heat everyone could tolerate. It felt even hotter than yesterday.

At the big house threshold, I braced myself during the zap and then walked to the dining room to find Kenneth. A table was laid with a buffet, but the family was out on the deck. I didn't have time to eat much, so I put a small wedge of artichoke frittata on my plate as I obsessed about the evidence and my theories.

Pauline and Marcella shared DNA as well as magical talents. Pauline also had some jute mixed in with her gold jewelry. They were so different it was easy to forget they were mother and daughter, the most powerful witch bond there was. Maybe Pauline had returned to see Horace, as angry as she'd been at dinner, and they'd fought. Weak from age and injury, he died. She fled, covering her tracks as best she could, inadvertently implicating her daughter. Or perhaps intentionally, and she counted on the power of the inherited wand saving Marcella from punishment.

By the time I walked out onto the deck, I was so eager to get access to the office that I was oblivious to the mood of the group outside.

Kenneth was sitting alone to one side, just as he had at breakfast, and the others stood near the stairs down to the lake, gathered around Pauline.

Belatedly, I realized she was upset, pushing them away and crying at the same time.

"What's going on?" I asked.

Kenneth got to his feet and pulled out a chair for me, his face grave. "You might want to sit down."

My stomach dropped. "What happened?" I looked over at the group—Isabel, Sage, Jack, Cullen. I stopped breathing. "Where's Marcella?"

Huxley appeared on the external staircase, jogging up from below. "Her stuff is still in the cabin."

Kenneth smacked the back of the chair with his palm. "You should sit. It's not good."

Heart racing, I touched my redwood beads and sent out a searching spell for my old friend. She wasn't in the house, she hadn't been in the cabin, she wasn't walking along the lake or sitting in a car…

"She's disappeared," Kenneth said. "I should've locked her up. There's no sign of her. Looks like she bolted."

Chapter Thirty-Five

Kenneth seemed sure Marcella had run away, but I couldn't believe it. She'd been afraid to abandon me at breakfast; she wouldn't leave me at the house altogether.

"How could she?" Pauline asked between sobs.

Jack put an arm around her, but she pushed him away and marched into the house, wiping her tears on a linen handkerchief. An experienced witch wouldn't use paper tissues that went in the trash; they held valuable, personal fluids that could be used in spells against her. Pauline would hold on to that handkerchief until she could wash it herself with a drop of lavender oil.

"Well, at least you're still here," Jack said to me. "When's the last time you saw Marcie?"

"She was bringing coffee to her mother's room," I said.

"When was that?" Kenneth asked.

"When I was talking to you at breakfast," I said.

"That was hours ago," Jack said. "Apparently nobody's seen her since she left Pauline's room around nine thirty."

"She didn't act like she was about to—" I cut myself off,

realizing I sounded stupid. If Marcella had planned on running away because she'd killed her grandfather, she wouldn't announce it beforehand, not even to me. "We need to look for her."

Sage sat next to her dad and scowled at me. "Please. As if you didn't know she was leaving."

"We don't know she did," I said. "She might be hurt. Huxley said her things are still in the cabin."

"I'm sure she thinks with all the money she's going to inherit, she can just buy new stuff," Sage said.

I didn't have time for Sage's antipathy. Valuable minutes were passing, and even her mother didn't seem to realize she could be in danger. "I'm going to go look for her."

Not waiting for assistance or an argument, I jogged down the stairs and hurried to the cabin. Being surrounded by her family and all their magic and emotional energy would make it impossible to get a clear tracking signal on her. But away from the others, with one of her belongings, I'd have a quicker time finding her.

I went directly to her room. Huxley's presence had left a mark; I could tell he'd used a key to enter the front door, touched the dresser and suitcase in Marcella's room, leaving a hint of Irish fiddle music, then moved her toothbrush in the bathroom. Thankfully he hadn't lingered, but I credited my own magic for making him hurry away.

I found a T-shirt of Marcella's slung over a chair. Moving into her room, I brought it to my heart. "Where are you?" I asked aloud. I could hear the agony in my voice. "Marcella, can you hear me?"

My breath was coming too fast, and I forced myself to slow down, relax, listen.

Nothing. The cocoon-like spells I'd cast around the cabin were blocking out too much of the outside world. I was already wearing all my beads, chains, rings, and pins, but I wanted as much power as I could get, so I stuffed a bag of herbs from my garden into the pockets of yet another borrowed pair of men's cargo shorts.

And then, at the last minute, I dug through my suitcase for a pouch the size of an apple that I'd crocheted out of wool and stuffed with random items that had washed up on the shore near Silverpool. They were useful in making sure the sea fae didn't compel me to drive off the steep cliffs along Highway 1 on the coast, but maybe they would be useful here as well—strands of dried kelp, a desiccated crab leg, a perfectly smooth stone, tiny shells, and a pencil-sized shard of driftwood.

With my pockets bulging, I went out to the vegetable garden, holding her T-shirt against my cheek. I imagined her laughing. I remembered her mumbling calming spells under her breath; I pictured her carrying the breakfast tray to her mother's room.

The fairies in the green beans were enjoying the hot weather, flying in and out between the vines.

"Excuse me," I said to them. "I'm looking for the witch who wore this shirt. Have you seen her?"

At first the fairies seemed delighted for me to address them. Most humans couldn't, and they gave up trying to communicate. But then they flitted over to the shirt and realized who it belonged to.

Before my next blink, they were gone. I walked around, looking for the telltale glimmer of their wings, and found them hiding beneath the shelter of a vining pumpkin plant. When I moved closer, they fluttered out and shot up into the trees.

I'd been worried before, but now a deep pit opened up in my stomach. Inhaling slowly, I turned my attention to the wood sprites up in the pines. They were larger, and although they disliked humans, they sang and talked and lived in complex social groups like us and were usually aware of us as individuals.

"Hello, good fairies," I called up, craning my head back so they could see my face. If they had any contact with coastal wood sprites, they might have heard of me, the witch in the redwoods who could communicate between them and the Protector of the Silverpool Wellspring. I held up Marcella's T-shirt. "I'm looking for my friend. This is her shirt. Can you help me find her?"

One of the larger fairies, a green one in a brown tunic, fluttered halfway down to me, paused, then flashed out of sight. The others higher up abandoned their branches, took to the air, and flew up and away.

Away from me or from the lake?

True fear set in. The others might think she'd left Lapis Lake, but I was afraid of the opposite. Taking my seashore pouch out of my pocket and holding it against my heart, I walked slowly around the cabin and approached the frozen beach.

I heard a low-pitched singing, almost a moan, coming from beneath the water. Closing my eyes, I focused on the sounds, squeezing the pouch in my fist so hard I broke the shells.

"Human," they were singing. "Human. Human."

With each step I took, their voices grew louder. They sounded happy for once. Celebratory.

I climbed over the rocks edging the shore and looked down at the boundary between hot and cold. None of the beach was visible, and I felt a cool breeze wafting toward me.

I looked back at the house, considering if I could trust any of the Gardners to provide backup, concluding that I couldn't. Except Pauline, any one of them might want Marcella dead. Possibly more than one.

Should I text Seth a quick goodbye, just in case? Tell him I… cared about him?

No, of course not. I was letting the lake fairies' mournful bullying get to me. They thrived on making humans scared. The trick was to show absolute confidence, display a strong front of magic, and not linger in their domain.

I crept down to the ice, feeling the boundary loom up before me. When we'd crossed in the Jeep, Marcella had simply walked through the enchantment. The kitchen and cleaning staff seemed to be able to come and go without a family escort, so I bet it wouldn't stop me from passing through.

After sucking in a deep breath and muttering a good-luck spell, I stepped out onto the ice.

Of course it was cold on the other side of the boundary, but my body was hot from the extreme summer weather. I cast a body-insulating spell around me to hold the heat in. I'd be all right for several minutes, like a Scandinavian witch fresh out of the winter sauna who'd enjoy a dip in the North Sea.

The sky was blue, but snow was blowing off the trees, dropping on my bare arms, face, legs. The singing was loud now, perfectly audible, coming from the middle of the lake.

I looked back at the house and cabins but saw nothing but white haze. The Gardners' vacation house was camouflaged behind an unremarkable patch of white under the towering pine and cedar. To make my way back, I'd have to memorize a landmark. The rocks on the winter side of the enchantment had a distinct pattern, with larger ones to the west where the mountain slope came directly to the lakeshore. I picked a white, pointy stone that was taller than the others at the edge of the haze and committed it to memory. Then I turned away from the safety of the shore and followed the music, no longer needing the pouch of beach flotsam to amplify the sound.

Human. Human. Human.

Oh, Marcella! In spite of the cold, I was sweating, terrified of what I might find. I thought of the abducted dog. I thought of Horace, hexed on the floor of his office. Gripping my redwood necklace with one hand while holding out the other arm for balance, I jogged and slid over the ice until I came to a dark patch in the middle of the lake.

Human.

Breathing hard, I bent down and wiped away the fog on the surface of the ice. It should've been cold, but it was oddly, terrifyingly warm, like a glass stovetop on simmer.

"Oh—!" I gasped, recoiling.

A face, Marcella's face, stared up at me. Her eyes were closed, her mouth open in a frozen scream. I pulled myself together, scrambled onto my knees, and crawled over to wipe away the fog covering the rest of her.

She was wearing the clothes she'd had on this morning, the last time I'd seen her—white shorts, floral tank top. So much bare skin looked horrible under the cold ice, but her complexion had enough color to indicate she was still alive.

I was careful to make sure there was nothing in her hands —no wand, for instance. The lake fairies hadn't taken her for the magic object they hated most. So why Marcella? How had she ended up in their cold, bitter possession?

A witch must've given her to them. Someone at the house.

But who?

And why?

Chapter Thirty-Six

I wouldn't be able to smash her out of the ice with my bare hands or my magic—the fae had locked her in a realm of their own, and although I could see her, she was beyond my reach.

"Hello?" I called out, knowing they could hear me. "Brilliant, beautiful lake fairies, would you talk to me?"

Their wordless song continued uninterrupted from below.

"Please?" I splayed my fingers on the ice. "Is there something you want? I could help negotiate between you and the other witches. I'm not the same as them. I'm a visitor. Please let me help."

Silence. I brought my hands to my mouth and breathed warmth onto them.

Seth. Would he help Marcella—for me? It worried me I had any doubt, but I did. His soul was of their kind, and he'd been forced out, but not willingly. If I was the one captured, I was sure he would rescue me if he could. But a woman I'd known years ago and had never introduced him to?

I couldn't be sure.

Fighting tears, I pounded the ice with the back of my fists. Then I got up and scurried, slipping every few steps, crying now, back to the shore. My spell having worn off, I was shivering in the winter air, imagining with horror how Marcella must feel.

The only person in the house I trusted with Marcella's life was her mother, and even that made me pause. Any one of the others might've given Marcella to the lake fairies if they thought it would benefit them; they were witches in an old, traditional family, and a streak of Shadow always ran through those. I knew from personal experience. Power breeding with power was not a method to create meek, Bright innocents.

Lungs burning from running in the winter air, I was relieved to burst back into the summer warmth of shore.

Sucking in deep breaths, I tried to come up with a plan. Before everyone found out Marcella had been taken by (or given to) the lake fae, I needed to talk to Kenneth—alone. She'd been abducted just before the time had run out on our arrangement. Was that relevant or just a coincidence?

Who else had he told about the evidence in Horace's office? I'd never expected the Gardners to actually hurt Marcella physically, or I would've protected her more carefully. Now that I'd seen her banished to a fairy prison by someone in her own family, I wished bitterly I'd been more vigilant.

Pauline wouldn't be able to help Marcella, so I could delay telling her about the abduction for a few minutes. But any longer than that would be cruel.

I walked to the big house and paused at the front door to glare at the blood-drop pattern. So much fighting over something as stupid as heredity. As I opened the door, I gripped the herbs from my garden and lashed out at the boundary spell. What good had it done Marcella to have this protective ward on the doorstep? None. The threat was inside the house or in the cabins, and their foolish threshold spell made a mockery of how they cared for their own family members.

When I was done with it, the Gardners' threshold spell sizzled like bacon, sending a tendril of white smoke into the cloudless blue sky. It wouldn't ever slow me down again.

The moment I was inside, I cast a seeking spell for Kenneth, magic I wouldn't have been able to do so easily before I'd destroyed the building's defensive wards.

His aura was downstairs—and seemed to be alone. Good. I heard voices coming from the living room, and I wanted to talk to him privately. I rushed down the stairs and walked in on Kenneth staring into the cold fireplace. He sat on the hearth as I had done, but he kept his hands to himself.

"Kenneth," I said in a rush, breathless. My face had to be blotchy with my crying. "I need to talk to you." I looked around, scanning for other people, finding none close enough to overhear.

He was a doctor used to emergencies, and he turned to me calmly. "I don't suppose you've come to admit you were wrong about my niece."

I sat on the bricks across from him and cast a silence spell around us. The proximity of the powerful hearth made it quick and effective even for an outsider. A hearth accepted many cooks. "Did you tell anyone about the evidence in the office? Against Marcella?"

He raised one eyebrow. "I shouldn't have given you any time at all."

"So you— I don't mean to insult or accuse you, but I need to be sure." I held his gaze. "You didn't tell anyone about what we saw? Not even accidentally? Could you have been overheard?"

"You don't mean to insult me or accuse me," he said coldly, "but you have."

His ego was going to need soothing. He was a cardiac

surgeon at Stanford—what did I expect, shrinking humility? "Of course, forgive me," I said, this time allowing my genuine fear to show in my face. "I've just found her trapped in the ice. The lake fae have her."

He stared, casting a truth spell over me to confirm what I'd said. It was insulting, which was why he'd done it. To get even. "Is she alive?"

"Seems to be," I said. "Hibernating. Eyes closed, her skin looks flushed. Under the ice though, so I couldn't be sure. She certainly isn't there by choice."

The truth spell snaked into my mouth, tasting like cinnamon. He was holding on to his skepticism. "And you think somebody here put her there out of vengeance for her killing Horace?"

"Out of a *misguided* vengeance, yes," I said.

"We can't be sure," he said. "She's weak, and your cabin is closest to the water. Maybe they took her the way they took that dog years ago."

"Maybe, but I don't think so." I wanted him to admit he was wrong about her making a run for it out of guilt, but he wasn't the type. "If you told someone, then we could ask—forcefully—if they had anything to do with—"

"But I didn't tell anyone, as I *promised*." He emphasized the word, subtly lecturing me again for questioning his honor. "Does Pauline know yet about her daughter? It might be some comfort to her to know she's probably innocent of her grandfather's death."

"Certainly innocent," I said, getting to my feet. "Do you know where she is? I'll tell her."

"I think she's in her room," he said. "But one of us should do it. You're not family."

My irritation got the best of me. "Oh really? Which one of you didn't have a reason for getting her out of the way?

Because from my point of view, I'm the only one who didn't have a reason to want her dead."

His face darkened. "I'll forgive you for that because you're upset. But if you ever accuse me of Shadow again, I'll hex your tongue out of your head. Do you understand?"

This time I didn't apologize. I turned without saying goodbye and jogged up the stairs to the bedrooms on the top floor. I hadn't been up there yet, but I wasn't surprised by the wallpaper pattern lining the long hallway: rust-red teardrops.

I scanned the doors and found Pauline's magical fingerprint on the one farthest from the stairs. I hesitated, bracing myself, then knocked.

She flung it open immediately, her face pale and splotchy from crying. "I knew it. She's dead, isn't she?"

Chapter Thirty-Seven

❦

"No," I said quickly. "No, I don't think so. Why did you think—"

"I can't feel her." Pauline put her hand on her chest, wrapping her manicured fingers around a gold-bead necklace. "Where is she? What do you know?"

There was no use in asking her to sit and try to break it gently. "The lake fae have her. I found her under the ice. Sleeping, I think."

"*In* the lake?" she demanded.

"Yes."

Pauline grabbed my arm, pulling me with her down the hall. "Show me. Then I'm going to hex the Shadow out of—"

Kenneth was standing at the top of the stairs. He held out a hand to stop Pauline. "Nobody is going to hex anybody." The silver belt buckle on his jeans flashed white-hot, blinding me for a second. "We don't know yet what happened."

Kenneth's magic made me lose my balance, and I had to brace a hand against the wall. "Has anything like this ever happened before?" I asked.

They both looked at me. "Of course not," Pauline said.

"We never bring our dogs up with us for a reason," Kenneth said.

"Don't try to convince me this is the fae acting on their own." Pauline tried to push past Kenneth, but his belt buckle had cast out a mesh screen of magic we couldn't pass. "That woman did this. Glenda."

"Until you calm down, I'm not letting you go downstairs," Kenneth said. "I've seen families kill each other over smaller misunderstandings than this one. The last thing we want is more bloodshed. Do you hear me?"

Pauline raised both hands and tried blasting through his spell one more time, then turned to me. "You believe she's still alive?"

"Yes," I said. "I can't be sure, but— Yes. I do."

Pauline took a deep breath and adjusted her blouse. "I won't hex anyone, Kenneth," she said. "I've never hurt anyone in my life. Now please let me by."

After a long moment, he touched his belt and the blockade dissolved.

Pauline strode past him, calling out, "How dare you stop me from seeing my only child in what may be the last minutes of her life?"

Kenneth and I exchanged a glance.

"Glenda is at the bottom of the stairs," he said quietly to me. "In her state, I was afraid—"

"I think you made the right call," I said. "A duel would've broken out."

He looked down at my bare arm where the bracelets had slid up, exposing the rings of black ink on my skin. "You've been in duels yourself, from the look of it," he said. "I didn't notice those before."

I pulled the bracelets back down. Was he worried he'd end up as my next tattoo? Should he? He'd seemed genuinely convinced Marcella had run away—and angry to think he was partially responsible.

"Self-defense," I muttered.

"I've already told them what you saw," he said. "Let's hope everyone has patience for the accusations Pauline is probably going to hurl at them." He walked downstairs, leaving me alone.

If he'd already told them, they would all want to go and see her. Every one of the Gardners—and the household employees too—would want to go see the frozen witch in the lake.

Yes—I heard footsteps, raised voices trailing away, a door slam. They were leaving to see for themselves what the lake fae had done to Horace's unwanted heiress. Some would be traumatized; others might be thrilled. I didn't think any of them would be able to free her even if they wanted to.

I paused where I stood on the stairs, trying to decide what to do. My body was primed to fight, my fingers tingling with magical energy. I wanted to run out on the lake and set the whole thing on fire to melt the ice and free her—but I didn't have the power, and it probably wouldn't work anyway. She'd just sink to the bottom and drown.

Options raced through my mind, but I had to be smart, move carefully. Whoever gave Marcella to the fae was here watching me—or they would be when they came back to the house. Right now I had it to myself.

I still had Kenneth's chamomile tea bag. There was so little time. Whatever state Marcella was in, it wouldn't keep her alive forever. Hours? Days? Years? Not even Seth could tell me. It would depend on the goals of the fairies who'd taken her, and they'd refused to talk to me.

When I thought the house was empty, I ran down the stairs and along the hallway to Horace's office door. I'd put Kenneth's chamomile in one of my pockets, and now I opened it and fished it out, still wrapped in its paper and dangling from a string.

I didn't have much time. Without any fancy spells, I pressed the dried-out tea bag to the door, tapped into the redwood beads around my throat, and said, "Open please" in my lowest voice. If the door was stupid enough—and how smart could it be?—it would think I was Kenneth. It was wood, and I'd developed a special talent with trees.

The door shuddered as if kicked. I waited a moment, tested the doorknob—and it turned.

Yes!

No time to celebrate. I went inside and closed it behind me, then immediately ran another scan on the room, looking for any individual magical marks—Glenda, Horace, Cullen, Jack, Marcella, Pauline.

They were all there, but Marcella's was the strongest. I got down on my knees and waved my hands over the floorboards, asking the oak to give me a vision of the past, any image at all.

First I saw nothing but a parade of feet moving in a meaningless blur, but then I saw a pair of distinctly colorful hiking sandals that I knew were Marcella's. They had little navy and yellow dots on the grass-green nylon straps— memorably playful shoes for a woman who lived in fear.

But of all the shoes, why would I only see *hers* clearly? On the day of his death, Horace had been there, Jack had been there, Sarah had been there—and probably several others. Why would the office want to show me only the fun sandals and with such obvious detail?

It felt like a setup. There were just too many small bits of *her* in the room for that. The jute, the hair, probably a used napkin I couldn't see—items like that were what a witch would use in a summoning spell.

And in the chair with most of the evidence against her, I

sensed a depletion of magic, like a pothole in the road. The rest of the office, especially near the desk and the box holding the magic wand, was thick with Horace's magic. He'd been killed in that spot, draining it of power. But maybe the hex hadn't been meant for him.

I heard a door slam in the distance and scrambled to my feet. As I strode back to the door, I thought of Marcella's panic attack the night her grandfather had died. Her terror at leaving the protection of the cabin. Her instincts had known what she hadn't let herself believe. Years of denying her fear had, in reality, hidden the truth.

I checked the hall was empty, stepped out, locked it behind me with Kenneth's chamomile as best I could, though it was much weaker now.

Everything was a mess, but maybe now, with Marcella under the bloodless protection of the fairies, she was safer than she'd been living and breathing with her family.

Maybe now I had time to go on a little trip.

Chapter Thirty-Eight

I ran to the cabin, put on winter clothes, and grabbed my purse. I left my suitcase, however—with my sweat and skin all over the fabric, my soiled clothes could act as a key to allow me back through the enchantment boundary when I returned.

In my Jeep, I set up my phone on the dash and called Zoe, knowing it hadn't been much time but hoping her extraordinary resources could work miracles. She picked up on the first ring.

"I'm sorry to bother you so soon," I said, "but we've got an emergency here. Marcella's in trouble. I think somebody gave her to the lake fairies who hate the family. They've got her locked in ice. I just found her."

Zoe let out a breath. "Oh no. I was looking forward to calling you," she said. "I've made progress."

I started up the Jeep and turned around. "You're amazing. Tell me."

"First big discovery," she said. "Lena is dead."

The news didn't surprise me, although I wasn't quite sure why not. Just a feeling. "When did she die?"

"Thirteen years ago," she said. "Interesting, isn't it? Horace would've had his hundredth birthday that year."

I didn't know if it was interesting, important, or irrelevant. "I wonder if he knew."

"Something else interesting," Zoe added. "That was the same year Bertrand Gardner died. A few months earlier."

"A boating accident," I said, driving up the hill to pass the house. If any of the Gardners saw me drive by, they would assume I was giving up on Marcella. Of course it wasn't true, but it was better than knowing I was going to chase down the truth no matter what it did to their family's reputation. If they'd known *that*, they might try to stop me. "That's what made Marcella the sudden heir. She said that's when things got stressful for her. All that pressure was suddenly put on her. Criticism, grief, fear she wasn't up to it."

"Poor thing."

A big question lingered, although I thought I already knew the answer. Another feeling. "Do you know if Lena had any children?"

Zoe let out a breath. "Yes, that's what you need to know, isn't it? Well, I'm not sure, but I think she had a daughter. The rather horrifying document that records Lena's death also mentions the transfer of her property, as spoken by the dying witch to a witness, to a Starling Moonbright," she said. "Lena seemed to have adopted several surnames during her life, and one was Bright. It seems likely she gave a version of the name to her child."

I was afraid to ask what about the document had turned Zoe's stomach, but I needed to know as much as possible. Any detail could be important. "How was it horrifying?"

Zoe hesitated. "Well, teeth have always bothered me. But I think we can assume they were removed after her death, not before, so there shouldn't have been any pain."

Shuddering, I put a protective hand on my redwood

beads. I'd reached the edge of the summer boundary. Just past my bumper was a mountain road in winter, plowed but narrow. "Right. Not the kind of will a nonmag trust attorney would put together. Unless he was a serial killer."

"Ah, no, this was strictly a witch document," she said. "The teeth were sealed into the paper, enchanted to, ah, *stick* forever. It ended up in a private witch library in Fresno because… well, because the witches there like gross things." Zoe cleared her throat. "Phil was able to lead me to it. The witches who own this library are always trying to summon demons. They keep a lot of Shadow magic, amulets, body parts, that sort of thing. You know the type."

I had indeed known that type. "Yes," I said.

"There wasn't much property. Seven hundred dollars and 'a large pine chest holding items of magical importance,' all to Starling Moonbright, age fourteen." Zoe sounded excited. "That would put her in her late twenties now."

Hearing that confirmation of Katharine's great-granddaughter—and the detail about a pine chest big enough to hold a hearth grate was a bonus—I hit the gas pedal and broke through into the unenchanted reality of winter in the Sierra.

"Thanks, Zoe. Anything else?" I asked.

"No, I'm sorry. Will that help?"

"Yes, yes, totally," I said, turning on the defroster. My breath was fogging up the windshield, and I didn't want to drive into a snowbank. "I think I know who she is."

"What's that?" Zoe's voice was distorted. "I'm losing y—"

I tapped the phone and then gave up. By driving away from the house, I'd lost coverage. I'd call her back later, hopefully with interesting information in return.

A twin magnet to the one I'd put on Sarah's car was under the hood of my Jeep. There was only one way to go until I got closer to South Lake Tahoe, but from that point on, she could've gone anywhere. She'd said she had a place on the Peninsula south of San Francisco, but that could've been a lie. She said she'd grown up outside LA, but that could've been false too. Until I had her in front of me under a truth spell, I wouldn't know if anything Sarah had presented to me or the family had been real.

Starling. Close enough to Sarah, and the age was right.

Had she killed Horace? If so, why had she left the wand behind? If she was the true heir under the blood oath, the wand would've recognized her as master and given her the power to escape punishment. As his PA, she would've had access to the office. But she'd been eager to leave as soon as possible—without it.

And if she'd killed Horace, then who had given Marcella to the lake fae?

About twenty minutes later at the first fork in the road, I set aside my ruminating and focused on listening to the magnet. I had to idle at the stop sign and clear my mind for a long moment before I felt an urge to go right. That took me through a residential neighborhood and then to a busier street that led to Highway 50.

I'd never tried the magnet tracking technique before— Helen, the crafty witch in San Francisco who lived next door to the Protectorate, had sold me the idea for a pound of shredded redwood bark—but so far it was working. If I drove without thinking too hard, the knowledge of where to go flowed through my fingers holding the steering wheel.

Sadly I was driving west, toward the Bay Area—and away from Seth and Random in the cabin on Lake Tahoe. It couldn't be helped. With each day that went by, the risk of the magnet falling off—or her discovering it—increased.

As I drove down Highway 50 through the old Gold Rush towns of the foothills, the last hours of daylight faded away, and it was dark by the time I drove past Sacramento. San

Francisco was over two hours away in the current traffic, which was heavy and slow. Tired and hungry, I was thinking about stopping for a hamburger and almost missed the magnet's pressure on my fingers to exit.

I shoved a trail mix bar into my mouth, sending a sad farewell to a hamburger, and turned all my energy into listening to the magnet's instructions. It led me through downtown Davis, which looked like it would've been a terrific place to get a real meal, around the University of California campus, and then into a residential neighborhood.

When the magnet stopped giving me any hints, I parked in front of a pale stucco house with a peeling white-picket fence and a dark door. On the corner, it was lit from above by a city streetlight. It was a single-story, gravel-roofed house identical to thousands of others in California built in the 1950s. And I was certain that behind the door of the one-car garage was Sarah's old SUV.

"Good job, magnet darling," I said, getting out of the car.

Chapter Thirty-Nine

Could Sarah sense I was there? If her poor security habits at the Gardners' house held, she wouldn't have a clue. I stretched and stomped life into my legs, then took off the sweater I'd put on for the drive. There wasn't any magic here, but the valley was naturally much hotter than the mountains or the coast. It felt like spring, even in the evening.

All the temperature shifts had given me another headache. A cheeseburger would be a therapeutic intervention—if I survived the conversation with Sarah. There was still a chance I'd underestimated her.

The short gate leading to the front door was open, and when I couldn't find any boundary spell, I walked through and rang the doorbell. Either she was as she seemed or was playing a very dangerous, sneaky game.

A yappy dog began barking as if his teeth were being plucked out of his jaws by a witch estate lawyer with pliers. But then it was abruptly quiet, and Sarah opened the door, holding a little dog in her arms.

"Hi," I said.

She sighed, brushing a strand of coppery hair out of her eyes. "I should've known. Did you put something on my car?"

I nodded, relaxing. She wasn't a killer. "Can I come in? We need to talk." My stomach rumbled. "Or we could go out to eat if you like."

She stepped aside and put the dog on the floor. "I don't want to leave Snowman. Come on in."

I hesitated, going in only after I'd scanned the threshold for danger. Her little dog, a white fluffball, sniffed me and then ran away to curl up in a bed by the refrigerator. The kitchen was inside the door to the left, and a small living room was to the right. It was as small as my own little two-bedroom bungalow. "Thanks. Can you guess why I'm here?"

"I hope it's not because you think I killed Horace," she said. "I understand you want to clear your friend's name, but I had nothing to do with his death."

"Then why were you so eager to leave?" I asked.

"Weren't *you* eager to get out of there?"

"Not yet," I said. "My friend might die without my help."

She frowned. "What do you mean?"

I told her about Marcella being trapped by the lake fae under the ice, concluding with, "I think somebody in the house gave her to them."

She shook her head. "That's horrible. I don't believe it. They can be annoying, of course, but nobody would do that. To Marcella? She's one of the family."

"They think she's the heir to the wand and everything else," I said.

She walked a few steps to an easel in the corner of her tiny kitchen. Next to it was a table covered with tubes of acrylic paints, cups, rags, bottles, and brushes. The painting she was working on was abstract, stripes of greens and blues. "I hope you don't mind if I keep working. The paint dries quickly, and I'm blending in some shadows." She picked up a paint-brush, her hand visibly trembling. "And it helps me relax."

The more her attention was on something else, the easier it would be for me to get the truth out of her. "Please go ahead," I said.

"Thanks. I hate to be a prima donna, but I'm really loving this painting so far." She put the paintbrush in her mouth, like a dog with a bone, and used both hands to adjust the large canvas on the easel. Then she took it out and swished it in the water jar.

Touching the redwood beads on my wrist, I asked, "So, you didn't kill Horace?"

She looked over her shoulder. "If I did, you think I'd just admit it?"

I waited until she relaxed and turned back to her painting again. Then I asked suddenly, "Was your mother's name Lena?" This time I wrapped my words with barbed, painful magic. Lying to me would be like pulling an embedded fish hook out of her flesh.

Belatedly she cast a stronger protective spell around herself and tried not to answer. She made a choking, gasping sound, waving the paintbrush in the air like the magic wand she'd left behind. Then she put a second hand on it, weakly attempting to draw magic out of the pine, but it snapped in two.

"Was it?" I demanded.

She shuddered. "Yes."

I wanted to release her from the pain, but I needed to know more. "I'm sorry this hurts," I said. "Marcella's life is at stake, and I don't have time to be nicer about it."

She dropped the broken paintbrush, gripped a kitchen

chair, hung her head. Her breath came in loud, heavy bursts. "Stop. Please."

I felt bad, but Marcella was locked in ice. "Tell me why you worked for Horace. Tell me why you put the grate in the fireplace and then took it out. Tell me why you left." Picking up the broken handle of the paintbrush, I brought it to my own mouth and licked off her spit to mingle with mine. She really didn't stand a chance now. "Let's sit down, OK? We'll both be more comfortable."

With her spit in my mouth, I wouldn't have to use the painfully barbed spell, but I had enhanced power over her speech. Her parents should've taught her better magic. Hadn't she learned anything about protecting herself? She was very lucky I was a Bright witch with an inconvenient moral code.

Staring at me with wide eyes, she staggered over to one of two kitchen chairs and fell into it, hanging one arm over the back as if she were drunk. I sat in the other and waited for the magic to pull her honest story out of her.

"I worked for Horace so I could get the chance to kill him," she said. With each word she became more relaxed, succumbing to the urge to chat. "I put the grate in the fireplace to help me kill him. And I took it out because he was already dead. And I left because I don't want to inherit anything." She leaned back in the chair, looking peaceful. I was making her enjoy talking to me. Talking to me was like writing in a secret diary. It was a relief to finally share the secrets with someone.

The fireplace grate had given off a magical fingerprint that felt older than just a few years. I suddenly remembered Marcella being brought to a gravestone as a child. "Did she work for the Gardners as a cook?" I asked.

"Y-y-yes," she gasped. "She cast the spell on the grate

then. T-t-to absorb their family energies. She couldn't get closer to Horace. He was too careful."

What would Horace have done to Lena or Sarah, had he known they existed, let alone plotted his demise? I thought about the day I'd arrived, when Sarah had said he'd put important correspondence in code, hidden from her. Had he suspected her of acting against him, or had that been standard procedure, typical witch paranoia?

"Did you ever manipulate his email or letters?" I asked. "When you were pursuing revenge?"

"Never," she said.

"And you truly couldn't decipher the encryption he used?" I had wondered if she'd been manipulating Horace to create a new will, which would cause chaos among her potential rivals for the wand.

"No," Sarah said. "I tried to use the grate to unlock it, but it didn't work. It was just letters and numbers, like a kid's game—nonmagical. I've never been good with puzzles."

So Sarah hadn't been manipulating the correspondence with the lawyers, but somebody else could've been. A children's game suggested something he'd played with his sons—Cullen, Ronald, Jack. And they could've taught their own kids.

"Tell me about your mother," I said. "Did she talk about the wand?"

"Oh, constantly." Sarah leaned an elbow on the table. "She was obsessed. Little things. It all revolved around Katharine."

"For instance?"

"Well, my mom was really proud she'd inherited Katharine's red hair. Obsessed that I did too." She stroked the hair at her temples, shaking her head. "She wasn't well. Kill, get the wand, avenge Katharine. Claim my firstling rights. That was all she cared about."

"You didn't do it?"

She averted her gaze. "No."

My magic assured me her words were true, but why did she look ashamed about it? Afraid I was using too much power, I eased off on the pressure I was putting on her. "Do you wish you *had* killed him?" I asked.

She still wouldn't look at me. "Here's my life: me and Mom, moving from place to place, never enough money for rent, food, school stuff, shoes," she said. "But instead of getting a normal job, Mom sold essential oils and tinctures out of the back of her car. Her stuff worked—she was good with potions—but it was never enough to cover the bills. This house was ours, but the title is in a stranger's name. Identity theft. I have the keys, but it's all an elaborate spell she set up when I was a kid."

"So you lied about the parents in Southern California?" I asked. There had been a chance her dad was part of the scheme and was still a threat I had to consider.

She gave a short, bitter laugh. "As if. Total fantasy. I used to wish for a life like that. My mom got pregnant at an equinox party in Portland with a guy with red hair. On purpose. She wanted to make sure I was a ginger like Great-grandma. She was too."

"Why did Katharine need to be avenged?" I asked. "Was her death unnatural?"

"According to Mom, her death was fated. Natural," Sarah said. "But afterward, Horace didn't believe he had a grand-daughter—that is, her. Lena. That was his crime. He didn't claim her and acknowledge her birthright. Instead, he got married and promised his new wife that *her* children would be the recipients of the blood oath. Mom had a copy of Horace's second marriage certificate and used to take it out sometimes and set it on fire. Losing her temper, you know.

Then she'd exhaust herself using magic to undo the fire, recover the certificate, and sleep for a week."

Her upbringing would've traumatized any child. "I'm sorry you went through that."

Sarah picked up various tubes of paint and set them down again. "She was cool otherwise. I didn't have to go to school if I didn't feel like it."

Given her poor defensive skills, she certainly hadn't gone to a private witch school. "Did she teach you any magic?"

"Sure, she taught me not to hurt myself by accident or expose my magic in public," she said. "And of course a few spells to cook and clean around the house."

"Didn't she teach you anything more advanced than that?" I asked.

"Only destructive magic," she said. "She was obsessed with the wand. I was supposed to take it by force, killing Horace and anybody else if necessary."

"Why didn't you? You must've had opportunity."

"I couldn't," she said. "I wanted to do that for her—I'd promised—but I just couldn't. I loved your story about leaving the Protectorate because you couldn't even kill demons. I thought *I* was pathetic. That made me realize I had a choice. As soon as his birthday party was over, I was going to quit and get rid of the fireplace grate. Without it, I'd never have the power to hurt him."

Well, I supposed it was worth her thinking I was pathetic if it had shown her she didn't have to kill anyone. "What could the fireplace grate do? What was your plan?"

"It wasn't mine! Brightness. I don't care about the wand. It was my mother's plan. Apparently, whatever I might've cooked or heated up over a fire in that grate would've killed him. She'd spent years researching a good hearthy-witchy way to hex him to death." Sarah got to her feet, which was allowed as long as she was talking. "How about I make us some spearmint tea?"

Since we'd just been discussing how heated consumables could kill people, I shook my head, even though I was thirsty as well as hungry. "No, thanks."

"Don't worry. I don't have the grate anymore," she said. "As long as I had it, I felt an urge to go after the Gardners, so I threw it into Lake Tahoe. It's iron. It'll rust out on the bottom. I hate to pollute, but at least it's not plastic. I just couldn't risk holding on to it any longer because—" She stopped abruptly.

I waited, knowing my truth spell was still active. She filled a glass with ice cubes from her freezer, poured water from a pitcher into it, tore a mint leaf from a small plant near the window, then sat across from me again. She lifted the glass and held it against her forehead.

"You couldn't risk what?" I asked finally.

"It wants me to be its master." She took a long drink of ice water. "I was burning up, fighting it off. The grate is also a hot magic, and between the two of them—well, I felt like I was dying of heatstroke. And now, just talking about it, thinking about it, I get hot flashes."

"When you left, the summer enchantment went into overdrive," I said.

"I was hoping it would just… fade away," she said. "I felt a little better as soon as I dropped the grate in Tahoe. I'm thinking about flying to Alaska or Norway or something. Maybe it'll get the hint and give up."

"Unlikely. If the wand feels you going farther away, it might try even harder," I said. "You have to claim it as its master and end the enchantment. Its magic is too wild now. It keeps getting hotter. It could set the forest on fire. People might die."

"But if I'm the master and I'm far away, doesn't it get weaker?" she asked.

"Apparently not. Maybe because it's still got all of Horace's life energy to fuel its desire for you. It's got to be incredibly powerful—it created an entire microclimate in the middle of a Sierra winter." I thought of Marcella, captive in the ice. But I also thought of the rest of her family—not my favorite witches in the world, but they didn't deserve to burn to death. "You've got to turn it off."

"I don't want the wand," she said.

"Too bad," I said. "It wants you."

Sarah covered her face in her hands. "Nothing in my life has been what I wanted it to be."

"Welcome to the human experience," I said, then realized that sounded unkind. "Sorry. Maybe you can give the wand to somebody else when you've got the hang of it."

Sighing, she got up and went over and picked up her dog, who had been watching us quietly from his bed. "Poor Snowman. He hates being separated. I had to leave him with a neighbor when Horace warned me about the lake fairies."

I watched as she picked up a green nylon dog carrier and slung it over her shoulder. Snowball didn't like that at all and began wriggling in her arms.

"You're doing the right thing," I said.

Sarah looked at me, her face shiny with sweat. "Marcella is really trapped under the ice?"

"The lake fae are holding her as captive or hostage," I said, "or maybe keeping her in deep freeze forever, I don't know. But I'm afraid she can't survive their prison much longer."

She got a treat from a jar on the counter, put it inside the carrier, then guided Snowman through the opening. "My neighbor will be happy to take him again, but I want to get back as soon as I can. The Gardners are going to hate me. I don't want to spend a lot of time with them and their drama."

The little dog peeked out at me through the mesh window of his carrier. It was wise to leave him in a safe place so he didn't become an appetizer for the frustrated lake fairies, especially if she walked out of the house, wielding the power they hated so much.

"With the wand, you can do whatever in Brightness you want to," I said.

"Yeah," she said, smiling slowly. "I guess you're right."

"That said, I'm relying on you to help me free Marcella," I said. She was still under my truth spell; I needed to know if I was right to expect her help. "Will you?"

She hugged the dog carrier to her chest. "If I can, but you've seen I can't do very much. The strongest amulet I've ever used is a silver ring my mom gave me, and even that didn't seem to do much," she said. "What if I can't control the wand? I want to help you, but what if I can't?"

I felt the sincerity of her words and accepted them as the best I could expect.

"You'll be better than nobody at all," I said, releasing her from my interrogation enchantments. "I'm sorry for the brute force. I won't do it again."

She let out a long breath, shook her hair, and gulped down a glass of water. "You won't be able to," she said, raising an eyebrow. "Not when I have the wand."

I gave her a sharp look, but she seemed to be kidding.

It didn't really matter to me. As long as she removed the summer enchantment, I had a chance of helping Marcella—especially with Seth's help.

He was my next visit.

Chapter Forty

I called Seth from the road. Sarah—Starling—would be taking her own car separately. An empty, crumpled-up cheeseburger wrapper from a quick pit stop in Davis was rolling around the floorboards behind my seat.

"Why didn't you call me earlier?" he asked. "Have you lost faith in me?"

"They're lake fairies," I said. "Like your family."

The traffic was lighter now, and I expected to be at his rental cabin at Tahoe before midnight. Starling might be able to control the wand, but nobody could control the fae. I'd need Seth.

"And so you think I want them to kill your friend?" he asked. "I wish you could see the disappointed look on my face. It's making Random nervous. He thinks he did something wrong." His voice drifted away; I heard him cooing to my dog about what a good boy he was.

My heart squeezed to hear his voice. It had been too many days apart. I had a sudden selfish urge to spend the night with him and then return to Lapis Lake in the morning. But the lake fae didn't follow modern human business hours—every minute might be Marcella's last.

"Do you think they actually want to kill her?" I asked. Sometimes the fae could be deadly for humans, but usually it was an indirect threat—driving us off the road, luring us out to sea, and unwittingly attracting demons, who could be dangerous to everyone. Except for extreme circumstances, they didn't attack humans directly.

"If they think she's the master of the wand, it's unlikely they'll ever free her," Seth said.

"They can't tell she isn't the master? That's Sarah," I said. "Actually, her birth name is Starling. She's the one. Not Marcella."

A car cut in front of me, making me brake, swerve, accelerate, change lanes again, check my rearview mirror to see if the car behind me was too close. I was going to have to talk to him in person if I wanted to survive the drive through Sacramento.

"You're going to have to talk to me in person if you're going to survive the drive," he said.

I hated it when he read my thoughts. "See you when I see you."

"*I* can see you right now," he said, his voice warm.

"No, you can't."

"But you're not sure," he said.

I hit the button to end the call. No, I wasn't sure his fairy powers wouldn't let him watch me better than a CIA spy gadget. But maybe it would be harder if I hung up.

I smiled at myself. Given our close personal bond—getting closer daily—it seemed unlikely a changeling fairy-human really needed a good cell phone connection to spy on his part-demon witch girlfriend. He'd known where I was before we'd even—well, when I was supposed to be hunting him as a Protectorate agent. He said we had a special bond because his fairy nature was hopelessly attracted to my demonic one. Since I'd never been a femme fatale in my life, I found that amusing. I did, however, have to admit the attraction between us had to be affected by our ancestry.

Taking a gulp from a tall can of caffeinated sparkling water—I didn't taste the pomegranate promised on the label —I moved into the fast lane and turned my thoughts to Marcella. Was she still alive? There wasn't anyone at the Gardner house who I trusted to tell me about Marcella. Even her mother was unreliable—she might lie for reasons of her own that I didn't know about.

So I drove as fast as I could and dug into my memories of lessons about fairy abductions. *Avoid the fae; they're unpredictable*, had been the general message of the lessons. I'd intentionally jettisoned from my brain many of the things I'd learned about fairies at witch school because reality had proven more complex, nuanced, and dangerous. But I did remember abductions were possible, during which death was likely because the fae didn't understand our mortal bodies were so fragile. Like Huxley had said, they'd pull you underwater, not intending to kill you—but you'd die anyway.

I was tired, but fear gave me the strength to enhance my speed through Sacramento with a jolt of magic. It was difficult to cast spells while driving, but easier if the focus stayed on the road, used for skills such as going faster without hitting anyone, rolling over, or getting a ticket.

It was only a little after eleven when nonmag technology got me to Seth's cabin in the deep snow. Before I'd put the Jeep in park, he and Random were already bounding out of the small building with a suitcase and a plastic sled—the narrow kind that held two human children. Or, I guessed, an adult man with a dog.

Had they been sledding without me? I felt a pang of childish jealousy.

After sharing a nuzzle with Random in the back seat, I pushed open the passenger door and started talking. "Hey, do you think you'll have any trouble with the enchantment boundary outside the house? The one I told you—"

Seth leaned across the seat and kissed me quiet.

After a few long seconds I pulled away. "No. No time. Don't tempt me."

"A few seconds won't make a difference," he said, but I felt him give the car a little jolt of fairy energy as he put on his seat belt. He was as worried as I was. That only made me worry more.

Driving off the main highway and making our way to Lapis Lake on a dark, narrow, snow-choked road made my muscles sore with tension. It was a relief to finally reach the snowdrift in the road that I knew was the summer boundary. There I stopped, leaving on the lights, and looked at Seth.

"This is it," I said. "Are you going to be OK? Do you want to try to approach the lake from the winter side? It's not too far from here."

He rolled down the window a crack. A second later, without me seeing him move, he was standing in front of the snowbank. A third moment later, he was gone. Breathing on my neck from behind my seat, Random whimpered.

"I think he made it," I said, moving the car forward again, flinching as we went through the enchantment.

I was back in the summer heat. It took me a minute to find Seth—lit by the Jeep's headlights. I saw him walking in the woods, looking up into the tall pines, his lips moving. Talking to the wood sprites, maybe. I turned off the headlights for ambiance and waited.

He returned several minutes later and climbed in next to me. "They don't know anything."

"You had a lot to say for them not knowing anything."

"Forest beings," he said. "It's rude to get to the point too quickly with them. They have a tree's perspective. Long timeline."

I drove slowly past the house to the cabin, giving Seth a commentary on the individuals I'd met inside. He'd already heard my story once on the drive, but now he seemed to listen more intently. At one point when I mentioned Kenneth, he rolled down the window and sniffed the warm air.

"Well?" I asked.

"He's here. I can connect your description to his aura." He wiped his nose. "Are you sure you can trust him?"

"Of course not," I said. "I don't trust any of them."

"So he might've killed the old witch and hidden the traces before you scanned the office?"

"He might've," I said.

"Right. Then I think it's best if we don't tell anyone I'm here unless it's unavoidable."

"Agreed." I parked outside the cabin and stroked my dog's head over my shoulder. "What about Random?"

"I'll keep him with me, enchanted if necessary. He's used to being in altered states. Nobody needs to know he's here."

I was tempted to argue—I didn't like Random being transformed with magic anymore—but the situation was too dangerous. With both of us using magic to muffle our presence, the Gardners hopefully wouldn't notice our return. I let us into the dark cabin, warm and stuffy, and turned on a light. Random trotted around the two rooms, sniffing curiously, then found the bed I'd been using, leaped to the foot of it, and curled up to sleep.

I watched Seth carefully for any sign he was talking to the fairies out in the lake just outside the window. He'd chatted with the forest sprites as if they'd been at a party. How would he approach his old kind?

Seth stood at the glass, staring into the night.

"You look cute with your hair like that," he said, making me realize he hadn't been staring thoughtfully at the lake fae but at my reflection next to his in the window.

Smiling, I touched my head and felt curls, tangles, and frizz. The rapid humidity changes had been as bad for my hair as a witch's hex. I wanted to throw my arms around him and go to bed, but of course that was impossible.

"Please focus on the important thing here," I said. "Marcella is out there under the ice."

"Yes, and her mother is sleeping on a blanket next to her on the ice," he said. "To keep her company."

I was touched by Pauline's show of motherly feeling. It had been more than I'd seen so far, and I hoped she'd continue with it after Marcella was recovered. "How do you know that?"

"The fae told me." He saw my mouth open and held up a hand. "Hold on, don't get your hopes up. I can't do anything until a witch claims the wand and ends the midsummer enchantment. Then I think I can get them to free her."

"You *think*?"

"I'm going to take the fairy way and promise them something in exchange, offering my existence as forfeit if I fail to deliver." He took my hand. "Do you have any beads you don't want? They might like those."

His existence as forfeit? A horrible corner of my brain suggested that price for an old classmate's life was too high. But I killed the thought.

Feeling myself begin to tremble, I looked down at my wrists, hesitating, then chose one of the strands of wood beads and put it into his palm. We held hands together, foreheads touching, saying nothing.

"When do you expect Starling?" he asked, using her birth name without being reminded of it. "I can't sense her presence. The wand might be protecting her already."

I reached into my pocket and wrapped my fingers around the twin magnet. A vision of white light cutting through a black-and-white world struck me. I felt the warm air of a car's defroster. The bump of a choppy road under my wheels.

"She's making her way around Lapis Lake," I said. "I'll meet her at the boundary."

"And then what?" he asked. "Just barge into the house and take the wand?"

I put the magnet back in my pocket and did a ritual check of my amulets and beads—redwood necklace, silver chain, bracelets, herbal sachets, stones. It was Starling who needed to be strong, but I needed to be prepared as well. Her training had been scattershot, and the wand was very old and powerful. If it blazed out of control, somebody would have to make sure an old family of witches didn't die tonight even if one of them was a murderer.

"That's the plan," I said.

Chapter Forty-One

In the dark, I walked past the big house to wait at the boundary on the incoming drive, silently greeting the fairies in the trees. Sarah's car arrived about fifteen minutes later. As Horace's PA, she'd been in and out of it many times and wouldn't have needed any help passing through the enchantment even without the wand's link to her.

After she drove through, she saw me on the shoulder, turned around, and parked facing the opposite direction.

"It'll be easier to get away in a hurry," she said as she got out. "Don't you think?"

It seemed she was finally learning to look out for herself. "Good idea," I said. "Why not closer to the house so you don't have to run this far, if it comes to that?"

"The Gardner boundary spells will be strongest around the house. I bet I can get away on foot, but not sure about driving."

She really *was* learning. "You're right. This is probably your best bet if things get sticky." We began walking along the drive toward the house. "Of course, if you're master of the wand, their spells won't hold."

"That's a big if. I might be worn out from taking down the summer enchantment. You're right—it's scary hot." She turned to me suddenly. "Did you check on Marcella? Is she still alive?"

I wasn't going to mention Seth unless I had to. "Yes, she's still alive."

Starling stopped walking a step behind me. After a long moment, her voice came, weak and afraid, out of the darkness. "I don't know if I can do it. What if I fail and she dies? Maybe I should try to give the wand to somebody else. *You* would know how to make it work for you—"

"Nope. It's yours. I bet you've been feeling its connection to you for a long time, am I right?"

She sighed. "Yes. Weird dreams at first, then just a weird buzz whenever I came into the room where Horace was. My mom never warned me I might feel that way. She'd never been close to the wand herself, so she didn't know."

"There's no fighting that bond," I said, feeling compassion for her. To have your life controlled by outside forces, especially before you were even born, was exasperating—as I knew from personal experience. "But I can support your energy levels, give you magical backup, hold your hand literally and figuratively."

"Thanks." She resumed walking, and I fell into step behind her. "Demon's balls, I wish I'd never come here."

"I doubt it was ever up to you," I said. "As Horace got older and older, the wand knew it needed to find its next master. For all we know, it drove your mother to raise you the way she did, giving you a reason to come here and find it."

We were at the house now, standing outside its lamplight. I'd already broken the boundary on the front door and walked up to it with confidence.

Starling, however, fell back. "What about the threshold wards?" she whispered. "Maybe it knows I don't work for—"

I pulled the door open and stepped inside. Nothing happened—no buzz of power, no scan. "We're good," I said, matching her low whisper. "Come on in."

Slowly she followed. "But— How?"

"I neutralized it earlier."

Shaking her head, she hurried inside. "Really is too bad you can't be the one to have the wand," she said under her breath.

The hallway to Horace's office was lit by a tiny moon-shaped nightlight plugged into an outlet near the floor, just like a nonmag family would have for the kids. Magic would've been more elegant, but the drain on the individual witch casting the spell would've been unnecessary and wasteful.

As we walked up to Horace's office door, I took out the dried-up tea bag I'd stolen from Kenneth's cup—*was that really just this morning? No wonder I'm tired*—and held it out to the door again.

This time, however, nothing happened. The essence of Kenneth had worn off. It wasn't going to help me break through his magical block on the door.

Panic swelled up inside me. I hadn't considered what I'd do if we couldn't get the wand by ourselves. The Gardners were hardly going to let us in to see if Horace's former PA could wave it around and claim it for herself. An outsider taking mastery of the family treasure was a nightmare they'd probably never considered. Even though Starling was as much Horace's descendant as any of them were, they wouldn't believe it until the wand proved it so.

And only the wand was going to save Marcella.

"What's the matter?" Starling asked.

"I thought I'd be able to get in, but I can't." I turned to

her, took her by the shoulders. It was a rare gesture of uninvited physical contact, but I had to get through to her. "You'll have to call the wand."

"What?" Her voice pierced the quiet.

Gripping her shoulders, I turned her to face the door and whispered in her ear. "It's bonded with you. It will feel you're here. Do you feel it? Concentrate. It will come to you."

She didn't speak for a moment. "Yes," she said finally. "I feel it."

"Good, good."

"It— It's angry," she said. "It's very hot."

"Don't be afraid. It's not alive. It's just energy and memories," I said, though I really had no idea what it was. Who knew what spirit it had? "Now try to call it to you. Tell it you're here and you want it to come to you."

"You mean literally?" she asked. "Won't it still be stuck on the other side of the door?"

I laughed quietly. "Look around, Starling. If that wand could turn a snowy mountain into summer, it can knock over one little human door."

"That's me," she said.

She was staring at the door, but I didn't know what she could see. "You're what?"

"I'm Starling. I've been calling myself Sarah for years, but it's not me." She took a deep breath, shook off my grip, and faced the door with her head high. "I'm Starling Moonbright."

With each syllable, her voice grew louder and more assured. She held up her hands, palms up, and I felt a tingling power rise up from her that I'd never sensed before, strong enough that I had to step back.

Nothing happened. Maybe I'd been too confident in her—

Bam. Something heavy struck the opposite side of the door. *Bam, bam, bam!*

The series of crashing sounds were going to wake somebody. Breath catching, I looked behind me, bracing myself for attack. My plan had not involved getting in a duel with the Gardner family—at least not just yet.

Bam!

The door was cracking.

"Stand back!" I grabbed Starling's arm and pulled her aside just as the door flew out and crashed on its back on the hallway.

Footsteps sounded upstairs. Doors pulling open. Voices.

"Hurry!" I held up my hand and made a hasty illumination spell. Resting on the door at our feet was Horace's box of valuable magic. The old pine looked unaffected by its impact with the door. "Get it in your hand before the others—"

The hallway lights turned on, blinding me for a second.

"What are you doing?" Jack appeared at the end of the hall in a T-shirt and boxer shorts. He had his hand on a heavy gold chain around his neck, and I felt the beginnings of a hex forming in the air around him.

I hastily put up a boundary spell between us and turned to Starling. "Do you have it yet?"

"I can't get it open!" She picked up the box with both hands and banged it on the wood floor.

Glenda, in a black nightgown threaded with silver, came running up behind Jack. "What's— Demon's balls, stop them!" She also began casting a hex.

I dug deeper into my well of magic to protect us, but I wanted to conserve as much of my strength as I could for ending the climate enchantment to rescue Marcella. Drained from the pull on my magic, my legs began to shake.

I felt a moment of despair. If we couldn't even open the stupid box...

"Got it!" Starling said.

Thank Brightness. I heard the box tumble to the floor, but I couldn't risk looking away from the advancing Gardners at the end of the hall. Kenneth and Ronald had joined them. The younger witches, in the cabins, were hopefully still sleeping.

"She is the master of the wand," I called out. "She is the great-granddaughter of Horace and Katharine."

"You snake!" Glenda cried. A white ball of shimmering light came flying at my head, but it bounced off my boundary spell. "We invited you into our home as a guest."

Maybe they'd stop attacking if they knew Marcella's life was at stake. "The wand is the only way to free Marcella," I said. "She'll die without it!"

Kenneth's magic was obviously stronger than Glenda's, because *his* hex came flying through my boundary spell like a bullet through whipped cream and knocked me to the floor. My vision went dark for two long seconds as I felt pain shoot through my left elbow and up into my shoulder. I smelled burning hair—my own—and tasted blood.

Well, he was a surgeon. Cutting people was their thing.

I lifted my hand to my mouth, then looked at it, my head spinning. I'd bitten my lip as I hit the floor. Kenneth had pierced a hole through the boundary but only enough to knock me down. The rest of it held, and the family stood on the other side of it, their mouths opening and closing.

Yelling. I couldn't hear them because I was still reeling from the strike. It wasn't too bad, kind of peaceful, though the sound of my blood pounding in my ears was a little alarming. Was I going to die? That might not be too bad. I was tired. It would be nice to put my head down and take a long, quiet nap.

"Alma! Wake up!" Starling's voice reached me through the

muffled throbbing in my brain. "I've got it. Should I take it out of the bag?"

I rolled over onto my side and looked up at her. She held the black velvet bag, wand-shaped, and was just staring at me, making no move to take it out. My hearing came back fully, and now I could hear the Gardners shouting *get them… put it down… back away… stop her… hands up…*

"Yes!" I gasped, too weak to add *Hurry!*

Starling tugged the drawstring open and pushed the velvet down over the bladelike section of the wand. The pewter, usually a dull metal, reflected the electric light but also added some of its own, making it glow white in Starling's grip, illuminating her face.

"Nothing's happening," she told me.

The wooden hilt was still wrapped with the velvet. "Take it out of the bag," I said, managing to get to my hands and knees, though I was still dizzy.

Starling shook off the bag but was holding the metal shaft. "Nothing's happening."

I rose to a squat. "Touch the wood with your bare ha—"

Starling grabbed the handle, and a blast of power knocked me back to the floor. Pale blue light flared from the wand—circular bands of light, one after the other, expanding out like the rings of Saturn.

Chapter Forty-Two

My head slowly cleared. I was lying on my side. I felt the wand's magic helping me, not hurting, though the shock had unbalanced me. Above me, the Gardners were pressing against my boundary, their faces twisted in anger, shock, and awe—but they weren't shouting anymore. Vaguely I noticed the younger witches had arrived. They were all here. One of them had put Marcella in the lake; one of them had killed Horace. Same witch, two witches, or a conspiracy?

I rolled over and got to my feet. The fighting had to stop so we could free Marcella. "She's the true master of the wand," I said. "There's nothing you can do about it. The blood oath—"

Starling screamed. The light flashed again, and she crumpled to the floor. As she landed, the wand rolled out of her hand and lay still, its glow fading.

Suddenly they were all there around us—Ronald, Jack, Kenneth, Glenda, Cullen, Isabel, Huxley, Sage. My boundary spells had been obliterated in the rings of power that had come out of the wand. There was nothing protecting us now, and Sarah was unconscious.

I *hoped* she was unconscious. Feeling sick—had I brought her to her death?—I bent down and felt for her pulse. Thank Brightness, it was strong. She'd just drained her strength. Well, the wand had. It would take her years to master its influence on her. Decades or centuries older, it had more experience than she did, but she'd learn.

"It was too strong for her," Cullen said.

"I've got it," Glenda said, picking up the wand. She immediately shoved it at Cullen. "This is yours. I know it is. Marcella killed Horace. It would never allow her to take it after that. It's yours, Cully. Take it. Show them."

Cullen looked reluctant to hold it. "This isn't the way, Mom. If Sarah really is—"

From all around came an unnerving sound—a creak, a pop—and then a hot wind began to roll in from all sides, surrounding them in scalding dry air. It was like a wildfire with just the heat. Within ten seconds, the hallway had become a sauna.

"What's happening?" Isabel cried.

"We need to get out of here." Ronald grabbed his children. "Come on, outside. Now." He caught them up in a command spell and hauled them away with him.

Jack and Kenneth did the same with Sage.

"But what's happening?" she cried.

The older witches didn't wait to find out. Experience had taught them to first get to a place of safety. Later, if ever, you might find out why the magic had almost killed you.

I couldn't just run away and leave Starling passed out on the floor with Glenda looking as if she was going to stab her with the pin from her gold-and-ruby brooch. And Cullen was still standing there with the wand in his hand, flinching as if it was burning a hole in his palm.

"Put it back in the bag!" I told him, finding it on the floor and thrusting it at him.

"The enchantment is malfunctioning," he said, dazed.

Sweat was pouring down my face. Without waiting for him to respond, I fitted the velvet bag over the tip of the wand and slid it all the way down to the hilt. Then I moved to secure the drawstring, but Glenda shoved me aside.

"Don't let her have it." Grabbing the velvet bag, she took Cullen by the arm and pulled him—and the wand—with her down the hall after the others.

With Starling on the floor in the stifling heat, I couldn't chase after them. I bent down, checked her pulse again, and gave her cheek a light slap—maybe not so light, given how stressed I was—and was relieved to see her eyes flutter open. Feeling light-headed myself, I was having trouble breathing in the heat.

Drawing upon my redwood beads for strength, I lifted her to a sitting position. "We've got to hurry. The heat might kill us."

She rolled her head sideways to look at me. "What happened?"

"Learning pains," I said. "Can you get up? You've got to get the wand back from Glenda and stop this. The heat might set the mountain on fire."

"But it tried to kill me," she said.

"No, it tried to bond with you." I got her to her knees. "But you weren't ready."

She touched her forehead. "My brain hurts."

"Par for the course." With hands slippery with sweat, I struggled to grip her arms and get us both to our feet.

"I can do this," she said, pushing aside my help and starting to run. "Let's go. I feel it calling me."

The sudden return of her energy was probably the effect of the wand. It wanted her to be strong so they could get on with the mind-meld. I hurried out of the house after Starling and was greeted with another wall of heat. Somebody had flicked on the exterior floodlights, lighting up the house and road. It was still hours until dawn.

It was even hotter outside than in. Death Valley heat. Would the fairies suffer as the flora and fauna suffered? I was afraid their fates were linked.

I saw a group of Gardners huddled on the ice at the lakeshore to escape the heat but didn't see Glenda and Cullen among them. "Do you feel it now?" I asked Starling.

Starling pointed behind me. "They're getting in a car!"

I spun around. Glenda, wand in her hand, was opening the door of a white SUV. Cullen was arguing with her, trying to pull her back. Before Starling and I could reach them, he grabbed the wand out of his mother's hand and—what was he doing?—*flung* it at us like a knife-thrower at a carnival.

"Catch!" he shouted.

Instinct made me duck and cover. Flying magical weaponry with a sharp edge wasn't something I liked to reach out for with bare hands.

But it wasn't aimed at me. Starling, partially attuned to the wand already, reached out a hand and caught it.

"What did you do?" Glenda was shouting at Cullen, pounding at his arm.

He pushed her back with a flash of magic, slowing her, and strode over to me. "Are you sure she's the great-grand-daughter of Katharine and my father?"

To my surprise, he looked willing to believe it. "Yes," I said.

"Others know about this?" he continued. I felt a truth spell lash out at me.

"Yes!" I wiped the sweat off my upper lip. "Let her try to use the wand. End this heat and save Marcella."

Cullen stared intently at Starling for a long moment, then something seemed to satisfy him. His body relaxing, he nodded. "Take it out of the bag. I'll keep my mother back."

I wanted to get away from Glenda, who might interfere any moment, and out of the worst of the heat and closer to Seth. "Let's get closer to the boundary first," I said, starting to walk.

"No lie," Starling said. "I'm afraid to touch it again."

I took her arm and pulled her away from the house, its blazing lights, the rest of her unpredictable, dangerous cousins. When we reached the first cabin, I led us down to the shore.

Starling pointed out at the middle of the lake. "Is that Pauline out there?"

The wand must've given her night vision. It was too dark for me to see that far. "Yes, she's counting on you," I said. *No pressure*, I added silently.

Starling glanced at me, took a deep breath, and pulled off the velvet with one hand. Then, flinching, she wrapped her bare fingers around the wooden handle.

There was another flash of light, almost as bright as the first time, and she threw her head back and let out a cry. Her hair rose to form a halo around her face.

I couldn't stop the wand, but I could give her some of my magical power. "Don't fight it," I said, sending her my energy. "Bend, don't break."

"It hurts," she gasped.

"It won't feel that way forever." I didn't know why I was so sure of that, but I was. The wand was hers to claim. Her resistance was only causing her more pain.

"I can feel it!"

"Good, good," I said. But unfortunately, so did I. Starling was pulling on the support I was giving her, drinking it, inhaling it, consuming it. Draining *me*. My legs started to shake.

"The summer spell is right… *there*," she continued. "I can taste it. Like ice cream. Isn't that funny? You'd think it would be warm, but it's not. It's cold and sweet."

Oh Brightness. She was taking every drop of power I was offering. "Good," I managed to say again, putting my hand on a large rock, hoping the granite could restore me a little.

"It's huge, like a galaxy of magic." Starling laughed. "I sound like I'm on drugs, but that's really what it's like. It's beautiful!"

I sank down and sat on the rock. It was cooler near the shore but still hot enough to make me light-headed. Or maybe that was Starling, sucking the energy out of me. I still could've turned off the spigot and revived myself, but she needed my help. The way she was floundering around with the power in her hand emphasized again how little training she'd had. Her mother had only trained her to kill Horace— the rest of Starling's life hadn't mattered to her.

The thought motivated me to keep giving. With a little time and practice, Starling would do fine. But right now—

My vision sparkled—

Right now she needed my help.

"I think I turned it off," she said. "The heat. It's a relief, actually. That's what was hurting. It was just blasting wild. I turned it off. It was like turning off a hose. I think."

I sent out a magic probe to the boundary nearby and didn't feel anything. To make sure it wasn't my own weakened state malfunctioning, I hauled myself to my feet and staggered over to the shore.

Cold, cold, cold. *Oh yeah.* The enchantment had been broken. What had been a wall before was now a tidal wave of winter, coming at me from all sides. Would the lake fae be happy now?

I looked out at the lake. The moon illuminated a figure on the ice coming toward us.

Pauline.

I was shivering. The shock of very hot to very cold was making the veins in my temples throb. And the muscles in my legs had turned into mashed potatoes. I sank to the sand and gravel at my feet and fought to keep my eyes open. After a magical effort like what I'd done for Starling, I needed hours, possibly days, of sleep to recover.

But I wasn't going to get it just yet.

"Starling?" I asked.

My voice was too weak for her to hear me. I had to repeat myself. "Starling."

Finally she came rushing over and put a hand on my shoulder. The wand's glow lit up her face. "Are you OK? I thought you were looking for something."

"Weak," I said. "Give me…" I gestured at the wand.

Hugging it to her chest, she frowned with a possessiveness she hadn't had earlier. "I can't give it to you. It's mine now."

I shook my head, laughing faintly. "Use it. Help me."

Her eyes widened. "Right. Sorry." She held it in both hands and closed her eyes. Unlike me, she didn't seem worn out at all. "Can you feel that?"

It took a second, but then I did feel a little… very little… zap. It was enough to get me off the ground and back on my feet, but not enough to restore my magic.

"That's great," I said, wiping sand off my pants. "Can you do it a little more?"

"It doesn't want me to," she said. "It wants to rest."

I could relate.

Pauline arrived, short of breath and shouting as she stumbled up on shore. "What have you done? I feel something. Why do you have the wand?"

"She's the true heir," I said. "Horace's great-grand-daughter by Katharine. She's—"

"*Sarah?*" Pauline asked.

"Her real name is Starling," I said. "She's turned off the—"

"But Katharine's baby died," Pauline said.

"As a teenager," I said. "She had a baby first."

"My grandmother, Violet," Starling said sleepily, gazing upon the wand. "I'm really tired. It was helping me, but now it's not. I think it's worn out. Can I lie down?"

"So she came here and killed Horace for the wand," Pauline said to me, her voice rising. She put a hand on a hoop earring. "And you helped her. You put Marcella in the lake to clear the way—"

"No!" I said quickly, unable to fight off her hex in my current state. "She's trying to save Marcella. She just ended the summer enchantment. That's what the fairies want."

Starling dropped to her knees and leaned against the large rock I'd used for support as well. She held the wand to her chest as she sank sideways, eyes fluttering.

"She's weak now and needs your protection," I told Pauline. "I'm going to try to get Marcella out of the lake, but you need to make sure nobody hurts her. Can you do that?"

"You're going to get Marcella," Pauline said.

"Yes, I'm going to try—"

"No, you're going to succeed." Pauline put a second hand on her other earring and gave me a current of strong, clear energy.

The magic poured into my well of power and allowed me to stand taller, breathe more easily. "Thank y—"

"Or else I'll kill you," Pauline said. The energy curled around my guts and sank in with a sharp, painful barb. "Got it?"

Flinching, I nodded, terrified she was serious. After a

glance at Starling, propped against the rock half-asleep, holding the wand up near her face, I decided I couldn't do anything more for her and ran off to find Seth.

We'd met our end of the bargain; the summer enchantment was destroyed. Now it was time to make sure the lake fae safely delivered my old friend.

Chapter Forty-Three

Rubbing my sternum where I felt Pauline's magical hook inside me, I walked into the cabin and was greeted in unison by Random and Seth.

"I have to go now." Seth kissed me, then drew back, frowning. "You're hurt."

"No, no. I'm fine."

He looked down at my chest. "One of those witches put something nasty on you."

"It's a mother's love," I said. "Don't worry about it."

He put his hand over the spot and held it there a moment. "It's horrible. It's all sharp and sticky. That's your friend's mother's work?"

"Just make sure you save Marcella, and I'll be fine."

He pressed his forehead against mine. "Oh, is that all?"

It felt good to have his arms around me, but there wasn't time. "The enchantment's broken. Tell the fae. Get Marcella." I pushed him away and sat on a chair near the window. It was the middle of the night, and the lake was a dark mystery beyond the glass. "Please."

"You're so weak…"

"I just need to rest for a minute." I could boil some water and make a tea out of my herbs, make a quick potion that would help. And being in the cabin, still protected by my boundary spells, would quicken my recovery. "Now go."

He gave me an agonized look. "Stay here with Random. Whatever you see, don't leave this cabin and don't leave him."

Random put his chin on my knee, begging for affection, and I ran my fingernails through his fur to the spot under his ears he loved to have scratched.

He leaned into my touch, and I felt an odd force around him…

"You've done something to my dog," I said.

Seth leaned over and kissed me. "Stay with him. Or else."

It was one thing to use magic to protect Random. But Seth had done something to make Random protect me. "You shouldn't have—" I began.

But in between one blink and the next, Seth disappeared.

"Stupid fairies," I said, resting my forehead on Random's. The fairy charm that Seth had given him soaked into my skin and warmed me through bone and muscle. It energized me enough to turn to the window, put my hands on my best redwood beads around my neck, and cast a night-vision charm on myself to see through the darkness.

The snow was blowing in. On the cabin's deck, the potted geraniums and dahlias were shriveling under the sudden onslaught of frost. And just beyond the deck on the flat expanse of the frozen lake—

Seth appeared, walking on the ice in a meandering way, head bowed, hands in his pockets. My heart squeezed, wishing he were with me, wishing we were both back at home in Silverpool, drinking hot chocolate, the kind he made with fresh vanilla bean, topped with brandy-spiked whipped cream.

He suddenly turned toward me and waved. Then, before

I could wave back, he leaped up in the air and dove headfirst into the ice.

And was gone.

"Be careful," I whispered.

I realized the temperature had dropped inside the cabin, that I was shivering. I tried not to imagine how cold it was under the ice.

After putting on my winter coat, I returned to the window to watch and wait. Random wouldn't let me out of his sight, and as soon as I stood at the window, he curled around my feet in a C shape. I smiled down at him, loving him and Seth's gesture, and felt some of my strength return.

We had to wait until dawn before it happened.

Chapter Forty-Four

Just before seven o'clock in the morning, the sun rose in the east—and the ice over Lapis Lake shattered into millions of sharp white pieces.

The explosion woke me from my shallow drowsing. I'd slumped sideways in my chair until my head and shoulder were resting against the glass, but the sound made me jump out of my seat and jerk the door open.

But going outside was not the smartest thing to do when millions of ice shards were flying through the air. Random, maybe acting on Seth's influence, barked and snapped at me, pushing me away from the entrance.

Belatedly regaining my sense, I recoiled and slammed the door shut. Icicles rained down, smacking against the glass.

Cursing myself for my stupidity—I wasn't hurt, but how about my poor dog?—I bent down to soothe Random. Still frantic, he licked my face and rubbed himself against my legs.

"Poor guy," I said, shaking head to toe from shock. "Good dog. Poor baby. Sorry to scare you." While I ran my trembling hands over his body to make sure he hadn't been impaled with icicles, I looked out with awe at the churning lake. The glass door was now spotted and blurry from the explosion, but through the clear sections I could see waves rolling across the small mountain lake. White-capped and wild, they were as big as those in the middle of the ocean.

I couldn't see the house from inside the cabin, and I wondered if the water was threatening the lower entrance. Just in front of my cabin, the waves were sloshing over the rocky shore, sending ice floes onto land.

Where was Seth? He had some fairy powers, but he was still stuck in the body of a man—more or less. I wasn't sure what his limits were. Up against pure lake fae, could he withstand an attack?

Had they taken his offer of a life for a life?

Feeling sick, I put both arms around Random and tried to stop myself from crying. I'd seen crazy things, but nothing had been as scary as an icy lake exploding a few yards in front of my face while people I cared about—a lot—were trapped inside.

Or were they?

I had to go out and see. And help.

Seth had brought a small overnight bag and thrown it on the bed. I dug through it for a rumpled T-shirt, unlaundered, and tore off my own top and sweater to wear his against my skin.

The smell of him triggered a surge of soft, squishy feelings. I didn't know what I'd do if he didn't survive, all because of my bringing him to the most dangerous beings on the planet for him—his own kind.

Random wanted to stop me from leaving the cabin, but my dog wasn't as well-trained as Seth had hoped. With a small piece of beef jerky, he trotted out the door with me and stayed close at my heels for more.

The ice shards were no longer flying through the air, but the waves were still swamping the shore. The wind on my face was cold, sharp with freezing rain. Comically my first thought was for the poor tomatoes in the enchanted vegetable garden.

The Gardners seemed to have gone inside; the only people standing above the rough shoreline were Pauline and Starling.

Pauline saw me and pointed at the lake. "You said she'd be freed!"

I turned my attention to the soft cotton of Seth's shirt, using it to search for his essence out in the lake. There was a faint sense of him coming closer.

The path between the cabins and shore was flooded, so with Random at my feet I ran up the road and then back toward shore, toward my sense of him, toward Pauline and Starling.

There. He was—

Walking out of the water with Marcella in his arms. She was limp, unconscious or dead, but all I saw was him. Waves came up to his hips—

No, he didn't have hips. Below the waist, he was water himself, and his hair was green, his eyes were blue, his complexion was a waxy, veiny gray.

Something ancient stirred inside me. My demon mother's influence, perhaps—the instinct to chase, bite, consume. I'd never seen him look so fae before.

Random barked a hello. He'd recognized him as a friend, not a threat.

But Pauline didn't. "Release her, fairy!" she cried, rushing out into the water and sending out an impressive blast of power at him.

Just before it struck, Seth looked at me with blank, unfamiliar eyes. And then the hex struck him in the face, knocking his head back. As he lost his hold on Marcella, the next wave rose up and swallowed him.

"No!" I shouted, desperate to use magic to catch him, pull him out of the small, violent sea before he was lost to me forever. But I knew I couldn't. He was in his element and with his kind, not mine, and if he was going to survive, it would have to be on his own power.

Pauline hadn't heard me. All her attention was on her daughter, now blinking awake in her arms.

She'd survived. The enchantment had kept her alive. The fae had powers over time, physical space, even mortality. But their motives were their own, amoral and secretive. They could've kept her in the suspended state for decades—or suddenly decided to let her freeze to death.

Starling took her legs and helped Pauline haul her out of the frigid water to shore. Just then Jack and Cullen ran out of the house, wiping icy rain away from their eyes, and the four of them carried Marcella inside.

She was alive, and she was with her mother. That was enough for me for the moment; I needed to make sure Seth was all right before I did anything else for anyone.

Putting my focus back on his T-shirt, I listened to its memory of him, his jokes and cinnamon rolls, his watery soul—and found my feet walking back to the cabin. Heart beating with hope—surely he had to be alive to get back there—I opened the door and heard the shower running.

I went into the bathroom, smiling, and slid the curtain back.

He was all man again, at least bodily. I smiled some more.

"I'm getting old," he said, kissing me. Hot water splashed on my face and shoulders. "That ice really gave me a chill."

"You scared the Shadow out of me," I said.

He looked me up and down, then shook his head, grinning. "Nope. Still got it, Demon Lady." He crossed his arms over his chest. "Mind closing the curtain? You're letting in a draft."

I felt better than I had in a long time. "I love you," I said.

"Then close the curtain before I catch my death of cold." He jerked the curtain closed between us. I was standing there, mouth agape, when he slid it open again, kissed me quickly, then put it back.

Feeling happy as well as annoyed, disappointed, and amused, I left him to his human pleasures.

A second later, reality set in. A killer was still on the loose and might strike again.

I made sure I had all my beads, herbs, and metal on me, then ran out through the freezing rain to the main house. Somebody had recast a boundary spell at the front door—I sensed Ronald's touch—and I had to pause and endure the nausea for a second before pushing through to the living room.

They were all there. The first thing I noticed was that Pauline had Marcella in a protective force field on the couch, warm and isolated. In a dining chair near the kitchen, Starling was sitting with the wand in her lap, looking pale and tired but alert. I thought it was smart of her to sit apart from the others, just as she had as Horace's PA—they couldn't be feeling kindly toward her.

Seeing that Marcella was safe allowed me to relax a little. One of her relatives had given her to the lake fae—was it Jack, standing at Pauline's side, offering a cup of echinacea tea? Or his daughter Sage, the cousin who hated her? Or could it be Cullen, who before Starling's appearance would've expected to inherit everything if she'd died?

I'd thought the witch to give Marcella to the lake fae must've also been the one to kill Horace, but now that Starling was there with the wand, everything was so much more complicated. Maybe I wasn't the first to discover who she was. But then—

My head swam. Marcella's eyes were closed, but earlier, at the lake, they'd fluttered open.

"Has she said anything?" I asked.

The gathered family all turned and looked at me. I met their gazes one by one—Jack, Kenneth, Cullen, Isabel, Glenda, Sage, Huxley, Ronald. What were they thinking? One of them had to be terrified they were about to be handed over to the Protectorate, but all were strong enough witches to hide their emotions. Only Pauline kept her full attention on Marcella.

"She told me everything," Pauline said, tenderly running her hand over Marcella's hair.

"When?" Ronald snapped. "She's still asleep."

Pauline lifted her chin and regarded him. "When she first came out of the lake. She told me who gave her to the water people." Her voice trembled with rage. "She told me who needs to be punished. And I'm quite prepared to do it myself. Brightness knows none of you monsters will help me."

"Of course we'll help—" Cullen began.

Pauline turned to him, her eyes flashing. "You don't fool me, golden child. Mama's boy. She never could've done this on her own."

Glenda, already on her feet, made a move to leave the room. "I'm not going to stay and listen to this."

I stepped in front of her, blocking her exit. "Sorry, but I think you are."

Pauline pulled Marcella closer to her. "You tried to kill your step-granddaughter, your husband's own blood. You deserve the curse that'll follow you the rest of your days."

Glenda gave me a wild look, probably weighing her ability to overcome me. Realizing she couldn't, she turned back to the others. "That's a lie," she said loudly. "Hear the truth in my words. Cast a truth spell. I never intended to kill her."

I did as she said and cast a spell, measuring her honesty. It was *almost* false. Which meant it was almost true. "You didn't want them to kill her, but you hoped they'd keep her for the rest of her natural life."

Cullen looked horrified. "Mom? Is that true?"

Glenda was trapped. Pauline on one side of her, me on the other. I felt her drawing power away from her appearance and putting it into her protective spells. The enchantment she used to make herself look younger flickered under the stress. Gray hair, wrinkles, stooped posture—previously hidden, now revealed.

"Nobody else was going to punish her for what she did!" Glenda pointed at Kenneth. "You knew but did nothing! This Protectorate friend of hers knew, of course she did, and she'd make sure there was no justice there either. Marcella's fingerprints were all over his office. She'd killed him, but nobody cared! Precious little Marcie, pathetic girl couldn't hurt a fly, except she did. My husband is dead by her hand—"

"That's a lie," Pauline said. "You're deranged. You want your son to have the wand. At any cost."

Cullen put his hand on Glenda. "Mom, if you did give Marcella to the fae, the family will forgive you. They know you were grieving. You thought Marcella was responsible—"

She smacked his hand away. "She *was* responsible! You told me yourself what you saw in the office."

I glanced at Kenneth, who stared back. So he hadn't broken his promise.

Glenda started pacing around the room. "There were bits and pieces of her all over his room," she said. "All over my poor, poor husband—when she wasn't supposed to have ever been there. How would that be possible if she hadn't been the one to kill him?"

Everything was starting to come together in my mind. I had to speak up. "Because it was a trap to hurt Marcella, not your husband," I said. "Marcella was the intended victim. Her magical fingerprints were planted there. And since you were the one to give her to the lake fairies, maybe you were the one to set the tra—"

"How dare you?" Glenda clutched a necklace and lobbed a poorly controlled hex at me. "You— You're an accomplice—"

I deflected her spell easily. "There was an accomplice, but it wasn't me."

Frantically, Glenda looked around the room. "Somebody back me up. She— This stranger has broken into our home and *killed* my hus—" Her mouth froze. Her eyes, too. A second later, lacking the subtle muscle movements necessary to balance on two feet, her body toppled over and banged against the couch. Cullen dove forward to break her fall, but it was too late; she rolled face-first onto the floor.

The stream of power that had come from Pauline hadn't seemed to require any effort. Without even looking, without stopping her caressing of her daughter's hair, without touching any of her metal or gemstone jewelry, she'd knocked out Glenda from across the room.

"She won't hurt you ever again," Pauline told Marcella, kissing her forehead.

Chapter Forty-Five

Cullen cradled his mother's head. She was still paralyzed, stiff as a board. "That wasn't necessary," he said. "She was just upset—"

"Pauline!" Ronald cried, jumping between her and Cullen.

I sensed a wave of defensive magic waft through the room; he'd stopped her next hex.

"Pauline," Ronald continued, wiping his brow. "Maybe you and Marcella could go upstairs. We'll resolve this."

Pauline hugged Marcella closer. "I'm not going anywhere. I want justice to be done. One way or another."

From the floor, Glenda groaned. Cullen cast a strength spell around himself and lifted his mother from the ground.

"I'm taking my mom upstairs to recover," he said, balancing her stiff body over one shoulder. "I'm overwhelmed by… by all of this. All I can say is I'm very glad Marcella is OK."

"She can't leave the house," Ronald said.

"Of course not. She's hardly in a state to go anywhere."

Avoiding everyone's eyes, Cullen hauled Glenda, appearing smaller in her gray-haired, natural form, out of the room.

Huxley spoke from a far corner of the room. "But it's still possible Marcie killed Granddad, isn't it? I mean, just because Glenda gave her to the lake fairies doesn't mean she didn't deserve it—"

Ronald deflected Pauline's hex even more quickly this time; his son was in the line of fire. "Really, Pauline," he said, short of breath. "If you can't allow honest speech, you'll need to be paralyzed as well."

"Agreed," Jack said. He'd put himself between Pauline and Sage. "Next attack spell you cast will be your last."

Pauline didn't look up, but she nodded.

My mind was racing, thinking about the evidence in the office, the details of the days before and after.

A trap had been set for Marcella. That I was sure of. But who had set it, and why had Horace been the one to die?

If I didn't resolve that question right now, Marcella would always live in fear of another attack. I didn't trust anyone else in the room to do it—not even Pauline, who was too enraged to think clearly.

Drawing upon the power of dried thistle in one of the sachets of herbs in my pockets, I stepped to the middle of the room and raised my voice. "Marcella didn't kill Horace. She never left the cabin. But—"

There was a murmur of dissenting voices. I held up my hand in a nonmagical bid for patience. When that didn't work, I put some magic behind it. After several seconds, their voices faded away.

I looked over my shoulder at Starling, who was sitting in a dining chair near the kitchen, an anxious look on her face. She still hadn't regained her strength since removing the summer enchantment. She looked pale, weak, heavy-lidded. The wand rested in her lap, but it wasn't giving her the energy boost it had given her grandfather. With time, maybe she'd learn how to use it as he had.

I turned back to the Gardners. "But she felt a strong, overwhelming pressure to go see her grandfather in his office that night," I continued. "Her reaction was kind of bizarre, actually. Just the thought of going to see him made her sick. Short of breath, sweating, chest pain—all the signs of a panic attack."

They stared at me, curious to hear where I was going with my argument, and I loosened my hold on their tongues to preserve my strength.

"That's Marcella," Isabel said. "She's always been like that."

"Has she?" I looked around the room, holding the gaze of the older members. "I heard she was a normal kid, not too anxious, before her father died. That's when things got hard for her."

"Understandably," Jack said. "She lost her dad."

I looked over at Marcella in Pauline's arms. "Hard in a different way. When she became the heir, her powerful grandfather got serious about trying to get rid of her. And he didn't hold anything back."

"That's a horrible thing to say," Kenneth said.

Ronald agreed. "Who do you think you are?"

I spoke faster, louder. "Things went wrong at home, at school, out in the world, in her own mind. She began to feel cursed. Well, we're witches. What if that's what was actually going on?"

The atmosphere in the room got colder. I didn't have much time before they lost patience with me—and I wasn't sure myself what I was getting at.

I went on, knowing the answers were there, but hidden. "There had been a trap to kill Marcella. She'd felt the summons. When she didn't show up, Horace died." I rubbed my forehead, trying to picture the office as I'd seen it the next day. The chair. His dead body, hair on end. "He'd already made it clear he wanted her eliminated from the will. He'd hired a special lawyer to argue she was unfit, one who was coming the next day. If Marcella had gone into that office—pushed to her limit, goaded, insulted—and finally lashed out at her grandfather, does anyone expect her to have won that duel?"

Nobody dissented. They'd never been impressed with Marcella's magical powers.

"No," I said. "And neither had he. That's why he summoned her. He *wanted* her to attack him."

Maybe I was crazy to challenge witches like this on their own turf. But seeing Marcella in her mother's arms had energized me. *That* was the loving, supportive treatment she'd deserved all these years and hadn't gotten it. And I believed it was because her own grandfather had taken it from her. Saddling her with unpopularity with her own family, punishing those who were nice to her, rewarding and encouraging cruelty. Now that he was dead, maybe she could rebuild her relationships with them. With new people, old friends, herself.

"I believe Horace was killed by his own magic," I said. "When Marcella didn't show, the trap lashed out at the only target in the room—him."

Silence greeted my theory. It sounded good to me, although something was nagging at me…

Jack's voice rang out. "I thought from the beginning he must've hexed himself," he said. "Like he did on the hike. He just wasn't able to control the wand the way he had when he was younger."

Ronald chimed in. "I don't believe for a second he would've hurt Marcella. That theory of yours, that he laid a trap? No. It would've put him too close to Shadow when he knew his days were numbered. Even if he'd wanted to hurt his own blood—and I refuse to believe he did—he wouldn't have risked the bad luck. None of us knows what lies beyond, but we expect we have a few years or decades to find out. But not him. He was afraid of death. Killing his own granddaughter would've been too unlucky."

"I agree. Never," Jack said. "He never would've done it. He lost control of his wand, and it killed him. This was all just a horrible accident."

I wanted to argue with them—Horace had been a Shadowed witch, horribly cruel, selfish—but they'd known him far better than I did. What he said about bad luck felt true. They certainly believed it.

A trap was set for Marcella, but Horace died.

Had it all been an accident? And bereaved Glenda had lashed out against Marcella because she'd honestly believed her to be guilty?

Looking for another point of view—from an employee, not a dependent relative—I looked over my shoulder to see what Starling thought.

She was gone.

Chapter Forty-Six

"Where is she?" I asked, my mouth going dry. "Where did she go?" Had she run away? Or had one of them hexed her while my back was turned?

In a flash, I remembered her printing out an email from a lawyer. The child's code. Sarah's walk down the hall, Cullen chasing after…

I should've made her sit closer to me, but I thought it would only be more dangerous for her. Plus she'd looked so tired, needing to put space between her and the family. I was sure she'd been tempted to go sit in her small office, her sanctuary among the Gardners, where she and Marcella had shared a bag of chips the day I'd arrived.

Huxley, who had been sitting in the back, spoke uncertainly. "She went with Cullen."

I never thought anyone would be able to take her out of the room without me noticing. Cullen hadn't seemed particularly powerful, but he'd overcome my strongest defenses. How?

The wand. It was the only explanation. He must be using it somehow.

I spun around to face Huxley. "What did you see?"

"It's all right." Huxley glanced at his dad for reassurance. "I think he just needed help with Glenda. They went upstairs."

I swallowed, feeling sick. The one person who was most vulnerable with the one person most likely to harm her. I'd been overconfident, thinking my defensive spells were strong enough to alert me to anything these witches attempted. But I'd been like Sarah, just as oblivious, vulnerable, stupid.

I hurried out of the living room and ran up the stairs two at a time. The banister with its blood droplet pattern inlay mocked me with each step.

Blood...

Starling had what the wand wanted. Cullen didn't. I heard some of the others follow me, but I didn't pause to see who. Every second counted.

How could I have let him get her...

Breathing heavily, I cast out my senses for the wand, finding a taste of it on a door halfway down the hall. Holding my redwood beads with my left hand, I drew all my power into myself and used a surge of magic to push the door open. I couldn't risk actually touching the brass doorknob.

It was a large bedroom, the master suite, with sweeping views of the lake and mountains out the windows. A massive four-poster bed stood to one side, Glenda rigid and uncon-scious on top of a white duvet. Starling, also unconscious, was lying on the floor behind Cullen, huddled in front of a fireplace. I realized the bedroom must be directly above the fireplaces on the first and second floors.

I absorbed all this with a glance—then saw nothing but the crimson blood on Starling's exposed arm. I ran over to her, tapping into my power to slam back Cullen's attempt to stop me, and knelt at her side.

"I swear to Brightness, if you've killed her…," I muttered, feeling for her pulse.

It was faint. And although the gash on her wrist wasn't deep, she was limp. Her life force was being drained away.

Jack was in the doorway. "Is she OK?"

"Get Kenneth," I said, putting myself between her and Cullen. She was alive now but would survive only if we broke whatever spell Cullen had on her.

He was huddled in front of a fire in the grate. "You're too late," he said, moving his arm. I couldn't see what he was doing, but I heard the sizzle and pop of water hitting the burning logs. He was using a cauldron hung from a hook in the firebox. "The wand is mine now."

"I don't give a demon's right eyeball about the Shadowed wand," I said. "You hurt Starling."

"Sarah will be fine. Well, probably." Cullen used a pair of fireplace tongs to pull the wand out of the cauldron and hold it before him, his handsome face beaming. "She didn't even want the wand. I do. With her help, I was able to break the blood oath."

Ronald came into the room. "Cullen, what are you doing?"

Flinching from the heat, Cullen opened the tongs, dropping the wand onto the hearth. When it struck the bricks, the wood handle dislodged, separating from the pewter handle and rolling to one side. The bath in the boiling potion must've weakened the seal.

Cullen snatched up both the wand and the handle, clearly worried he'd destroyed it. But then he pushed them back together, tested it with a little wave, then lifted the restored wand up into the air.

"The blood oath is broken. Forever. My father wanted me

to have it," he said, smiling. "And now I do. There's nothing to get upset about."

"You killed your own father," I said.

Cullen rolled his eyes. "My family knows that isn't true."

Maybe he even believed it himself, just because he'd intended the hex for Marcella. But it was Cullen's magic that had killed Horace.

Kenneth came into the room with a small first aid box and knelt at Starling's side. He studied the wound on her arm for a moment, then pushed back on his heels. "The cut will heal, but she's under a draining enchantment." He looked over at the bed. "I don't suppose anyone has made sure Glenda is still alive?"

"She was making a lot of noise." Ronald went over to her, looking down, not seeming very concerned. "Yes, she's alive."

Cullen continued to hold the wand aloft, gazing at it proudly. He stroked a finger along the metal. "Of course she is. She's my mother." He waved it back and forth. "The hearth would've rejected me if I'd hurt her. This is old magic —I bet you've heard of it, Alma—hearth witch and all that. Father's body, mother's fire. Very powerful stuff."

I guessed he'd used Starling's blood in his potion to break the chain of the old oath and was continuing to drain her energies to maintain his hold on the wand. His mother's hearth, his mother's life energy, and his father's body (what part had he taken from the corpse—Hair? Fingernails?) would wield a lot of power. The blood oath would never have been broken without all of it put together. If it had been just a matter of taking the heir's blood, Horace would've done it decades ago.

Jack walked into the room and addressed me. "What did you mean about Cullen killing our father?"

"She's just making things up to protect her friend," Cullen said. "I forgive her. She's loyal. The world needs more people like you, Alma." He smiled, his dimple flashing.

I wanted to throw up. He hadn't resisted Horace's favoritism; he'd internalized it. "You've probably used the wand before," I said. "Horace wanted you to practice. Did he give it to you sometimes?"

Cullen, calm and confident with the wand in his hand, walked over and sat on his mother's bed. She stared at the ceiling, moaning softly but apparently unable to move. "Since I was old enough to hold a rattle. It knows me. It's always wanted me to be its master, and now I am." He gave Starling a pitying glance. "Thanks, Kenneth, for bandaging her up. I'll see to it she gets a nice bonus for what she's been through."

His self-protective boundary magic felt impenetrable. I risked a quick probing spell and discovered a river of power between himself and not only Starling but his unconscious mother. He was using their lives to fuel his energy stores. If he needed to do that, then the wand was not yet in his full command. The bond was not as complete as it had been with Horace.

There was still a chance to overcome him.

"Break the connection you've got with your mother and Starling," I said. "It's killing them."

He waved aside my concerns. "Mom will probably be fine. Sarah might be, but we'll have to wipe her memory." He looked at Kenneth. "You're a doctor—you must know a good amnesia spell, right? For when you screw up?"

I was thinking furiously. If Cullen had had minor control of the wand, he could've affected the trap Horace had set for Marcella.

"You read the email the new lawyer sent. It was bad news, right? Something about it made you panic." I thought about Horace's speech at dinner, how confident he was. "But you didn't share it with your father. You changed it so he wouldn't give up hope. You wanted him to tell the family you were the heir."

"The stupid woman," he said. "So famous. So expensive. The witch lawyer who was supposed to be able to fix anything. Father promised me, and I believed him. Why wouldn't I? It's what he told me all my life. I knew the wand would be mine."

"What did she say in the email?" I asked.

He stroked the wand, his lips curving in a sneer. "*She* didn't think a blood oath could be broken. Which is obviously false since I've just done it. My father wasted his money on so many of those lawyers when all it needed was a little direct action."

And Shadow magic. I'd sensed a burning in the fireplace on the ground floor. That's where he must've changed the document—using hearth magic to change the words on the page—safe enough to hide the truth from a man who only read his emails on printouts.

I cast my gaze around the room at the Gardners paying rapt attention. They might believe me, they might not, but they were listening. "You got desperate. You lost hope in a new will. You suddenly realized there wasn't a legitimate way to change the line of succession," I said to Cullen. "Horace was nearing the end of his life. You decided it was time to just kill Marcella so you would inherit everything, nothing complicated about changing the will or the blood oath."

Cullen shook his head. "I'd never hurt Marcie. That's a terrible thing to say. Poor girl didn't have any friends in the family except for me."

"You encouraged Horace to set the trap and summon her. But then you modified it to be deadly." I looked around. At least one of them had cast a truth spell to screen Cullen's words and would know they were lies.

"I was never in the office that night," he said.

"You didn't have to be," I said. "You were partially bonded with the wand, using it from another room. No wonder the weather was going haywire—you, Horace, and Starling were all giving it mixed instructions."

"I totally agree it was a bad situation," Cullen said. "That's why I had to take it for myself. Jack, Ronald—this is good for the whole family. For us. We can't let an employee have it. And nobody wants crazy Marcie in charge."

"That's the sort of thing you and Horace said to each other," I said, "but Marcella surprised you both by being strong enough to resist the summons. Hours went by, and the trap only got more and more dangerous. Horace was an old witch and too proud to ask for help disabling the trap he'd set. When he realized Marcella was never going to come, he tried to take it down by himself. And it killed him."

"Demon's balls," Kenneth muttered.

I looked at the others—Jack, Ronald, their kids—they believed what I was saying. Cullen's actions to get the wand had killed their patriarch.

But would they punish him…?

Or kill me to hide the truth from the world?

Chapter Forty-Seven

I would have to appeal to their Brighter natures. They were witches, raised with privilege; it would be a hard sell to risk their necks and sacrifice for the greater good.

"He's killed his father, and he's about to kill his cousin," I said, gesturing at Starling. "Is this going to be the Gardner family's legacy? A bunch of liars, thieves, and murderers?"

Jack and Kenneth put an arm around Sage but didn't answer. Ronald turned his gaze on Isabel and Huxley, who were looking at him for guidance.

They would lose a lot with the wand leaving the family. Its power and wealth would drain away and with it possibly their homes, their social status, their magical, exclusive winter getaway.

Holding the wand upright, Cullen walked to the window, pushed open the sash, and leaned out. Cold air blasted in.

"It's freezing out there," he said. Tucking the wand under his arm, he sat on the sash and swung his legs outside. "I'll take care of that. Jack, Ronald—deal with Alma. Kenneth, you probably won't need to wipe the girl's memory after all. I don't think she's going to make it."

Oh Brightness. I rushed forward. He was going to need Starling's energy to recast the summer spell—and from the looks of her pale and still form on the floor, she didn't have that energy to spare.

Before I got to the window, he bent down, climbed out, and dropped from sight. Sage got to the window before I did and looked down.

"He's OK," she said, coming back inside. "He's alive."

I couldn't tell if she was relieved or disappointed. I leaned out to see for myself.

Below on the ground, just inside the bank of snow and ice, Cullen stood with the wand. A cloud of magical energy was forming around him, strong enough for me to feel from two stories above. He was rebuilding the summer enchantment.

Feet planted in a wide stance, he held the wand up like Arthur with Excalibur. A white light glowed around his hands, then flickered—on and off like a worn-out fluorescent light bulb.

He lowered the wand, tapped it against his palm, lifted it again. It continued to flicker until, shaking his head with frustration, he took the wand in both hands and twisted off the loose wooden handle.

Ah. Now the wand glowed steadily. He hurled the broken handle into the lake, took the pewter wand in both hands, and went back to his Excalibur pose.

The sleet turned into a warm mist. The wind on my face had become balmy.

As long as he had the wand—and Starling's body feeding energy to him—I wouldn't be able to subdue him.

Not by myself.

I left the window and cast a frantic eye over the Gardners. Would they support me over their own kin?

"Please," I said. "We've got to stop him. We can do it together. Please."

My heart was pounding in full flight-or-fight mode now. I wanted to reach for my beads, pull up all my defensive spells, get Seth and Random, run away—but that would leave Starling to die. And soon, with the wand, Cullen could kill Marcella too—I was sure of it.

"He's dangerous," I said. "Anyone who gets in his way will end up dead. You think he'll share the wealth, the power? He won't. Anyone who isn't any use to him will become a threat."

They seemed to be listening. At least they weren't attacking me. Yet.

"After Marcella, the youngest will be the next to die," I said, gesturing at Huxley and Isabel. "He can't be sure he's broken the blood oath. He'll start to worry one of them might have a child that will grow up to take the wand from him. He'll expect them to do what he did. Plot and kill to get it."

Ronald's jaw tightened. He looked at Jack. "She might be right about that."

"But he's just... Cullen. Little Cullen," Jack said, turning to Kenneth. "You scanned the office. Could he have done that?"

Kenneth put his arm around Sage, his face hard. "It fits," he said.

Sage buried her face in his chest. "Let's go home."

"Easy for you to say," Isabel said. "You're not the one he's going to come for next."

Before another argument broke out, I strode across the room and grabbed Glenda's nightgown off a chair. "I've got a plan. Do what I say. Please." I brought the nightgown—it felt like pure, old-fashioned cotton—over to the fireplace and pushed it into the bubbling cauldron.

Water overflowed and sizzled on the burning logs. I grabbed the fireplace tongs and dipped them into the hot water, shoving the nightgown around to absorb as much of the water—and other stuff—Cullen had put into his potion. "Somebody get Glenda's water glass. It's on her nightstand. Over there. Hurry."

There was a pause that felt like an hour as I waited to see what they would do. Would they do the Bright thing?

Jack reacted first. He got the glass and started to empty it into a vase.

"No!" I said. "Don't pour it out. We'll use her spit. Bring it over here."

Jack walked over to me with the glass. "It's not big enough to catch much of whatever's in that thing," he said.

I pulled the dripping nightgown out of the cauldron. The logs hissed, spattered. "If it broke the blood oath, it must be potent." I waited for him to set the glass on the hearth, then held the nightgown over it. The potion dribbled into it, mixing with the existing water, and overflowed onto the rug.

"We'll all drink," I said.

"Ugh," Isabel said.

"Form a Circle," I said. "We'll put Glenda in the middle. She brought Cullen into the world. She'll have more power over him than anyone."

It took me longer than I wanted to get the witches to form a ring around the bed. Glenda, moaning with eyes closed, was hopefully still under Pauline's hex and wouldn't rise up and fight us.

"Me first," I said, lifting the glass to my lips. "So you know it's safe." It was the best way to get them to trust me.

Of course, I myself didn't know if it was safe, but Starling would still be in Davis with her little Snowman if I hadn't dragged her back. Now she was on the verge of death.

As soon as the hot, bitter, disgustingly chewy liquid hit my tongue, I had regrets. What did I owe Starling? She was an adult. She could make her own choices. I wasn't responsible for any of these people, not even Marcella.

I hoped my face didn't betray how nasty the potion tasted on my tongue. Forcing a smile through gritted teeth, I handed the glass to Ronald at my right.

He choked but gagged it down. Then a competitive spirit arose, and one by one, everyone drank.

I don't know what the others saw, but I was greeted with a clear vision of Cullen Gardner in his birthday suit. The apparition floated over Glenda's body, empty-eyed and expressionless.

"Why is he naked?" Huxley asked.

I couldn't help but smile. It was working—I wasn't the only one to see him. There was hope.

"What he was born with," Kenneth said. "I've seen it in surgery before when a mother's in the waiting room."

"Now what?" Jack asked.

"We pull him back inside before he kills Starling," I said, "and take the wand from him."

"Sure," Huxley said. "But how?"

I reached out to take the hands of Ronald and Isabel in mine. "Take your neighbors' hands," I said. "Skin to skin. Then we'll tell him to come."

As soon as they did as I said, the floor shook as if a giant had stepped on it.

"What was that?" Isabel asked.

"The Summoning Circle just went online," I said. Usually the object of a summons was a demon, but it would work on people as well. Hopefully. I raised my voice. "Cullen, come here. Now."

My voice sounded funny to my own ears—and then I realized my words had been spoken through Glenda's mouth.

My knees wobbled. The potion was burning the back of my throat. If this didn't work, I wasn't sure I'd have any energy left to try something else.

"I've got you," Ronald said, tightening his grip on my hand. Warm energy poured into me.

"Thanks," I whispered. To my relief, the words were spoken in my own voice.

The apparition of Cullen flew up to the ceiling and floated over to the doorway, hovering above it. A moment later, the door flew open and Cullen stormed in, enraged.

"What are you doing? Why did you stop m—"

The apparition sank down into Cullen's body, disappearing into his T-shirt and jeans.

Then Cullen fell over with a thud.

I spoke through Glenda's mouth again. "Bring me the wand."

The apparition, now wearing clothes, sat up from Cullen's prone body. Holding the wand, it floated over to the Circle and dropped it on the bed next to Glenda's right hand. Then it curled up beside her and disappeared.

"Now what?" Ronald asked.

"Starling needs it first." I looked around the Circle. "Do I have your permission to touch it?"

Still holding hands, everyone glanced at each other, unsure.

"I'm just going to put it in Starling's hand," I said. "She'll die without it." When they didn't argue, I freed both my hands, picked it up with the hem of my shirt, and hurried over to Starling.

I peeled her cold fingers apart, arranged them around the metal rod, then stepped back.

The real Cullen sat up. "What's happening?" He looked down at himself. "Why am I naked?"

Starling rolled over and curled her body around the wand, cradling it like a mother nursing an infant. Then she let out a long, ragged sigh.

I leaned over and met her gaze. "Feeling better?"

"I hate this thing." Pushing up to a sitting position, she grimaced at the wand in her hand. "It gives me the worst dreams."

"Is she OK?" Isabel asked.

"So far," Kenneth said.

Cullen hunched himself over to hide his nakedness. "Why is everyone in my mom's— Hey, is she sick? What's happening?"

"What's the last thing you remember?" Kenneth asked.

Cullen stared at him. "Who are you?"

Eyebrows raised, Jack looked at me. A smile twitched in the corner of his mouth.

"He's going to be a bit out of it for a while. Can you control him now?" I asked. "I want to get Starling out of here."

I felt Jack set up a sizzling magical boundary around Cullen, still naked and huddled on the floor.

"Got him," Jack said.

Ronald looked miserable but put his hand on his silver belt buckle to help support the magic of the cage.

Before they could remember how desperately they wanted the wand for themselves, I helped Starling to her feet and hurried her and the wand out the door. Then I escorted her down two flights of stairs and out to the lake.

We staggered across the mud toward the shore. Once more the air was hot, bright with unfiltered sunshine.

"I'm sorry to ask this, but you'll need to undo the summer enchantment again," I said. "Cullen tried to turn it back on. The fae might reclaim Marcella if it's enacted again. She's still too weak to fight back."

"I can't," she said, leaning heavily against me. "I can barely walk."

A wave rose from the lake, taller than all the others, and splashed over us.

We jumped back, soaked. The fairies were going to fight the enchantment. Would they try to abduct any human they saw on shore?

"You've got to try," I said. "Please."

"It's sharp inside me. It's not like before. It hurts." She held out the wand. "I don't want it. Take it!"

Cullen had broken the blood oath. Starling was still connected to it enough for it to revive her, but maybe it wasn't hers any more than it was mine. Maybe now it was like any other magical object—to be used and abused by the witch holding it.

Touching my beads for support—although I feared they would be too weak to defend me from the wand if it attacked me—I reached out and lifted it from her fingers.

Chapter Forty-Eight

Unfamiliar power struck me in the chest, making me gasp for breath. My fingers felt sticky, as if I'd shoved them into a vat of melted caramel, and I realized I wouldn't have been able to drop the wand if I'd wanted to. It was glued to my hand.

When the shock of the sensation had passed, I rolled over and pushed myself up to a sitting position.

Interesting. It had knocked me down. Brushing mud and sand off my chest and legs with my free hand, I got to my feet, wavering slightly, and braced my legs for the next jolt of power.

It didn't come. I studied the wand in my hand. It looked like just a stick of bare pewter now. I risked casting a probing spell past its matte, warm-gray surface.

Delicious magic, sleek power, strong and uncomplicated force. Like all modern witchcraft's favorite metals, it had a pure flavor. Unlike the botanical ingredients I preferred for magic, metal was uncomplicated by mud, insects, drought, bird droppings, disease, or weather.

It was an interesting piece of metalwork. Mostly tin, a

little copper, some lead. From my time with the Gardners, I'd expected something Shadowed, sinister, twisted. But it was just a strong piece of metal. Lots of it—it was heavy in my hand—but disappointingly ordinary for an amulet that had led to blood oaths, generations of lust and conflict, and murder.

It was still stuck to my skin, which I didn't like. More confident now that I wasn't dealing with a supernatural object beyond my skills, I put my left hand on my redwood beads and let my thoughts sink into the aura of the metal wand.

I saw the strings that swept out of the pewter and hooked through my skin into…

With disgust, I saw the strings had woven themselves around my veins and arteries.

Blood again.

The impulse to cut them all away and be free of the thing was overpowering—but first I had to end the summer enchantment one last time.

It was big, going deep into the earth, high into the clouds. But… I sensed it wasn't as steady as it had been. It was struggling to hold on, to regain what it had lost when Starling ended it. Cullen had done a poor job of reestablishing it.

Afraid I might fall down again, I sat on the bench of the picnic table, then closed my eyes, tapped into the well of my power, such as remained, and visualized a cleansing rain pouring down, washing away the enchantment.

First the mountains, then the trees, the creek, the waterfall, the rocky shore, the grasses and weeds, the vegetable garden, the house.

All clean.

I found the insects and animals who were most vulnerable to the sudden winter and cast a protective charm over them. They would have time to adjust.

I felt wood under my cheek and noticed with pleasure it was from a redwood tree. The picnic table. I'd collapsed, but I had to keep the rain flowing, wash away the last of Cullen and Horace.

The wand wasn't attacking me—I wasn't hurt—but wielding it was draining my well of power. Even if I'd had a full night's sleep and hadn't been doing magic for days, I would be feeling weak after breaking the summer enchantment.

But I *hadn't* gotten enough sleep, and I *had* been overextending my internal magical resources all week.

My vision faded out.

The last thing I remember was the feel of snow on my cheeks.

Chapter Forty-Nine

I woke up in a familiar attic. Unlike then, however, when I'd been a prisoner lying on the bare floorboards, I was now on a soft bed. Next to the bed was a nightstand with a glass of water, and beyond that was a view of Sutro Tower jutting through the foggy hills in San Francisco. I guessed it was late afternoon.

I was at the Protectorate office on Diamond Street.

And my head felt like a mountain troll had dropped a boulder on it.

"The princess wakes," Raynor said.

Raynor, now the Director of the Protectorate in San Francisco, had been a famous colleague, an employer, a neighbor, and a friend. For a little while, he'd been the Protector of Silverpool, living within walking distance of me, but he'd returned to the city. Although he looked like The Rock, and the agents under his wing were distracted by his nonmagical good looks, he was a serious, all-business witch, and I'd come to trust him.

"Who hit me?" I asked, lifting a hand to my forehead. Even the touch of my own hand felt like an assault.

Somewhat reluctantly, I stretched out my arm and counted my tattoos. As I'd come to expect, there was a new dark mark above my wrist next to the others. A sixth ring. Would I ever get so many that I forgot the names of the witches who had given them to me? Should I write them down, just in case?

The idea made me squeeze my eyes shut and drop my arm with a groan.

"You smacked your head when you fell. Drink this." Raynor moved the glass over to my face, but before I could sit up, he poured it on my face.

I gulped a mouthful as it splashed over my lips. The rest of the liquid soaked the pillow, trailed down my neck, ears, hair. A second later, the pain in my head faded away, and I sat up.

"You couldn't, you know, try a straw? Help me sit up first?" I asked, wiping my face.

"You'd rather I dunked Glenda Gardner's nightgown in it and squeezed it into your mouth?"

So he'd already had time to interrogate the Gardners. That meant hours—or a day or two—had passed. "Yes, actually."

"Sorry," he said. "I thought you'd open your mouth faster."

I tucked a damp strand of hair behind my ear. It was tangled, making me wonder again how long I'd been unconscious. "How did I get here?"

"The boyfriend who shall remain nameless gave us a call," he said. "We arrived just as the snowstorm hit."

That explained why he'd dumped water on my face. The Protectorate was pledged to kill beings like Seth, and although Raynor wasn't actively trying to get him anymore, he didn't like me being involved with him. He also got annoyed when I put myself in danger—although it was fine if *he* was the one doing it.

"When did Seth call?" I thought back. If the Protectorate had arrived that quickly, he must've called them… much earlier.

"Middle of the night before last. One of the Flints woke me. They have standing orders to reach me anytime if your name is mentioned."

I smiled, almost forgiving him for pouring water on my face. "That's nice."

"Don't take it as a compliment. You attract disaster. It's more efficient to keep an eye on you than to watch everybody equally."

Ignoring his jibe—I really didn't have any defense, because it was true—I took the glass out of his hand and took another sip of the healing potion. The ache in my head was replaced with a soft, fluffy sensation. Lovely.

Seth must've called them before he'd gone out to free Marcella. Without asking me. Given how relieved I was to be in a soft bed over a hundred miles away from Lapis Lake, I couldn't be too annoyed with him for being sneaky. Though I'd let him know not to do it again.

I tucked the covers over my lap. "Tell me everything."

Raynor raised an eyebrow. "I'll do the questioning, Witch Bellrose. Or have you forgotten how the real world works outside that forest of yours?"

"Come on, have a heart. Drop the formalities. Is Marcella OK? Did you have to kill anyone? Is Cullen in custody? Did you get the code to read the encrypted emails from the lawyers? Where's the wand?"

He crossed his massive arms over his chest and leaned back in his chair, making it creak. "Marcella was here watching you most of last night," he said. "At her mother's insistence, we finally kicked her out of the room. I believe your crazy friend has given her a bed for the night. For a price, of course."

He must've meant Helen, the mercenary witch who owned the big Victorian next door. "And Cullen?" I asked.

"I sent him to the Protectorate office in LA," he said. "They were glad to have him. Apparently, the late Horace Gardner has old enemies there. Just as well. I didn't want to deal with the paperwork. His advocate is trying to keep him out of a Mojave jail, but it won't do any good. He's already confessed."

Imagining Cullen locked up, I indulged in a long, slow smile. "Death Valley hit one hundred and twenty-five degrees last summer, you know."

"Well, those Gardners do like their warm weather," Raynor said.

I let out a laugh but stopped abruptly as other worries caught up to me. "What about the wand? The other property?" There was still a chance the family was standing by Cullen and was pressing for his release. I pictured Marcella and her mother here in San Francisco, too impoverished to get a hotel room.

"Well, the Protectorate will have to study the wand for some time to evaluate its safety to the general population," he said. "Until we are certain there was no Shadow involved with that old blood oath, it will have to remain here with the Emerald mages."

I laughed again. The Gardners had been right to avoid calling the Protectorate for help. Would they have ever called, even knowing Cullen was a deranged killer?

No, I didn't think so. To hide the family secrets and retain the wand, what might they have done with me?

I was grateful to be in the attic on Diamond Street.

"And Horace's will? The house, all the money…?"

"Not my department," Raynor said. "But Pauline

Gardner seemed relaxed about her future. She's staying at the Four Seasons."

That didn't mean much. She might be putting it all on a credit card. I'd have to talk to Marcella.

"The wand is no longer ensnared in any blood oath though," he continued. "Whatever the will had to say about that is moot. The wand is usable by any witch strong enough to wield it."

"Which means you guys can have it," I said.

He frowned. "For the world's safety." Raynor took out a pouch and pinched some herbs between two fingers. "But without the bond to its ancestral masters, it will never be as strong as it used to be." He sniffed the herbs into his nose—a habit he'd had as long as I'd known him.

"That's good. One person shouldn't have so much power." I leaned back in bed and closed my eyes. Things had turned out pretty well. Now I just needed to get back home. "When you got to Lapis Lake, did you happen to see… my dog?" I avoided mentioning Seth outright.

"No, and I was wondering how you got up there, because your Jeep wasn't there either," he said.

Which meant Seth had driven home in it. And was there now, waiting for me. "I need a ride up to Silverpool," I said.

"Tomorrow. After the Emerald mages put you through a few hours of formal questioning," he said. "Darius has offered to drive you back up north. He wants to tease you about passing out with that wand. He was surprised a hearth witch like you would try to use such a big, powerful piece of metal."

Darius was my former partner. "Needs must," I said, irritated to know Darius, not always my biggest fan, had seen me knocked out from magical effort. "I hope he realizes how strong and ancient it was. How much talent it took for me to disarm it and terminate the climate enchantment."

"Sure, sure," he said, getting up, bored with my insecurities. "I'll have a Flint get you a meal before you have to face the Emerald interrogation. What would you like—burrito? Buddha bowl?"

The thought of interrogation made my stomach clench. I'd survive, but they'd make it as unpleasant as possible. "Dry toast please." I pulled the covers over my face.

Chapter Fifty

I was heading out the front door of the Protectorate office the next morning, after surviving the typically unpleasant routine of suspicious, officious Emerald-level Protectorate employees picking through my mind, when Marcella hailed me from the porch of Helen's house next door.

"Helen told me you were heading home now," she said. "She's been super nice, giving me tea, listening to my stories."

I frowned, knowing Helen was only nice if she thought she'd get something out of it. In Marcella's case, that could be money, information, or both.

"I'm glad to see you're feeling better," I said.

Marcella looked like a completely different person—relaxed, bright-eyed, happy. Thawed. Smiling, she jogged down the steps to meet me on the sidewalk, then stopped when she saw something behind me. "Oh, who's that?"

I turned to see Darius Ironford, my old partner, running up with his fingers splayed, flinging a protective spell around my body that was so strong I couldn't hear the conversation that followed.

"Hey!" I shouted from inside the bubble. "She's not dangerous. That's Marcella."

Darius ignored me. He walked over to Marcella, spoke to her, scanned her, then finally nodded and removed the magical shield over me.

Sound whooshed back into my ears. "I can protect myself, thanks," I said, smiling. Darius and I hadn't spoken in months, and I'd missed him.

Darius stood up taller, frowning at me. "I found you unconscious next to that lake. You don't know your own limits."

Still smiling, I introduced Darius to Marcella.

"I know who she is. I interrogated her." He regarded her with hostile skepticism. "Next time you're afraid of other witches, ask the Protectorate for help, not civilians."

"Hey, leave her alone," I said.

But Marcella was nodding. "No, he's right. I am so sorry, Alma. Grateful, but sorry."

"So what happened when I…"

"Collapsed from magical exhaustion and cracked your head open?" Darius offered.

I shushed him and pulled Marcella over to one side. "Are you OK with money? Your mom?"

She gave me a hug. "Witch Buck says I'm getting all the money. Remember when he read the will, the first one? It gives everything to the firstborn daughter of the firstborn *son*." She reached up and touched the jute cord I'd given her. The sense of friendship flashed stronger between us. "At the time we didn't know about Katharine's line, so it didn't mean anything that he specified a son. But by mentioning my father specifically, it excludes Sar—I mean Starling. I'll help her, of course."

"You think the others will accept what Buck says?" I asked, skeptical.

"He insists that now that the oath is broken and the Protectorate has the wand, the money follows the instructions in his original will. The alternative is to let the Protectorate take everything just because they have the wand," she said. "But I know I'll have to be really, really generous to stop the others from suing me."

I cast my mind back to that day in the office with Ambrose Buck reading from the big binder. "What if the Protectorate returns the wand? Do you get it?"

Marcella shook her head. "Buck thinks I have a strong legal case to get the wand, now that the blood oath is erased, but the Protectorate thinks Starling has a claim. I honestly don't care."

"That wand will be tied up in legal wrangling for the rest of our natural lives," I said.

With a laugh, she tucked a strand of her blond hair behind one ear. Diamond earrings glinted, and I wondered if Helen had tried to steal one. "Just between you and me," she said, "I might ask the Protectorate to keep it so my relatives stop trying to kill each other."

"That would be sensible of you," I said. Would I have the willpower to do the same? I doubted it. Even though the wand was metal, not my specialty, I was a witch—curiosity alone would make me take it if I could.

"Every penny and property and rare orchid goes to me. So silly. Why would I want to keep everything for myself? I've already told Ambrose to distribute it equally. After that, I'll take what's left and give away as much as I can. I want to be a force for Bright in the world." She took my hand and touched the tattooed arcs around my wrist. "I can't believe you're still talking to me. I nearly killed you and your boyfriend. I hear he's the one who called for help?"

I glanced at Darius, worried he'd heard mention of Seth

being at the scene, but he just rolled his eyes. He knew already.

"You didn't do anything," I said. "It was your family. And they were victims of the Shadowed curse your grandfather put on you years ago. He wanted them to isolate you, cast you out, make you unworthy of the wand so he could give it to his golden boy."

"It's hard to believe, but I think you might be right," she said. "Sage sent me a text that didn't actually wish me dead. It was almost nice."

"Over the next few weeks and months, their behavior should get nicer," I said. "As your grandfather's curse fades away completely. You're probably going to be the one with the most to relearn. Next time you feel the urge to get off a train or avoid driving, listen to it. It could save your life."

"Just like when you got me at the airport." She shook her head wonderingly. "Remember when I made us get off the BART train early? Helen told me there was a shooting. We might've been shot."

"There you go," I said. "Listen to your instincts."

"I think that's what Starling did. She disappeared right after that conversation with me." Marcella smiled, glancing at Darius. "It made your Protectorate friends mad. They wanted to talk to her."

"Still do," Darius said. "We believe she's in a house in Davis. I'm going there after I bring you up to Silverpool."

How could Starling disappear without the wand when a dozen Protectorate agents at the highest levels were trying to find her?

Seth. Fae magic was always unpredictable. He'd zipped out of there with the Jeep, my dog, and Starling. Raynor hadn't mentioned it, which meant his pride was wounded.

Suddenly I had a craving to see Seth more powerful than a demon craving fairy kebabs.

"Take me home," I told Darius.

Chapter Fifty-One

"Will you please tell that gnome to find a new hobby?" Seth mumbled, his mouth pressed against my shoulder.

It was morning the day after I'd returned from the Protectorate.

"What's he doing now?" I asked, peering out into the dim light of a cloudy day. Willy was usually a night owl, but sometimes he was busy at dawn.

"He's singing," Seth said, rolling away from me and pulling the pillow over his ears.

I laughed. Willy, unique among the fae, had the ability to hide what I could see and hear from him. If Seth could hear him singing and I could not, it was because Willy wanted it that way.

He disliked Seth. Seth might have to continue living in the house next door and never with me in mine. Willy could make it inhospitable and impenetrable to other magical creatures.

"What kind of singing?" I asked.

"It's all bad," Seth said.

"Is it about his long-lost love? The one who was here on the winter solstice?"

He grunted and rolled away from me. "Maybe you could ask him to be quiet."

"He'll know it's you who's complaining," I said. "I can't hear it. He might sing louder if I say anything."

Seth groaned and flung the pillow across the room. "It's not right. He's just a gnome. Why does he have the power of a thousand river nymphs under a full moon?"

"I've often wondered that," I said.

Seth got out of bed and pulled on his jeans. Random, belatedly realizing the breakfast providers were awake, jumped off the bed and ran to the kitchen where he'd stare at the empty food bowls until the kibble rained down.

"I was going to wait until your birthday, but apparently the diminutive garden monster has no patience." Seth stomped off into the kitchen. I heard the sound of dog food landing in the metal bowl.

My birthday? A childish glee came over me. I called out, "Did you get me a present?"

If Willy was finding it difficult to wait, it must be food. Willy loved human treats of all kinds. But my birthday was a month away, and food would spoil. How would Willy know what Seth planned for the future?

How was Willy able to do anything? He was godlike in his powers.

I shouted again. "I could eat an early breakfast!"

Seth could make anything. Scones, Belgian waffles, fruit tarts...

An array of delights passed through my mind. I was as bad as Random staring at his food bowl.

One cost of performing large feats of magic was exhaustion. The other was hunger. For the next week, I'd eat like a woman breastfeeding quintuplets while training for a triathlon.

But Seth didn't answer. And the only sounds from the kitchen were the back door opening and closing for Random to get out. I didn't hear pots and pans or a blender, mixer, food processor or even the refrigerator door opening.

I turned on the light and sat up in bed, disgruntled. He'd welcomed me home yesterday warmly enough, but I'd had the feeling he was holding something back.

Of course my first thought was that he'd fallen in love with Starling and was moving to Davis that afternoon. She was cute and didn't have any domineering gnomes in her backyard. Unlike me. Who did. Recently I'd even had two.

"Seth! What's wrong?" My head was still rattled from the concussion. The potions and spells at the Protectorate had helped, but they weren't as good as the magic I could cook up at home in my own kitchen. If he didn't bring me a cup of something hot to drink in the next few minutes, I'd go into the kitchen and brew myself an herbal concoction that would smell horrible but work beautifully to clear my head.

I flopped back on the bed with a sigh. It was so nice to be home. Early wildflowers were arriving—the yellow sticky monkey flower, the orange poppies in the patches of sun beside the road, and the redwood sorrel with its white, five-petaled blooms. I'd go out and harvest a small amount of leaves, pollen, and petals for my collection of dried botanicals.

My head throbbed, reminding me of the rock it had collided with a few days earlier. Where *was* that changeling? A lemon thyme scone would work wonders on my headache.

I heard the door slam. Then footsteps. Random bounded into the bedroom and jumped onto the bed, then Seth walked in behind him. I pushed up to sitting, my pulse picking up with childish anticipation. He was really good at surprises.

Seth held an envelope and a drawstring gift bag, glittery-pink with white stripes and a white bow, about the size of a coconut.

"The first thing you can do is evict the little man in the garden," he said. "That'll teach him to interfere." He sat on the bed, a lopsided grin curving his lips, and set the package in my lap.

It was heavy with magic. My smile fell. "What is it?"

"Don't worry," he said. "It's just a hunk of wood. I've noticed you liked things like that."

I ran my fingers over the lumpy object under the synthetic fabric. It was wood, like he said, but it was infused with power. For a moment I was reminded of my childhood when my father would steal something from a rich man's collection, then pretend to give it to me as a present before turning around and selling it on the Shadow market.

Seth wouldn't do that. But one thing I knew—the object didn't belong to him. It had been stolen, taken from its old home. I could feel it longing for its previous owner.

"I don't think I want this," I said. "Whatever it is."

Seth kissed me on the cheek. "Just open it, my demon darling."

I gave him a side-eyed frown. There was no need to remind me of my annoying ancestry when I'd just woken up. What would he do if I left it unopened and went to make myself blueberry-leaf and yarrow-root tea?

In the end, my curiosity won out. Of course it did. I was a witch. He sat there, trying to hide his grin, as I pulled the drawstring bow apart.

Inside was a cylinder of carved wood, dark brown, badly scratched.

The handle of the Gardner magic wand.

"Cullen threw this in the lake," I said.

"Stupid witch," Seth replied.

When he'd boiled the wand in the cauldron, the handle had come loose from the wand, but everyone had assumed the metal was the only important part. The pewter was stronger, and the Protectorate would investigate its powers, but the handle held its own magic. A lot of it.

Heart pounding—the aura of the thing was lovely, mysterious, loud with magical buzzing—I wrapped my fingers around it as if the metal wand were inside and held it up.

Random jumped up and hopped over to me, his tail wagging. Then he started barking.

Seth grabbed his collar and pulled him away from me. "Easy, Rando. It won't hurt you."

"Did you get it yourself, or did the lake fairies give it to you?" I asked.

"You seriously think my lake fairy cousins would give up a thing they hated so much?"

I scrambled off the bed to play with it better. It was like the staff I'd made from redwood beams I'd found in the attic of my house. Wood just made sense to me, blended with my thoughts, my talents. Pretending the wand was inside, I pointed it at the kitchen and imagined a plate of chocolate éclairs.

Random got away from Seth, landed on the floor, put his front paws up on my thighs. Smiling, I imagined a cheeseburger, room temperature, no bun, no onions—his favorite —and set it in his dinner bowl.

And then for Seth…

I looked at him. He was watching me with a wide-open, loving expression that took the breath out of me.

"What would you like?" I asked, waving the wand handle.

He continued to gaze at me. After a long moment, he smiled. "You," he said. "Just you."

Epilogue

I propped the bamboo poles together in the front garden, hoping the gap in the trees would give my green beans enough sun. So close to the coast, Silverpool was cool in the summer, with foggy mornings and nights—good for the redwood trees, not so great for a summer vegetable garden.

"There are fairies you were bringing here that will be glad for that, I am thinking," Willy the Gnome said. He was a small creature, no taller than a house cat, but he dressed to impress in a red velvet coat and pointy cap. He held a pipe in one hand, standing in a beam of spring sunshine near me.

"I brought fairies here?" I asked, wrapping the twine around the poles at the top to make a teepee.

Willy pointed to the east. "From the cold lake of your beloved. They were tiring of the long wait, for you could be planting those beans in the ground a week ago yesterday. We are both knowing it is almost summer now. The little ones are being tired of sleeping in the oleander."

I frowned at the large bush along my driveway. "The Lake Tahoe fairies followed me home?"

"They are of course believing you were the one with the power of sun and beans," Willy said, "and there are no smart words that I am sharing with them that they are capable of understanding. And so they are staying here, even though the oleander is poisonous."

I smiled, eager to meet them properly when the seedlings sprouted and sent bushy vines up the bamboo poles. "How sweet." I took out my seed packet and tore off the top. "I'll plant extra beans for them so they have a nice, thick little shelter."

Inside the house, Random whined through a gap in the window. Whenever he saw me digging, he tried to help—and no magic at my disposal would make him stop. He'd been banished to the kitchen with Seth, who was making his sixth batch of cookies for Birdie's bookstore.

Not surprising to anyone who knew human nature, most days she was selling far more of Seth's cookies than her books and was getting permits to put up a few tables and sell coffee and tea as well. The books sold during witch holidays like the winter solstice, and she was planning a huge event for the summer equinox, but the other days of the year had been slow for magic literature retail.

"There is some raisin, I am thinking, in the warm flat cakes today," Willy said. "Your beloved is not using too much of the sour things, I am hoping. They make me very angry. There is the thinking you should be warning him I am not liking them, so he knows to do better, for me and for dear Birdie, who doesn't like them either."

"Sour things?" I asked, looking up from the soil.

"They are shriveled and rusty and very nasty indeed. I am sure you are thinking as the same way I am also thinking."

"Do you mean dried cranberries?" I asked.

Willy spat the pipe out of his mouth and shuddered. "I

am hating them very much and even to be saying the word is making me very sad."

Last week, Seth had developed a new cranberry-walnut cookie. "But they're sweetened with sugar," I said, poking my finger in the dirt around the pole. "And you love nuts."

"The nasty neighbor to a good friend is not being a good friend no matter how perfect and beautiful is being the one you are visiting," he said.

"I have a nasty neighbor?" I asked. There were only three houses on our rural street—me, Seth, and a nice nonmagical couple.

"It is the red sour balls that are the nasty neighbor," he said. "It is sad for the excellent nuts to have them nearby."

"Right. You really don't like them." I nodded. "I'll tell Seth."

"Your beloved gave you the new, powerful present that is made of wood," he said. "Maybe I am thinking you can use it to be sure he is not using the bad things in the food."

"I don't need the wand handle to make him stop using cranberries," I said, looking at the house with a sweet feeling in my heart. Ever since we'd come back from Lake Tahoe, Willy had started calling Seth my beloved. He wouldn't let him into the house unless I was around, claiming our courtship was not yet advanced enough for that, but he wasn't actively attempting to harm him. "I'll just ask him to use raisins instead. Is that OK?"

Willy's face broke into a wide, delighted grin. Pointing his pipe at me, he nodded vigorously. "How much are you being intelligent and kind, my dear Alma. Of course you are knowing what is right and good. The grapes are what we are eating, wet or dry, young or old. The red balls of unhappy nastiness are never forgetting they are sour."

"No more cranberries," I assured him. I'd lost track of where I'd already planted beans, then decided I'd plant the entire packet all around the teepee and let the fairies cultivate them to their liking.

"Your new toy is good at bringing here a loud wagon," he said.

"My new toy?" For a second I thought he meant Seth. But then I remembered *loud wagon* was Willy's expression for car. And the toy was the wand handle. "Somebody's coming over?"

"I am thinking your beloved is not always being wrong, even though he brought the nasty red things into your dwelling," Willy said. "He is wanting you on the two wheels so your human form is not dying tomorrow, which would be sad for the fairies, who are wanting somebody to water the beans. And if you are being dead, your beloved is being too sad for making cookies that are not having nastiness in them."

I was unable to translate what he was trying to tell me. Brushing off my hands, I got to my feet and looked around for the hose. If I was going to die tomorrow, I'd better give the seeds at least one drink before I kicked off. "Does Seth know what you're trying to tell me?" I asked. Now that Seth and Willy weren't complete enemies, I relied on my changeling boyfriend to interpret his odd speech when it was beyond me.

But Willy was already halfway inside his illusory door in the bottom of the redwood tree. "You are telling him what cake I am wanting, is this the truth?"

"Yes, but—"

In a blink, he was gone. I was about to walk into the kitchen door at the back to ask Seth for help interpreting Willy's words, but then I felt a tingle in my shoulders as somebody tried to enter my driveway. With a stainless-steel spade in my hand, I strode around the house to meet the intruder. Well, sometimes I didn't mind people coming by. I should call them visitors, just in case I didn't have to hex them away. Nevertheless I had the spade ready to fire just in case.

There in my driveway was a small, completely empty SUV with metallic green paint. The high shine made me think for a moment it had been enchanted to blind human eyes.

Seth appeared at my shoulder. "Nice, isn't it? It's electric. Do I get the Jeep?"

I looked at him. "Did you buy this?"

"I helped you earn it, in a manner of speaking," he said, kissing my cheek, "but Marcella put just your name on the registration."

I remembered her promise of payment. "But I don't need a new car."

"She was afraid she might not get a chance to buy one later," Seth said. "She's giving away all the money now before she loses her nerve."

I walked to the Escape and put my hand over, but not touching, the hood. The magic that had delivered it to me was wafting off the metal like heat after a long drive. "Where am I supposed to plug it in? I don't have the hookups."

"Sure you do," Seth said, nodding toward my detached garage. "I had it put in yesterday when you were helping Birdie with the café permit paperwork."

"How did you override my boundary spells?" I demanded. After all the trouble I went to, one rogue changeling could just snap his fingers and let strange men with power tools into my precious, private workspace?

"Willy helped," he said. "I had to promise not to use cranberries anymore."

"He's really covering all his bases," I said. "He just lectured me all about that too."

"I don't think he likes them very much," Seth said.

I shook my head. A new car was totally unnecessary. I had my Jeep, and as Willy had said, riding a bike around town was better for my health. Especially now that the rain had stopped for the summer and the roads were dry and free of flooding or mudslides.

After a moment's hesitation—I *could've* sold it for rent money—I opened the door and got in. There was a white envelope on the dashboard. Feeling Marcella's magical fingerprint, I picked it up and tore it open.

Inside was a jute bracelet entwined with a strand of blond human hair. I took it out, remembering the triumph of her bravery against all odds.

"I got Random," Seth said, climbing in beside me. "Let's go to the beach."

Giving both of them a delighted, goofy smile, I pulled the bracelet over my left wrist, feeling Marcella's friendship send deeper tendrils into my soul, and started up my new car.

Books by Gretchen Galway

SONOMA WITCHES (Paranormal Mystery)

Dead Witch on a Bridge (Sonoma Witches #1)

Hex at a House Party (Sonoma Witches #2)

A Spell to Die For (Sonoma Witches #3)

Charmed to Death (Sonoma Witches #4)

Murder by Magic (Sonoma Witches #5)

Hexed in Show (Sonoma Witches #6)

Dead Witch in the Library (Sonoma Witches #7)

The Sonoma Witches Series Box Set: First Three Novels (Sonoma Witches Books 1-3)

OAKLAND HILLS SERIES (Romance)

Love Handles (Oakland Hills #1)

This Time Next Door (Oakland Hills #2)

Not Quite Perfect (Oakland Hills #3)

This Changes Everything (Oakland Hills #4)

Quick Takes (Oakland Hills Stories Boxed Set)

Going For Broke (Oakland Hills #5)

Going Wild (Oakland Hills #6)

Oakland Hills Romantic Comedy Boxed Set (Books 1-3)

RESORT TO LOVE SERIES (Romance)

The Supermodel's Best Friend (Resort to Love #1)

Diving In (Resort to Love #2)

About the Author

GRETCHEN GALWAY is a *USA Today* bestselling author who writes mystery, fantasy, and romance. She lives in Sonoma County, California.

For more information:
www.gretchengalway.com